Fighting Absolution

A NOVEL

AUTHOR'S NOTE

Fighting Absolution, while a fictional story, deals with the subject of the war in Afghanistan and how it impacts the lives of soldiers and those who are left behind. The utmost care has been taken to write this story with respect for those who serve or have served their country and the families that love them.

Special Acknowledgement

To the former and current soldiers of the army who have assisted me with ensuring the accuracy of the following fictional events, thank you so very much.

DEDICATION

To Sergeant First Class Jeremy Hodson
US Army Retired

The best friendships are the unexpected ones.
The ones you never saw coming.
The ones that change your whole life.
Thank you for changing mine.

This book is for you.

"All that I am, all that we were,
is here in these pages.
This is me. Screaming to the world …
I was here.
I loved you.
I was happy.
It mattered.
~ Ranata Suzuki

1

JAMIE MURPHY, 15 YEARS OLD

*P*erth, Australia, 2006

I step outside the back door and down the three cement stairs leading to the brown, patchy grass. The rusty old screen door slaps closed behind me. I tilt my head to the sky. The sun warms my face, the sensation breathing life into my body. And there lies the problem. Because the sensation reminds me I'm alive, and with that reminder brings an ache so deep it steals my breath.

My eyes burn and I squeeze them shut.

Oh, Dad.

His image flutters through my mind. Dark hair. Strong jaw. Fierce brown eyes. The love in them. The way they shone whenever he teased me. My father was a fighter. Literally. He was signed with the Ultimate Fighting Championship—the UFC. He travelled the world in competition, claiming the title of middleweight champion. His was a meteoric rise to fame. Forbes listed him as one of the greatest fighters of all time. *Of all time.* He wasn't the flashiest fighter around, but he was the deadliest. He radiated power and confidence, his eyes savage as he took down opponent after opponent like they were nothing.

Despite the success, he made it hard for anyone to like him. He was rude and aggressive, shoving a reporter who had the gall to call his fights all hype and no substance. He once fired his manager in a spectacular public rant, right outside the cage after a fight that won him a title. The media dragged all the sordid details of the divorce from his wife, my mother, including counts of cheating—on both sides—money grabbing—my mother—and worst of all the custody battle, which my father won with ease. I was the subject of his adoration. My mother was not. She hated me for it. And all this by the age of thirty.

He took sole custody of me when I was six years old, while my mother took all his money and disappeared to Europe, never to be seen or heard from again.

I was the only one who saw his smile. I was the one he laughed with and carried on his broad, muscular shoulders. The one he took to the beach and tossed in the water, watching with amusement as I learnt to ride the waves. My father taught me everything he knew, including the kind of moves that could put a guy in the ground if he looked at me the wrong way.

Seeing my father win a fight was like watching a star shooting across the sky—extraordinary and untouchable. But the problem with shooting stars is that they burn too quick. Too bright. Too fast. And far, far too hard.

Great success in sport equals injuries of similar proportions. And soon after came surgeries and painkillers. Comebacks. More injuries. More painkillers, this time downed with alcohol. He lost his title. He lost his fans along with it too, because fans are fickle creatures; they devour you until you're nothing but an empty husk before moving on to the next great success.

Medical bills eventually took what money he had left. And while I had been the light of his life, it wasn't enough, because the fight was the *love* of his life, and all the fight left inside of him was gone.

"Jamie!"

My eyes shoot open, the voice cutting through the memories. I ignore it and limp towards the back of the yard. My feet crunch across the dead grass, the sharp little blades poking my tender skin. Reaching the fence, I turn and slide my back down the timber panels until my butt hits the ground.

Now what, Dad?

I thump my head back against the fence.

Thwack!

The fence hits back. My body jerks forward, my arm jostled inside its brand-new cast.

"Ouch!" I yell. "What the …"

I twist around, peering through the tiny gap in the panelling. At best I can see a flash of golden-brown hair well overdue for a cut. It has a slight curl and hangs out from beneath a red ball cap. The sliver of a bright hazel eye peers back at me. At least I think it's hazel. There seems to be some green and gold mixed with the brown.

"Sorry," comes the reply. I catch the flash of a rugby ball as he tosses it back and forth in his hands.

"Jerk," I hiss, my entire body aching. "Watch where you're throwing that stupid thing."

"Hey." His voice sounds taken aback. "It was an accident. The ball hit the fence. I didn't know anyone was sitting against it."

"Well, I've had enough accidents to last a lifetime," I snap, furious. "Go kick your ball somewhere else."

I turn back around, but he doesn't leave. "What happened to your face?"

Heat pricks my eyes, and I palm my swollen cheek, knowing my body has a thousand bruises beneath the clothes that match this one. *Damn you, Dad. Goddamn you.*

"Nothing," I retort with a heated lie. How can he even see my face? "It's perfectly fine."

"Did someone hurt you?"

"Don't be so nosy. No one hurt me." A shuddery breath escapes me. "Get lost."

"Wow, okay."

I hear grass crunching, and I turn for another peek. He's moving away … I think. The gaps in the timber make it hard to see. I know there's another backyard behind this one; the houses flank each other all the way down the street.

Silence returns and I close my eyes.

Time passes.

"Jamie!"

As much as I want to, I can't sit out here forever. I struggle to my feet and limp my return to the house, the midday heat causing a trickle of sweat to wind its way down the centre of my back.

I yank open the crappy screen door. I'm greeted by Sue standing in the kitchen, wiping her hands with a tea towel. Her frizzy blond hair is tied in a knot on the top of her head, and her cheap cotton dress flutters beneath the overhead fan. She nods towards the bathroom. "You're a mess. Go shower. It will make you feel better."

I don't answer. I simply head towards the bathroom like she asked, knowing no shower in the world will make anything better ever again.

THE NEXT DAY I return to my spot by the fence. I turn and plonk down against it, closing my eyes, but the sound of screeching metal assaults my ears. Glass shatters, spraying my face, cutting it into a thousand pieces.

I gasp, my eyes blinking open and chest pounding. I brush at my face but there's no metal. No glass. Just healing cuts and bruises. A mess that didn't wash away in the shower yesterday.

Another shuddery breath escapes me. And another.

"You're back," comes the same voice from yesterday.

I ignore him, hoping he'll go away as I work at calming my racing pulse.

"Did you just move in?"

My nostrils flare but I don't engage.

"What's your name?"

"None of your business!" I burst out with heated aggression. I came here for peace, not an inquisition.

"That's okay. I can just make one up for you."

A frustrated snort escapes me.

"I'll call you Little Warrior, because you're kinda like a rabid animal."

Do not engage. Do *not* engage. "I'm not little."

"Sure you are. You're like, what, thirteen?"

I go to fold my arms and wince at the spike of sharp pain. A reminder that the bones in my forearm are shattered and a couple of pins and papier-mâché are all that holds it together. "I'll be sixteen in a few months. And you're what, ten?"

"Older than you. Seventeen."

"Pffft." I twist around, peering through the tiny sliver. It's hard to tell, but he *does* look older. Big. Broad. Maybe. I gently press my face to the fence and squint, but I can't get the full picture. I barely get any picture at all. All I can see is his stupid hair. "Bear."

"What?"

"That's my made-up name for you. Bear. Because you look like a freaking grizzly." My comment is mean and harsh and doesn't feel good. It just makes my insides sink lower than they already have.

Bear only chuckles, not seeming bothered by my snark at all. "Yeah, I could probably do with a haircut."

"So why don't you go do that and leave me alone?"

"Because I'm curious."

"Curious about what?"

He turns his head away, his voice softening. "About how you got those bruises on your face."

For a moment I'd forgotten they were there. The pain throbs anew. A wound that will never heal. I turn and sink back against the fence. "Go away, Bear."

The quiet returns.

I close my eyes.

THREE DAYS later and I'm back at my usual spot by the fence. I like it here. It's shaded by a big tree and mostly quiet apart from the occasional harassment by Bear. Inside the house is messy and loud, the noise grating. My jaw aches from biting back the urge to scream at them all to shut up.

I get almost an hour of alone time before the voice comes from over the fence.

"Hey."

Surely he's not so hard up for conversation that he has to harass me for it.

"So, what school are you going to?"

I sigh. Apparently he is.

School starts in less than two weeks, and I couldn't care less. New teachers. New faces. The start of a new year. People talking about summer break, all tanned and relaxed and *happy.*

"Are you going?" he asks when I don't respond.

I ignore that too.

"Why don't you talk?"

I contemplate this question for a moment. "Because it feels better not to talk. To anyone. About anything." Talking means remembering and remembering just hurts.

"Okay."

The fence jolts. I twist around. Bear is sitting with his back against the fence, mimicking me. My stomach tightens at his proximity. "What are you doing?"

"Sitting here, not talking to you. Trying to see if it feels better."

How ridiculous. Who is this guy? Then I remind myself that I don't care who he is and turn back around. Now we're sitting with our backs to each other, the fence a barrier between us.

A half hour passes and I risk a peek. He's still sitting there. I'm not sure what irritates me more: his quiet presence or all his questions. I fidget with a blade of grass, shredding it between my fingernails.

"Fine," I burst out, unable to handle the loaded silence a moment longer. "I'm going to Chatsworth High."

His voice shows no hint of triumph at my answer. "That's a girl's school."

"So?"

"I go to Bayside State. We won't be study buddies."

"I don't want a study buddy."

"We could always study together after school."

He sounds thoughtful, as if he's seriously contemplating it.

"No. Not happening."

"Don't be like that, LW."

"LW?"

"Your name's a bit wordy. Thought I'd shorten it."

I roll my eyes. He can't see it, but I hope he feels it.

～

"How was your first day at Chatsworth?"

Seriously? I sigh, tipping my head back against the fence. "It was fine."

If fine means fielding rude stares from students all day long. I'm not just the new kid, I'm also covered in faded cuts and bruises, casts and bandages—though my leg is better so at least the limp is less pronounced. The worst part? They all know *why*. They *know* what happened. Who I am. Pity leached from their staring eyes until it suffocated me. It's almost a relief to be back by the fence with Bear and his teasing questions and warm voice.

"Make any new friends?"

A huff of disbelief escapes my mouth. Who would want to be friends with some broken, angry girl? "No, Bear. No friends."

He hums quietly. "Maybe tomorrow."

"Sure. Maybe tomorrow."

～

"Hey, you got your cast off!"

I look down at my arm, wondering how Bear even knew I had one. It's not like you can see properly through the fence. The cast had been on for ten weeks. Now my skin is pale, the muscle tone gone, angry red scars marring the once smooth, tanned flesh. It looks horrible and I don't care. The mirror doesn't show much better either. My once healthy, happy face is now pale and thin. A fine red scar decorates my right cheekbone, just below dark brown eyes that once held warmth and happiness. I'm assured it will fade in time, as if it's important my face is the unmarred perfection it used to be. I used to long for freckles or rosy cheeks—anything to make my face more interesting. Be careful what you wish for, I guess.

My long brown hair sits in a ponytail now because who can be bothered to wash it? Sue suggested cutting it, but Dad used to braid my long hair before bedtime. He would smooth the thick strands with battered hands and tattooed arms that were trained to cause damage, weaving made-up fairy tales as he plaited, ones where the girl beat her foe alone and ended up saving the boy instead.

I ignored Sue's suggestion.

"Yeah. I got my cast off."

"How does it feel?"

I test the arm, lifting it up and down. "Really light. Like it's made of air."

"How did you break it?"

I don't answer.

"Come on, LW," he pleads. "Give me something."

I open my mouth, finding myself about to give him something because his voice tugs at me as if he cares. It's hard not to respond to that. Then I close it.

"I'll come over and knock on your door," he threatens.

"No!" My heart pounds at the thought. I like the anonymity we have with each other. It makes everything easy. With Bear I can pretend that nothing ever happened. Except for times like now, when he pushes, poking at the hurt. "Please don't."

"I feel like I should be offended." His tone is teasing but there's something more beneath it.

That something has me scrambling to reassure him. "It's not you. It's just …" I blow out a sharp breath, my cheeks puffing. "I was in a car accident." There's a beat of silence. "That's all." I brush it off like it's no big deal because I don't want to dissect the details.

But I still feel the glass cutting my face and the screeching metal tears through me. I scream and scream until there's silence and the car rests upside down. I try to unbuckle my seat belt because I know I need to get out—to run, to escape what happened, until I see bones poking through my skin. *"Dad!"* I cry out, horrified, eyes shifting from my arm to my father. *"Dad!"* He's stuck in his seat, same as me, his head hanging unconscious.

A sob climbs my throat. I choke it back, hunching over on myself. I have to be strong like my father always taught me to be.

Bear's gentle voice reaches out. "Don't cry, Little Warrior."

His words ease their way around my heart. I press my hands against my eyes, pushing the tears back in.

"I was in an accident once," he confides.

"You were?" I choke out. I want to hear more. Did it happen slowly for him like it did me? Did the world tilt? Did he feel the same terror?

"I had a run-in with a quad bike down at my friend's farm."

"A quad bike?"

"You know, the four-wheeler things? I can be a bit competitive, and we were racing. I saw a huge mound up ahead. Thought I'd jump it. Don't know why. Looking back, I figure it only would have slowed me down had I actually made it."

I press my lips together, picturing Bear hitting the mound and flying through the air like Evel Knievel. Then his words register. "Wait a minute. You didn't even make it to the mound?"

"Not even close. I revved the bike and it shot out from under me."

My mouth opens. "You fell off?"

"Yeah."

"That's so *lame!*"

"Yeah," he repeats, laughing at himself. "The worst part was that the bike kept going."

I laugh with him, picturing Bear on the ground as his bike shoots off in the distance, escaping him like a wild horse. The laughter builds and builds until it aches, and I'm holding my sides, and then suddenly it's not funny anymore. It just hurts and there's nothing left but agony and grief.

I whisper my confession, my voice hoarse and broken. "My dad died."

Bear sucks in a sharp breath. I hear it over the roaring in my ears.

A beat of silence passes between us as my words ricochet through my head, sounding ugly and wrong.

"I'm so sorry," he says quietly. And after another moment, "Do you want to talk about it?"

"No," I answer, curt and rude.

"Okay. You don't have to."

That night as I lie in bed, I stare at the ceiling of Sue's house and hear Bear in my head.

"Don't cry, Little Warrior."

For some reason it feels like Bear is all I have in the world now, which is stupid because he's just some boy from the other side of the fence that knows nothing about me nor I about him.

All I do know is that when I push him away, he doesn't leave, and it feels like a lifeline.

My eyes prickle with heat.

"Don't cry, Little Warrior."

2

———————

JAMIE

"Make any new friends today?"

"No, Bear. No friends."

Yelling comes from inside the house. A female shriek followed by a male bellow. I close my eyes, wishing they would all disappear.

"Who's that?" he asks.

"The other foster kids."

A heavy silence follows, as if Bear is unpacking those four words and examining them with great care. I'm so attuned to his presence now, I miss nothing, not even the quiet whoosh of air that leaves his lungs.

"They're loud," is all he says.

"Yeah." And I hate it. I should be grateful I have a roof over my head, but Sue fosters up to six kids at a time, me being one of them. The state released me into her care when I left the hospital three months ago, and I'll likely be here until at least sixteen—or when I decide what I'm going to do with my life. I haven't worked that out yet. All I know is that I want to leave. Every kid here has their issues, though we at least know better than to poke at each other over them.

The general consensus is that we leave each other alone until we each make our own escape.

"So what's your favourite subject at school?"

"None." Every day passes painfully slow, and each lesson is just as boring as the one that came before it. "They all suck. I mean, maybe one day those polynomial equations might come in handy, but I'm pretty sure there's a better chance of a meteor falling from the sky and hitting me on the head. Wouldn't we all be better off learning how to change the oil in a car?"

He laughs. "You just told a joke, Little Warrior."

"Huh." My dad is gone and I'm here making jokes as if I'm actually okay. The thought leaves a sick lump in the pit of my stomach. "I guess I've met my quota for the year."

"I'm sure there's more in there somewhere."

Ten minutes pass in silence and I'm left wondering why Bear bothers coming out here to talk to me at all. Isn't he sick of my surly attitude? I am. I'm sick to death of myself, but I can't escape me. *He* can. Doesn't he have better things to do?

"Bear?"

"Yeah?"

"Shouldn't you be out playing rugby?"

"Games are on weekends."

It's Wednesday. "Oh." Another minute passes. "What about practice?"

"We train Tuesday afternoons and early Friday mornings."

"Oh," I say again. "Why?"

"Why what?"

"Why do you play?" It's a rough sport. There's a lot of hard-core contact and violence and no padding or head gear. Just a mouthguard and a mass of blazing testosterone.

"Because it's fun. And it keeps me fit."

I get that. My sparring sessions were something I anticipated. They weren't easy, but I left feeling strong as if I accomplished something.

"But it's not just that," he adds.

It's not?

I don't voice the question, but he answers regardless. "We're a team. A family. Brothers. That's why we win all the time. Because all that matters is giving it everything. We don't let our mates down."

I pluck at the blades of grass while I sit cross-legged, listening to Bear, his voice infused with enthusiasm for the sport.

"Mateship is everything, Little Warrior."

"Is that why you keep banging on about me making friends?"

"Yeah, but at least you've got one, right?"

I'm pretty sure I just told Bear I've made no friends.

He huffs loudly, as if he can see my confusion from the other side of the fence. "Me, LW. Geez!"

"Oh."

"You don't think of us as friends?"

Friends? He's so much more than just a friend. He's … Bear is … I sigh. "I don't know what we are."

My eyes burn.

But I do know my world would be a little darker without you in it.

~

"So I was planting flowers the other day and—"

I snort. "You? Planting flowers?"

"Come on, LW, you're interrupting my story. So I was planting these flowers, and it was so bloody hot—"

"What kind of flowers?"

There's a pause and I tip my head back against the fence, appreciating the sun's warmth as I listen to Bear tell his story.

"What does it matter what freaking flowers they were?"

"Because I'm trying to picture your story in my head, and I can't do that if I don't know what kind of flowers they were."

We're sitting back-to-back against the fence. It's late on a Sunday afternoon, and I'm tired. Sue is slowly renovating her house. I offered to help chip out the old tile from the second bathroom. It wasn't the best time I've ever had, but it gave me something to do.

"They were purple ones," Bear says, and I can practically *feel* him rolling his eyes at me. It almost makes me chuckle. "So, like I said, it was bloody hot and I was sweating and getting sunburned, and my old neighbour from next door stops in and says you need to wait until the sun goes down. Either that or plant them in the morning when it's coolest. So, I say I can't do that. The instructions said to plant them in full sun."

My lips press together, fighting the smile. But it comes, and then I laugh, and he laughs right along with me. "That's the lamest thing I've ever heard! You didn't really plant any flowers, did you?"

"God no, but I made you laugh, didn't I? And that's better than purple flowers any day."

I suck in a sharp breath. "Bear."

"What?"

My heart pounds a little harder. *You're so ... everything.*

I RUSH to the fence straight after school, squinting through the slats, looking for movement. Nothing. "Bear, are you there?"

I made a friend today. Her name is Erin Tennyson, and I hit her with a text book. I was throwing it in my locker when it bounced off the open door and whacked her as she walked past.

"Hey, what did I ever do to you?" she asked jokingly, stooping to collect the book from the floor before I got the chance. When she straightened there was a teasing look on her face. It dropped a little when she handed it over, recognising who she was talking to.

"Sorry," I said.

"That's okay." She went to move on and hesitated.

Don't, I thought.

"You're Jamie Murphy, right?"

My heart began to pound so hard in my chest it hurt. The need to slam my locker door shut and scurry off was strong, but I thought of Bear and his repetitive question. *"Make any new friends today?"* Maybe today I could give him a different answer. Shock him a little. The thought almost made me grin.

I arranged a smile on my face, my lips curving slowly. It felt forced and she could probably tell, but it was better than none at all. Wasn't it? "That's me."

She smiled back. It was bright and beaming as if my response gave her a thrill. Did she not read what happened in the tabloids? *No one* smiled at me like that. "I'm Erin Tennyson." She even held out a hand. I shook it. "Walk to class with me?"

"Why?" I asked before I could stop myself, turning to close my locker. I wasn't sure I wanted to hear the answer.

"Honestly?" We started walking together down the hall. Erin was tall, at least a head higher than me, with a blond braid and blue eyes. She had that wholesome look to her. Athletic. I was pretty sure she played volleyball. "You've got this whole *fuck off* vibe going on, but I decided today that maybe I wouldn't."

"Wouldn't what?"

She looked at me sideways, giving me a *duh* expression. "Fuck off."

"Oh." I laughed a little.

"Wow." She waggled her brows. "You have a great smile."

"Yeah, Dad spent a huge amount of money on my ..." I faltered, caught off guard at my slip.

"Sorry," she replied, wincing as she re-shouldered her bag. "I meant you're really beautiful. It sort of smacks you in the face when you smile."

"Kinda like my text book?"

"Yeah." She laughed. "Like that."

Bear was right, of course, like he always seemed to be. Human beings aren't made to be isolated, yet here I was, pretending to be the only person in the world. Walking back to Sue's house after school that afternoon felt a little less ... solitary.

"Bear?"

There's still no response. Then I remember it's Tuesday. He's at rugby training.

My shoulders sag against the fence.

~

THE NEXT DAY I'm back at the fence after school. I still haven't told Bear about Erin. I sat with her 'group' at lunch today. I didn't say much, but that sense of belonging with people made the day a little easier to bear.

"You there?"

Nothing.

Where are you?

~

THURSDAY I'M BACK AGAIN like a sad little puppy missing its owner.

"Bear?"

~

SUNDAY AFTERNOON I stare at the fence from the kitchen window, where I hold a cereal bowl under the sink, rinsing it absentmindedly. The other fosters eat like a famine is imminent and Wheaties was all I could find for afternoon tea.

The lack of food never usually bothers me, but that empty growling from my belly was my first hunger pain in months. All because I decided to join a Goju-ryu Karate school yesterday, taking along my old uniform and the black belt it took me eight years to earn. And today I quit. Because yeah, it seems like I'm a quitter now.

The smell of the mats. The muscle memory. The entire discipline.

It was too much being there without Dad. I almost threw up all over myself.

I set the bowl upside down on the rack and open the window. The sound of laughter rings out. Two bodies are moving in the yard behind ours, shouting friendly slurs as a ball flies between them both. Bear is back. And he has a friend over.

I grip the edges of the sink as longing swells in my chest. I haven't lost the urge to tell him about Erin, but there's a new urge there too. One that wants to tell him about my failed attempt at returning to karate. But I can't do that without talking about Dad, and talking about Dad means he'll know what happened too. And maybe if he knew …

If he knew …

He might decide I'm not worth talking to anymore.

Reaching over, I grasp the handle of the window and slam it shut.

3

———————

JAMIE

"Are you pissed off at me?"

"No." I'm sitting against the fence, knees drawn up, text-book open in my lap. To be honest, the moment I saw movement in the yard beyond mine, my heart skipped a small beat. I grabbed my books and made my way out, plopping myself down in a fashion that's become more familiar to me than brushing my teeth. But now that I'm here, I don't know what to say. It's been a whole week. We've never gone that long without talking to each other before.

"You're not saying anything."

"It's better not talking, remember?"

"Are we back to this?"

I can hear the scowl in his tone, and the atmosphere is tense. Bear isn't in a great mood. Is this how it is for him when I'm always surly? It makes me want to reach under the fence and grab his hand. Obviously, I don't. Boys don't hold girls' hands to make themselves feel better do they? Or do they?

"No," I say instead. "We're not. I'm sorry, Bear."

"What did you say?"

"I said no."

"Not that. The other part."

My brows rise. "Ummm, we're not?"

"No. The part after that one."

"I'm sorry?"

"Yeah, say that again."

"Bear!" I laugh and whack the fence, hoping it jostles him.

"Hey!" It does but he laughs too. His inevitable question comes soon after. "So, did you make any new friends today?"

My heart swells. I have a positive answer for him today. "Actually …" I drag it out.

There's hope in his tone. "Actually what?"

"I kinda did."

His shout is loud. "No shit, LW! Tell me."

"Tuesday last week at school. Her name is Erin. I threw my textbook at her."

Bear snorts. "Only you could make a friend by punching them with a book."

I chew the inside of my cheek, sort of grinning but trying not to. The pride in his voice is unmistakeable. It lifts me up, making my heart a little lighter, making me feel a little taller. A little stronger. "Yeah."

We talk about Erin for a minute until shouting comes from inside the house, ricocheting outward and filling the yard. Sue is mad. One of the fosters took off three days ago without a word. She's been out driving around for hours, searching. She might not be the most kind or loving person, but sometimes I get the impression she cares. Just a small bit. Either way, the fighting makes everything tense.

I sigh. "Bear?"

"Yeah?"

"Do you have any brothers or sisters?"

"Nope. It's just me."

"Same."

"Kinda wish I did though." His voice is wistful.

"Why?"

"I like people, Little Warrior."

"Why?"

He laughs and it dies off slowly, leaving me hanging for his answer. "I don't know. I guess I don't like being alone."

"Are you alone a lot?"

Bear sighs. "Not really. Just … sometimes it feels that way. Even when there are people there. Does that make sense?"

The whole feeling lonely in a room full of people? "Yes."

He exhales, a sound of relief. "Good. Because it sounded kinda stupid in my head."

"Umm …" I hesitate. "Is everything okay? With you?"

Bear is my rock, but sometimes I forget even rocks need the ground to hold them up. He's unknowingly reminded me of how self-absorbed I've been. Most of the time I can't see beyond my own pain in order to recognise it in someone else.

"No." His voice dips. "I'm not okay."

Oh god. *Bear.* My stomach drops. "What happened?"

"I lost my rugby ball."

"You …" My mouth opens. That's it? "You lost your freaking rugby ball?"

"Yeah." He sounds forlorn as if he lost his best friend.

"Bear!" I turn and whack my fist against the fence. Again. And *ouch!* That hurt. "Dammit!"

"What?" His defensive tone has me rolling my eyes. "Haven't you ever seen Castaway with Tom Hanks? Wiiillllsonnnn!"

I palm my face, shaking my head. "What am I going to do with you?"

"You could kiss me," he says from left field.

"What?" I blurt out, even though I heard him clear as a bell. My cheeks burn hot beneath my hands, and my heart begins a steady gallop. "Why would you say something like that?" I squeak, holding my breath for his answer.

"To hear your reaction." There's a grin in his voice. "You sound so embarrassed. Have you ever been kissed, Little Warrior?"

No. "Yes. Have you?"

"What was his name?"

"Tom," I throw out.

Bear busts out laughing.

"What?"

"You're so making that up. Tom was the first name that came to mind because we were talking about Castaway."

"*You* were talking about Castaway," I retort.

"Are you sure you're almost sixteen?" he asks. "Because you sound ten."

"Har har. Yes, I'm sure. It's my birthday in four weeks."

"What date?"

"Next month. The tenth."

"LW?"

I sigh. Maybe I should tell him my name.

But then he'll know, cautions the niggly little voice in my head. And you don't want him to stop talking to you, do you? But maybe … maybe he wouldn't care?

Or he would.

It's your risk.

"Yes, Bear?"

"I could be your first."

"First kiss?"

"Yeah."

"I told you—"

"Don't lie." His voice softens. "You can keep stuff from me, but don't lie."

A minute of silence passes between us. I count the beats of my heart, knowing it's still fast. "You don't even know what I look like."

"You have brown hair and brown eyes."

"But—"

He cuts me off again. "Why do I need to know what you look like? Isn't what I feel enough to know what I want?"

He has feelings for me? Does that mean he likes me? In *that way?*

My face feels hot as I ask the question, my voice cracking on the words. "And you want to kiss *me*?"

"Maybe not today. One day? Soon?"

I run my tongue over my lips, as if testing whether they're kiss worthy. Then I imagine Bear pressing his mouth to mine. My eyes close, the image stealing my breath. The sun beating down. The dappled shade from the tree above. The buzzing of insects. The warm, musky scent of his skin. His lips soft, their touch gentle but sure. Shivers skate across my skin.

"Okay," I croak. "One day. Soon."

Dad would flip his lid. The usual wave of pain rises up, and I shove it away. Not today. Please.

～

"So what are we doing for your birthday?" Erin asks, unpacking the wrapper on her sandwich.

We're sitting out on the grass in the common area at school during our lunch break. It's been our favourite spot for weeks now since the weather started getting cool. The sun is bright and warm and chases the goose bumps away.

Time has passed quickly as I get to know my new friend, and now my birthday is only ten days away. The first one without— No. Sorry, Dad. But it's easier to shove you out.

"Sweet sixteen," she adds with an excited shake of her shoulders, as if I'd forgotten. Erin is a permanently happy soul. I'm guessing she was pushed out of the vaginal canal with a giant smile on her face and hasn't stopped since. You would think it annoying, but I don't seem to mind. It's almost as if she smiles enough for the both of us. She has an older brother, Matt, who's equally as cheerful. He's blond too, with blue eyes. Cute, if you liked cute. But I like deep, teasing voices and messy golden-brown hair. I like humour and complexity. I like—

I realise the path my thoughts are taking me down and catch my breath.

Bear.

I like Bear.

"Jamie?"

My eyes shift from the distance and focus on Erin. "Huh?"

"Birthday?" she prompts. "What are we doing?"

"I hadn't planned on doing anything." Except talk to Bear.

"We could have a party at my place?" The waggle of her brows suggests she finds this an excellent idea.

"My birthday falls on a Tuesday." And Bear has training that day. My shoulders sag. He won't be home until late.

"I know that, silly," she retorts, tossing one of her sandwich crusts at me. I'm wearing my hair down today, and it catches in the long strands, dangling there, smearing butter and tomato seeds everywhere.

"Erin! Gross."

She laughs and rises to her knees, reaching across to snatch it free and toss it to the grass. Then she tries wiping the mess from my hair. I slap her hand away, laughing too. "Oh my god. Stop. You've done enough damage."

Erin sits back down and picks up the other half of her sandwich. She takes a massive bite, talking around the mouthful bulging from her cheek. "I was thinking the following Saturday. Maybe you could invite…" she hesitates "…Bear? Is that his name?"

My brows snap together. "Why would I do that?"

"You talk about him all the time. Bear said this. Bear did that."

"I do not!"

"You totally do."

"I don't, do I? Really?"

"Yes."

I purse my lips.

It's Monday afternoon, the day before my birthday. I'm standing in front of the bathroom mirror, assessing my hair and face. The scar on my cheek has faded. It's thin now and maybe an inch long. Barely noticeable. But maybe … maybe I could cover it with a bit of makeup for my birthday party.

I run fingers through my hair. Erin trimmed it for me today. She brought her mum's hairdressing scissors to school, and we sat outside during lunch break while she chopped off about three inches. It only reaches halfway down my back now, but there's more life to it now. The colour looks richer. More vibrant.

I take a step back, getting a sense of my overall appearance. My skin is tan from sitting out in the yard all the time, my brows thick and even, my eyes dark. Lips full and rosy. But I don't see beauty. I don't see hope in my eyes. Or warmth. Or love. I still see a girl who failed.

I swallow thickly and leave the bathroom.

Who cares what I look like anyway?

Bear probably won't come to my party. I can't imagine anyone wanting to.

After grabbing my textbooks from my school bag, I ignore the other fosters like I usually do and trek my way out to the fence. Finding my groove, I sit down and open my books, flicking pages as I find my place while I wait for Bear.

"Happy birthday Eve."

I jolt, not realising he was already there. It was too quiet. Usually he's stomping about, or kicking a ball, or flicking a pen. Something.

"Thanks. I'm uh … having a party. At Erin's."

"Wow, cool, Little Warrior. Look at you go. A real member of society now."

"Hardly." I let out a shaky breath and forge ahead. "No one will probably come. But I was thinking that maybe you—"

"You're kidding, right? This is Fremantle. You'll get a packed house. Any chance for a party."

He cut me off unintentionally, but now I've lost my nerve. "How was school?" I ask instead.

"Same old shit, different day."

"You sound like me," I tease, rubbing sweaty hands against the knees of my old, faded jeans. Why am I so nervous? "Bear, I wanted to—"

"Sorry, LW. I can't stay today. There's stuff I have to do." My body deflates like a popped balloon, leaving a sad, empty feeling inside. "I just wanted to tell you I'll be here tomorrow after practice to wish you a happy birthday. If that's cool?"

I swallow my disappointment, pushing it down deep inside. "Of course that's cool," I say with forced cheer. "Go do your stuff," I add, as if him leaving early is no big deal. As if I haven't been looking forward to 'seeing' him all day while at school, counting down every painful minute, watching each second tick over until I was ready to scream my frustration.

"I got you a present."

My breath catches, surprised. "You did?"

"Yep." Bear sounds really pleased with himself, and my curiosity rises. I bite down on my bottom lip, a grin forming.

"What is it?"

"As if I'm gonna tell you. You'll find out tomorrow. Think you can hold out until then?"

"No," I quip.

He laughs and I hear the grass rustling from the other side of the fence, catching a shift of movement. "I've got to go."

"So go," I say, feigning indifference.

He pauses, his big frame lingering behind the fence. "LW?"

"Yeah?"

"I miss you when we're not together. Is that weird?"

His admission sends flutters through my belly. He misses me the same way I miss him. I'm not alone in this, whatever it is. "No," I say softly. "It's not weird."

Bear leaves and it's not until he's gone I realise I didn't get a chance to invite him to my party.

4

JAMIE

"*H*appy birthday, Little Warrior."

I close my eyes, a tear tracking its way down my cheek. I wasn't sure how I'd feel waking up today, knowing it's my first birthday without Dad here. Without him cooking his horrible birthday pancakes with the chocolate drops plonked in to make a wonky smiley face. They tasted like rubber, but I didn't care. It was enough having Dad in the kitchen with a spatula and a grin, along with a pile of wrapped presents waiting on the counter. I used to get all the latest gadgets and toys. Nothing ever girly because he didn't know about that stuff. Neither did I. I still don't. But none of that matters. Material things feel so meaningless now.

I clear my throat. "Thanks, Bear."

"You're not crying, are you?"

I open my eyes, scrubbing a hand across my face. "Of course not."

"Is it …" He hesitates and I know why. When it comes to talking about anything personal, I'm a freaking cactus.

"Yeah." Air leaves my lungs in a *whoosh.* "Today just feels … wrong."

"Do you want to talk about it?"

It's dusk and cold. Shivers track across my exposed arms. There's no dappled sunlight at this time of year. No chirping crickets. No bees hovering from flower to flower, taking their fill. I've always thought of winter as the saddest season. Everything is dark and gloomy. Cold. Windy. It's harsh and unforgiving, whereas summer is beautiful. It might get hot enough to blister your skin, but it's bright and full of hope.

Bear is like my summer in this cold, crappy season.

"Nope," I say. "I don't." His disappointment is almost tangible. If it were a brick, it would hit me in the face. It's been five months, and I'm still closed up tighter than a clam. *Dammit, Bear.* Why do you poke and prod me so? And why do I feel this urge not to let you down? "I wouldn't even know where to start."

"Start wherever you want to."

I draw a deep breath inside my lungs and picture the first thing that comes to mind. It's me in the Dojo. The mat beneath my bare feet is cool, the scent of old sweat wrinkles my nose. Dad stands across from me, taunting me, eyes gleaming with anticipation as he waits for me to put him on the ground. Not that I could. His strength and size made it impossible, but he expected me to give it a red-hot go regardless. "I have a black belt in karate. I used to love it in the same way you love your rugby."

"Wow, that's pretty cool, LW. Are you telling me you could kick my butt if you wanted to?"

"Totally. I could take you down like *that*," I say, snapping my fingers.

"Ha! I'd like to see you try."

"Is that a challenge?"

"Hell yes. I love a good challenge. How long did it take to work your way up to a black belt?"

"Eight years. I got it last year, a couple of months after I turned fifteen."

"And what made you choose karate?"

"Not what, but who."

His voice softens. "Your dad."

"Yeah. He was one of the best fighters there was. One of the greats."

The image of my father and me in the Dojo fades like smoke in the wind. I want to replace it with the image of Bear, but I can't because I've never seen his face. Anger tightens my chest. Anger at myself. I never used to be this way. Never. That face I saw in the mirror—the one with the scar and the empty eyes—used to hold determination. Confidence. I was a fighter like my dad. Now I'm nothing but a timid mouse, too scared to feel anything anymore.

"What happened?" Bear prompts.

Is he already starting to connect the dots? "He got injured and everything went downhill from there. He started on drugs and alcohol. They got him through the pain when I couldn't. I wasn't enough to help him, Bear."

A pained sound leaves his throat, and I wipe at my eyes. "Don't say that. You were just a kid. What were you supposed to have done?"

"I don't know. Something. Anything. I was strong. I could have handled it."

"You're still strong, Little Warrior."

"Not anymore."

"How can you say that? Life brought you the biggest fight of your life, and you know what you did?"

"What?"

"You showed up. Every day. You showed up. You're still showing up. One day you'll look back and realise how much strength it took just to do that."

I swallow the sob climbing my throat. I would have never showed up if it weren't for Bear. Life would have beat me to the mat, and I would have stayed down, defeated, never to get up again. "You don't understand. I killed him, Bear." My voice cracks. "My father died because of *me*."

He sucks in a sharp breath. "Jesus, LW. You can't take that on yourself."

I jerk my head, nodding. "Yes I can, because it was my fault. I was the one driving the car. It was *me.*"

There. Connect the dots now. His death headlined every paper across the world. News reports covered the story on television. You couldn't turn on the radio without hearing something. They spun his story into a tragedy. Dead at just forty years old, his daughter at the wheel. One of the greatest fighters to ever live. So handsome. Fierce. Vital. Now gone. There was an outpouring of grief—all of it utter bullshit. Where was the love when he was spiralling? When he needed it most? None of them were there to pick him up when he hit rock bottom. There was only me. And I failed.

"Jamie," Bear whispers. "That's your name, isn't it? Jamie Murphy."

Hearing it on his lips for the first time is too much, like I want to claw my way out of my skin. I sink down against the fence, wiping my face, my stomach clenching in a sick, hot ball.

"It was a freak accident. An *accident.*"

A snort escapes me. It's a horrible, bitter sound. "Maybe so, but I was the reason he was in the car to start with. If I hadn't made him go, he would never have died."

"What happened?"

"He took something. I don't know what it was. He was shaking and slurring his words. I was so freaking scared." He was failing right in front of my eyes. Falling apart. And it broke my heart. "I called an ambulance, but they were taking too long. I should have waited." I curl my arms around my knees and drop my head. "I should have waited."

A few seconds pass as I rock painfully into myself. "Jamie?"

"Yes?" I whisper against my legs.

"Neither of you would have got in the car if he hadn't taken anything."

Anger rises swiftly, hot and bright. My father was everything. *Everything.* He simply went too far, and tried too hard, and it broke him. "So what ... I should blame him?"

"No. But I think you're angry at him and you don't want to be.

You're angry because he died and left you alone. But you can't stand being angry at him, so you take it out on yourself instead."

My protest rises swiftly, sweeping his words away. "That's the dumbest thing I've ever heard!"

Bear's voice softens. "It's okay to be mad."

"I'm not!" My cheeks grow hot. "It was *my* fault. He didn't want to go, but I *made him.* I didn't know he was going to jerk the wheel while I was driving, trying to get me to turn the car around. He didn't want the publicity of an overdose. I jerked the wheel back, only I jerked it too far and lost control." I scrunch my eyes shut, hearing the almighty bang all over again, the sound like a thunderclap, the screech of metal, the shards of glass splintering my face. "We hit a tree. The force made the car flip, and he died." My voice breaks, my jaw chattering. "He d-d-died."

Bear makes a noise that's deep and heavy and sad. "I'm sorry. I wish I could fix it for you. I wish I could do something."

I wipe at my face. "Being here is enough in case you didn't know."

"Maybe this will help?"

"What?"

"Look down."

My eyes shift down and to my right, seeing nothing. What the— I look over to my left. Bear is pushing something underneath the fence. His hand is already large for seventeen, his big knuckles scraping the timber panels as he nudges a small pouch towards me. It's pale blue in colour with a thin gold ribbon tying it together, complete with a little bow. It looks tiny and delicate in his hand.

My birthday present. Just like he promised. I reach for it. My fingers graze his, and there's an urge to grab hold. He releases the little pouch, and I don't think. Before he can retreat, I put my hand on his. I don't know how he manages it, but he twists his wrist until his palm is open. My hand slides in easily, and his fingers wrap around mine, warm and rough.

The small bit of intimacy has my breath catching in my throat, but I like it. I'm grateful for that small contact. I can't remember the last time I openly touched someone.

It feels good.

It feels *so good.*

My eyes burn as the sweet bloom of something big and beautiful begins to unfurl in my chest. "Bear."

His voice is gruff. "I'm here."

We sit there quietly for a long moment as if absorbing each other, my hand in his, my heart pounding, unwilling to let go.

He breaks the silence eventually. "Are you going to open your present?"

My fingers slide from his, slow and reluctant, and they reach for the pouch. "You didn't have to get me anything."

"I know. I'm gift enough," he says, laughing.

I snort. "You have no shame!"

"I thought you could have this for when I'm not here," he continues as I tackle the sweet little bow, pulling it until it slips free.

"You're here almost every day." I roll my eyes, but there's a smile on my lips as I wedge my fingers inside to loosen the gathered fabric. It opens and I reach inside, my fingers brushing against what feels like a scrap of paper. I ignore it when I feel something cool and metallic. "Oh, Bear," I breathe, pulling out a silver chain.

It's a necklace, the metal delicate yet somehow substantial, as if he wanted to make sure it was strong enough to last forever. On it dangles a little silver rectangle, and I realise there are words stamped into it. I place it on my palm for a closer look.

Capital letters spell out LITTLE WARRIOR.

"Do you like it?"

My hand shakes. I couldn't imagine anything more perfect if I tried. "It's beautiful."

"It's a reminder," he tells me. "So you never forget who you are."

"Thank you, Bear." I undo the clasp, sliding the pretty chain around my neck and securing it in place. "I won't ever take it off."

◡

MY BROWS SNAP TOGETHER as I twist against the fence, peering through the slats. It's the Wednesday afternoon following my birthday, and the yard behind me has felt eerily deserted for over an hour now—at least until I heard an odd noise. The sound of a bucket being dropped on cement or something.

"Bear?" I call out.

I get nothing in return.

My hand shifts to my neck, grasping the cool metal, warming it beneath my fingers.

"Bear?"

◡

I DON'T EVEN WALK inside the house after school the next afternoon. I walk straight to the fence, dumping my bag by the back door on my way. He's always there first on Thursdays, waiting for me. My skin tingles with anticipation. I still haven't asked him about the party yet, and it's only two days away now.

"Bear?" I press my face against the timber, peeking through as best I can. "Are you there?"

Still nothing.

A small knot forms in my belly.

Where are you?

I go back for my bag and bring it back to the fence, doing my homework while I wait. We have required reading for class, and I pull my tattered copy of *The Catcher in the Rye* free and find my place, slowly immersing myself in the story. Time passes and when I look up it's eerie and dark.

Shivers skate down my spine.

I twist around in my little groove. "Bear?" I whisper, confused.

◡

FRIDAY AFTERNOON COMES AND GOES, and there's a sick sense of panic in my belly. Today was my last chance to ask him to my party, and he isn't here.

Shoulders slumped, I shove my hands in the pockets of my shorts and head inside. It's enough to have me reaching for the phone and calling Erin.

Her mum answers. "Oh hey, Jamie. Happy birthday for Tuesday, sweetheart."

"Thanks, Mrs. Tennyson," I reply dutifully while busting inside with impatience. I need advice. *Now.* "Is Erin there?"

"She's upstairs. I'll call her down."

A muffled crackle comes down the line then a *clunk.* "Eeeriiiinn!" Mrs. Tennyson hollers. "Jamie's on the phone."

"Coooommmiinnnng!" I hear her yell.

The sound of a teasing sibling fight gets closer, and then the phone *clunks* again. "Hello?" she answers, breathless.

"It's me."

"Who's me?" she sing-songs.

"Erin," I whine.

"Actually, I'm glad you called." Her voice is now all business. "We have to talk party stuff."

My brows rise. "What kind of party stuff?"

"The best kind," she retorts. "The *food* kind. Mum was thinking instead of doing the frozen party pies and sausage rolls, she could make mini hotdogs for us. Maybe even some mini burgers. Sliders, I think she called them, although she mentioned putting some kind of foreign festy cheese on them so we might have to rein her in a little."

"I like all kinds of cheese." But it sounds like a lot of work for her mother. And money. Especially for some random girl she barely knows. "She would do that for us? For me?"

"Umm yes! Mum loves to fuss, and it's our duty as her offspring to let her."

"If you're sure. I'll come over early to help."

"Yes! Then we can do our hair and makeup together."

"Makeup? Gross, Erin. I don't want that stuff slathered all over my face."

"It's not like we're putting pancakes on our face. Just a little mascara. Maybe some blush and lipstick. I have to see what I can hijack from Mum's makeup case. Then we can put it on just before everyone arrives. That way she won't have time to make us go upstairs and wash it off."

It sounds like a lot of work, but it's obvious my birthday party is the Erin Train now and I'm just along for the ride. Not that I mind. I have no idea how to plan a party. "Well okay."

"Did you ask Bear yet?"

Erin knows I haven't been able to catch him this week. It's obvious, she told me. Apparently my face hangs lower than "a pair of old lady's boobs" whenever he doesn't show up. "He wasn't there again, Erin. That's why I called. I don't know what to do."

"Can't you just … go over there?"

My heart pounds at the very thought. "You mean just walk on over and knock on the front door?"

"Yeah."

"I don't … I can't."

"Yes, you can. It's not like your legs have fallen off. Just grow a ballsack and walk over there."

"Erin!" I wail, shuddering at the word *ballsack*. "Gross!"

She busts out laughing. "I know." Her voice lowers as though she's trying to muffle her words from others. "How freaking hideous. Imagine one day having to actually touch a set of wrinkly, hairy, sweaty balls— Ouch!" The sound of a *thump* comes down the line. "Matt!" Erin yells.

Her brother's voice is muffled. "Better than having two airbags hanging off your chest."

"At least our airbags look good. Yours are just—"

"Kids!" Mrs. Tennyson whips out, as if she had a whole bunch of straws at the start of her day and now she's reached her last one. "Enough. It's time for dinner."

"Woohoo! Food," Erin says into the phone. "I have to go eat. Go ask him, Jamie. Be like Nike and just do it. Then report back."

She hangs up.

I put the phone down and contemplate walking over to Bear's house tomorrow morning. Just walking right up to the front door and knocking. I'd have to walk down the end of my street and then all the way back up to his house, but it wouldn't take more than ten minutes—fifteen at the most if I take my time.

I have to do it someday. And I want him with me at this party. I'm not sure I can do it without him. My hands shake at the thought of sitting in a room with a bunch of kids from school, all of them pretending they're not watching me. Watching the kid who killed her dad in a car crash.

Taking a deep breath, I decide to go first thing tomorrow. I don't have a choice. I'm one hundred percent sure I can't do this party without him. I just can't. Not unless I bring the party to the fence, and not only is that too ridiculous to imagine, the fence is *our* spot.

Lying in bed that night, my head on my pillow, eyes trained on the ceiling, I remember the feel of his hand on mine.

"Never forget who you are."

I reach up and clutch the necklace in my fist, feeling the cool metal turn warm beneath my touch. Soothed, I slowly drift to sleep.

5

JAMIE

I step outside the front door, knowing the morning is getting away from me. If I don't make the trek to Bear's house, he'll be gone for rugby and I'll be too late. My head tilts up, contemplating the sky. It's overcast and a faint rumble echoes in the distance. An angry storm is bearing down. I should grab an umbrella, but if I take the time to hunt for it, I might change my mind about going at all. Instead, I pull the door closed and lift the hood of my sweatshirt, letting it cover my head and half my forehead, hiding my long dark hair from sight.

Hunching against the cold brittle air, I tuck my hands into the torn, faded denim shorts that only reach the tops of my thighs. The wind bites my legs as I start to walk, prickling my skin. I shiver and shove my hands deeper into the pockets.

Cars whiz past as I walk alongside the road, their occupants eager to beat the rain home. *I can't believe I'm really doing this.* Walking to his house. Putting one foot in front of the other, my heart pounding with every step I take. Erin's voice is an echo in my head. *Be like Nike and just do it.* How easy she's made it seem, this friendship of ours. I just know she'll be my best friend for life.

I have Bear to thank for that. There's so much hope in my chest now, where before there was none. Hope that he'll come to the party. That maybe he *will* be my first kiss. My first love. Maybe even the greatest love of my life.

Before I know it, I've turned down his street. Breathing comes a little harder now. My stomach churns and my palms are sweating. Anxiety is taking hold, but I continue on. Bear told me once that I was strong, and if I do this, then maybe I'll believe it.

His house looms. It's weatherboard and a little rundown, like most of the properties along the street. Like the one I live in. The one I still can't bring myself to call home.

I pause at his front path, hesitating, fighting the urge to run. I glance behind me, an instinctive need to ensure my getaway is clear. There's a noise inside. A bang and crash. My head swings back. Someone is home.

Just do it.

I wipe sweaty hands against my shorts then shove them back in my pockets, forcing my legs to move towards the front door. I reach it, my chest so freaking tight it's a wonder I can breathe at all as I knock on the screen door. The noise inside the house stops.

I can see partially inside. The floors are timber and worn, the furniture minimal. Footsteps make their way towards me, bringing an older woman into view. She's wearing tatty clothes, her greying hair tied into a knot on top of her head. Strands have escaped and hang on her forehead, sticking to the sweaty sheen of her face. Is that Bear's mother? She looks so tired.

She peers at me from the other side of the door, and I realise my hood is shadowing my face. I swipe it from my head with my palm, mussing my hair. I attempt to smooth it as I arrange a polite smile on my face.

"Can I help you?" she asks.

"Umm yes. I'm looking for uh …" Crap. I didn't think this through very well. "… The boy who lives here. Your uh, son?"

"Oh, honey." She chuckles and even that sounds tired. "My boys are grown up and long gone."

My brows pull together, confused. "I'm sorry." I take a step back, looking at the house to my left and right. "I must have the wrong house."

"Oh, I don't live here. I'm just the cleaner, love."

Bear has a cleaner? Nothing seems to compute.

"You're probably looking for the young man who used to live here with his mother."

I pause, my voice the faintest whisper. "Used to?"

She clucks her tongue in sympathy, and I know she's about to deliver something I really don't want to hear. I really don't. "Never mind." I jerk my thumb over my shoulder as I take another step backwards. "I'll just—"

"Don't you know?"

I take another step. And another. She's talking and I just want her to stop. "Never mind. I'll just—"

"This row is all government hospice houses."

"Hospice?" I echo, pausing.

"Housing and care for the terminally ill," she clarifies. "The young man lived here with his mother. She died a few days ago." An expression of sympathy is aimed my way. "I'm sorry, love. You knew them?"

Shock steals my breath.

All this time.

All this time.

My stomach churns. A rioting hot mess as memories hit me in the face.

"Go kick your ball somewhere else," I'd hissed at him so furiously.

Bear met me by that fence, day after day, talking about anything and everything except the one thing that mattered most. He lifted me up when I was down. He was there for me. He saved me from myself when all along …

My eyes burn and anger rises, swift and hard and hot, faster than the incoming storm. *Damn you, Bear. Why didn't you tell me?*

"No." I shake my head at the cleaner, hands clenched into fists. I swallow furious tears, except they're rising too fast. One slips free. Then another. I scrub at my face. "I didn't know them."

I turn blindly, stumbling my way back down the front path, knowing the words I spoke were painfully, heartbreakingly true.

Reaching Sue's house, I make my way inside towards my room. Grabbing the necklace from around my neck, I rip it free and toss it across the room, enraged.

"Fuck you, Bear!" I scream as loud as my lungs will allow. "Fuck you!"

A bang comes against my wall. One of the fosters trying to sleep the day away. "Shut up, Murphy!"

"You shut up!" I yell, kicking the wall. It felt good. I kick it again and scream.

Bear is gone.

He's nothing except smoke in the wind now, just like my father. I swallow, fighting back tears, but it's too much. A jagged sob escapes, and I sink to the floor, my head dropping to my hands, tears falling until I can barely see. When I open my eyes, they land on my necklace where it rests broken on the floor.

"I won't ever take it off."

I can't wear it, at least not right now, but I collect it from the floor. After finding the small pouch it came in, I open it wide and let the little chain drop inside. It emits a crinkling sound. My brows draw together as I peer inside and see a bit of paper. I reach inside and pull it out. It's a note. A tiny folded note. I unwrap it, almost tearing it in my haste.

It's handwritten. To me. The words marked out with what seems like painstaking care.

Little Warrior,

I'm sorry. I suck at goodbyes and you deserve a better one than this, but I'm not strong like you. It's easier to be a coward and leave you this note instead.

My mother died today and it hurts so fucking much. She had cancer. I'm sorry I didn't tell you. You deserved to know, but I couldn't bring myself to talk about it because it made everything too real.

I'm joining the army. I know it looks like I'm running away, maybe I am, but I don't know what else to do. I need to find out where I belong. My purpose. And I feel like maybe I'm holding you back from yours. You need to leave our fence behind and join the world again, Jamie. It needs strong people like you.

I wish I met you under different circumstances. And that I could be your first kiss. Maybe one day I'll regret that I wasn't. In fact, I'm pretty sure I already do. Please find yourself a good guy. There are too many assholes in the world already—perhaps I'm one of them—but you deserve the best.

I'll never forget you.

Yours always,

Bear.

6

———

JAMIE

*wo years later.*

"THE FUCK DID YOU JUST SAY?" Erin pales beneath the dusting of blusher she's sweeping across her cheekbones.

She turns from the bathroom mirror to look at me, her eyes rounding like dinner plates and her mouth wide open. I'm seated on the closed lid of the toilet seat, watching her do her face. We're getting ready for a night out, my first *real* one, because I turned eighteen four days ago. Apparently it's the age the Australian government deems you mature enough to handle parties and alcohol—legally at least. I'm on board with that. School is done with me and I'm more than done with it. It's time I found my purpose, just like Bear.

"I joined the army."

"Jamie," she breathes, clearly at a loss for words. I watch her shocked expression slowly evolve into one of pity.

"Don't."

She shakes her head. "You don't even know his name. Or what he

41

looks like." The hospice service wouldn't provide the information for privacy reasons. God knows Erin tried after she found me on the floor of my room the afternoon of my birthday party, the letter crumpled in my hand.

"I'm not looking for him."

"Then what *are* you looking for?"

"Myself."

Her eyes fill. "Dammit, Jamie. You can't leave." Her chin lifts, the makeup brush in her hand forgotten. "In fact, you're not going. I won't let you. Go un-join or whatever it is you do."

"It's too late. I leave tomorrow."

"This is the stupidest thing you've ever done," she bites out, turning back to the mirror as if she's too pissed to even look at me right now. "And you've done some stupid shit."

"Umm, I think you mean *you've* done some stupid shit," I say, chuckling. "You know, like the time Maria Medina said your eyebrows were huge so you shaved half of them off."

Erin flattens her lips, but I see them twitch. The hairs grew back in all wonky after that particular disaster. "Or the time you stole the blusher from that store, the high-end place where they looked down on us for asking what a lip liner was. What was that colour called again? Watermelon ripple?"

"Watermelon slushie."

I snort. "And then your mum found out and made you wear it on your cheeks so thick you looked like a clown and then took you out to the shops with it on."

Erin shakes her head, picking up her tube of mascara from the bathroom counter. "I wanted to die."

We're silent for a moment as she fiddles with the wand. Then she turns back around, looking at me. "It wasn't crazy, though, not like the time you jumped off that cliff because Michael King dared you."

"He was a jerk."

"He liked you though."

"He had a strange way of showing it," I retort.

Erin hesitates. "All the boys liked you. You just never noticed. You're so … unobtainable. And so reckless. And beautiful as all hell."

"Erin—"

"But still so freaking stupid." Her eyebrows turn to angry slashes. "Like the time you set fire to the back fence in your yard and the fire brigade got called."

My heart jerks at the mention of it. I'd wanted to destroy every memory of Bear I had. I thought burning the fence would stop his voice inside my head. All it took was two shots of vodka for courage and a packet of matches. But he still speaks to me. And here I am, two years later, talking back to him as if he's still here. "I was angry."

"You know most people don't turn into arsonists when someone pisses them off. And now here's your stupidest stunt of all." Her arms sweep out wide, and an eyelash curler clatters to the tiles below. "Joining the freaking army."

"It's not stupid. It's—"

"Stupid."

"Erin." She turns back to the mirror and tilts her head, brushing the mascara wand over her lashes. "Maybe you're right." Her hand stills and her eyes flick to my reflection in the mirror. "But I don't know what else to do."

A frustrated sound escapes her throat, and she spins back around. "In case you forgot … there's a war in Afghanistan! Soldiers are getting sent to fight. Some of them aren't coming home alive!"

Fear twists my stomach. It's all I've thought about. Apart from Bear. "I know, but there's something you seem to have forgotten."

"And what's that?" she throws out, her tone bitter.

"I was raised by the greatest fighter there was. It's what I do best."

Her bottom lip wobbles, and I know it's the right time to tell her the second phase of my plan. It will take her mind from the first. "There's just one thing I need to do before I go."

She breathes in, her nostrils flaring. "What's that?"

"Lose my virginity."

Her eyes widen all over again, flickering with a hint of something that looks suspiciously like excitement. "Girl," she says and holds up a hand. We high-five each other, and she giggles. "I have no idea how you held out this long. My clit would literally explode if I waited like you have. But with who?"

Make sure you give yourself to a good guy.

My breath escapes in a huff. *Shut up, Bear. This is the one thing I was holding on to for you, the one thing I kept safe, but you left and you never came back like I hoped you would. You have no say now. It's mine to do with what I will.*

"I've thought about it," I say. "And I'm leaving tomorrow. I don't want a relationship. I don't want it to be special. And I know what an orgasm feels like." My cheeks heat at the admission, and Erin's lips form a smirk. "I just want to know what sex is like, and I don't want to join the army a freaking virgin."

Erin nods. "Okay." I can see her mind ticking over, her eyes sweeping over my face and body as if assessing what kind of work I'll need. A lot, I imagine. I want to look sexy and sure. I definitely don't want to look like a virgin. "It needs to be with someone who knows what they're doing."

Erin told me her first time was a complete dud, even though she tried to make it special. Most girls do, right? She said it was messy and awkward, but it was his first time too, so neither knew what they were doing. Their budding romance fizzled soon after. She moved on to Bradley, a boy from our neighbouring school. He was already a rumoured player at seventeen and apparently those rumours appeared to be true, considering Erin described her first two proper orgasms in precise detail.

She rifles through her makeup bag, plucking out an eyeshadow palette with smoky shades. The dark colours scream *sex*. She swipes a brush through the charcoal square first and comes at my face. Before the little implement touches my lid, she pauses, her gaze flicking down to my eyes. "Are you sure about this?"

"One hundred percent."

A gleeful grin widens her lips. "Sweaty hairy ballsacks and all?"

"Oh god." I laugh. "Bring it."

It takes an hour to complete the transformation, but when Erin steps away from me for the last time and I check the mirror, my hair hangs down my back in loose waves, as if I swam in the ocean and left it to dry in the sun. My eyelids are shaded from black to metallic brown, my lashes dark and curled. Erin swept powder along my cheekbones, forehead, and chin, giving me a sun-kissed glow. The look was finished with a nude lipstick, masking the natural pink tone and allowing my eyes to be the focus.

My face appears confident and sultry—so basically nothing like me —and definitely not a girl anymore. More like a woman who knows what she's doing. "It's perfect."

Erin nods because of course it is. She's already a master before even starting her cosmetology training next year. Erin will study makeup, hairstyling, and skin care, and one day open her own spa. My best friend already has her purpose. It's time to find mine. "Let's go."

~

"WHAT IS THIS PLACE?" I half-yell as the cab zooms off behind us, burning rubber in the quest to reach his next lot of passengers.

The bar in front of us is crammed with people. It features a windowless front, exposing its patrons to the chilly evening air and the wind sweeping in from the ocean across the road. They seem unaffected as the music ricochets outward. Its heavy beat vibrates my body, from my face to my boobs and straight to my vagina—where an anticipatory tingle begins to form. I want this. I do.

Erin grins and wiggles her shoulders, her eyelids flashing a glittery green, which only emphasises the blond of her hair. "A bar, Murphy." She always uses my surname when she feels the need for sarcasm.

"Of course it's a bar, *Tennyson*. I've just never noticed it before."

"I'm told it's where a lot of the army guys hang."

I grit my teeth. "And that's a good idea?"

"It's a brilliant idea. They're here for the same reason you are. A good time, not a long time." She links her arm with mine. "There are no boys in this bar. Only men. Ones who've seen shitty things. Trust me. The men in here are the kind who are all about finding pleasure wherever they can get it."

I rub my nude-painted lips together. "How do I look?"

She gives me the once-over, from my hair to the strapless black corset top, skinny black pants, and pointy nude heels. I feel so … *exposed.* "Hot. Like you'll singe the skin off anyone who dares to touch you."

We make our way inside, and Erin is not wrong.

Men.

Men everywhere.

Big ones.

All I see are broad shoulders and masculine bodies decorating every corner and crevice. My stomach clenches with nerves, but they're definitely the good kind. I immediately catch a flash of golden-brown hair, and my heart stops. My eyes flick to the man. His gaze is on my boobs, his eyes brown when I'm looking for hazel.

Dammit, Bear, I growl internally, *get the hell out of my head.*

We reach the bar and order vodka sodas with lime. When they're handed over, we clink them and grin at each other. "Cheers!"

"To losing your virgin status," Erin adds, and we both giggle and clink again because this can't happen soon enough.

I gave you two years, Bear. That's more than enough time. Now it's time to join the world again, just like you told me.

Taking a deep pull from my straw, I swallow, and warmth blooms in my belly. It feels good. I take another. And another. Soon the drink is gone as we talk and move a little to the music. We order more and Erin leans in as we wait, talking loudly into my ear. "Seen anyone you like yet?"

I turn around, my eyes scanning over the men in the room. They land on one who's watching me. He's tall and good-looking, his hair dark and eyes blue, the complete opposite of— No. Not going there. I feel the guy out, offering a small smile.

He smiles back and I look away, my cheeks getting hot.

"Okay, don't do that," Erin says, taking my empty glass and handing me another.

"Do what?"

"Look away and blush. It screams 'virgin,'" she air-quotes.

"Well I kinda am."

"Well duh, but you said you didn't want to look like one tonight, so try not to act like one either or he won't approach." Erin sneaks a look from the corner of her eye as she collects her drink. "He's not looking anymore."

My eyes find their way back to where he stands. He's talking with a group of his friends now. One of them is just as tall, his shoulders broad, hair blond, his back to me. He's wearing a grey cotton tee shirt, the lighter colour showing off thick muscle. I watch it bunch and flex as he gestures, my gaze stuck as he tells his story to his friends. They all laugh loudly. Then the dark-haired guy says something and glances my way, and I know he must have said something about me staring.

The blond man turns. He looks right at me and my heart skips a beat, something hot and impatient building inside me as he holds my gaze. I know in that instant.

Him.

I want *that one*.

There's something in his green eyes, something intense and warm that sets my insides on fire. My lips find my straw, and I suck. He watches, those eyes flaring as I swallow. His jaw is strong and stubbled, his skin golden, his chest clearly defined beneath the casual cotton.

Then he releases my eyes. But only to track his own further down to my breasts pushed up and outward inside the corset top, my waist, hips, legs, and slowly back up. An extremely thorough, heated inventory. When that gaze returns to mine, it's inflamed, but there's also a hint of cheekiness, as if he wants to do wicked things to me and he'll enjoy every minute of it as he does it.

Shivers skate down my body and across my arms, raising goose bumps.

"Excuse me," I see his lips say to his friends, and then he starts towards me.

I take another sip of my vodka—a big one—as he gets closer.

"Oh Jesus, that one?" Erin says and turns away, lightly fanning herself in a way that only I can see. "It's getting hot in here."

"So freaking hot," I mutter.

He's attracted attention. Women are tracking his movements, and they aren't being subtle, but his focus is on me, not deviating once as he walks my way. I lick my lips, nervous as he reaches my side, one of his big hands wrapped around a beer bottle.

He grins and right there I know that *it is on*. My legs turn to jelly beneath me.

"Hi," he says, his voice deep and confident.

It makes my body parts throb with instant need. He waits for a response, but I can't for the life of me remember what I'm supposed to say. Words seem foreign right now.

He leans in a little, and I breathe him in, catching the faint scent of cologne and soap. "Are you here with someone?"

"Just my friend Erin." I wave my hand in her general direction. "No one else," I think to add.

He nods, glancing from her and back to me, something like a satisfied glint in his eyes. Then he offers his hand. "I'm Jake. Jake Tanner."

I slide my hand in his, and his fingers wrap around it, firm, warm, rough. My imagination instantly puts those hands on my bare skin, roaming downward, inside my underwear, one of those thick digits pushing its way inside me. I need to know what that feels like.

My cheeks heat and Jake squeezes gently, expelling a breath, waiting for something. "I'm Jamie," I tell him. "Murphy," I add after a pause.

"Would you and your friend like to join us, Jamie?"

Holy crap.

I'm really doing this.

This is happening.

His hand still holds mine, and it feels strong. Capable of things I've never even felt before.

"We would love to," Erin says on my behalf, because it's becoming apparent that I'm a massive failure when it comes to flirting.

Jake leads me over to their table, guiding me around groups of people, tables, and harried bar staff. I glance behind to make sure Erin is following. She catches my gaze and widens her eyes as she keeps pace behind us. "Hubba hubba," she mouths and makes a kissy face. "You got this." I get a discreet double-thumbs-up.

We arrive at our destination, and Jake introduces us to his friends. I briefly catch their names, but they flitter right out of my mind because he's yet to let go of my hand. Instead, he pulls me closer and leans in again, his breath tickling my skin in the most delicious way as he speaks. "Tell me, Jamie Murphy. What are you doing in here tonight looking like that?"

I turn my face and it brings us close, close enough that when I whisper back he hears me over the noise. "What do you think I'm doing here?"

"Seems like you're planning on breaking a whole bunch of hearts."

"Not a bunch. Just one, maybe."

Jake grins, clearly liking my response. "Tell me about yourself."

I don't want to mention my joining the army. I'm not sure why. Probably because the whole idea of leaving the only home I've ever known is terrifying. New faces again. New people. It's going to be a whole different way of life, and I don't want to think about it right now. I just want to live in the moment until I leave. "I've just finished school."

Jake pulls back swiftly, releasing my hand with a furrow on his brow. "How old are you?"

"Eighteen."

His furrow clears. "You had me worried there for a minute."

"How old are you?"

"Twenty-two."

"And you … live around here?" Smooth, Jamie. What a great question. I take a sip of my drink. Maybe more vodka will loosen me up a little better, ease some of the awkwardness.

"I do. Are you asking for a tour?"

You wanted this.

It's now or never.

I draw in a deep breath of courage, trying to dispel the nervous energy. "That depends."

"On what?"

I take another sip and realise my glass is empty. "On whether you're offering one."

Jake exhales heavily, his lips curving. "So it's *my* heart you plan on breaking tonight then, is it? After I give you a tour of my place?"

"Jake, I …" My eyes cast downward. I know he's teasing. He doesn't literally believe I'll break his heart, but I should probably tell him I only want tonight without somehow sounding like I sleep around with *all* the boys. Though who am I kidding? He probably wouldn't give it a single thought. Guys are all about one-night stands, aren't they? I need to stop overthinking this.

He tucks a thumb beneath my chin and tilts my head back up. I meet his eyes, seeing hesitation in his. "Maybe some other time?"

"No," I say quickly and set my glass on the table beside us. "Tonight is good."

Jake nods. "How about I buy you another drink first?" He takes my hand, lacing our fingers together. "Come to the bar with me?" I turn to let Erin know. She's deep in conversation with one of the guys and another girl, who appears to be a friend of Jake's friends. I lean into her ear so she can hear me better. "We're just going to get another drink. Do you want one?"

She shakes her head and lifts her half-full drink with a wave.

"Be back."

Jake leads me away, keeping me close as he forges a path through the throng. My bared cleavage rubs against his arm from behind. The contact sends a buzz of electricity through my body. He turns his head as we walk, giving me a heated glance, and I know he must have felt it too.

God, is this how all sex begins? Because it's almost unbearable. I want to push him down on the floor of this place and grind on him until pleasure rips me apart. I don't think I'd even care who sees.

We reach the bar and Jake tucks me in beside him. He hasn't quite thrown an arm around me in a territorial move, but it rests gently at my back, a subtle gesture to show we're together. I like it. If anything it makes him hotter.

"What are you drinking?"

"Vodka and soda."

He orders my beverage of choice and a beer for himself. Then he looks at me while we wait. "So, Jamie, I'm gonna be a little cliché and say I haven't seen you in this place before. You grow up around here?"

"Mostly. We travelled a lot when I was younger, so I was home-schooled by tutors here and there, but otherwise, yeah, this is home. I've lived here all my life."

"Same here, apart from all the travelling part. When did you turn eighteen?"

"Four days ago."

"Only four days?" Jake grasps my chin and leans in.

He's going to kiss me.

My heart stops.

"Happy birthday, gorgeous girl," he says, and as the music beats heavily around us, and people yell loudly in their groups and glasses clink, his lips touch mine. I close my eyes and everything fades. I press myself into him until there's no space between us.

For a moment it's just us, his mouth on mine, his hand moving to grasp my hip, branding me with heat. He draws back and it's like surfacing from beneath the ocean. Suddenly I'm breathing again and the din around us becomes loud once more.

"Thank you," I croak and clear my throat.

It was the barest touch of our lips, but if that's what kissing is all about, why is everyone not doing it all the freaking time?

"For what? The birthday wish or the kiss?"

"The kiss, but the birthday wish was almost as good."

"The pleasure is all mine."

The bartender sets down our drinks, and Jake hands over a couple of notes in exchange. Then he picks up my drink and holds it out towards me. "For you."

"Thank you," I say again and take it. The glass is icy, and I want to rub it over my chest to cool off my feverish skin.

After managing to manoeuvre the straw into my mouth, he watches as I suck the vodka down, his brows rising until the liquid disappears and there's nothing left but chunks of ice. There's a small slurp at the end, and then I'm placing my empty glass on the bar. I notice he's barely taken a sip of his beer, but I'm not sure I have the patience for him to finish it. I take it from his hand and set it next to my empty glass. "So … how about that tour?"

Jake's lips curve slowly, wicked and hot.

My girl parts clench.

Holy mother of God.

7

JAMIE

Goose bumps prickle my skin as we step outside, moving from the packed heat of the bar to the chilly night air.

Jake notices, his brows drawing together. "Where's your coat?"

I rub my arms, an attempt to keep warm. "I didn't bring one."

"Jamie," he tuts and wraps an arm around my shoulders, drawing me close as we walk towards the cab rank. The weight of it is heavy, his gesture wonderfully intimate. For the first time in so many years, I feel safe and protected, despite being with a man I barely know. Leaving with Jake is probably another tick in my list of reckless pursuits, but my gut is telling me I've inadvertently found a good guy.

Maybe it was the way he took me with him to the bar so I could feel safe drinking my vodka without worrying about what could potentially be slipped inside. Or maybe it was the way he stole my phone and took a snapshot of his licence with it, telling me to message it to Erin before we left. Or maybe it's the way he's walking slowly with me right now, allowing me to take my time in my dainty heels.

Does that make you happy, Bear? That I found a good one? Or are you out there nursing a lifetime of regret?

A wave of sadness engulfs me, making my stomach clench in a knot. Two years later and I still miss him. I still think of him every day and talk to him in my head. Why does everyone who ever matters just up and leave?

Jake gives my shoulder a squeeze as we reach the kerb. "You okay?"

I turn and face him, tilting my head, meeting his eyes. His arms come around me, warm and strong, and I realise that perhaps nothing will ever be okay, and maybe that's okay too. Maybe that's what life is all about. Snatching moments like this. Ones that get you through when you have nothing else.

"I'm feeling *very* okay right now."

Jake smiles and looks over my shoulder, lifting an arm as he hails a cab. It pulls alongside, and he lets me go, opening the back-passenger door. "You sure?"

I step down onto the road and take hold of the door, slipping one leg inside before turning back to look at him. "One hundred percent."

Taking a seat, I scoot across so Jake can slide in beside me. He does, pulling the door shut behind him. His bulk crowds me, making me hyperaware of how his body brushes against mine.

"Where to?" asks the driver.

"Lilly Street. Thanks, mate."

We roar off into the night, and Jake slides his palm across the top of my thigh, holding me there. My breath catches and holds.

"Tell me about your travels," Jake says, talking like it's completely normal to be in a cab in the middle of the night, a hand intimately placed on the leg of a girl he barely knows. He turns to look at me. "You mentioned doing a lot of it when you were young."

Right. Casual conversation. I can do this. Just pretend guys have their hands on your upper thigh every day of the week. No biggie. Ha!

"We did. Travel a lot that is."

"Who's we?"

His palm begins a slow rub. I let out a shaky breath. "Me and my Dad. For his work."

"What kind of work?"

"He was an MMA fighter," I reply, the admission coming a little easier now than it used to. My past is old news to the general public now. No one connects the dots anymore, not unless they dig a little deeper, and no one apart from Bear and Erin have ever bothered to do that. "You know, mixed martial arts?"

"That's impressive." Jake's palm continues its slow rub. Tingles erupt all over the place. "Did he teach you any moves?"

"He taught me all of them."

His beautiful green eyes flare, and he leans in. I turn my head and it brings us a mere inch apart. "I knew there was something about you."

"What do you mean?"

"You carry yourself differently. Like you have confidence in your body and what it can do. There's no fear." His palm slides inward, and my pulse begins to race. "It's incredibly sexy."

I swallow, barely able to think. "Is that why you came over?"

"You want to know why I came over?"

"Yes please," I breathe.

"Because after I saw you, I couldn't see anything else."

My heart gives a steady thump, starting to *feel* things.

Don't even go there.

My heart thumps again in protest.

It's a line, Jamie. One he likely uses with all the girls.

The cab arrives at a small cottage situated three blocks away from the beach. Even at night I can see it appears in desperate need of a renovation with its worn and faded little picket fence, weeds in the garden, and sagging porch.

Jake pays the driver before I can offer any money. Then he has my hand and he's helping me from the car.

"This is where you live?" I ask while he shuts the door.

The driver speeds off, and we make our way down the cracked cement path. "I rent it, but it's in such a great spot that I'm hoping to make it permanent. My sister and I have talked about buying it together and renovating it."

"You have a sister?"

"I do. Her name's Finlay, but we call her Fin. She's younger than me, but she's crazy smart. She's studying to be a research scientist," he says with some measure of pride. "She wants to focus on climate change in the arctic."

"Wow, that's amazing. I think the world needs more people like her."

He sticks his key in the lock of the front door and turns it. "One day all the ice in Antarctica will melt and be no more. I hope I don't see it in my lifetime. But maybe her research will make a difference."

Jake pushes open the door and guides me inside, his hand on the small of my back. "So," he says, shutting it behind us. "You really want that tour?"

"Maybe later." My fingers slide through the belt loop of his jeans, and I drag him close, surprising myself with my boldness.

Jake ducks his head. "Later," he whispers against my lips.

Then his mouth is on mine, his tongue sweeping inside. He nudges me backwards with his body until I'm pressed against the front door behind me. My first real kiss is hot and hard, and for a moment I'm suspended in shock. It disappears quickly and I don't hold back, hoping he doesn't notice my inexperience.

He groans at my enthusiasm and I slide my hands slowly up his chest, looping my arms around his neck. His slide down, reaching around until they grip my backside. His tongue pushes deeper, kissing me like I'm air and he's drowning. It doesn't feel like enough. I need *more*. I know he feels the same when he frees a hand and uses it to fist my hair violently, ramping my pulse up and into the stratosphere.

I'm struggling for breath when he draws his mouth from mine. A panting, trembling mess with legs made of jelly.

"My room," he croaks, turning me around.

He walks me backwards down the hall, kissing me.

Every part of my body is throbbing, screaming yes, yes, YES!

But somewhere in my heart speaks a little voice so small I can barely hear it. *Wait.*

What? Did you just say wait? Wait for what?

Bear.

No. I want this. I want Jake.

Jake is a good guy. He won't mind if you ask him to stop.

I don't want him to stop, dammit.

We reach the end of the hall, and Jake stops me by the doorway, pulling back, his eyes unfocused and hair mussed. "Do you want me to stop?" he asks as if he can hear the conflicting thoughts in my head.

"No." I kick off my shoes and it drops my height down a couple of inches, forcing me to tilt my head even more to meet his eyes. "Hell no."

I grab his shirt, shoving it upward. "You need to lose this." He gets on board and tugs it over his head, baring his chest to my gaze. For a moment I stare, transfixed. His body is like an endless ripple of sand dunes. Rugged, golden terrain that somehow defies reality.

Jake bunches the shirt in his hands with an impressive display of biceps before he tosses it away. I'm still staring when he's done.

"You okay?"

"I don't think so." My mouth opens and closes like a fish gasping for air. "I'm just not sure that …"

"That what?"

I wave a hand over the gift he's shared with me. "All that is real."

He grabs my hand and plants it on his stomach.

His abs do a little ripple. "What was that?"

Jake grins. "Your hands are cold."

"I didn't have a coat, remember?"

His gaze drops to my cleavage, heating. "I remember."

"Take off your pants," I demand.

He arches a brow. "You take off yours."

I reach for my pants button, unfastening the little clasp before I can think. I yank the zipper apart and shove my pants down. Jake watches, his eyes sparkling gems of amusement as I perform what I'm sure is the most unsexy strip in the history of stripping. Freeing them from my ankles, I kick them away. It leaves me in nothing but my little black bustier and a scrap of lace with black straps around my hips that masquerade as underwear.

When I'm done, I straighten, huffing as if the effort of disrobing was equivalent to a hundred-yard sprint. Jake is watching me, and I feel like he's restraining the urge to laugh. Am I doing this wrong? Fuck it. I plant my hands on my hips, feigning bravado. "Let's do this."

"You sound like you want to get it over with." A smirk spreads across his face like warm, melted butter. "Sex isn't laundry, Jamie."

"I know that," I mutter, defensive.

"How about we have another drink first?"

"A drink. Yes!" I leap on the offer, swinging my arms and lightly clapping my hands together in a ridiculously obvious attempt to appear casual. "A beer if you have it."

Jake turns and walks further down the back of the house. I follow, down to where the hall opens up into a little kitchen on the right and living area on the left. The back doors might be old, but they're framed white French doors that open wide onto a timber deck that further looks out onto a yard too dark too see. His couch is wide and plush, the kind you sink inside like quicksand, and thick cushions invite you to lie down and rest your head.

"Make yourself at home," he calls out, his head stuck in the fridge.

I do, taking a seat on that cosy couch in nothing but my little bustier and sexy knickers. I hear the clink of glass and a fridge door slamming shut, then he's walking over, two bottles of pale ale in his hand. He holds one out to me—I take it—and sets his on the scarred coffee table in front of us.

He takes a seat, twisting his torso to face me and resting his arm along the back of the couch.

"So …" I bring the beer to my lips. I'm trying to think of something clever to say, but my insides are bouncing all over the place. I've got nothing. "What do you do?"

"I'm an army boy."

Erin *did* say the bar would be full of them. I should have guessed by his build alone. His muscle doesn't appear carved out of regular gym reps. Rather it appears earned by the great outdoors—running up mountains with rucksacks, long-distance swimming, obstacle courses so difficult you pray for an injury just so you can stop and rest. It's what awaits me, and the thought has my nerves ratcheting up another notch.

"Is that a problem?"

"Not tonight it's not."

Jake grabs his beer and takes a swig before he sets it down, shifting a little closer. "But tomorrow it is?"

"I won't be here tomorrow."

"Yeah? I was kinda hoping I'd be waking up with you tomorrow."

Waking up with someone like him? I'm pretty sure I could do that every day.

"I'm leaving town."

He frowns. "Why?"

"I guess you could say I'm an army girl."

"Jamie, baby, why?"

"I could ask you the same thing."

"You could, but it's dawning on me that if you're leaving tomorrow, we need to make the most of the time I have you."

Jake takes the bottle from my grip and sets it down beside his. Then he takes my hand and tugs me close until he's able to grip my waist and lift me, setting me astride his lap. My hands splay out across his chest, the heat of his body vivid. I tremble with a mixture of nerves and anticipation. "This is how we're going to make the most of it?"

"Hell yeah it is." He tilts his hips upward, rubbing his crotch against mine. The friction eases the ache between my legs and heightens it at the same time. It's unexpected and exciting. The surprise must show on my face because he stops.

"Don't stop."

"Jamie, have you…" he gives me an uncertain look, "…have you done this before?"

Dammit. How can I be so bloody obvious? "Not this," I reply, waving a hand between us. Hopefully he thinks the gesture means just this particular thing we're doing right now and not well … everything.

Jake's hand on my thigh slides inward, and he palms the warm achy place between my legs, rubbing firmly over my underwear.

Ugh.

So. Good.

I moan.

"What about this?" he asks, his eyes intent on my face.

Dammit. "Not this either."

"Jamie," he says, groaning. His head tips back against the couch, and he closes his eyes, releasing a frustrated, husky chuckle. He removes his hand, leaving me bereft. And even though I'm still on his lap, I can feel him withdrawing. "When you said you planned on breaking someone's heart tonight, I kinda thought you were teasing."

"Jake." I grab his hand, putting it back where it was. "I'm not here to break your heart. I just want you to …"

His head straightens, eyeballing me. "To what?"

My voice lowers as if there are people around who can hear me. "Fuck me."

He sucks in a breath.

"Please?" I beg, because yeah, it can't get any lower than this, right? My cheeks feel hotter than the sun right now. "Fuck me, Jake."

His hand withdraws again, and I feel so ridiculously frustrated I want to throw a hissy fit right on this couch. "Can I just get one thing straight? You've never done any of this before? You're a…" he hesitates as if the word is foreign before forging ahead "…virgin?"

"Only in the physical sense."

"Only in the …" Jake scratches his head.

"I've watched porn. I know how it all works."

He laughs. "Okay."

"So in the mental sense, I'm one hundred percent de-virginised."

"What about the emotional sense?"

I shift my hips forward, mimicking the way Jake was rubbing me before. He groans.

"What about it?" I ask.

My hips are grabbed in vice-like hands, fingers digging in like he's trying to stop me and urge me to keep going all at the same time. "It should be special. With someone you care about."

"I care about you," I throw out brazenly because the friction still feels so damn good. I'm pretty sure I'll say anything at this point to keep this train rolling forward.

Jake gives me a look.

"Well." I rub and grind some more. "Given the chance I could."

His chuckle is throaty and thick with frustration as the hands on my hips lift me up and set me back on the couch beside him. "You're incredibly stubborn."

I reach behind me for the little hooks that hold my top together. Perhaps taking it off might help my cause because seriously, I've been geared up for sex all day and I'm not leaving until I get it. "Damn right I am. This is happening, Jake." My lips purse, arms straining as I struggle with the first hook. I tug at it. "It's so…" tug "totally…" tug, tug "…happening. Then I'll leave tomorrow…" tug "…and you won't have to…" frustrated growl "…see me again!"

"Jamie—"

"Arrrgghh!" My arms flop as I give up, huffing. Sweat dots my brow and hair sticks to my hot face. I can't even begin to imagine how incredibly unsexy I must appear to him right now. A desperate, sweaty, stubborn, virginal mess. Let's face it. I've embarrassed myself enough tonight.

"I think I should go." I start to rise, swiping my beer from the table because I'll be needing one for the road.

Jake grabs my wrist and I halt. "Don't." He shakes his head. "We should…" his eyes look around, searching for something "…watch TV or something. I've got a PlayStation."

My eyes narrow on his face, my little heart bleating at the rejection. "You want to play computer games?"

"Well, I'd rather be doing something better than that, but I'd rather you not leave either. What about Call of Duty?"

"You've got the latest version?"

He nods.

"Well why didn't you just say that? What could be better than playing Call of Duty?"

Jake gives me a look as if to say yep, you clearly have *not* had sex before. My hand is released and after setting down my beer, I walk over to his television unit, hoping like hell his eyes are on my ass, the one that could be gripped in his hands right now if only he wasn't more stubborn than I was.

I know my cheeks are mostly exposed. The underwear is definitely not designed for practical purposes.

Eat your heart out, Jake!

I turn my head slightly as I bend, reaching for the entertainment console. From my peripheral vision, I can see he's looking. Oh, he's definitely looking, his hands rubbing up and down his thighs as if he's trying to calm himself down.

Good.

I switch on the PlayStation. The green light flashes, the device *whirring* as I pick up the headsets and controllers. Then I turn to face him. Appearances are deceiving if we're going by my excessive makeup and feminine clothes tonight. Little does he know, I was raised a tomboy and Call of Duty is my jam. In Advanced Warfare, my pro team is called The Black Keepers and we totally dominate.

An evil grin lights my face, one hundred percent forgetting that I'm standing here in my unmentionables, a sexy, half-naked guy on the couch watching me. "You are going down, Tanner."

His answering grin is downright fire. "If you play your cards right, Murphy, you can bet your sweet ass I'll be going down."

8

———————

JAMIE

"*H*ostiles have destroyed your UAV," says the monotone female voice simulator as I manoeuvre through old ramshackle buildings in the jungle.

"Dammit," I mutter.

"I'm behind you but I think someone's in the house on your right," Jake replies.

He's sitting cross-legged on the couch, wearing nothing but a pair of black boxer-briefs—I finally convinced him to *get a little more comfortable*—and a gaming headset. It shouldn't be sexy, but he looks like a half-naked GI Joe. I'm sitting the same way except on the floor beside him, my back against the couch. Ten empty beer bottles litter the coffee table and rug around us, evidence of my current inebriation, which funnily enough has not affected my playing ability at all.

We've been talking all night while we played. Jake use to play rugby just like Bear did, and it made me wonder if they knew each other. Not that I could ask. Jake also likes Guinness. It's something he's made me promise to try, telling me it's satisfying and smooth. Kinda like going down on a girl, he said, which made me clench all

63

over. I very much liked the idea of him doing that to me, but I didn't quite like the image of him doing that to someone else. Jealousy much?

He told me about the time he and his best friend since childhood, Ryan Kendall, took a small bar fridge out into the middle of nowhere, filled it with fuel, stuck an electrical detonator in it, waited for the gas to evaporate, then set it off and watched the door blow into the sky on a huge column of flame.

"That is so ridiculously dangerous!" I told him, laughing so hard I completely missed shooting up an all-terrain vehicle and got a tree instead.

"Completely stupid," he agreed, laughing too.

"I would've loved to see it, though."

"I'll take you with us next time we decide to blow up a household appliance," he joked, as if we were actually going to see each other again.

I found myself telling him about Bear and how he left. And how I got so mad I set fire to the fence. "It got replaced, but I …"

"You what?" he prompted, taking a hand from his controller to swipe his beer off the table and take a long guzzle.

"I kept a piece of it. How stupid is that?"

"Stupid is blowing up a fridge when you're thirteen. Keeping that bit of fence is a memento. A reminder of how someone made you feel."

"Yeah, well all it does is remind me of how angry I am."

"At you or him?"

"I don't know. I don't look too close."

We moved on to talking about his family, and it sounded like the type of childhood you saw in the movies. His dad, Mike, was fit from playing rugby for years at national level, getting Jake and Ryan into the sport after settling into a career of physiotherapy. His mum, Julie, worked as a personal assistant but was involved in team administration: sorting uniforms, sign-ups, and coordinating schedules. His sister, Fin, was studious, her nose always stuck inside a textbook.

So I told him about my dad. We didn't discuss the accident, but Jake mentioned he knew who he was. That he'd seen him fight. So I'm pretty sure he knows what happened, yet he didn't make it into a big deal or expect me to talk about it.

"Look out," Jake shouts, drawing me back into the present.

I duck down, narrowly evading a bullet, and jog through rocky terrain and muddy water, taking cover behind another building. A dog joins the scene from behind a cluster of trees on our right. My eyes narrow and a tipsy little *hiccup* escapes me. "I don't think that's one of our dogs."

"I don't want to kill it."

"Don't be a baby." I open fire and blood splatters the ground, the dog decimated. I run forward, leaping over the top of its mangled carcass. "If you don't kill them, then they just kill you."

"Baby, you're so heartless!"

"Hey, I saved your life!"

I keep moving forward at a fast clip, and an enemy soldier climbs up onto the bridge in front of me. Bullets rain down, and he falls off the side into a bloody heap.

"We have the advantage," says the voice simulator.

I whoop. "Damn straight we do."

We jog through jungle and more rocky terrain, guns at the ready.

Jake yawns.

"Nooooo, Jake. You can't possibly be tired."

His voice is low and sleepy. "What's the time?"

"Still early," I lie because I'm pretty sure it was two in the morning last time I checked. My eyes are burning in my head, and I've got nothing left in the tank, but we're on a roll. While I've always played in a team, I've never sat down and played Call of Duty with another person like this and it's So. Much. Fun.

I don't want it to end.

"Christ, it's three in the morning," he exclaims, scratching at that gorgeous chest of his absentmindedly while he yawns a second time. "We should wrap this up."

"Not yet. We've still got—"

He leans across and hits the button on the console. It powers down, the screen going black. The air stills around us, the little device beginning to *tick* as it starts cooling down from our epic gaming marathon.

I gasp. "Jake, nooooo!"

He tosses his headset and controller towards the coffee table then rises from the couch, reaching for me. "C'mon, pretty girl."

Despite my protests, Jake robs me of my electronics and lifts me up, putting me in a fireman's carry over his shoulder.

"Jake!"

He walks off with me hanging over him like a sack of potatoes, my ass copping a light slap when I continue to protest. Then he rubs it, his big palm warm and scratchy against my half-bared cheek. "Mmm," I moan and fall against him, giving in like a puppy being offered a treat. "Now you're talking," I say, blood rushing to my head.

"Oh, you like that?" He rubs some more and heat blooms between my legs.

Jake steps through a doorway, and then I'm falling, weightless for a single moment before my backside bounces onto a mattress beneath me. I barely get a moment to take in the room around me. The bed is plain, the sheets white, with sheer curtains billowing against an open window, leaving the air chilly. A few pairs of shorts and a couple of tee shirts dot the surrounding carpeted floor.

He stalks across the room and slams the window shut. The curtains stop their dance. After switching off the light, he comes back to me, the light of the moon revealing the heated intent in his eyes. My heart begins to pound. This is it.

It's finally happening.

Jake crawls onto the bed, and my pulse skyrockets. He snakes an arm around my middle and drags me towards him until I'm the little spoon to his big one. Then he sighs deeply. I feel his chest pushing against me as it fills with air. Then he lets it out. "Get some rest, army girl."

Umm, what?

He reaches down and grabs the sheet from the end of his unmade bed. He pulls it up and over us, and then his whole body relaxes as if he can actually go to sleep right now.

My eyes widen in the dark. I can literally feel *every single inch* of him against me. Every. Damn. Inch. I'm basically *on fire*. I'm sure my clit will explode if he so much as *looks* at it. And *he's going to sleep?* Oh hell no.

"Jake?"

He rubs his nose against the back of my neck, breathing me in as if I smell better than a baked croissant. "Mmm?"

"My top is seriously uncomfortable right now." Not even a lie. The boning and hooks are digging in, and I—conveniently—need it off. "You think you can undo the hooks at the back for me?"

"I can do that," he says quietly.

His fingers fiddle gently in the dark. I hold my breath as each hook releases, one by one, slowly easing my discomfit and baring my naked back to his eyes. He finishes and I grab it from the front, easing it away from my chest and tossing it towards the floor.

Jake's palm splays on my back like a hot brand. He rubs me up and down. "Feel better?"

I moan. "So much better."

His hand explores further, across my hip and then upward, travelling along my waist and higher, until his fingers brush the underside of my boob.

I moan again, shivers skating across my skin. How can such a simple touch feel like heaven? I want more, but I don't know how to ask for it.

Don't be so timid, Jamie Murphy, I can hear Erin say in my head. *Just grab his hand and put it right there on your tit, for the love of God!*

I lift my arm, intent on doing just that, but he must have taken my move as an invitation to give him better access because his hand roams higher, inch by painful, nail-biting inch, until my breast is cupped in his palm. He rubs his thumb over my hardened nipple, his hand squeezing gently, and he groans against the back of my neck.

Holy shit. Jake Tanner has his hand on my naked boob and I. Have. Found. Nirvana.

My entire body squirms with raging need.

"Jamie?" His voice is low and husky. "I want to touch you so bad and taste you on my tongue. Can I—"

I roll onto my back in an instant. "Yes."

Jake chuckles.

He rises up over me, hovering above, his eyes on my breasts. He lets out a breath, and they lower all the way down and back up. "You're so incredibly beautiful."

"So are you."

Because he is. Jake Tanner is like a Greek god. His skin is like sunshine, the kind you could bask in all day and never get cold. His shoulders broad and arms strong, as if he's the sort of person who could weather any storm and come out fighting. His teeth are white and even, biting down on his bottom lip as he studies my face.

"I meant what I said before."

"You said a lot of things."

"Jamie. I said this should be special. With someone you care about."

I reach up, cupping his face in my palm.

My heart gives a little bleat, like a baby lamb being led to slaughter. In the space of one night, this army boy has made me feel something. Something that makes me ache at the thought of leaving tomorrow.

I care about you.

I don't say it aloud. Surely it's impossible to care about someone you've only known for one night? He wouldn't believe me anyway. Not after I teased him about it earlier. Jake is supposed to be my *tonight*, not my *forever*.

"I meant what I said before too."

His lips curve at the corners. "You said a lot of things."

"Jake." My hand skims down his neck, over his chest and lower, until I'm cupping the visible bulge in his boxer-briefs. "Fuck me. Please."

His nostrils flare and he shudders beneath my touch. "I like it when you say please."

I rub his cock over the underwear, hoping like hell it feels good for him because I have no idea what I'm doing. "Please."

With his palms planted on either side of me on the bed, he ducks his head and kisses me. When he draws away, I slide my hand around his neck and tug him back down, lifting my head to capture his lips. He groans and his tongue thrusts inside my mouth, his passion intense.

I sink down as the kiss goes on, seemingly endless. He lowers himself, allowing his weight to press me into the bed. It feels better than I imagined it would. Hotter. Harder. All-consuming.

I claw at his shoulders, fingers digging in.

God, so good. I want to crawl inside him and never leave.

"Please be sure," he says against my lips before moving his mouth across my cheek and down my neck, an urgent caress that makes me shiver.

"I'm sure. I want this."

Jake shifts down, his mouth travelling across my chest. He takes a nipple in his mouth, sucking deep. Sucking *hard*.

My head tilts back, an involuntary gasp leaving my throat as pleasure hits, so sharp it almost hurts. Jake's eyes flick up, watching me, eyes hungry like I've not yet seen before. Then he moves across to my other nipple, and I'm subjected to the same delicious torture. "Oh, you definitely like that," he murmurs, his voice thick.

His mouth resumes its downward trajectory until he reaches my little scrap of black lace. "These definitely need to come off." He hooks his fingers in the sides and tugs, but they go nowhere because I'm stuck watching his arms flex, the pale glow of the moon highlighting each muscle in high-definition. "Up," he commands.

My butt lifts and he sweeps them down and off, throwing them over his shoulder. I shoot up and snap my thighs closed, suddenly feeling shy and exposed for some strange embarrassing reason.

"On your back, army girl," he demands. "And spread your legs."

My lungs deflate with a shaky exhale. "Jake."

He grins at me and rubs my thighs as if the caress is a trick that will magically open them. "You've got to get used to taking orders, so you may as well start now."

"Jake!" I drop back on my elbows. "You know very well I won't be taking those kinds of orders."

His nostrils flare. "You better fucking not be."

His tone is growly and almost possessive. And *abra-fucking-cadabra*. My legs fall open and my clit throbs because I don't think I've ever heard anything hotter in my life.

"So beautiful," he murmurs and glides his thumb through the slick heat.

I jerk, my breath hitching. Jake looks up at my face, a slow smile forming on his lips. There's a wealth of satisfaction in his expression. It's wicked yet sweet, like thick melted chocolate. I tuck it deep inside my memories. It's a look I don't think I'll ever forget. Not for the rest of my life.

Then he dips his head and a kiss lands on my inner left thigh, the thick stubble on his chin scratching the soft skin.

I fall back against the mattress, swept away in a tidal wave of fevered lust.

A kiss lands on my inner right thigh.

He's killing me. "Jake," I gasp. "Please."

His tongue flicks my clit, and my entire body shakes as if an earthquake just hit. I gasp and before I can recover, he does it again and again. I think I just died. Jake Tanner has his head between my legs, and I'm floating outside my body. Dead. Why did I wait so long for this?

Jake sucks and licks me and my hips rock against his mouth. I can't keep still.

"You like that, army girl?"

"Yes," I croak, moaning, a boneless quivering mass. My sweaty palms tangle in his sheets. "I'm going to lie here while you do this for the rest of our lives. Okay?"

He laughs against me and even the vibration tickles me in the best possible way. "Okay."

Then Jake pushes a thick digit inside me, and his mouth returns, sucking hard while he slides in another. And I'm done. I'm so done.

Pleasure rushes through me like a freight train, and my back bows as I explode, an orgasm gripping me so hard I cry out. "Jake," I pant, rubbing against his face, never knowing it could feel like this with someone. It's so much bigger and brighter, and so much more intense. It's fucking *wonderful*.

He continues, prolonging the sensation for as long as he can. "Jake. God. So good."

"The best," he says, giving me a final lick.

My insides twitch, wringing every last drop of pleasure left in my body. "The best I've ever had."

Jake busts out laughing, his amusement flickering bright, and it feels good being the one to bring that light to his eyes. If I was his, I'd make him laugh all the time.

"It's true," I joke with a chuckle. It dies clean away as he steps back from the bed and tugs his underwear down and off. I swallow, trying not to stare but staring anyway. He's hard *everywhere*.

"You are something else," he tells me as climbs back on, rising up over me on his hands and looking down.

"You make me feel like something else."

Jake's expression sobers, and there's a beat of silence between us, a sense of desperation rising. As if we've just realised how short our time is getting. "You make me feel like something else too."

He watches me as he rubs his cock between my legs, through the wet swollen heat. It juts out, thick and hard, and I'm not leaving until I know what it's like having it inside of me.

"Fuck me?" I ask, and I swear to God it's the last time I will. A girl can only handle so much rejection.

Jake reaches across as if me asking enough times has finally sunk in, and he yanks open his bedside draw. He rummages through it, cursing, before finally drawing back, a square foil packet in his hand.

A condom.

My insides quake, sudden nerves making me sweat. "Soooo," I drawl as he sits back on his legs, tearing the little packet open. "We're really doing this, huh?"

Jake pauses, looking at me as if I just kicked his puppy. "Not if you don't want to."

I rear up, grasping his cock in both hands. A little too tight, I think, because he flinches. My face burns as I loosen my hold. "I want to."

Jake puts his hand over mine and moves it up and down, showing me how to add pressure, how to set a teasing pace. He lets go and I take control, gaining confidence, flicking my wrist at the end in a way that makes him groan. He's so silky and hard.

My hand is nudged away, and he rolls the condom on in quick, jerky movements. I fall back on the bed, and he hovers above me. I feel him, a sense of pressure between my legs. My eyes flick down. He's guiding his cock inside me, pushing his way in. It's incredibly uncomfortable.

Jake grimaces as if it hurts him to hold back. "Relax, Jamie."

"Oh my god!" I gasp. "That's easy for you to say."

"Should I stop?"

"Hell no. We're doing this."

"So damn stubborn."

"Because I know what I want, Jake. And I want you. So no stopping." My hips rear up, taking more of him in. I wince.

"Don't do that!"

"Too late. I'm already doing it."

Jake groans and thrusts deep, all the way in. I cry out and freeze. He freezes with me. We lie there, our breathing ragged, me not daring to move in case it hurts again and him not daring to move in case he hurts me again.

We're at an impasse.

I can feel him pulse inside me. *Throb, throb, throb.* My insides give a flicker like a candle sputtering back to life. I shift my hips.

"Don't," he mutters, gritting his teeth.

So of course I shift my hips again. He grinds against me, an involuntary reaction. It doesn't feel … bad. It feels like it's not enough. "Do that again."

Jake grinds again. Not quite a hard thrust but a gentle roll of his hips.

My eyes close.

Holy. Freaking. Shit.

What the hell was that?

"Again," I moan.

This time he thrusts a little.

Fuck. *Yes.*

Lava floods my veins. I'm burning up like a shuttle on re-entry into Earth's atmosphere. I am *on fire.* Somehow he seems to know this because he rocks into me again. "Jamie. Open your eyes."

He thrusts into me, harder this time.

My eyes open.

"That good?"

"Best … thing … ever."

Jake laughs and I didn't expect this. The intensity. The intimacy. The talking. The laughter. He's right. This *should* be done with someone you care for. Someone special. But I can't shake the feeling that he is. No matter that he's mine for just tonight.

"More," I whisper, my hips rising in jerky movements, my clit aching and my need for friction becoming this wild, desperate thing.

Jake pumps hard and deep, and my hands clutch at his back, fingers digging in, impatient. I expect him to laugh at the frustration he's evoking in me, and my crude, inexperienced movements, but his brow is creased and his breathing erratic as if he's barely holding on.

Am I doing this to him? My lungs flood with air.

"Jamie, fuck," he rasps in my ear, drawing back out and punching back in. I gasp, the bed bouncing from the force.

"Yes." My head falls back. "That. Keep doing that."

Jake does and I'm so ever-loving grateful.

"Don't stop," I add. "Ever."

"Don't ever want to." He ducks his head, nipping my earlobe with his teeth.

What kind of sexual fuckery was that? "Do that again."

He does.

"Jake." It leaves me delirious and shaky as the bed judders.

He pounds into me, again and again. Sweat sheens our skin. It's intense and messy, the sheets damp beneath us, hair sticking to my neck. Then he's sweeping his arms beneath my thighs, pushing them against me like he can't get deep enough.

Leaning in, his lips find mine, kissing me as he goes rock solid, every muscle rigid. He groans into my mouth, his body straining. "Jamie," he pants, his breath ragged as he ducks his head, his mouth brushing against my neck. Rather than draw away, his arms pull tighter, a steel band locking me close. "You okay?"

Am I okay?

How is that even a real question?

I just had sex. With Jake Tanner.

My body feels used. My mind a little fucked. My heart a little battered.

"I've never felt more okay in my life."

9

———————

JAMIE

I make my way down the front path of Sue's house, all my worldly possessions in a single bag slung over my shoulder. It's only a ten-minute walk to the bus shelter, which will take me to the airport. Then I'll fly across the other side of the country to Sydney, where my new life will begin.

My heart gets heavy with each step I take, memories weighing me down, keeping me from letting go.

You need to leave our fence behind and join the world again, Jamie. It needs strong people like you.

Oh, Bear, how easy you make it sound! As if it's just like going to the store for a loaf of bread.

My lips mash together as I walk, so very determined yet so utterly, achingly *alone*. No Dad to push on the handlebars of my bike as I learn to ride without training wheels, having him whoop and punch the air when I succeed. No Bear on the other side of the fence, reminding me how important it is to live again. No Jake, his green eyes solemn as we lie looking at each other in bed, him tucking a lock of my hair behind my ear as he reminds me how to *feel* again.

A sob climbs my throat, fighting to break free. I swallow it down, blinking back tears. *You're a born fighter, Jamie,* Dad says in my head —the way he always did before a karate tournament, or when I snapped a finger in training, or on my first day at a new school. *Prove it,* he would say, and I would hold in all the fear, the pain, the anxiety —hold it all in so hard my eyes would burn with effort and muscles shake—because the thought of disappointing him was terrifying. *You have to train your mind to be stronger than your emotions, Jamie. Or else you'll lose every time.*

I reach the bus shelter with fifteen minutes to spare, a little sweaty and a whole lot tired. I barely have a moment to set down my bag when a *"beeeeeeeepppppp! beep! beep!"* rips through the air. I jolt, turning towards the source of the noisy blast.

A beat-up little Mazda 323 in faded bronze roars to the kerb, loose gravel flying and dust kicking up, coating the air. It clouds me and I inhale a lungful, prompting a coughing fit. I wave a hand in front of my face, dispersing the haze.

The car belongs to Matt, but Erin alights from the driver's side, indicating she probably stole it from her older brother. She rips off her sunglasses and jogs over, her eyes red and swollen. I'm swept into a hug that squeezes the last of the dust from my lungs, her face burying itself in my neck.

"Jamie!" A tear plops on my shoulder. "You can't go."

"Erin." I squeeze back, her warmth and familiarity making me wonder what the hell I'm doing. "I don't want to leave you." But I know I have to do this. Erin has her family, a sense of belonging. So does Jake. He has everyone he needs right here. But Bear and I … we're the same. We have nothing left. No family to leave behind. No roots tugging us back home. We need to get out there and find our own.

"So don't!" She steps back and wipes at her face, sniffing. Her blond hair is a little wild and mascara is smudged beneath her eyes.

"You're a mess."

Erin snorts. "You're no better." She brushes a hand over my tangled hair and lightly touches a finger to my cheek. "Look at you. You've got sex face." I'm grabbed into another quick hug. "I'm so proud of you." Erin releases me equally as fast, and I stumble. "How was it? Wait, don't tell me." She collects the bag I dumped on the bench seat of the bus shelter and starts for the car. "Tell me on the way. I'm driving you."

I baulk. "What? Erin, that's like a four-day drive."

"Ha!" Erin dumps my bag on the backseat and slams Matt's car door so hard I wince. The thing looks held together with a wing and a prayer. A swift wind could possibly blow the door clean off. "I love you, but not *that* much. Screw the bus. I'll take you to the airport." She gives her shoulders a sexy little shimmy. "You can tell me all about Jake."

God, Jake. Where do I even start? Maybe with the fact I'm a walking zombie. I barely slept last night, but who could after a night like that? It was eye-opening. My world has been turned on its head. It's no wonder I couldn't switch off. I know I did eventually, because I woke with the harsh light of the morning blaring into the room, warming the air around me.

My brows drew into puzzled lines as I shifted in bed, fuzzy, disoriented, and tangled in white sheets. I turned my head, feeling it thud with the slight movement, and encountered Jake. Every moment from the night before flooded me like a burst dam.

He was asleep, facing me, his expression relaxed and sheets pooled around his hips. What he did to me last night … They say you never forget your first. Is that true? I hope so, because I don't want to forget a single minute. Thank god it was Jake at the bar. I couldn't imagine it being someone else.

His eyes blinked open as if he could feel my stare. I watched awareness come over him, of our night together. A slow smile curved his lips. "Mornin', army girl."

There was something between us. Something that even I—young, naïve about men, and never having been in love before—knew was special. A seed that if watered and placed in filtered sunlight had the potential to bloom into something incredibly bright and beautiful.

And I had to let it go.

Let the seed die.

My pounding heart began to ache.

"Mornin', army boy," I whispered back.

He reached over and tucked a lock of hair behind my ear. The gesture was gentle. "How do you feel after last night?"

I stretched a little, feeling parts of me ache that never had before. It was a good ache. The kind I wanted to feel again. I returned his smile. "Like I want to do it all over again."

Jake laughed and I loved how his eyes crinkled at the corners, as if he laughed often. "Is it weird that I don't want you to leave?" His palm skimmed over my bare shoulder and down my arm, leaving a delicious shiver in its wake. "I just found you."

The smile on my face died away. "I don't think it's weird. I feel the same way."

Jake took my hand in his, twining our fingers together, and tugged. "C'mon." I was pulled from the bed, both of us still naked. He waggled his eyebrows, giving me the once-over. My face burned, even after last night's antics, yet I giggled and pushed against him, the brush of his naked skin against mine thrilling. "I'll introduce you to shower sex before you go."

"You did not!" Erin screams, interrupting my recount.

"Don't interrupt me!"

"Who even are you right now? You were a virgin yesterday. A *virgin*," she enunciates slowly as if I somehow wasn't aware of my own sexual history—or lack thereof. "And now you're like, getting pounded against the tiles in Jake's shower?" She leans across and punches me in the arm.

I suck in a breath, the offending thump sending a sick lurch to my belly. I rub the pained area. "Ow, Erin! What was that for?"

"For not telling me this sooner."

"How could I have told you sooner?"

Her chin juts out. "You could have called. All I got was a lame message telling me you were alive."

"You were lucky to even get that."

She glances across at me, a smirk on her face. "What? Because you were so busy playing computer games all night long? How did you two even manage shower sex between all those important missions?"

"Shut up."

"You shut up."

"No, you shut up."

I fold my arms. "Okay. I will. Then you won't hear what happened *after* the shower sex."

"I'd prefer to hear what happened *during* the shower sex."

"That part is private."

Erin glances across at me again. "Okay, I'll give you that," she says, letting it go a lot easier than I thought she would. Maybe it's the tone in my voice. Maybe the look on my face. Every mile she drives takes me farther from Jake, and it feels wrong, like I'm throwing a rare gift into the trash, something I'll never receive again.

The shower sex wasn't anything wild like she's probably envisaging, or smooth like something you'd see in the movies. It was intimate, a little bit awkward, and a whole lot slippery. But it was one hundred percent perfect. Jake basically lowered himself into a squat, and I climbed onto his legs as he instructed, my thighs hugging his hips and ankles crossing together at his back. He slid inside, breathing heavy as hot water beat down, before straightening, bringing me with him as if I weighed a feather.

Then he pressed me against the tiles, biceps bulging in a ridiculous display of strength. I kissed him, my tongue rubbing with his as he rocked his hips gently, his body surrounding me until he was all I could feel.

Jake began to thrust and a small amount of pain mixed in with the pleasure—but it only heightened everything I was feeling.

"Is that good?"

All I managed was a useless gasp. I was too far gone. My body was tingling, and I was coming from the endless friction of him rubbing against my clit. He came soon after, burying his face in the crook of my neck as I held on.

Jake set me on my feet after, and we laughed and soaped each other, learning each other's scars and ticklish spots.

"This is some kind of torture device," he said after we were clean and dry, him standing behind me as he tried to hook me back into the bustier from the night before.

"You seemed to like it just fine last night."

"It's definitely sexy, but Christ it left red welts all over your back. I'm not sure I can bring myself to put it back on you."

"You have to. I can't leave here in just a pair of pants."

He threw my bustier away. I watched it sail across the room in front of me, landing in the corner of his bedroom. "Jake!"

Laughing, he palmed my boobs from behind, his large hands covering them completely. The touch had my head tilting back against his chest, my lungs drawing in a shaky breath.

"How about if I just cover them like this?" Jake gave them a firm squeeze, his strong fingers digging in just a little bit. "Then no one will see."

I swatted him away, turning to face him. "You can't do that!"

"There's no such thing as can't." He grinned. "You'll learn that in the army."

"Jake!" I hugged my arms across my chest, covering myself as if he hadn't seen it all before.

"You don't need to hide all that from me." His eyes darkened a whole hell of a lot. "You're beautiful."

Jake shifted closer, wrapping me up in his arms, lifting me until we were eye level. He was clad only in boxer-briefs, and I could feel him pressing against me, hard and hot. "One more time?" I whispered, utterly addicted.

He smacked his lips to mine. "I want to, but you're too tender. You'll be even more sore tomorrow than you are now."

"I don't care about tomorrow."

"Well *I* care about your tomorrow." Jake set me down and reached around me, pulling open a drawer from a tallboy from behind me. He plucked a folded shirt free and gave it to me. "You can wear this."

I took it even though I knew I couldn't wear it, hugging it to my chest. It was soft and worn and smelled freshly laundered. "Thanks, but I can't take your shirt. I won't be able to get it back to you."

"There you go with saying can't again." His voice was gruff, and he swiped a thumb across my cheek. "Keep it."

We pulled to the kerb out the front of Sue's house, Jake having drove me home. He cut the engine and twisted in his seat, ducking his head to look out my open passenger window. "This where you live?"

I looked at the house with fresh eyes. It was small for the amount of fosters Sue took in. The exterior needed work, the porch sagging and the paint peeling. It was on the to-do list, the crazy long one that I helped her with whenever I had the time. The little cement path leading to the front door was aged and cracked, and the lawn overgrown. She wouldn't be happy about that. We each had our allotted chores, but it wasn't mine to mow.

I sighed. I was grateful for Sue. She wasn't loving or affectionate, but I'd heard worse stories. She gave me a roof over my head. "I used to."

Jake took my hand, and I turned to look at him. "You nervous?"

"About the army?"

"Yeah."

"I'm more worried about finding my place there. What if I hate it?"

"You won't." He gave my hand a squeeze. "But can I give you a piece of advice?"

"Please."

"Don't hold back out of fear. Challenge yourself. Get skilled while you're young. Get promoted. It means better pay and more privileges, more opportunities and the freedom to choose assignments. Listen to your training officer, and your sergeant, because when you screw up—and trust me, you will—it'll be because you weren't paying attention."

It was good advice.

"When does your basic training start?"

"The day after tomorrow."

Jake winced. "You're not giving yourself much time."

I lifted my chin. "I'm ready."

"You're not." He shook his head as if I had no clue what was coming for me. But I'd be fine, wouldn't I? I was healthy, young, fit. I felt like I'd been preparing for this moment my entire life. "Everything you thought you knew is going to change from the moment you step off the bus and fall into basic formation. You're going to get yelled at. All the time. They'll tell you you're lower than a piece of garbage stuck to someone's shoe. They'll insult you where it hurts. Your family, your dad, hell, even your hair. You'll never get enough sleep, or food, and you'll be doing push-ups in your sleep."

I swallowed, feeling the urge to poop. "Ugh, okay. Why am I doing this again?"

"Because it's the best thing you'll ever do. Go find your family, Jamie."

Jake leaned over and fisted the shirt he gave me to wear, tugging me towards him. His scent surrounded me, and I breathed it in—clean, warm, delicious—knowing it would be the last time I could.

I tilted my head and he touched his lips to mine, the pressure light and sweet, and yet I felt it down to my toes. "Mmm, I'm gonna miss this mouth." He brushed a finger over my bottom lip. Then he kissed me again, his tongue rubbing with mine, lazy, deep, as if we had all day. But we didn't, and as if we both recognised it at the same time, the pace kicked up a notch. My lips pressed harder, growing more urgent. His hands gripped my waist, pulling me closer, anchoring me against him, the handbrake digging into my hip.

"Jamie," he groaned, sucking in a breath.

Our gazes locked and my heart actually hurt. "I should go." But instead, I kissed him again. His arms tightened around me, hugging me to him as if were special.

"Thank you for last night," he whispered between kisses.

"Thank *you*," I retorted, my hands finding their way under the navy-blue Henley he unfortunately covered his chest with this morning. My fingers traversed the warm, muscled ridges, and he sucked in a breath.

"What time's your flight? I could drive you to the airport."

"You don't have to do that. I've got a ride."

I didn't, but I couldn't drag this out any longer. It was literally making me ache. I kissed him again, my fingers fumbling for the door handle. It opened and I pulled myself away, forcing my legs to step out of his car.

I shut the door behind me and turned, ducking down to rest my arms on the open window. "I'll be seeing you, Jake Tanner."

He held my eyes. "See you, Jamie Murphy."

I walked up the cracked path wearing my tight tailored pants and heels, his tee shirt hanging off me. My hair was a mess and my makeup washed clean away. A mirror inspection after our shower revealed a red rash all down my neck. I'd never looked worse, and I didn't care.

I glanced behind me. He was watching, waiting for me to go inside.

My heart pounded as I forced a smile and a brief wave.

Then I stepped inside Sue's house, hearing his car drive away as I walked to my room. My bag was packed, sitting ready on my stripped bed. All I needed to do was change, which I did, keeping Jake's shirt and exchanging my pants and heels for gym tights and sneakers. When I folded up the pants, a piece of paper fluttered to the ground. I picked it up, a puzzled frown on my brow.

Email me any time, army girl.

Jake.Tanner@defence.gov.au.

xo

My thumb glided along the handwritten words, my belly fluttering. With a smile pulling at my lips, I took the piece of paper and slid it into the zip-pocket of my bag.

"I'm off, Sue!" I yelled.

"Got everything?" she yelled back from somewhere in the house.

I thought of Jake's note as I left my bedroom for the last time. "Yeah!"

She came out and after an awkward half-hug, I left, shooting one last glance to the fence before I made my way down the street.

See ya, Bear.

10

JAMIE

My first day of basic training is The Worst Day Ever. I knew it was going to be tough; I was warned. But this is next level, and it all starts with the yelling.

"Recruits! Put your paperwork on your left, bag on your right!"

And we have to yell back. "Yes, Drill Sergeant!" If it isn't loud enough, we have to do it again. "Yes, Drill Sergeant!"

Our phones are confiscated on arrival. We get them back after we earn the privilege, whenever that will be. Meanwhile, we're allowed to email on two separate occasions.

"Call home, say the following three sentences and no more: I have arrived at Kapooka Training Centre. I am safe. I will call you when I can."

"Yes, Drill Sergeant!"

And while everyone lines up to make their call home, I stay behind and get yelled at some more. "Can't you hear, Recruit?"

"I can hear, Drill Sergeant!"

"Then go call home!"

"Uh, I don't have one."

"You don't have one what?"

"I don't have one, Drill Sergeant!"

"You think I care?" he yells in my face. "No special treatment for charity cases, Recruit. Go make the call. I don't care who it's to."

So I call Erin and thankfully she's the one who answers. I mumble the required words and hang up before she can respond, my face burning as I turn and make my way back down the line. They all hear the drill sergeant yelling, and I know from here on out I'll be known as 'Charity Case.'

We train well into the night on our first day, running in our brand-new uniforms, the fabric thick and stiff, the boots big and heavy. We run until my legs are numb. Until I can't feel my face. When bedtime comes, my head is pounding, blisters burn like fire on my toes and the backs of my ankles, and I'm actually starting to question whether I'll survive this place. It's just lucky I don't have it in me to quit.

Each day is the same after the first one. Routine, structure, order, rules. We learn our weapons. Not just how to hold them or fire them but how to disassemble them, clean them, and put them back together until we can do it in our sleep.

Week after endless week, we immerse ourselves in army life. Learning the culture, customs, and training. We complete endless drills, and the value of teamwork is drummed into us until our heads ache. We navigate obstacles and barbed wire at night, wading through mud and over rocky outcrops, while flares and machine guns fire repeatedly in bursts above us.

I pay attention every single day, just like Jake told me to, and I keep up, and sometimes I even excel.

And yes, Bear, I make another new friend.

His name is Colin Wood. He's extra tall and gangly, and incredibly unco-ordinated. I might not be their star recruit, but I'm pretty sure he won't last the week. Only he does, surviving the physical training by the skin of his teeth. It's everything else he excels at—the rifle range, first aid, exams.

We become friends on a most unfortunate day for him. It's just six days into basic training. We're in the chow hall, tired, sweaty, hungry, when he gets called out by the sergeant for carrying his flashlight on his belt.

"Is that where you keep your flashlight, Recruit? You think it's a light sabre?"

His red face lights up the room. "No, Drill Sergeant!"

"Go stand by the door!"

"Sir?"

Uh oh. Our drill sergeant scowls, his lips pressing flat. "What did you say, Skywalker?"

"Yes, Drill Sergeant!"

All eyes are on Wood as he sets his uneaten tray of food down by the nearest table and jogs to the door, long arms and legs swinging as if he has no control of his limbs.

"Get your light sabre, Recruit."

Wood plucks his flashlight free, his brow pulling into puzzled lines. We all watch on like a car crash is unfolding before our eyes.

"Now hold it at the ready. I want you to strike dead all the recruits as they leave."

Laughter bubbles up in my chest, but I hold on to it for dear life, otherwise I'll be right up there playing Star Wars alongside him. I look away as I eat my lunch.

"I can't hear your light sabre, Recruit!"

Oh no. He's actually forcing him to make the sound effects.

I almost choke on a mouthful of lamb stew the first time I hear it. *"Bzzzzzhmmmm!"* And again. *"Bzzzzzhmmmm!"*

By the time I finish eating and am ready to leave, he's still at it, his hot lunch congealing on the table nearby, his toasted bread roll growing cold and soggy where he dipped it in the bowl. I know Wood must be starving; his stomach is always growling at the worst moments. I shoot him a sympathetic look as I make my way out the door. He waves his light sabre at me as I step out, only I think he's a bit delirious from hunger because his arm flails upward and his flashlight whacks me in the eye.

The *crack* is loud—louder than his little light sabre sound effect—and my head snaps sideways.

"Arrghh!" I cry out and put a hand to my brow. It comes away red and sticky.

"Oh shit. Fuck." In his panic, Wood makes the unfortunate mistake of putting his flashlight back on his belt so he can reach for me with free hands. "I'm so sorry."

"Jesus Christ, Skywalker!" yells our drill sergeant. "Go take Charity Case to the infirmary."

The infirmary isn't far from the chow hall, but it's busy. Wood apologises a thousand times on our walk to the onsite medical facility. According to the brief assessment from the harried medic, all my brow needs is a bit of glue. Maybe some ice for the eye I can already feel swelling. The staff seem to know Wood and allow him to fix me himself, his bony fingers surprisingly nimble and proficient. "Where did you learn to do that?" I ask as he focuses on his task, placing a small patch over the wound.

"My father is a doctor. So was my grandfather before him." He pats the edges of the adhesive, making sure it sticks. "He wanted me to follow in his footsteps."

"And you ended up here because ..."

"I don't want to be a doctor. I want to be a combat medic."

And suddenly *I know*, like a lock clicking into place. The army isn't just about the fight for me. It's about saving lives. Maybe if I can do that, it will make up for the one I lost. I'm not sure I'll ever forgive myself for what happened in my past, but what I do from here on out can make a difference. Can't it? Maybe it really *is* possible to leave the world a little better than I found it.

"What about you?" Wood asks.

"Same," I reply, warming to my fellow recruit for unintentionally helping me find my place in the world—despite the fact he punched me in the face on my sixth day of basic training. I'll be spending the next two days completing obstacles with only one functioning eye. "I want to be a combat medic too."

He gives me a look, the dubious kind, the one that says females can't do that. They aren't strong enough. They aren't tough enough. And they sure as hell aren't built to carry those seventy-plus kilogram packs on patrol. And maybe he's right. I'll have to work harder than anyone else. I'll have to build muscle. Endurance. Mental strength. Not to mention females on the front line, in combat, are rare—and likely unwelcome. I probably have rocks in my head choosing this life. And then Jake's grinning face swims in front of me. *There's no such thing as can't.*

And although he was applying it to something more sexual in nature, he's the kind of guy you just *know* applies that motto to every aspect of his life.

So I return Wood's look, my jaw set tight, my brow bandaged, my eye currently swelling faster than a river in flood, and my hackles rising. "I can do anything you can do, Wood. Only I'll be doing it better."

He grins at me, seeming to like my mettle. "Except maybe wield a light sabre."

My lips twitch. "Yeah. Except that."

"Right on, Murphy." He offers me his fist, and I bump it with my own. And just like that, Wood becomes family.

I don't have time to email during our first four weeks, but by the fifth we get our phones back. Late that night I switch mine on, and *ping* after *ping* rings out as my screen fills with messages from Erin.

I have to swallow the lump in my throat, grateful to Bear for forcing me to make a friend. I flick through her messages quickly, trying to soak in as much as I can before I pass out from exhaustion. Most are just stories about her day but a couple stand out.

Erin: I'm moving out! I found a share apartment in the city and it's only a small walk to college every day. I can't wait for you to see it! PS I love you!

I smile, knowing she's following the plan she carefully laid out for herself.

Erin: I saw Jake in the bar last night. He asked after you! Naturally

I told him nothing BECAUSE I HAVEN'T HEARD FROM YOU! He told me that was normal though. And he totally left the bar alone even though every woman in the place had their tongues hanging out low enough to touch the sticky floor. GROSS!

My belly flutters and then I sigh, smushing my face into the pillow. *It's never going to happen, Murphy. Get over it.*

I send her one back before setting my phone aside and going to sleep.

Jamie: I'm alive! They confiscated our phones, sorry. The good news is that I made a new friend. His name is Colin. I think you two would really hit it off. The bad news is that I've decided to become a medic, which means another two years or so of training (at least) out at Bonegilla in Victoria. And then I'll probably get a placement in Townsville. PS I love you too.

Townsville is on the far north coast of Queensland, which is still on the other side of the country to home. It's beautiful if you care about the tropics and spend your days diving the reefs, but it's also hotter than Satan's anus. Unfortunately, I have no choice in the matter. I enlisted for six years minimum and go where they tell me to. It just sucks there are only three locations for combat medics in Australia, and home is not one of them.

Her reply is sitting on my phone when I wake at five in the morning, so she must have had a late night out. I don't get a chance to even look at the message for another two days.

Erin: Townsville? WTF? I hate you right now. You suck worse than sweaty, hairy ballsacks.

Erin: You can at least come visit though, right? When do you get a break?

Jamie: Of course I can come visit. I just don't know when, but as soon as I do you'll be the first to find out.

It's not like I have anyone else to tell anyway. I'm pretty sure Sue isn't interested in a reunion, and while I hung out with some of Erin's friends from school now and then, we were never close. And Jake, well he may have left the bar alone that night, but it wasn't because he was waiting for me.

❧

GRADUATION DAY EVENTUALLY COMES. We stand in formation during the ceremony, uniforms pressed and shoes shined. Speeches are made as the hot sun beats down, long and arduous, and sweat trickles down my back. Finally, we're dismissed and everyone around me cheers, my fellow recruits, their family and friends clapping and whooping from the stands. They pour down onto the field, surrounding their graduating loved ones, admiring the smart uniforms, laughing and talking.

My eyes fall to my shoes, blinking, alone in a sea of people.

I turn, walking away.

"Hey! Wait! Murphy!"

Wood is pushing his way through the throng of people. He grabs me by the shoulder, his bright face happy. He jerks his thumb towards the parking lot. "We're going for beers. Come with us?"

I peer around him, looking for the *us*. There are two other guys waiting. Civilians, we call them now. Neither are as tall as Wood, but they aren't far behind. They all have the same eyes, but Wood is the only gangly one. "Your brothers?"

"Yeah. Pains in my ass," he mutters. "If you come along, they'll be easier to put up with."

"Umm why?"

His eyes widen on me as if I'm stupid. "Umm because you're hot. Surely you know you're the most beautiful girl any of us have ever seen?"

"Wood, that's crazy." Because it is. My nails are chipped, my brows overgrown, my legs unshaven, not to mention my body is an entire bruise. I'm covered in them from my face down to my toes. Big ones, little ones. I look like the plastic mat in a game of Twister.

Tugging the hat from my head, I smooth a few stray hairs that have escaped the tight bun at the nape of my neck. Then my thoughts take a sharp turn. "Oh, you don't …"

He physically recoils. "Oh god, no!"

I whack him with my hat. "Well you don't have to say that like I have leprosy!"

"You're not my type, Murphy."

Suddenly I'm curious because we've never talked about that stuff before. "And what *is* your type?"

Wood grins. "I like sweet girls."

"And I'm not?"

"You're a bit too badass for me, Murphy." He flexes one of his stringy arms. "I don't have much to work with, so I need someone who's easily impressed."

I shake my head and he laughs, linking his arm with mine. "C'mon. Let's go drink."

11

JAMIE

I don't get to go home after basic training. Graduation parade was Friday (yesterday) and the last chance for recruits to see their loved ones. Today we have local leave, tomorrow is maintenance and clean up, and Monday Wood and I depart for the Army School of Health in Bonegilla, Victoria, where we'll complete seven modules of training over the next seventy-six weeks. When finished, we'll have a Diploma of Nursing under our belts, along with a Diploma of Paramedical Science.

My future is mapped out for the first time in my life, and it's a relief. Rules, structure, plans—it's comforting in some strange way. I've taken to this life like a duck to water. Except leave time is scarce —at least it is during training—so Wood and I are taking advantage of our day off.

We're out at a local café, seated outdoors in the sun. I'm in civilian attire. It feels ridiculously *light*. I'm wearing a pair of short shorts after weeks of heavy uniform, my legs stretched out to get a little tanning action in while we drink our coffees.

Wood takes a long, noisy *slurrppp* from his takeout cup, reading the local paper that was left behind by a previous patron while I sit with my eyes glued to the screen of my Blackberry, trying to focus on sending an email to Jake.

I shoot him a look. "Wood, that's gross."

"You're gross."

My brows rise. "How old are you? Ten?"

His brows rise back just as coolly. "Are you forgetting about the other night when you ate dinner so fast after PT you barfed it all back up again?"

Ugh. I shudder. The assessment was gruelling. I choked on so much muddy water during our crawl beneath barbwire—in the dark mind you—I thought I was literally going to die. I shrug at Wood as if it were nothing. "Are you forgetting about the time you punched me in the face with your light sabre?"

His eyes flatten. "I can't believe you told my brothers about that yesterday."

I smile sweetly. "Hey, I was four beers in by then." And we hadn't had alcohol for well over eighty days, which was basically a lifetime for someone who's barely just become legal to drink. "I can't be held accountable for what I say under the influence."

He *harrumphs* and I re-focus on my email.

Jake,

I survived basic training, so yeah, thanks for all the advice. I'm heading straight to Bonegilla now so I don't get to come home.

Dammit. That sounds incredibly stilted and boring. Wood's phone beeps little message alerts in the background as I delete what I have and try again. He sets his paper down and picks up his phone while I stab out little letters, hating the fact that I'm no good at this type of stuff. When I was with him, it felt so effortless and fun, but I suck at written communication.

Thanks for giving me your email address. Basic training is finished, and I now have another two years of advanced training ahead of me. Hope you're well?

Ugh. My second attempt is no better. I'm hitting delete again when Wood gives me an odd look. I pause. "What?"

He jerks his head towards a cab pulling up to the kerb by our café. I stare, searching the exterior for whatever it is Wood seems to think is worth my attention. Then the back door opens, and my heart explodes as Erin steps out. "Oh my god. What?" I'm standing up, saying to Wood, "How did you …" and trailing off from shock. I set my Blackberry down, the half-deleted email forgotten.

She's grinning wildly, dressed in a pretty spring dress, her blond hair out and flowing down her back as she starts towards us. I run at her and we hug and squeal while pedestrians step around us with irritated expressions. I pull back, inspecting her as she does with me. "How did you …" I'm still in shock.

"Wood. He stole my number from your phone. I'm sorry I couldn't get here yesterday for graduation but I had an exam."

We gravitate towards the table where Wood sits. He rises and I introduce them officially. He holds out a hand. "Colin Wood, ma'am. Nice to meet you."

Erin smiles slowly. It's her flirty smile. I know because I've seen her practice it in the mirror and on boys everywhere. "Erin Tennyson."

He drags a chair across from an empty table so she can take a seat, and then he runs off to order her a coffee, doting on her as if she's the Second Coming.

We watch him at the counter for a moment and before he comes back, she grabs my hands in hers, excitement dancing in her eyes. "He's cute, don't you think?"

I frown and look at him. He's still tall and gangly, but maybe he's filled out a little since we met. All we did was work out and eat, and eat, and then eat some more, and it still felt like they weren't feeding us enough. His hair is dark and buzzed short, his skin a beautiful olive, and his lashes belong on a girl, but still, there's nothing there to make me giddy and I *know* giddy, because even now when I think of Jake I can't catch my breath.

I look at my new friend as he returns to our table, limbs flapping as he manoeuvres around chairs filled with people. He's just the guy who wielded a light sabre and punched me in the face with it. "Umm, it's just Wood."

"They're bringing it over," he says, his chair scraping on the pavement as he pulls it back out and seats himself. "And don't you dare tell her the light sabre story."

I bust out laughing. "Oh my god, Erin, you have to hear it."

I can't even blame my loose lips on alcohol this time as I share the story, but Wood did himself proud. He would make a great Skywalker. By the time I finish, Erin is laughing too, but her eyes are lit on Wood with admiration.

"You can't go there," I tell her after brunch is done and we're out shopping, Wood getting dragged along. He's ducked off to the bathroom, and I'm seizing the moment. I don't want my best friend caught up in a long-distance relationship with my other best friend. I'll just end up the little piggy in the middle when it all goes to shit, which it will, because as much as I love this girl, she's fickle. I hear about a new crush every other week.

"It's not against the law to flirt, Murphy." She picks up a little black dress and holds it to her body, poking out a leg to see where the hem reaches. "It doesn't mean anything."

"Sure it doesn't."

She blinks at me, her best attempt at an innocent expression.

"Pffft." I snatch the black dress from her hands and return it to the hanger. "You don't need this. You have like, ten already."

Erin snatches it back up as if another customer is about to pounce and steal it out from under her. "It's not for me. It's for you."

I snort. "And where am I going to wear that?"

"Don't think I see what's going on here." She waves a finger over my body. "You think because you're army now you can let yourself go?"

My brows draw together, and I look down, giving myself the once-over even though I know what she's referring to. But training is hard on the body. There was no time for girly face masks, waxing sessions, or exfoliation scrubs. I barely had time for sleep. "Tidy yourself up, babe. Put on a sexy dress while you're in Adelaide." Her shoulders do a shimmy. "Get some action."

I glance over her shoulder, praying for Wood to return and save me from this conversation. "I don't want any action."

I can't help but feel no other man would measure up to the one that came before him, and it would just end in disappointment.

Erin gives me a look, the kind that says she knows where my head is at. It's probably written all over my face. "Jamie …"

There's something in her voice, something serious. It makes my insides clench tight. Her expression is solemn, as if she's about to deliver news that I do *not* want to hear. I lift my chin. "What?"

"Jake is gone."

Her words take a moment to sink in, and when they do, my body plummets through an open trapdoor beneath my feet. "Gone?" My voice is sharp and high. "What do you mean *gone*?"

"He's been deployed to Afghanistan."

I suck in a breath. *Of course* he's been deployed. He's army and there's a war going on. It's what we train for. And even though it's not *our* war, we should be there. People—ones like us who have hopes and dreams, and friends and family—are being mistreated and tortured. Even killed. How could our nation hold its head high if we sat back and did nothing?

And yet a sick knot forms in my belly. In my head Jake was still back home in Perth on leave, maybe working on buying that cottage, doing the renovations he said he wanted to do. I didn't even ask where he was stationed.

"How do you even know that?" I ask.

"I heard it from a friend of a friend who saw you two together at the bar that night. She thought you and Jake were a thing."

I shake my head. "We're not a thing."

"Maybe you could be."

Jake would have known of his deployment before I even met him, and yet he never said a word. I guess it's not the kind of light-hearted talk you have with your one-night stand. Which is all I was, right? Just someone he slept with that one time.

Plucking my Blackberry free from my pocket, I call up the email and delete it entirely, vowing to forget the email address Jake gave me. Then I snatch the dress from Erin and march it to the counter. "No. You're right. I need to put this on and get some action."

Wood sidles up beside us, leaning his elbow on the counter and huffing a long breath, bored with our shopping expedition when Erin has barely just begun. "What'd I miss?"

"We were talking about Jake."

I elbow Erin in the side.

"Who's Jake?" he asks.

"No one," I retort, paying for the dress, tapping my fingers while I wait for the sales assistant to finish wrapping it in tissue paper. She slides it carefully inside a bag and hands it over with a smile. I don't even know if the dress fits. I don't care. I don't want to be here anymore.

ME AND WOOD leave for Bonegilla the following Monday, and the next two years fly by as if we've only been there weeks.

Our training is delivered by a combination of military and civilian contracted staff. There's barely time for a module to sink in before we move on to the next—covering the history of ADF health services, advanced first aid, infection control, primary health care, resuscitation, treatment control, and minor skills such as how to complete the boring paperwork no one wants to do.

They save the hardest module for last: army specific training and experiences in a deployed setting. They're preparing us for treating patients in a war zone. At one point in my assessment, there's a crowd of soldiers yelling over me while I attempt to triage a 'wounded soldier' on the ground. My hands shake and my heart pounds the entire time, but I get it done, thriving under the challenge.

We still have our PT and drills and room inspections, but it's a little more relaxed than Kapooka. I return home only once during training, spending Christmas with Erin. Wood comes with me. We spend four days hanging out on the beach, opening presents, and drinking beer under the sun before returning to reality, and eventually, another graduation.

They station the both of us at Townsville, medics being in high demand. My first deployment is to East Timor. It isn't a war zone, but it's eye-opening. Our troops are teaching soldiers how to weld, operate diggers, and build bridges. The Timor soldiers are learning how to help their nation rather than just secure it, which is important in stabilising their future.

I treat minor issues while stationed there—soldiers suffering dehydration, sprains, minor cuts and bruising, and basically handing out Band-Aids. It isn't the kind of trauma I'm trained to treat in the midst of a hectic combat zone, yet it feels good. I'm doing *something*.

The best part? I make a difference by helping treat the general population. It's *me* who they walk for miles on bare feet to see, giving them injections that will save their lives and the lives of their children.

My first deployment to Afghanistan comes two years after my initial station in Townsville. The battalion I'm assigned to has five medics. I'm one of them. Wood another. We're being sent as part of the mentoring and restructuring taskforce, flying into Kuwait first. We spend a week there being briefed and learning special drills, body armour, and identifying IEDs.

From there we fly to Tarin Kowt, coming in under the cover of darkness. My heart pounds as the plane dips and lurches, making us less of a target to enemy gunfire. Bile rises in my throat. I swallow it down and close my eyes, fear a living breathing animal inside me.

"Murphy."

I blink.

"Murphy, we're here."

I blink again and turn to my right. Wood is beside me. Our plane has landed, and my hand is holding on so tight to his I fear I've broken bones. Jerking free, I glance around the plane. Battalion soldiers smirk. They think we're a thing, Wood and me. They also don't want me here. They haven't outright said so, but I feel it in the way they look at me and the way they make an active effort not to talk to me. I might be a favourite in our unit back home, but it's active combat here and I have a vagina. I'll have to work twice as hard to earn their trust and prove I belong just as much as they do.

Rolling frustrated eyes at my unit, I stand, reaching for my pack. It's heavy. Heavier than what they have to carry because mine doesn't just include general supplies, sleeping gear, and food and water for patrols; it also includes medical equipment, of which they may possibly be thanking me for one day.

My first day is spent getting situated, and I find myself looking carefully at every Australian soldier who passes me, searching for Jake and seeking out hazel eyes and shaggy golden-brown hair. Wondering. Always wondering where Bear is, even now, over six years later. Did he end up joining the army? Is he here? Is he okay?

The next day I'm thrown in the deep end. As one of the few females, I've been tasked with searching local women and providing them with health checks. The females are quiet, but their eyes speak more than words ever could. It's clear they appreciate our presence and the medical care we provide.

From there I move to the Tarin Kowt hospital, treating countless trauma cases. It's when I get assigned last minute to assist a remote patrol base that I get the full effect of being in a combat zone.

It's forty kilometres away, requiring a three-vehicle convoy. I'm in the second armoured vehicle when the first hits an IED. We're following too close behind and the force of the blast is enough to send us careening off the road and rolling on our side.

My combat helmet cracks against the window and dust fills the vehicle, coating our face and bodies as we skid metres off the road. The truck comes to a sudden stop, and I jerk against my seat belt.

"Is everyone okay?" our driver shouts.

I stare blankly at the seat in front of me. For a moment I'm fifteen again and my father is unconscious in the seat beside me. Splintered glass covers my face, slicing and jabbing tender skin. My arm. The bone is poking through. My lungs wheeze.

"Dad?" my voice is a low rasp. I can barely hear myself speak. "Dad. I can't—"

"Private Murphy!"

I blink. It's not dark out. There's no bitumen road with painted white lines, rolling green hills, and leafy trees. No houses or street lights. It's midday and everything is red and hazy. I look down. I'm in an army uniform, combat armour protecting me from serious damage.

Jesus. Our convoy was hit by an IED. I touch a palm to my face then look at it. There are no shards of glass. Just dust and a smear of blood.

"Private Murphy! Doc!"

"I'm okay," I croak and cough. "Just a little shook up."

The soldier beside me, Private Connor, scrambles for his seat belt. "We gotta get out of here."

12

———————

JAMIE

*P*rivate Connor climbs out the top of the truck and reaches in through the window, offering a hand. I go to grab it, disoriented, then my training kicks in as if a switch is flicked. "Wait. My rifle." I scramble for the weapon, tucking it in beside me as I'm seized in a strong grip and pulled free of the truck. I jump down, doing a quick assessment for personal injury, but I'm fine. My combat armour and helmet have kept me safe.

Connor reaches in for another soldier. That's when the first shot rings out. A loud *crack* that seems to echo across the earth.

"Get the fuck down!" someone yells.

Soldiers from our convoy jump down beside me, and we use the truck as a shield. I move around to the side, time slowing down as I raise my rifle. The weight of it is familiar in my hands as I risk a peek. My throat is coated with dust, my voice a rasp when I speak. "An ambush?"

"Looks like it. Sons of bitches," comes the voice beside me. It's Corporal Marsh—his face coated with dust, his teeth dazzling white in comparison. I peer through my scope at the crop of crumbling cement buildings where it seems the shots came from. Blood thunders through my veins as I take aim, just like I've done a million times before during training. I don't even have to think about. My body is operating on autopilot, my mind clear. My finger pulls back easy and the rifle fires.

"You need to get to the lead vehicle. I'll cover."

"I need my medi pack!" I take aim and fire again. Once, twice, three times. Four. A body falls. I don't have time to process what I've just done before I'm firing again. "It's in the truck," I yell.

"Private Connor," Marsh barks. "Get the doc's pack."

It's a risky move. It means climbing back inside the truck, leaving him exposed, but he doesn't hesitate. He leaps up and jumps inside with barely a blink. We fire off more rounds for cover as he climbs free, tossing my pack out beside him.

"Doc Murphy, you need to get to the lead truck." He pushes in front of my position, his own rifle raised as I secure my pack. "When I say, go, you go."

They begin to fire, raining a volley of heat. Enemy fire ceases.

"Go!" Marsh shouts. "Go, go, go!"

I don't even blink as I run, my adrenaline pumping as I zigzag my way towards the crippled truck. It's crumpled, having rolled more than once before landing upright. Three wounded soldiers are on the ground, one still inside—the driver—and another dragging his comrade to cover. I reach him first and help drag the fallen soldier without breaking stride.

"The driver?" I bark.

He shakes his head.

"Dammit." I wrench the truck door open and lean in, jabbing my fingers in his burnt and bloodied neck as I check for a pulse. Nothing. A sickening cocktail of fear and panic begins to bubble up inside me. I swallow it down.

Not now, Murphy. You need to focus. This is what you're here for.

I move to the fallen soldier next, dropping beside him.

He blinks, coming to, and croaks. "What happened?"

"You're going to be all right, Private," is the first thing out of my mouth. The one thing we're trained to say first in order to keep our patient calm. The second is to explain the situation in a concise manner because there's fear in the unknown. "You were hit by an IED."

His eyes are bright blue like the sky, and I read the panic in them in an instant. They tear up. "I can't feel my toes." His nostrils flare and his arms start to flail. "I can't feel my toes!"

I look down. The soldier's legs are intact, but there's a lot of blood —shrapnel the likely cause. When I look back he's blacked out again. Grabbing my pack, I pull out a C spine collar and gently place it around his neck. Corporal Marsh skids to a stop beside me. "Is he okay?"

"We're going to need a medevac," I tell him as I check vitals, shining a light into his eyes. Both pupils are dilated. "Possible spinal fracture and head injury." I reach inside my pack for bandages and scissors, my breathing harsh as I focus on what I need to do.

"Already radioed it in. They won't come out until they have the all clear. We need to take those fuckers out."

"Maybe they'll run out of bullets," I reply with grim hope, slicing my way up the soldier's pants leg. "Shit." I assess the wound, it's jagged and gaping, more blood oozing out than I'd like, but at least it's not pumping out. "Grab me a tourniquet, will you?"

He hands one over and I fix it around the soldier's thigh before applying a bandage. There's not much more I can do for him in the field, so I grab my pack and move to the next soldier. He's conscious. I patch him up and move to the next, and the next. There are burns, more shrapnel wounds than I can count, fractures, and bullets firing so close I can feel the heat of them tearing past.

I hand out green whistles for pain, doing everything I can even though it doesn't feel enough.

It's dark by the time we get the all clear. The medevac arrives and after our patients are secure, I jump on board and the big camouflaged beast lurches into the night sky. The rotor blades are loud, the *whoomph, whoomph, whoomph* filling the open cabin as it carries us back to base.

Someone hands me a bottle of water. I take it, rasping, "thanks," before guzzling it down so fast it pours over my face and dribbles down my chin and neck. I wipe my mouth with the back of my hand. It comes away smeared with blood and dirt. I stare it, turning my palm over, watching as it slowly begins to shake. I look down. I'm covered in blood. The sticky, metallic substance coats my uniform, my body armour, every bit of exposed skin.

Jesus. Holy Mary Mother of God.

My head tips back against the seat behind me, my whole body beginning to shudder. A sob rises, the dam inside me ready to burst. I hold it back by the skin of my teeth.

"You okay?" someone yells.

I don't open my eyes. I can't. Not yet. But I give the thumbs-up.

Wood is there when we land, running across the tarmac with a gurney and a face filled with panic. A medical team follows behind, bearing more gurneys. I've never been more grateful to see his flapping limbs in all my life.

I stumble out of the Blackhawk, and he grabs both my arms in a vice-like grip, yelling into my face to be heard. "Are you okay?"

I manage a nod. "Fine!" But I choke on the word, and Wood seems to know I'm hanging on by my fingernails because he gives me a task. Something to focus on. I go back on autopilot while I help the injured soldiers out of the chopper, my teeth chattering as shock takes hold.

The wounded are shipped inside the hospital, and I follow behind, pushing through the doors behind Wood. I run through the list of injuries with the on-call doctor, swaying on my feet as I outline the treatment I implemented out in the field.

"Get Private Murphy out of here," he says to Wood and looks at me. "You did good. Go get a shower and something to eat."

But I have to go debrief first, so Wood walks me over.

"What the hell happened out there?"

I shake my head. "IED blast on the lead truck. It all happened so fast. I mean, you hear about them happening, but experiencing it …" I trail off, shaking my head again. "We got ambushed and stuck for hours waiting for extraction." I check my watch. It's four in the morning. Dawn will break soon on the longest night of my life.

We make our way to the debrief building, garnering plenty of stares along the way, including more than a few double-takes. News of our ambush is all over base. A camera flash comes from out of nowhere, blinding me.

I hold a hand to my eyes.

"Dude, what the fuck," growls Wood. "You can't do that."

It's one of the male foreign correspondents from Sydney, putting a documentary together for the BBC on the war in Afghanistan. I've seen him before, questioning one of the doctors in the hospital. "We won't post it without permission." I blink away the dots and find him walking backwards in front of us. "Tell us about the ambush, Murphy."

"Are you for real?" I shake my head, hastening my stride. He keeps up with us. Wood tries tucking me into his side, protecting me from any more photos, but I'm tired and pissed off, and I know I need to handle this myself. I'm not here to hide while the big, strong men provide protection.

I grab the camera that hangs from the guy's neck and yank it towards me, dragging him with it as we come to a halt. His nostrils twitch. It's because I stink of sweat and blood and a whole lot of anger. "You wanna hear about the ambush?" My eyes narrow. "People died." I try sounding harsh, but my voice cracks on the word. "The end. Go write your fucking story."

I'm shoving him away when Corporal Marsh steps out of the debrief building. I straighten and give him a nod.

He nods in return and grips my shoulder for a quick moment. "Good job out there last night, Private. You saved a lot of lives," he says before walking off.

It's not until after the debriefing, when I'm alone in the shower, the water flowing brown and red as it circles the drain, that it all sinks in.

You saved a lot of lives.

You saved a lot of lives.

You saved a lot of lives.

My back slides down the shower wall as I sink beneath the spray, holding both palms against my head as I hold in the pained, heavy sob that threatens to escape.

I took a life last night. Maybe two. It somehow feels worse that I don't know the count. I always thought I would be okay with it as long as it was in defence of my own life or others. Survival at its most basic. Yet I feel … exhilaration at being alive. And powerful. And sick. Because it also feels wrong. So utterly, unspeakably *wrong*.

My stomach heaves and I throw up water and bile until there's nothing left. When I step out of the shower I'm wrung dry. My eyes are swollen with fatigue, my face cut and bruised, my chest red and purple from the force of the belt holding me in my seat. I stare at my face in the mirror. It looks foreign to my own eyes.

You're a born fighter, Jamie. Prove it.

I take a deep, shuddering breath and it sends a stabbing pain down my chest.

I'm trying, goddammit. I'm trying.

I push all the emotion back down inside and dress in a fresh uniform. Orders are to eat before getting sleep, so I make my way to the mess hall. It's five-thirty in the morning and the place is a hive of activity when I step inside—soldiers coming and going, laughing and talking, chef's cooking, utensils scraping, and boots thumping across the floor. Even the dust particles swirl busily above my head, alive with the scent of combat.

Heads turn as I make my way to the chow line; they track my path as I collect a tray of scrambled eggs, beans, toast and coffee. I keep my head down, hiding my battered face and swollen eyes, but I feel them watching and hear their hushed voices. Members of my unit are already seated and eating breakfast. Instead of glares I get nods and a handful of greetings as I pass them.

Finding the last empty table available, my chair scrapes across the floor as I pull it out and take a seat. I pick up a piece of slightly burnt toast, take a bite, chew, and swallow.

I've never felt more alone than I do right now, never longed more for that spot by the fence with Bear, his voice deep and comforting. Instead I'm here—on the front line in one of the world's most harsh and hostile environments—by choice.

My stomach churns but I force another bite of toast, chew, and swallow. I'm reaching for my coffee when a commotion comes from the building entrance. I turn my head, counting five soldiers, all of them large and bearded, their clothing filthy and rumpled. They look like wild beasts, as if they don't belong inside mere structures made of timber and plaster.

I force myself to look away and focus on my plate, but I hear them. Their boots are heavy as they clomp between tables and chairs towards the chow line. I take a sip of coffee, but it's impossible not to stare, my eyes tracking thick muscled limbs and low, rumbling voices. The noise rises, exposing laughter and teasing. They've returned from a mission. It's obvious in their light-hearted banter and plates piled to the ceiling.

I see the first of the group turn with his tray from my peripheral vision. He starts towards my table. My eyes glue themselves to my plate, my body tensing, radiating *fuck off* vibes like gamma rays. The exact same ones I learnt how to use in high school with great success.

And yet he takes the seat opposite, his tray slapping down adjacent to mine. I jolt at the sudden burst of noise as he sits with a thump and an audible sigh. Then I feel him looking at me, really *looking* at me, and I find myself reaching for my necklace. I wasn't sure I'd wear it again after Bear left, but I was drawn to it constantly, until one day I made the effort to fix the little clasp. It felt good when I put it on. A comfort and reminder of who I was. *Little Warrior.* And I found myself unable to take it off.

I stop myself from reaching for the silver chain—I'm not supposed to be wearing jewellery. I reach for my mug instead, risking a peek at the soldier opposite me as I lift it to my lips.

His face is covered with dried sweat and dirt, his blond beard thick with it, so it takes me a moment to fully recognise him. When I do, my eyes widen in shock, my voice a croak. "Jake?"

After all this time. Here? Now?

There are more crinkles around his eyes now and a scar on his fore-head. My gaze travels down his uniform. It's worn and muddy, covering wide shoulders and thick biceps. The sleeves are rolled halfway up his forearms, baring tanned skin and scars.

I realise then that he and his team are SAS. Legendary creatures in the army. Deadly, like venomous snakes they hide in the grass, striking before you even know they're there. They're also notoriously slow to trust, and yet so fiercely loyal they would sooner lose their own life than betray you.

Jake clears his throat and my gaze shoots up from its inspection, meeting surprised green eyes. "Army girl." He seems frozen to his chair, staring as if I'm an apparition.

My heart pounds like a jackhammer in my chest, but I try to keep cool. "You uh, come here often?"

His lips quirk beneath the beard, his voice deep and rusty. "That sounds like a line."

"How can you tell?" I ask, my lips twitching.

He picks up a piece of buttered toast and tears off a huge bite with his perfect teeth. He grins at me before chewing. "My powers of obser-vation are legendary around here."

"Excuse me." My lips form an outright smile. I can't stop it from spreading across my face. "I didn't realise I was seated in the company of a legend."

"The important thing is that you know now." The toast in Jake's hand pauses halfway to his mouth. He lowers it to his plate, his gaze settling on the red cross attached to my uniform. "You're a combat medic." A frown mars his brow, and I know what he's thinking.

The medic's job is hardest of all. It's not just seeing bodies torn apart by IEDs, people in agony covered in burns and open head wounds, it's being the one who fights against the clock to treat them all. And after we finish a twenty-mile ruck and everyone gets to rest, I'm the one treating sprains and blisters and working twice as hard to earn the respect of the soldiers I work with because I'm a woman on the front line.

My knuckles whiten around the mug in my hand. "And you're SAS."

"I see my powers of observation are not exclusive."

He's so incredibly witty, while I feel incredibly uncool. Surely he can see how hard my heart is beating beneath my uniform? Heat is already pooling between my legs, remembering what he did to my body, how alive he made it feel.

My eyes drop to his hands. They're wrapped around his knife and fork. Those hands gripped my naked hips, holding on tight as he thrust his cock inside me in the shower.

I take a shaky breath. This. Is. Not. Good.

The path my mind is travelling down right now is a forbidden one. You can't get naked with your fellow soldier, even if it *is* for the good of morale. *My* morale. Obviously.

I shake my head internally. It might be best if I don't look at him for a few minutes. It'll give my body time to chill.

I drop my gaze to my plate.

"Jamie?"

I pick up a fork, feigning interest in my now cold eggs. "Mmm?"

"What happened to your face?"

I shovel in a large bite and grimace, staring at my food as if it's about to make an escape from my plate. I speak around my mouthful. "IED."

"Fuck." His voice is harsh and low. "What about the rest of you? Are you hurt?"

After chewing a little, I swallow the horrid, cold lump of eggs. "Looks pretty much the same as my face."

He curses a blue streak, and my eyes lift without permission. He's looking at me, his gaze roaming over my face as if he can't believe I'm actually here.

Another soldier takes the empty seat beside Jake, slapping down an overloaded breakfast tray. Jake rolls his eyes towards his comrade, a man filthier and more bearded than he is. "So, being a combat medic, you'd know how to treat a pain in the neck, then?"

"Fuck off, Tanner," the big soldier mutters before shoving an entire piece of bacon in his mouth. He looks like a giant grizzly bear, one who wandered in from the wilds in search of food.

"That depends," I say to Jake, setting down my fork and picking up my mug.

His brows rise with humour as he chews his toast. "On what?"

"On just how big this pain in your neck is."

"It's *big*. And hairy." He winks at me, making us co-conspirators in his joke. "Stinks too, like a dead donkey. It's also getting a little pudgy around the middle."

The big soldier snorts and lifts the hem of his shirt, baring a thick set of washboard abs. Not a hint of pudge to be seen. "The only part you got right about any of that is that it's big," The man nods at me knowingly. "In *all* the ways that count."

I set my coffee down before I spill it.

Jake gives him a look. "Don't you have somewhere to be, Brooks?"

"Nope," he gives his cheerful reply.

Jake shakes his head at me as if to say *can you see what I have to deal with?*

"I'd probably suggest some ibuprofen," I tell him, lips twitching, "but I can see your pain appears rather … persistent."

"You're right," Jake replies. "It's definitely persistent. I may need something a little stronger."

The soldier scowls. "I'm a persistent pain now, am I?" His eyes narrow on Jake. "That's rich, coming from the asshole who makes our ears bleed with his shitty guitar playing skills."

"You play guitar?"

"I do," Jake says and cocks a brow. "I can teach you."

"Oh good lord," the big soldier beside him mutters before shoving another fork load of bacon in his mouth. He looks between the both of us while our table fills with more SAS soldiers. All of them ridiculously large. I feel like Frodo amongst the Fellowship of the Ring. "You two know each other?"

"Kyle Brooks, this is Jamie," Jake says, introducing the two of us from across the table. "Jamie Murphy."

Kyle's knee jerks into the table and tips his coffee over. Hot liquid unloads all over his tray and half his plate. "Fuck," he mutters, grabbing for his mug with another curse, his eyes darting to my face and back as he sops up the mess with a paper napkin. "And yes," Jake continues as Kyle dumps his wet napkin on his tray. "We met a long time ago. Before Jamie joined the army." His eyes heat on mine. "The night before she left for Kapooka, actually."

My pulse speeds up and my hand clutches involuntarily at my necklace, the cool metal soothing.

Kyle's gaze drops to the chain fisted in my hand, and I realise what I've done. I let it go, tucking it out of sight. His eyes shoot back to mine and he stares for a long uncomfortable moment, so long my face begins to burn.

I shift in my seat, brows wrinkling in confusion as his eyes slowly harden to stone. "You should probably take that thing off."

My jaw tightens at his tone and his irritated expression, as if my female presence suddenly offends him. And I realise he's one of *those*. One who can't handle a *delicate flower* like me on the front line.

"Brooks." Jake glares, but there's surprise in his tone. "Don't be an asshole."

"No. It's okay." I shake my head, embarrassed at exposing my rookie error. I meant to put the necklace somewhere safe and forgot. "He's right. I shouldn't be wearing it." We wear camouflage for a reason. The slightest glint of jewellery flashing from behind a crop of trees is all it takes to make me, and everyone around me, a target. I rise from my seat, bringing my tray with me. "I should go."

"Wait." Jake rises too, and my eyes traverse his wide shoulders and down. Then I realise I'm ogling and snap my gaze upward. "I'll walk with you."

"No!" I blurt out. He's barely made a dent in his breakfast. "Stay. Eat." My knuckles whiten on my tray, grateful there's a table between us. If there wasn't it was highly possible I might latch on like a monkey and do something wildly inappropriate. "I have to go and … heal some stuff."

After returning my tray with its empty coffee mug and half-eaten breakfast, I step outside into the early morning light.

Heal some stuff? You suck, Jamie Murphy.

13

JAMIE

The air is fresh, the horizon a palette of pale blue, orange, and deep rose as I walk towards my sleeping quarters. I breathe in deep, hands in my pockets, heart racing as if I just completed a marathon.

Jake is here. *Really here.*

And I made a fool of myself. I couldn't drag my eyes off him as if he were iced water and I'd just made a three-day trek through the sandy desert.

So pathetic, snarks the voice in my head.

Oh shut up, I tell it. *I'm allowed to look. I never said anything about touching.*

"Army girl. Wait up!"

My breath quickens as I stop and turn.

Jake is jogging towards me. I take a moment to appreciate the sight. He's so blatantly *masculine.* So hard and roughened. But it suits him. It only makes him hotter. And remembering how that stubbled jaw scraped the insides of my thighs? Imagine it now with the beard covering his handsome face. I almost lick my lips.

He's not fried chicken, Murphy.

God no. He's way better than that.

The thought has my lips twitching.

Jake catches up and wraps his arms around me, lifting me. I gasp at the unexpected embrace as he twirls me around once before setting me back down. "I wanted to do that as soon as I realised it was you." He doesn't let go immediately. He holds me to him, breathing in the scent of my hair before releasing me.

"What's so funny?" he asks, drawing back to look at me, and I realise my lips are still caught in a smirk.

"I was just thinking that you looked like fried chicken."

Jake lifts his brows, laughing a little. "I'm not sure if I should be flattered or insulted."

"It's just … I'm pretty hungry."

"Oh Jesus." He takes a deep breath and looks somewhere over my shoulder as if maybe that was too much. It probably was, but I'm tired and have no control over my filter. After a short moment, his eyes return to mine like he can only look away for so long. "I'm pretty damn hungry myself."

Well okay then. His admission has just ratcheted up my longing to a whole new level, which is still. Not. Good. It could spell a loss of rank, or worse, a court martial, if either of us ever get caught in the other's room. The penalties for that kind of fraternisation are *severe*. We both know it.

I jerk a thumb over my shoulder. "I should go and, um …"

"Heal some stuff?"

A silly grin forms on my face. "Yeah. That."

He stares for a moment. "Jamie?"

"Mmm?"

"You never emailed." Jake sounds a little tentative, as if he's not sure he should even mention it. "Did you get my note?"

"I did. I just— I wasn't sure you wanted me to."

His brows snap together, clearly confused. "I don't understand. Why would I give you my email if I didn't want you to?"

I scratch at the back of my neck, having no idea how to answer. "Well, when you put it like that."

Jake shakes his head. *Women!* his expression seems to say. I can't blame him. We read more into things than we should, creating some kind of complex algebraic equation out of a simple addition.

"I guess I thought maybe you were just being polite. You know, like when you ask someone in passing how they are? You're asking because it's a courtesy, not because you're expecting an in-depth answer."

"Well, I wanted you to email."

"I'm sorry. I wanted to."

He grins. "You're just saying that to be polite."

My chest shakes with a silent laugh, my lips pressing together. "I think maybe we're a bit past the point of being polite, aren't we? I mean, you've had your mouth on my—" I cut myself off. I shouldn't be allowed to speak sometimes.

His grin widens further. "And I'd like it there again."

I suck in a breath. "Jake."

"Jamie."

I shift uncomfortably and wince, my uniform suddenly feeling too tight and heavy for my body.

"Are you okay?" he asks, concerned eyes moving over my face and down. "I heard talk about the IED before we made it in for breakfast. They said your convoy was ambushed?"

And just like that, my bubble of need deflates like a punctured balloon, replaced with the staccato of gunfire and the bitter, metallic tang of blood in my mouth. Bile climbs my throat just that fast, coffee and eggs rising on a tidal wave. "I need to go," I whisper, swallowing as I turn blindly, making an abrupt departure. I start walking in the direction of my sleeping quarters, my pace rapid.

"Jamie!"

"It sure was great seeing you again, Tanner," I say without turning around, using his surname to create some kind of distance.

He lets me go and I'm pathetically grateful. How embarrassing would it be to barf at his feet? For him to see how weak I am, and how brittle I feel, like a twig that could snap at any moment.

You're a born fighter, Jamie.

The reminder has me shoving it back down as I walk. I'm almost there. *Just a few more steps,* I tell myself, focused on my destination like I'm adrift in a storm and the looming building is my life raft.

"Murphy." Wood appears from nowhere like he was lying in wait. Worry flashes on his face, brighter than a neon sign.

"What?" I snap, on edge and in a hurry.

He frowns. "I just wanted to check on you."

"I'm doing great, Wood. Just had a leisurely breakfast in fact, and now, if you don't mind, I'm going to get some goddamn sleep."

"What the hell?"

Anger builds. I'm tired and sick of the hovering. "I don't need you checking on me every five minutes. I'm not some delicate flower that's going to die if it isn't watered, Wood. I did my job. That's all."

"I never—"

I plant my hand on the door and push it open. "I'll catch you later."

"Dammit, Murphy. I'd check on any of my unit if they'd gone through what you did last night." His tone is rife with anger, making me pause in the doorway. "I'm the last person in this fucking war that thinks you don't belong here."

God. He's right. Wood has always had my back, and I'm being such a bitch to him right now. I take a breath. "I'm sorry, Wood. I—"

"Save it," he snaps and walks off.

Great.

Good job, idiot.

I make my way down the hallway and find my room. It's narrow and horribly claustrophobic, with a closet on one side, two bunks on the other, and a small window at the end. I have the bottom bed, which suits me just fine. After taking care of my weapon, I close the blind and crawl onto the mattress, falling asleep minutes after my head hits the pillow.

I'm hoping for sexy dreams of Jake. Instead I get his friend, Brooks, which is incredibly random. We're by a stream in the jungle somewhere, both in uniform. It feels real—the pretty tinkle of water rushing over rocks, the rich smell of dirt and leafy trees, and the heat. A bead of sweat trickles down my chest. I look down. The top two buttons of my shirt are undone, exposing my collarbone and dog tags, along with my necklace.

Brooks is standing in front of me, the sun glinting across his heavily bearded face. His eyes are hooded on mine, their colour gold with flecks of green and rimmed in dark brown. They glint like an angered lion, as if he hates me for being here.

The *crack* of a rifle echoes through the trees, and my body jerks as if a hot poker just jabbed me in the gut. I look down in horror. I've been shot. Blood is spreading across my uniform. I clutch my stomach and it pools in my fingers and spills over, pouring down my hands. I sink to my knees, gasping, my eyes rising to the soldier standing over me.

He shakes his head and leans his big bulk down, reaching out. For a moment I think he's reaching for me. But he doesn't. He takes my necklace in his massive paw and yanks, ripping it free.

"Brooks, help me," I plead, gasping for breath.

"I told you to take that thing off," he growls, his nostrils flaring. "There's no helping you now."

A single tear spills over, tracking down my cheek. He brushes it away, cocking his head as he looks at me. Then his eyes drop to the necklace dangling from his fist. "You aren't supposed to be here, Jamie."

"What do you mean?" I wheeze, coughing. Blood sprays from my mouth.

Brooks wipes it away with calloused fingers. "Joining the army was a mistake, and now you're going to die because of it."

"I don't want to die." My teeth begin to chatter. "I don't want to die."

"Then fight," he says.

My hands loosen slowly from my middle, and my lids begin to lower. I don't have the strength to hold them open any longer.

"Fight, Jamie."

"I can't."

"Fight."

The world begins to fade.

"Private Murphy!"

My voice is a mere whisper on the wind. "What?"

Bang, bang, bang! "Private Murphy. Report for duty!"

I come awake with a start, jerking upright, wheezing, my eyes darting around the room. I'm in my bed on base, lying above the sheets in my uniform. I reach for my necklace. It's still there. *It's still there.* I clutch it tight, taking long deep breaths. "I'm up," I call back, pushing the dream away until it's forgotten. "Give me five."

~

THEY SEND me back in another convoy to the remote patrol base still awaiting a medic. I literally have to go back there, having barely slept, along the same path I travelled yesterday. I don't get to choose where I go. Medics are in high demand here. There aren't enough to go around, making time off rare, even now, tired and bruised as I am and desperate for a day off.

I stare out across the red plain as we drive. Corporal Marsh is up front and Private Connor is seated beside me, just like last time. Connor is talking and laughing with the guys in front as if we never hit an IED yesterday. That's the trick to surviving this place, I guess. Not only do you have to work out like a demon possessed just to stay sane, you have to forget about what happened the day before and not worry about what's coming for you tomorrow. Only think of the now.

I tune them out, my mind sending me back to the time I competed in the Australian Open Karate Championship when I was twelve. My dad flew home all the way from L.A. to be there for it. He made the national news just being there, raising the championship's profile to a whole new level. The great Lucas 'the Maverick' Murphy turned heads everywhere we went. His size. His muscle. His temper. He was named for being a rebel. For doing the unexpected. For blazing a trail so bright through the UFC it blinded you.

I made the finals in my age division that year. I don't know how. Maybe because I had something to prove. I was the Maverick's daughter and I couldn't let him down.

Despite the protective gear we had to wear at that age—head guard, mouth guard, chest guard—I came into my final battered and sore. My opponent was taller and a little bigger. Her eyes a little harder, as if she needed to win like she needed her next breath. I felt defeated before I even began.

Dad pulled me aside before the bout, crouching a little so we were eye level, and took hold of my shoulders. I waited for the pep talk. He was full of those. Great ones. The best.

"You're going to lose."

My mouth fell open. That was *not* what I expected to hear. "Dad, I—"

"Listen to me," he said in a voice that brooked no argument. I huffed, my little twelve-year-old nostrils flaring with a volatile cocktail of anger and embarrassment. "You've assessed that girl over there," he said, referring to my opponent across the mat, "and decided that she wants this more than you. She's bigger too. And more confident. So up here," he tapped at my temple, "you're already letting her win. You're already seeing it in your mind. Manifesting it into reality. But deep down in here," he jabbed at my chest, "you have more heart than she does. You've worked harder. For longer. You've earned it. You're tough. And it pays to be a tough son of a bitch, Jamie. The world belongs to the strong." He pushed me towards the mat, towards the girl whose eyes were narrowed on mine as if she owned me. As if she owned this bout. "Go and get it."

I won the match. Then I had to wait an hour after the trophy cere-mony while Dad talked to fans and gave autographs. He took me out to celebrate that night. Dinner in the city. His entourage came with us—

coach, manager, his two training partners, and more. He got roaring drunk because his career had already peaked by then. It was a slippery slope down the other side.

I won't be like you, Dad, I vow as the convoy arrives at my new home for the next few weeks, driving through the gates. *You told me the world belonged to the strong and yet you gave up. You stopped fighting.*

I step out of the truck, masking the wince of pain as I stare at the modest buildings. When they say remote, they definitely mean it. I'm the only female here, but that means I get my own room, which is actually more spacious than my room back on base.

My days here are spent on the 'Hearts and Minds' mission. I work in the local village, providing health care to families as best I can; most suffer malnutrition, which is harder to treat than a simple injury. The children here are small, their eyes too big for their little faces, but their smiles when they see us each day could light up the night sky. Private Connor packed colouring books and pencils, and he gives me half. We hand them out, sharing a bittersweet smile as they chatter excitedly, tugging on our hands to get our attention and show us their art.

I make another friend while I'm here.

What do you think of that, huh, Bear?

His name is Arash. He's about seven but he looks five. He's the loudest of all the children and keeps trying to touch my hair because it isn't covered. His drawings are atrocious, but he presents them to me one at a time, as if he's unveiling a gallery at the Louvre. He's very proud of himself and it's incredibly cute. I want to tuck him inside my pocket and take him home with me. My heart gives a little tug every time I leave him behind and head back to our remote base.

My only form of communication here is email. I send one to Erin while the boys sit at the rickety outdoor table playing cards.

Hey girl,

I have a new best friend now. You've been replaced.

I attach a photo of me and Arash. Connor took it. He was seated on the ground with the other kids while Arash and I sat on an old broken log so we're looking down into the camera. The sun is behind us, casting an orange halo around our heads, and his little smile is fierce with pride as if he's getting a photo with his favourite celebrity. His tiny arm is slung up over my shoulder. "Cool?" he asks Connor when it's done, trying to see the digital image on the back of the camera.

"You look seriously cool," I tell him as I check the photo because it seems important.

He beams when he hears the word 'cool.'

Winter will be here soon. It's getting cooler. Can you believe it actually snows here? I've lived my whole life managing to never see snow, and now I'll see it here in this arid hellish place!

I'm on a remote base right now.

I'm not allowed to specify any of my locations, but I can at least tell her that.

I'm spending a lot of time performing health checks on the locals and playing cards.

Which is boring. The cards part. What I wouldn't give for a night out, a few beers, and Jake Tanner's hands on me like I'm his own personal playground.

My thighs clench together. It's harder out here. The constant ache for physical intimacy is so sharp some nights I can barely sleep. I lie in bed almost shaking with need and having to take care of it myself. I feel no better when I'm done because it isn't enough. Sex is not what I need.

I'm missing the warmth. The connection. Another human being. I haven't captured that feeling again since Jake, and his reappearance in my life has rekindled what we once had, flaring it bright inside me like a lit match.

Jake is here. How crazy is that? I ran into him at breakfast, but I haven't seen him since because I got assigned off the main base. I don't even know if he'll be there when I get back. There wasn't time to talk.

How goes the saving?

Erin is trying to live a frugal life, which is hard for her. She likes pretty things. But she's saving for the spa retreat she plans to open in the mountains outside of Perth one day, and I know she wants it more than trinkets and pretty dresses. We've talked about me being a silent partner. I'm not spending any of the money I earn in the army. Everything is provided—food, accommodation, uniforms. Money has been accumulating in my account since the moment I arrived in Kapooka for basic training years ago.

Have you met any cute guys lately? Speaking of cute guys, how is Matt?

She hates it when I refer to her older brother as cute. It *icks* her out.

I miss you. Talk soon, okay?

Love, Jamie

After hitting send, I head outside and join the card game. I don't get a chance to check my emails for another two weeks. There's a response from Erin sitting in my inbox. I click it open, greedy for anything to read. I don't even care if she talks for a whole page about a dress she bought at the local shops.

Miss Jamie Murphy,

Arash looks ridiculously cute. You on the other hand look like a liar liar pants on fire. Seriously. Your face needs a punch. In the jaw. Preferably with my fist. How dare you write me as if you're on a freaking holiday?

You do know Wood and I keep in touch, don't you?

I do. They've done so ever since graduation at Kapooka. I don't pry though, keeping my head buried firmly in the sand because it appeared harmless. Until now. Wood and his flapping limbs and stupid flapping gums. My jaw locks tight as I continue to read.

HE TOLD ME ABOUT THE IED.

I can't even with you right now.

You can't keep me in the dark like this. I deserve to know what's going on, and I'm stuck here knowing nothing. Do you have any idea how that feels?

It's not freaking fair.

You seem to have forgotten that I AM YOUR BEST FRIEND.

Remember the fence fire? Bad things happen when you bottle everything up inside. You eventually lose your shit. It's that Murphy temper. Please don't bottle all of this up inside you. Talk to me. Be real, okay? Please.

You know I miss you too. I love you.

Erin

PS. I can't believe Jake is there! You need to board that train and ride it all the way to the station, booyah!

I sit for a moment, staring at the laptop. She's right. I'm keeping her in the dark. It's a fine line between sharing everything and sharing just enough for her not to worry. Damn Wood for telling her about the IED.

Taking a slow, even breath, I hit reply.

Dear Best Friend,

I'm sorry I didn't tell you. I don't want you to worry while I'm here. I am totally okay. Just a bruise, nothing more. And I'm not bottling anything inside because there's nothing to bottle.

If I need to talk about anything you'll be the first to know, okay? I promise.

So ... You didn't mention about meeting any cute guys. That's usually your favourite topic. What's going on? Let me live through you! God knows there'll be no boarding ANY trains at all while I'm here. THAT is what's freaking unfair!

A smart rap comes at my door, and I smother a yawn. It's early morning. Dawn hasn't even broken. We're leaving today, heading back to base. My thoughts are filled with Jake. He's probably gone now. I'm already kicking myself for walking off, cutting short our conversation.

"Murphy?" It's Connor.

Miss you, I add quickly.

Love, your best friend.

I hit send and rise to answer it.

"There was a Taliban attack during the night," he says through the closed door, his voice loud. "In the village," he adds.

My throat tightens with a sense of dread. I stalk to the door wearing my army pants and white tank top, not fully dressed. My feet are bare and my hair is out and tousled from sleep when usually it's pulled into a sleek plaited knot at the nape of my neck. I've always cared about looking respectable around the guys, the less feminine the better, but right now I couldn't care less.

I yank the door open. "A Taliban attack in the village?"

His eyes skim over me quickly, but he says nothing about my disarray. His face is pale. "Yeah."

"Jesus." I swallow. "How bad?"

He shakes his head. "We don't know. Suit up. We're heading out."

I'm tense during the drive. It takes too long, as if time has slowed to a crawl. I feel like I could get out and run faster. Instead, I sit there, hands fisted on my lap, potential IEDs not even a thought in my head.

We screech to a stop at the west end of the village, dust flying up and coating my skin as I leap from the truck, turning to grab my medi pack. I'm shouldering it, running behind Marsh and Connor as smoke rises from buildings, the scent singeing my nostrils. Wails render the air. Sobbing. I don't know where to start. Bodies litter the ground everywhere. Burnt, stabbed, bleeding out. There are kids. God, little babies cut down and bloodied.

Bile floods my throat. The soldier beside me veers off and bends at the waist, vomit flying from his mouth.

I turn in a circle, frantic and lost.

I can't do this. I can't be here. I can't.

"Doc!" I stop turning and my eyes find Marsh kneeling on the ground beside a body, checking for a pulse. "He's still alive." He looks up, brows snapping together. "Doc, goddammit! Get over here now!"

His shout jolts me like an electrical current. I start towards him, spurred into action. The man is on his stomach. I press my fingers to his neck. He has a pulse but it's thready. "We need to roll him over."

But when we do, his insides spill out all over himself, covering my hands. There's no hope. I shake my head at Marsh, and we move on to the next body. And the next. Then there's a shout through the village, my name being yelled in a high-pitched Afghani accent.

"Jah-mee! Jah-mee!" I stand quickly, searching in the direction of the sound. It's Arash. "Jah-mee!"

He's running towards me, and I'm so relieved to see him alive that my legs almost give out. He yells again, frantic. "Jah-mee!"

I reach for him and he grabs my hand, tugging me backwards with all his might. "Fix!" he shouts, desperate. "Fix!"

He drags me and I follow along with a glance behind me. "Marsh," I jerk my head in the direction I'm going, indicating for him to follow.

We reach a man on the ground. Arash drops to his knees in the dirt by his side and looks up at me. It's his father. "Fix!"

I crouch beside Arash, pressing my fingers to his neck. There's no pulse. The man is cold to the touch, his eyes closed and lips purple. I lift his bloodied shirt. Two bullet wounds decorate his chest, both not bleeding. His heart has stopped pumping. Likely hours ago. I can't fix this.

"He's gone, Arash." My jaw trembles. "I'm sorry."

"Fix!" he screams, gesturing violently at the man. His face is twisted in anguish, not understanding my lack of action.

"I can't, Arash. I'm sorry." I shake my head and he seems to get it. "I can't."

His little face crumples. "Jah-mee."

Marsh puts his hands on his hips, cursing under his breath. His struggle for composure is almost lost, and he turns his head.

I rise to my feet and fold Arash close, brushing my hand over his soft dark curls. I know what it feels like to lose a father so violently, and my heart aches for him. I take his face in my hands and he looks up at me. "Where is your mother?"

He shakes his head, not understanding, tears a river down his cheeks. I wipe at them. "Madar?" I try. "Maman?"

"*Nekyehr!*" he says in Farsi. "*Nekyehr!*"

It means no. He has no mother.

"Private Murphy."

I shake my head at Marsh. I can't leave him.

"Private Murphy," he says again, harder this time. "There are injured people here. You need to help them."

But Arash is clinging to me, his fingers twisting in my uniform.

"That's an order," he barks.

I set my jaw and peel his little fingers away, feeling sick as I set him aside and walk away. Yet Arash screams and clings to me, not letting me go. "I'll take him," Marsh says and grabs the little boy up in his arms, freeing me to leave.

I walk away, knowing I shouldn't glance back, but I do. His arms are outstretched, reaching for me. He's crying and screaming as if I'm all he has left in the world. My heart breaks into pieces as I leave him behind.

14

JAMIE

It's early, not even five a.m. I'm in the gym back on base with only two other people doing their own thing, sweating through my long-sleeved fitted sports shirt and full-length tights, ear buds in and iPod blaring Cold Chisel because the music reminds me of home. It's Australia. "Flame Trees" more so than any other song. It was Dad's favourite.

Winter has hit, and while it's not quite snowing yet, it's freaking cold. My hair is piled in a messy knot on top of my head, and my face is flushed and damp.

I'm on the stair climber after finishing up a weights session, and it feels good, stretching out my legs, taking step after step, muscles working, thighs straining, calves burning. There's little else you can think about during a workout. Your mind is focused on your reps, your form, your breathing, and pushing through the burn.

My legs start to wobble. I'm reaching the point where I can't continue, but I don't want to stop. I flick to an upbeat song and close my eyes, holding on to the rails as I push through, squeezing every last drop of energy I have left until I achieve fatigue. Maybe then I'll sleep tonight.

The music reaches an end. I open my eyes to find a soldier standing in front of me. A big one. I don't recognise him for a moment. There's a distinct lack of dirt and beard. His jaw is clean-shaven and strong, his face startlingly appealing. And his eyes. They're focused on me, clear and striking and fringed with wonderfully thick lashes. I jerk, almost falling off the climber. It's Kyle. Chest hair peeks out from the muscle shirt he's wearing, and biceps thick with corded muscle are on display. A towel is slung over his shoulder and drink bottle in hand, proclaiming him workout ready.

"You look like you're done," he says.

Damn him. I *am* done. But the way he says it, as if I should just run along now like a good little girl, means I have to keep going until I pass out. I don't know what it is about this dude that rubs me the wrong way. He just leaves me feeling like I have something to prove.

I hit the speed button and the stairs ratchet up another notch. Then I point to my ear buds and shake my head as if I can't hear him.

The jerk has the gall to laugh at me. "Your iPod isn't even playing."

I look down. The screen is black. The battery life on the stupid thing has exposed my little lie, and he seems thoroughly entertained.

"I'm not done."

Kyle doesn't move. The stair climber is popular. The training is necessary for those on constant patrol. "I can wait."

I climb a few more steps and my legs scream in protest. "Seriously? You're just going to stand there?"

He shrugs. "You won't be much longer."

"I'll be ages yet," I reply, trying for a 'sorry not sorry' smile and failing because I'm puffing as if I'm in the final leg of a triathlon.

"When did you get back?" he asks, folding his arms. Muscles bulge everywhere and it looks ridiculous. Is he aiming for The Hulk aesthetic?

I pull the earbuds from my ears. "How did you even know I was gone?"

"I haven't seen you around."

My brows knit, confused. "You were looking for me?"

"No. Tanner mentioned you'd been assigned off base somewhere."

"Has he—" Crap. I was going to ask this guy if Jake had mentioned me. I've truly lost my mind.

Kyle grins as if he knows exactly what I was going to ask. *Damn* him. "Maybe you can ask him yourself," he says, jerking his head towards the gym entrance. Jake is walking in. I almost miss a step. He's just so … golden. It's like basking in sunshine. He sees us and a happy smile lights his face. He starts our way and I'm suddenly realising how much I stink, lamenting the sweat patches on my workout clothes and the hair sticking to my face. I free a hand to swipe at the damp strands and almost lose my balance.

I quickly grab the rail as he reaches my side. "Hey. When did you get back?"

"Yesterday."

"How was it?"

An ache grips my belly, the simple question undoing everything my workout was designed to achieve. I paste a smile on my face. "It was great."

"Are you sure about that?" Brooks interjects, cocking his head as he watches me gasp and puff through my steps.

I shoot him a dirty look, not even having to wonder how he knows. This base is a cesspool of gossip, as if there's nothing better to do than act like a bunch of high school kids with too much time on their hands.

Jake looks between us both, frowning. "What do you mean?"

"I heard the village was—"

"He means nothing." I hit stop on the machine and it powers down, the stairs slowing to a stop. I grab my towel where it's slung across the side, my legs almost giving out beneath me as I climb off.

It puts me in close proximity to Jake who, thankfully, doesn't take a step back after getting a full whiff of my sweaty stench. I look up at him from beneath my lashes with what I hope is a sultry smile, though it probably looks like I'm having a stroke. Either way, it distracts him from asking any further questions. "Machine's free if you want it."

"Thanks." Jake grins down at me. "Maybe we can catch up this afternoon? Play some cards or watch a movie?"

A ripple of pleasure flutters over me. "That sounds fun."

"Great." He jumps on the stair climber, placing his water bottle in the drink holder before looking at me. "I'll come get you later."

"Wait. I should wipe the machine down."

"I'm not worried about a bit of sweat, army girl," Jake says, punching the buttons on the machine to fire it up. "Especially from you."

"Well okay then." I start walking backwards to leave, wiping at my face with my towel. "Catch you later."

I glance over my shoulder before exiting the gym. Jake winks at me, his eyes dropping to my ass. Kyle is watching my face as if he knows exactly what that was all about.

I shake my head in warning, and his lips press flat. With Jake now occupying the stair climber he was waiting for, he moves off towards the squat rack. I jerk open the door, cool air blasting me as if I opened a freezer door. After a shower and breakfast, I spend the day at the hospital, assigned the task of stocktake, alongside Wood and two admin staff, for our medical supplies. It's tedious but joking with my best friend makes the day go faster, and I have Jake to look forward to this afternoon.

When we're done for the day, I race back to my room and tidy myself up, which basically means re-doing my hair from a bun to a braid. I'm lamenting the fact I can't change into something a little sexier than a bulky uniform in desert camouflage when a knock comes at the door.

My pulse leaps. I open it and Jake is on the other side. I want to fist my hand in his shirt and drag him inside my room. The gleam of frustration in his green eyes suggests he wouldn't be averse to the idea. "Ready for a game of cards?"

I sigh audibly, the tone inferring I'd rather be doing something so much more fun. "Ready as I'll ever be."

I step out into the hall because all hell will break loose if he steps one foot inside, and he gestures in front of him, letting me lead the way towards the games room.

"So, I'm assuming you're based in Brisbane or Townsville?" he asks as we walk.

"Townsville. And you're Perth, right?" Because that's where the SAS are stationed. Campbell Barracks at Swanbourne.

"Yeah, that's me. The other side of the country to you." His tone is rueful. "We had to fly all the way to Afghanistan just so we could play a game of cards together."

I laugh, brushing at my neat braid when I'd rather be reaching for his hand. "FYI, I'm just as good at cards as I am at Call of Duty."

He grins. "I wouldn't expect anything less."

We start with a simple game of Snap, just the two of us, but sexual tension crackles in the air every time my hand slaps his or his mine. And then he'll slide his palm away slowly, a caress that sets my blood on fire.

My eyes meet his over the cards I've held up to cover my hot face. "Maybe we should try a different game."

He swallows. "Good idea."

We move on to Gin Rummy, and Wood joins us soon after, taking a seat at my side. I'm about to introduce him when Kyle joins us, followed by one of the other SAS soldiers who joined us at the breakfast table the morning I first ran into Jake.

It turns our cosy twosome into a rowdy group as introductions are made all round. I half-rise, reaching across the gaming table to shake the hand of the infamous Ryan Kendall, the best friend Jake grew up with, before I let go and sit back down. He's clean-shaven, his cropped hair dark and eyes darker, though they're friendly as he takes my hand. "You're the one who blew up the fridge."

Ryan laughs as he takes the seat opposite mine, slapping his friend on the back. "Ahhh good times."

Wood is taking his time looking at Jake, eyes narrowed as he rubs at his jaw. "And you're the one who—"

My elbow jabs him sharply in the side. Obviously he knows who

Jake is after Erin ran her mouth off after basic training. My friends have a lot to answer for.

"Who what?" Kyle asks.

Wood snickers from beside me, and I want to punch him in the nuts. "You're so immature," I hiss under my breath so only he can hear.

"Who pounded my friend here at Call of Duty," he says across the table.

"Pounded?" I hiss again. "Nice choice of words, Wood." He snickers again as if he's having a merry old time. "Why are you here?"

"To play cards," he tells me with an innocent expression before speaking louder for the whole group to hear. "How about poker?" He reaches into his pocket and pulls out a pack of soft, chewy jelly beans. My eyes narrow on the large plastic packet he tosses onto the table. I know for a fact that Erin sent him those. She sent me a care package with the same exact things. "Jelly beans are the stakes."

"I'm in," Jake says.

"Same," Kyle echoes.

Ryan simply reaches across and takes the packet, ripping it open. He tips the colourful, squishy beans on the table and counts them out into an even group of five.

I cup my beans in both hands and drag them towards me. Jelly beans are a high commodity here. The sugar hit is enough to keep a soldier going for hours. "You all are gonna lose."

"No offence, GI Jane, but you don't have a poker face," Kyle taunts from across the table.

"You think you can heckle me?" I flick one of my jelly beans at his face. It *pings* off his forehead and onto the floor. The soldier on the couch by our table snatches it up and pops it in his mouth, grinning as he chews before returning his attention to the movie playing out on the television. I'm pleased with my aim. It was worth the loss. "Don't call me GI Jane."

There are various 'oooooh's' around the table, and I roll my eyes as the cards get shuffled and dealt. The rules of the game get looser as the afternoon progresses and our group a little rowdier. Jelly beans 'accidentally' get eaten by sore losers—which is mostly me—some roll off the table and get snatched up by vultures, and others seem to mysteriously disappear.

I'm down to two beans when it comes time for dinner. "Brooks was right," Wood jokes. "Your poker face is for shit."

I look across at Kyle's pile, which is non-existent, while Jake's haul of jelly beans is a mini-mountain. "It's not the worst though." I smirk at Kyle. "Tanner whooped your ass."

Everyone laughs and Jake eyes me across the table, waggling his eyebrows. "Looks like you're my good luck charm." He halves the pile with his hand and pushes them across to me. "You can be my poker buddy any day," he says to a burst of ribbing from his mates.

My face burns hot because all I can think about is gladly being his buddy any day where there's poking involved. I know Wood is hearing everything I'm not saying by the way he kicks me in the ankle while smothering a shout of laughter.

"Thanks, Jake," I say sweetly and pop one in my mouth, chewing and grinning at him as I pocket the shared half.

We finish up and eat dinner in the mess hall as a group, though Jake seats himself at the end of the table next to me, which means we have our own private conversation and manage to tune everyone out.

It's late when I realise they've all gone, even Wood, leaving just the two of us. I glance around. The dinner rush is over. There's only a sporadic bunch of soldiers left grabbing a bite to eat. "We should go."

Jake stacks my tray with his and dumps it off. Then we leave together. I look up as we step outside. The stars are bright tonight and pretty. Even here in a war zone there's beauty to be found somewhere.

We start for our sleeping quarters, both with our hands tucked in our pockets. It seems safer that way. "I've thought about you a lot since that night," Jake admits after a few moments of quiet between us both.

I can't hide the warm burst of pleasure from my expression. "Really?"

"Yeah."

"What have you thought about specifically?"

He grins across at me. "Nothing you need to know."

"Jake!" I bump his shoulder with mine, our hands still pocketed. "You can't do that."

"Do what?"

"Think stuff about me and then not tell me what it is."

After a quick glance left and right, Jake frees his hands and grabs my arm, pulling me down behind an unlit building. He nudges me in front of him until we reach a dark corner. I'm pushed up against the wall, his chest pressing into me, warm and hard.

We stare at each other for a single heartbeat.

Then his mouth hits mine.

Yes. *Yes.*

My arms come up around his neck, grabbing at hair, at skin, holding him tight. There's nothing else but Jake surrounding me. His lips, his tongue in my mouth and mine in his, his erection pushing up against my belly. We come up for air, a brief second, before we're kissing again. He yanks the tie from my braid, unravelling my hair and fisting it in his hands as his mouth moves on mine.

"This," he gasps against my lips. "This is what I've thought about." Jake rips my shirt free of my pants and slides his hands up my bare stomach. His fingers dig under the wire of my sports bra until my naked breasts fills his warm, scratchy palms. He rubs and pinches my nipples, and sharp bolts of pleasure shoot through me. I moan, my head tilting back and hitting the building. "That feels so good."

"It feels fucking amazing," he mutters into my neck as he touches me, our warm breaths puffing into the cold night like little clouds. "I want to be inside you so bad."

"God, yes," I gasp.

Jake nudges my thigh, and I wrap it around his hip. He grinds into me, the rigid length of him hitting all the right spots. Heat erupts between my legs. "Jesus, I could come just like this."

"Me too."

It's so much harder this time. More desperate. Frantic. We don't have all night. Just this. A snatched moment in time.

Voices and bodies hit our peripheral vision.

"Shit." Jake pulls back with a groan, adjusting himself while I shove my shirt back inside my pants.

"Where's my hair tie?"

He hands it to me and I quickly pull the tousled mess into a low ponytail. Reasonably respectable, we walk back past the building and into a more lit area, moving back in the direction of our bunks, and I'm so frustrated I want to cry.

"So that was a bad idea," he mutters with a half-chuckle, though he sounds like he wants to cry too … and maybe punch something.

"Totally."

And yet it wasn't, because I forgot everything when he was touching me. Every damn thing. I want more of that as much as I want more of him.

15

Commander Bowen glances up at me from across his desk. "I'm referring you for a mental health evaluation."

My brows snap together, confused, while he goes back to reading the open file on his desk. It's the day after our marathon game of poker. I woke at three in the morning and couldn't get back to sleep. A check in the mirror found dark circles forming beneath my eyes. I shrugged it off. My bed is narrow and hard, my pillow thin. No one could sleep properly in those conditions. I lay in bed for two hours, replaying Jake's kiss in my head over and over, before I forced my tired body up and into my gym gear.

After a lengthy bicep and shoulder session on the weights, Wood came in, finding me in the far back on the stair climber.

"You have to report to Commander Bowen. Five minutes."

"What the hell?" I griped, grabbing my sweaty towel and making a run for the door. "What for?"

He shrugged but wouldn't look me in the eye. I didn't have time to question him. Instead I raced to my bunk, changed without showering, and exactly five minutes later I was knocking on my commander's door.

"Sir, I'm fine. I don't think—"

He doesn't look up from the file. "I'm not asking you if you think you're okay. I'm asking the mental health officer to make that particular assessment."

I baulk, stuck between wanting to protest and following my commander's directive.

"That's an order, Private Murphy," he barks to my lingering form, looking up with irritation.

My nostrils flare. He doesn't care about my mental welfare specifically, he cares about the overall health of his team. It's like contracting gangrene in your foot. It's just in the one spot, but it can make your entire body sick. And if it can't be treated, you cut it off. "When, sir?"

"Now. Dismissed."

Shit.

I snap a salute and leave his office, twisting to shut the door behind me. I don't care how tedious the medical supplies stocktake is, I'd rather be there with them right now than on my way to a mental health evaluation. No doubt they'll survive without me for a few minutes. Surely it won't take longer than that.

Starting forward, I slam into a large body and literally bounce off it. I look up, righting myself. Freaking Kyle seems to pop up wherever I am, like a mole surfacing from a hole in the ground.

I scowl, suddenly remembering the way he looked at me yesterday in the gym. His awareness of the village attack and my involvement. Then there were the taunts throughout our game yesterday. And the way he spoke to me at breakfast that first morning, as if I don't belong here. The pieces of the puzzle click together. "You," I hiss.

Kyle holds up his hands in a gesture of surrender. "My bad. What did I do?"

"You're trying to get me kicked off base and sent back home."

"Wow." He cocks his head. "You think I'm trying to get you kicked out? What kind of asshole do you think I am?"

I take in his size with narrowed eyes. "The big kind."

His own eyes narrow in return. "Whatever wire you have crossed, you better uncross it."

My brows fly up. The freaking *audacity*. I'm not the one in the wrong here. I take an aggressive step forward, folding my arms. "Or else what?"

Kyle shakes his head. "What's going on, Murphy?"

"I'm being sent to mental health, no thanks to you. *That* is what's going on. What did you say to my commander? Did you mention something about the village attack? Because you don't know what happened. You weren't there!"

"I didn't say anything, but it seems like I've already been found guilty in the court of Jamie Murphy without a fair trial."

I stare him down, trying to find evidence of guilt on his face. Then his expression gentles, as if he's trying to approach a wild animal. "I know what went down because I'm friends with Corporal Marsh," he says quietly, watching me carefully. "He told me what happened. He might have mentioned you'd made friends with the some of the kids who died, one in particular who was orphaned in the attack. Arash, I think? I'm sorry. It's never easy, but when it's kids? It's the fucking worst."

Fucking hell.

My eyes hit my feet, blinking rapidly. "It really is."

"Murphy."

I can't look up.

"Murphy."

"What?" I snap, lifting my chin, my eyes hitting his.

"For what it's worth, I didn't mention it to anyone," he says, and I know he means he didn't mention it to Jake. "It's up to you what you choose to share."

And I'm choosing not to share at all. I don't want to keep Jake in the dark, but it's too hard to talk about. The images flood my mind, and the ache of leaving that boy all alone rips at my heart. With Jake I don't have to think about any of it. It's just me and him and nothing else. I want to keep it that way.

I brush past Kyle. "I have to go."

"Wait," he calls out and reaches for me. Then he stops himself.

I pause, lips mashing together for a moment before I turn, waiting for him to say whatever it is that's so damn important.

"Being a combat medic …" he trails off for a moment like he's thinking carefully about what he wants to say. "Mental health checks can be common for you guys during deployment. You see more than most because that's your job. You're not just there during combat, you get called in when everything turns to shit. And everything turns to shit a lot around here. Just …"

I shift impatiently, his advice unwarranted and just plain pissing me off. "Just what?"

His eyes soften in a way I don't understand. "Just talk to someone, Murphy. Anyone. Don't take it home with you when you leave."

"I get it, okay? But I'm fine. There's nothing to talk about."

I stalk off.

"Murphy?"

I pause and turn. "What?"

Kyle shakes his head. "You can't save everyone."

A FEW MINUTES LATER, I'm knocking on another door, my chest tight. I don't like strange therapist-type people poking into my business, trying to find something wrong so they can blame it on family issues and feel like they've done their job.

"Come in," calls a male voice.

I turn the knob and step inside. The man behind the desk also has his head stuck in a file. It seems to be a common theme today. He doesn't look older than forty in his face but he has a head full of grey hair and reading glasses. "It says here you went to Chatsworth High School all the way over in Melville, Western Australia," he says, perusing the papers in front of him. "From there it was straight to basic training." He pulls his glasses off and looks at me. "And you chose to be a combat medic."

"Yes, sir."

"Take a seat." He gestures across the desk. "And inside this room you can call me Michael. May I call you Jamie?"

"Yes, sir. Michael. Sir." Ugh. First naming in the military feels incredibly weird.

"Do you enjoy your role?" he asks as I take the seat opposite, my back ramrod straight.

"Yes, sir. Michael."

"What is it you like so much?"

"I like helping people, and I should get back to doing that. So maybe you could tell me what this is all about?"

Michael leans back in his seat, settling his arms on the armrests as if he's ready to chat the morning away. "You've been through a lot already on your first deployment here. Handling trauma cases in the hospital, combat, IEDs, not to mention your efforts on the Hearts and Minds mission. You spent weeks there," he says as if I didn't already know. "Treating the locals. Gaining their trust. Even making friends. Did you like that part of your role most, Jamie? Helping them with their health care needs?"

I nod, lips pressed together. It was the highlight of my time here. They took their time opening up, learning English words, speaking them tentatively. And the gratitude in their eyes after giving life-saving vaccines and wound care on minor issues like cuts and boils, things that eased their comfort and helped them sleep at night, was incredibly rewarding. I felt ten feet tall at the end of every day. But finding them all struck down after the village attack will stick with me for life.

The image of their bodies flash before my eyes, the scent of their charred flesh hitting my nostrils.

Bile rises.

Jesus.

"Jamie?"

I swallow it down, knowing there's no changing what happened.

There's no bringing those people back, no matter how much you talk about it.

Michael seems to sense my unwillingness to travel down that path and changes tack. "You and Colin Wood are friends? Your file says you went through training together and were both deployed here in the same unit."

"That's right," I croak and clear my throat. "We met in basic training."

"It must be nice, having a friend here with you?"

I nod. "It's great."

"What about back home? You have friends there?"

"Erin. We went to school together."

"Do you keep in touch with Erin while you're here? Phone? Email?"

"Email mostly."

"That's good." Michael nods. "Good."

"Is that it, then?" I half-rise. "Because I should get back to work."

"You do seem eager to get back into it." He scribbles something in my file. "How about I ask you three quick questions before I let you go."

Three quick questions. Great. I can do that easy. Relief loosens my shoulders, and I relax back in my seat. "Sure. Go ahead."

"I'm empowered by the army to determine if you're operating in an impaired capacity in your current role. To do that I need you to be truthful. So tell me, Jamie, have you spoken to any of your friends about what you've been dealing with here during your deployment?"

"I'm pretty sure they know."

He shrugs. "Maybe they do, but I'm after a yes or no."

My teeth grind together. "No."

"Do you think maybe you *can* talk to them? Or me, if you need? My door is always open."

"Sure. Absolutely."

Michael draws in a deep breath and scribbles in my file again. "Do you think getting out there and performing further duties under your role as a combat medic is best for your current mental status right now?"

My nod is firm. Sure. I couldn't imagine doing anything else. "I know it is."

"Okay then." He sets his pen down and eases back in his chair, steepling his fingers. "Get back out there."

"That's it?" I was expecting him to delve into every nook and cranny of my life—from the abandonment of my mother and her choosing a cash settlement in lieu of custody to the spiralling health of my father and his subsequent death. If Michael had asked, I would have told him I'm glad my mother left. Who wants to be raised by someone who values money more than human life? I would have told him my father was a great dad. He taught me everything I needed to know. We had a great life, however short our time was together.

Michael smiles. "That's it."

～

WEEKS PASS BY. I spend it working with my unit and with the hospital and trying to find information on Arash. He was sent to a neighbouring village. That's all I can find. I've been trying to get on patrols heading out that way, but it's not that simple. This is the army. I do what I'm told, and consequences are severe if I don't. Getting locked up for insubordination won't help my cause.

"You okay?" Wood asks, watching me pick at my dinner from his seat across the table.

"Yeah."

"You're in a mood. And you're not eating."

How can I? I've been Googling orphaned children in Afghanistan. Knowing the conditions Arash will be faced with makes the food in my mouth taste like sawdust. "Thanks, Captain Obvious. I'm not hungry."

"You're always hungry."

"I had a big lunch."

"You've been Googling again, haven't you?"

I shrug. Wood caught me on Google the other day, and I couldn't eat for the rest of the day after that. Statistics swarmed in my head like an angry bunch of bees. Afghanistan has been identified as the worst place in the world to be a child. Arash was facing an uphill battle just by being born. There's no foster care system. Kids without family are subject to labour, violence, illiteracy, and worse … enrolled in terrorist groups and brainwashed or used as child suicide bombers. Danger, poverty, and death is their normal.

I have only four weeks left before returning to Australia, and there's nothing I can do to help him. Call it a hunch, but I'm pretty sure they'd notice if I tried smuggling him home on the plane—that's if I could even *find* him first.

"This place sucks."

"Agreed." Wood looks around the crowded mess hall. "I can't wait to get home."

Jake sets a tray down beside me and takes a seat, close enough to give my shoulder a brief nudge. His proximity has my heart leaping like a pole vaulter at the Olympics.

"Did someone just say the magic word?" he asks.

"Home," Wood says again.

I look sideways. Jake is grinning. "No place like it."

"Speaking of home …" I clear my throat. "I've been thinking—"

"Don't strain yourself," Kyle quips as he takes a seat opposite, beside Wood.

My lips mash together, despite his teasing tone. Jake doesn't know about our altercation. I'm glad Kyle didn't say anything because I feel like a fool. I owe him a long overdue apology after my outburst. It was ludicrous to assume he was trying to have me sent home. He just happened to be there during a moment of frustration, and I lashed out. I realised it soon after calming down, but Kyle is making it impossible to say sorry.

"As I was saying," I continue, ignoring the loutish soldier, "I was thinking of returning to Perth after we finish up here. I could stay with Erin."

It would give Jake and me a chance to spend some time together. We haven't discussed a future. It's hard to envision a long-distance relationship when we're based on opposite sides of the country. I'm not sure it would work, but a date or two would be nice. Maybe some time between the sheets if I'm lucky.

At the moment we're stuck playing card games with friends and stealing kisses in the dark. It's Frustration City.

Judging by the gleam in Jake's eyes, he's a hundred percent on board. "Oh yeah?"

I reach for my coffee—a double shot because my day isn't over yet—and smile over the rim as I take a sip. "Yeah."

Wood sounds affronted. "You never told me that."

Because I only just decided. Playing in a pit of snakes sounds more appealing than being stuck in Townsville for a month of leave right now. It would be four entire weeks to sit around on my own and think about how I failed Arash and the other children of the village. It's unfair how I get to board a plane and leave them all behind as if they never mattered.

I set my mug down and look at Wood across the table. He's finished eating, his plate scraped clean. Mine is full. I push it away, my stomach knotted. "I'm telling you now."

My best friend rolls his eyes. "How long for?"

"The full month. You'll come too, right?"

"I guess," he says, acting a little too casual. Wood is *never* casual when it comes to the subject of Erin. I'm pretty sure he's developed a small thing for her over time, and yet he won't admit to it. "I mean, it could be fun," he adds for extra effect, as if he's only going because he has nothing better to do.

A smirk stretches across my lips. "You don't have to come. We won't be doing much. Just hanging out at the beach, sunbathing," I say, putting the visual of Erin in a bikini in his head. "Swimming, drinking beer, maybe some shopping, and I know how much you hate shopping."

The sharp planes of Wood's cheekbones turn a little pink. "I uh, actually do need a few new things."

"Really?" I shouldn't tease, but I can't help myself. It's fun to see him flustered over a pretty girl. I'm pretty sure Wood would never go there. The three of us are best friends. A casual fling between the two would upset the dynamic. "Last time I asked you to come shopping with me you said you'd rather poke your eyes out with a rusty fork."

Wood's gaze narrows on mine, taking my measure, catching on to my game. "I need to buy condoms. Lots of condoms. And socks."

Jake chokes on his dinner. I give him a thump on the back while I speak to Wood. "Thanks, but you don't have to buy me condoms. I have heaps. Enough to cover every dick in Australia."

Kyle outright laughs, startling me. A strangled sound emerges from Jake's throat. I give his back another thump, and he coughs.

"The condoms are for *my* dick, Murphy."

"Don't you mean your light sabre?"

The table erupts. Of course they've heard the story of Wood channelling his inner Skywalker at basic training. Wood isn't the only one with flapping gums, and a story like that is legendary. It's almost a crime *not* to share it. I even picture myself telling it to his future kids one day.

Jake's palm lands on my upper thigh beneath the table as the laughter and ribbing continues around us. Heat burns in that singular spot, building into a fire that travels straight to my centre. I squirm as he leans in, lips brushing my ear. "I hope it's just *my* dick you plan on covering with all those condoms, army girl, and not the entire male population of Australia."

My body clenches. "Yes," I whisper thickly. "Hell yes."

His voice is firm with male satisfaction. "Good."

I take a breath, feeling a little removed from everyone and everything around me. Jake has stolen my focus. I rise to my feet. "I need to get back to work."

Jake looks up at me. "Tonight?"

"Yep. I'll be working nights for a while. The hospital is short staffed."

"I'll walk you over."

He starts to rise alongside me, and I put a hand on his shoulder, halting his upward progression. "No, it's okay. Stay. Finish your dinner." He still has half a plate full left to eat.

"Nah." He pushes his plate away and stands. "I'll eat something later if I get hungry."

"Wood?" I look over at my best friend. He's on shift with me. "You coming?"

He shakes his head. "I'll be along in a minute."

Thank you, I say with my eyes, knowing he's doing it so Jake and I can have a minute of alone time.

You owe me, he replies.

I'll sneak him a pastry and a hot coffee later tonight when we start flagging.

"You don't really have to walk me over," I tell Jake as we step outside.

The back of his hand brushes mine as we start towards the hospital. "I know, but I know how much you like it when I do."

Pleasure warms my insides, yet I feign indifference. "I guess it's okay."

"You won't give me an inch, will you?"

I snort. "Of course not. I give everyone I like a hard time."

"Is that your way of testing whether they'll bother to stick around?" My eyes whip to his, coming to a stop. He halts in front of me. "You have a tough veneer, Jamie Murphy, but it's not tougher than me."

I fold my arms, struggling with his declaration. There's very few in my life who've managed to batter down the walls I've erected around myself. Bear was the first, by sheer persistence. Then came Erin, who took a chance and ignored my hostile demeanour. Wood was next, and so easy to like, with his gangly limbs and laidback nature. Arash was impossible to resist, with his big eyes and the way he said 'cool' as if it was the most important word in the English language.

I let go of a deep sigh. And now Jake. Proving day after day that the perfect man might possibly exist. I decide to give him an inch. A small one. "Remember that night in the bar when I asked why you came over? You said it was because after you saw me, you couldn't see anything else. I figured it was just a line. One you told all the girls. But that was how I felt when I saw you." I look down at my feet, thoroughly embarrassed, my face hot against the cool night air. "Like there was no one else."

I risk a peek. Jake's eyes are flaring beneath the lights in the street. "It wasn't just a line. I've never had a night like that before with a girl. I never have since." He reaches for me and stops himself, cursing quietly, before tucking his hands in his pockets. "We should keep walking."

"We should."

"So …"

"So …"

We both laugh at the same time.

"Are you really going to take your leave in Perth?"

"If it's cool with Erin, which it probably will be. I have a standing invitation to crash at her apartment whenever I want to, for however long. I'll check in with her later and book flights."

"Does that mean I can take you out?"

My pulse takes a giddy little roller coaster ride. "On a date?"

"Yeah. Dinner. Movies. Normal stuff."

It sounds incredibly appealing. The normality of it. Spending time with a handsome man, one that gives me flutters in my belly. "Or we could do a beach picnic and swim."

"That too."

"Like two dates?"

"Maybe. I mean, I might decide I don't like you after the first one."

"Jake!"

His teeth gleam white in the dark. "Ahhh, you can dish it out…" he pokes his finger in my side and I leap away "…but you can't take it."

Our private little alley looms ahead, and I bound away, laughing as

I disappear into the dark. Jake gives chase. My heart is racing when I glance behind me. He's bridged the gap and grabs my arm, twisting me and pushing me up against the wall.

His fingers go for my buttons without a breath, starting their way from the top down. He's never done that before. Usually it's kissing and hands fumbling beneath shirts. My chest is rapidly exposed, the chilly air penetrating my bared skin. I shiver.

"Warm me up, Jake, it's cold."

He ducks his head, his mouth moving along the swell of my breast until he reaches the middle, where my dog tags and necklace rest. He lifts them, impatient, but then his eyes snag on the delicate chain, reading the words that are stamped onto the little metal rectangle. "Little Warrior," he reads, his brows drawing together in a puzzled frown.

He looks up at me, searching my face for something.

"What?" I ask.

"It's just …" Jake shakes his head, his gaze returning to my birthday gift.

There's something about the way he's looking at my necklace that makes my heart jackhammer in my chest. "Jake, what?"

"It's nothing. I just thought I'd seen this somewhere before."

"Seen what? My necklace?"

He brushes a thumb down the letters. "No, not the necklace. These words."

I grab his hand, the one holding my silver chain. "Jake, where?"

"I don't know," he murmurs, seeming deep in thought. Then he lets it go and my hand falls away. The alarm on my watch beeps, the shrill tinny sound indicating my shift starts in five minutes. I silence it.

Jake sighs and starts re-doing the buttons he almost ripped apart moments earlier.

"Soon," I tell him, my lips curving.

"Soon," he replies and plants a swift kiss on my mouth. I press forward when he goes to pull away, extending the intimate caress, lingering just a few moments more.

"Jamie," he whispers.

"Jake," I whisper back.

"You totally like me." His grin is slow. Teasing. It's on my lips to deny his statement, but I can't and he knows it. "You give everyone you like a hard time, remember?"

I grab his shirt in my fist, dragging his face to mine. I brush my lips against his, gentle and sweet, and my heart thumps hard and loud in my chest. "I like you."

His breath catches, the sound so soft it drifts away on the wind. "I like you too."

My insides melt like chocolate in the sun. Then I remember I have to report for duty. I look down, fixing my rumpled shirt. "Will I see you in the gym in the morning?"

"No." We walk together, out of the shadows and into the well-lit street. "I have a patrol. That's why I wanted to walk with you. To let you know I'll be gone a couple of weeks, and when I'm back we're shipping home. I'm not sure when I'll see you next."

"A patrol?"

Jake nods. "In the mountains."

He can't tell me more than that, but he's SAS. They go in first, before everyone else, doing reconnaissance and gathering intelligence. It's dangerous but his team is a well-oiled machine. They know what they're doing.

I brush my hand against his, so brief no one walking near us would notice. I don't ask him to be safe like I want to. Or tell him to take care. Instead, we reach the hospital entrance and stand just off to the side, out of the way. "Come find me when you get back."

He raises his fist with a grin. "If I don't catch you before I ship out—"

I bump it with my own. "Then I'll see you on the other side."

Jake winks. "Roger that, army girl."

16

JAMIE

"Drew, you need to be more careful," I say to the army cook, immersing his forearm beneath the cold water gushing from the hospital tap. "I can't live without your fried chicken. It's the only thing keeping me going until I get out of here."

The poor man winces. He tripped while carrying a small vat of hot oil in the kitchen this morning. "I'm not usually such a fuckin' klutz, Doc. Danger Mouse was unpacking a box on the ground, and I didn't see it," he says, referring to the head cook, named for his round ears and freakish knife talents.

"Well, it's lucky you fell on your side, otherwise that oil would've gone all over your face and chest."

Drew chuckles, a derisive sound. "That woulda sucked. This face ain't that pretty. Adding burns won't help my cause."

"What are you talking about, Drew?" I pat his shoulder and shift away, grabbing a packaged sterile bandage roll. "You're married. You've already locked that girl down."

"I'm not so sure," he mutters.

"What do you mean?"

"This army life. I don't think it's for her." He shifts his stance, inspecting his burn beneath the cold water. "You got a guy, Murphy?"

My mind turns to Jake. "Maybe."

"Well, let me give you some advice. Make sure your guy understands this life. If he don't, then strap in because it's gonna be a bumpy ride."

"Oh, he understands it."

"Good." Drew nods, seemingly satisfied with the safety of my romantic future. "How long do I gotta keep my arm under this tap?"

I set the bandage on the narrow patient bed and walk over, examining the blistered wound. It's not third degree, but it's not minor either. "Give it another five minutes."

"Five? Doc, you're killing me."

"I'm trying not to."

"I gotta get back. Everyone'll be screamin' for their hash browns, and Danger Mouse thinks cookin' them is beneath him."

"This won't take too long. It's more than just a minor burn, Drew. You'll have to—"

Squadron Leader Irvine, an Australian doctor at our base's medical facility, rushes past, stops, and pokes his head in. "Private Murphy. Radio came in. Multiple casualties. Need you on the medevac."

Wood charges in before I can respond, already suiting up, armour in place, helmet going on. He looks sick, his face whiter than snow. "I got it. I got it," he keeps saying. "I got it."

I look to Irvine as Wood jogs off, already disappearing down the hall. "Where?"

"Somewhere in the mountains. Khaz Uruzgan, I think." He checks his watch. "I have to get to surgery. Seven-year-old girl with massive internal injuries. The local hospital can't treat her." He shakes his head and rushes off from where he came.

I turn back to Drew where he stands by the sink, forearm still stuck beneath the gushing water, his expression resigned. The army cook has seen a few deployments already. No doubt he's heard a thousand stories of combat and casualties. "You on the medevac a lot?"

"A bit," I say, feigning a smile as I inspect his arm.

"You get shot at?"

It's still red, blisters popping up everywhere. "Some. I've had bullets hit the ground near my feet."

"Jesus. It takes balls to be a healer in this place. You shot your rifle?"

"I have."

"Jesus," he mutters again. "How does that work in your head?"

"What do you mean?"

"Well, you're like a weapon on one hand and a saviour on the other. How do you do both?"

I shrug and take his wrist, turning for a better view. "Knowing how to save a life and end one are two completely different things. It's like wearing two different hats, I guess."

Drew's gaze shifts from his inflamed arm to my face. "Your hand is shaking, Doc. You okay?"

"I'm fine." *Multiple casualties. In the mountains.* My lips form a professional smile, and I push Irvine's words from my head. "It's been a long shift is all." I reach over and flick the tap off before guiding Drew to the bed. "Take a seat."

He eases himself up. I try taking a closer inspection of the wound but Wood's pale face swims in my vision. *I got it. I got it.* I blink it away and focus on the blisters. "You'll need some antibiotics." I lean across to Drew's file, where it lies open on the bed beside him. "Tetanus is up-to-date. I'll just put a sterile covering on the wound, and you can come back and get it checked in twenty-four hours, okay?"

"Okay, Doc."

I rip open the packet, and the bandage falls on the floor. "Shit," I mutter under my breath. I crouch for it, picking it up from where it rolled beneath the bed. A wave of dizziness swamps me when I rise.

"Whoa." Drew grabs me and I brush him away, leaning my side against the bed for a moment.

"I'm okay. Just stood up too fast."

"You don't look so good. Maybe you should be up here on the bed, Doc."

"I'm fine. Really." I paste on another reassuring smile as I set the bandage aside knowing it's no longer sterile. I collect a new one and remove the packaging. Beginning at the wrist, I wind it gently around his arm. "Hungry and tired. Bring me some hash browns later, okay?"

"I can do that."

I finish wrapping Drew's wound and send him on his way with some ibuprofen and antibiotics. I'm starting towards the medevac station when I'm waylaid by a nursing officer. "I have a wounded Afghan soldier in the intensive care unit and we're short staffed. Again. I need you to monitor his breathing for me."

I change direction, swallowing my rising frustration as I follow her down the narrow hall. The soldier's head is bloodied and bandaged, tubes winding out from his nose and mouth. I take the stethoscope from around my neck and place the tips in my ears, pressing the chest piece to his torso.

I'm trying to listen but an age-old panic begins clawing its way upward, taking hold of my throat. I take a few deep breaths, but it won't let go, leaving me jittery and sick.

Something is wrong.

An hour passes unbearably slowly. When I'm free of intensive care, I rush out, jogging towards the medevac station, not giving anyone the chance to grab me for another task.

A sense of urgency engulfs me, pushing me faster. I burst through the doors as the Blackhawk lands, wind and dust kicking up, the early morning sun blasting me in the face. Wood steps out first as I run towards them, his uniform splattered red, before he turns and reaches back inside the big mechanical beast.

Kyle steps out beside him, staggering a little, and my legs almost buckle beneath me. Blood drenches the side of his shirt and pants. It smears his dirty brow and bearded jaw. My eyes search inside for Jake, but I'm too far away to see.

C'mon, Jake. Step out. Please.

The pushy breeze blows hair across my face. I shove it behind my ears, my steps beginning to falter. I slow until I come to a stop, shading my eyes with my hand as another medic steps out. Someone pushes past me, rushing towards the chopper with a stretcher, but I can't move. My feet have frozen to the ground.

Both Wood and the other medic slide someone out on a portable board. My eyes snap to their patient, and I flinch. Blond hair, tousled and dirty, glinting in the sun. Shirt steeped in blood. Muddy boots still laced and splattered red.

I take a step forward, my eyes shifting to Wood as they start towards the hospital entrance. He reads the question in them, and his lips mash together. He shakes his head.

The stethoscope clutched in my fist falls slowly as my fingers lose their grip. It hits the ground, soundless beneath the deafening whir of the rotor blades.

"God, please. Not Jake," someone whimpers, but there's no one next to me, and I realise the prayer has come from me.

Ryan steps off behind them, his hands crusted with dried blood, his expression hollow. He takes Wood's position on the patient board and nudges my friend towards me.

"Jamie." Wood's mouth is moving as he gets closer, but I don't hear it. I take a step back as he comes forward.

I shake my head violently. "No."

"Jamie."

"Wood, no," I croak.

He grabs me when I jerk away. I need to get to Jake. I need to—Wood's arms fold me up tight, an iron band that locks me to his body. My face is mashed against his chest, and I can't see. I turn my head as they move Jake past me. His eyes are closed, his face pale and void of expression. A bullet wound punctures his neck.

I want to scream at them to get him to the ER, but the rational voice in my head knows why they're moving so slowly.

The wound isn't bleeding.

His heart isn't beating anymore.

Jake is gone.

The whirring blades of the chopper start to slow as a loud keening wail rips from my throat. I feel my legs give out, and my body sags against my best friend.

"Jamie, I'm so sorry," Wood mutters thickly, his arms the only thing keeping me upright. A shuddering breath rips out of him. "I'm so sorry."

"Noooooo!" I cry out, pushing against him, trying to escape this insidious ache inside. "Wood, no."

He only holds me tighter, his hand rubbing the back of my head. "I'm so fucking sorry."

I grab at his shirt, squeezing the fabric in my fists as a sob rises up inside me. It rises up so hard and so fast it hurts. I choke it back, my body shaking with so much effort it almost crumples me. His hold tightens, curling around me as if he could protect me from the pain. "They c-c-can't take him, Wood. They *can't.*"

Heartache fills his voice. "Oh, Jamie."

"Fuck this p-place." I shove against him, pushing myself free. "Fuck this place!" I scream, my heart pounding so hard in my chest it *hurts.* I am done. I am so *done* with being here. I'm done with this war. With this whole goddamn *life.* "It takes from you. And it takes. And it fucking *takes!*" My chest heaves, and I wipe at my eyes with the heel of my hands. Wood stands there, arms hanging by his sides, a helpless expression on his face. "Soon enough they'll take *all* the good," I croak, my voice a hoarse, broken sound, "and there'll be nothing left."

I turn, starting for the hospital entrance.

"Jamie, wait!"

Wood grabs my arm from behind and I shrug him off, my steps hurried. I burst back through the doors and come to a halt. My throat aches as I stand there, unable to breathe as I take in the room.

Ryan is in the ER station, his face dirty and eyes red. He sinks into a seat and holds his head in his hands, fingers trembling against his dark hair. A nurse is taking Kyle into a treatment room, and the rest of Jake's team—Galloway, their sniper, Tex, their patrol signaller, and

Monty, their troop commander—mill around, lost and a little broken, as if their minds are somewhere else.

"Jamie." Wood catches up with me.

I turn. "I need to see Jake."

His bottom lip wobbles, and it takes him a moment to speak. "They'll be taking him to the morgue, Jamie."

I nod, my vision starting to blur. "I know, but I need to see him. I need to make sure he's okay."

"Oh, Jamie." He drops his head, rubbing at the back of his neck. "Give it a minute. They still have to …"

Wood keeps talking, but I tune him out as I start down the hall. My ears ring and my legs falter the closer I get. It's like an IED has gone off at my feet. I pass Kyle in the treatment room. He's sitting on an ER bed, hands fisted in his lap as a nurse inspects his injury. He looks up when I walk past, grief dark in his eyes.

I look away, forcing myself to keep moving until I reach the room where Jake is being held. Dr. Irvine is leaving as I step inside. "Private Murphy?" I see his lips move as he comes towards me, but I don't hear. "Jamie?"

He lays a hand on my shoulder, giving a gentle squeeze. "Did you know this soldier?"

My eyes shift to the prone figure on the portable bed and then away, blinking. "Jake," I croak. "His name is Jake."

Dr. Irvine nods. "I'll give you a minute," he says and leaves.

My heart hammers in my chest as I make my way towards him. He's been placed in the corner, beside a medical supply cabinet, and I shift across until I'm standing beside him, the wall at my back.

I'm not ready to look at his face, so I focus on his hand, gathering it up in mine. His palm is dry and unbearably lifeless, and it flashes me back to meeting him at the bar all those years ago, when I held his hand for the first time, his touch so warm and vital.

"I'm Jake. Jake Tanner," he said, offering his hand. I took it in mine and his fingers wrapped around it, firm, warm, rough.

Now those fingers will never touch me again. They'll never brush a wayward strand of hair from my face, trace a thumb across my bottom lip, or curl around my upper thigh in a cheeky caress beneath the dining table.

Silent tears slip free as I set his hand gently back on the bed and reach across, brushing shaky fingers over the bloodied hem of his shirt. My thumb skims across the thick cotton where it's frayed a little at the corner. I move my gaze down his legs to his worn, muddy boots. I don't know what it is about seeing those laces tied so neatly, but suddenly my chest aches, and I can't breathe. When he woke this morning and put those boots on his feet, it was the last time he ever would, and the thought absolutely breaks me.

"You have a tough veneer, Jamie, but it's not tougher than me."

A great big hulking sob steals my breath. And another. Painful. Clawing. Heavy. My body can't hold the weight of it, and my back slides down the wall, knees pressing to my chest. My head tilts back as the tears pour out, gushing as if a dam has burst.

"You're a virgin?"

"Only in the physical sense."

Jake was my first. Deep down inside I was starting to think that maybe he was it for me. The one. I wanted him to be my last. I wanted it *so much.*

"You are going down, Tanner."

"If you play your cards right, Murphy, you can bet your sweet ass I'll be going down."

Jake pushing inside me for the first time. *"Relax, Jamie."*

"Oh my god. That's easy for you to say."

"Should I stop?"

"Hell no. We're doing this."

And I never regretted a moment of it. I relived that night over and over in my head like I was watching my favourite movie on repeat.

"You totally like me."

How could I not? He made it impossible not to.

"If I don't catch you before I ship out—"

"Then I'll see you on the other side."

He winked at me and something beautiful sparked big and bright inside my heart. *"Roger that, army girl."*

The sobs come harder. Someone collects me from the floor and rises, cradling me gently against their body. I don't care who it is. Or that I'm on duty. I can't be a soldier anymore today. There's no strength left inside to care about rules and regiment and war, when the result of it all is lying cold and lifeless beside me.

I grasp the shirt of the man who holds me and burrow in. "I c-can't."

The voice is gruff and belongs to Kyle. "Can't what?"

"S-s-say goodbye." I'm not ready for Jake to leave.

"You don't have to say goodbye now. You can do it later."

I nod, a rough jerky movement against his chest. Later.

Kyle sets me down, steadying me with gentle hands as I set my feet on the floor. I straighten my spine, gathering up all the grief, and I hold it all in so hard my eyes burn with effort and my muscles shake, because that's what I was taught. *You have to train your mind to be stronger than your emotions or else you'll lose every time.*

But it's too late, isn't it? I've already lost.

We all have.

Kyle lost his brother today.

So did Ryan.

And Finlay.

The entire world has lost today. Something beautiful. Something incredibly vital. Something we'll never get back.

17

KYLE BROOKS

We step outside the room, and I shut the door, my jaw tight and body throbbing with pain. I'm not sure which hurts worse, the wound on my hip or the ache in my chest. My brother is lying in that room because my cover fire wasn't enough. He was the best member of our team, the glue that held us all together, and I let him down. I let him down so fucking hard.

Jamie's brows knit together as she glances down, pulling her uniform away from her side with her fingers. "What the …"

It's covered in blood. My blood.

She looks at me, her sad, swollen eyes dropping to my hip. "You didn't get that seen to?" She lifts my shirt and inspects the wound. "Brooks." Her eyes widen. "You've been shot."

"It's nothing." The devastation on Jamie's face was so much worse. I couldn't sit there without making sure she was okay first. "Just a flesh wound."

"I'll be the judge of that." Her eyes harden. I can see her medical training snapping into action. Good. It will give her something else to focus on. "Get back in the exam room."

She follows me to the treatment room where I take my seat back on the bed, shifting backwards with a grimace. Jamie fusses with the tray on the cart beside her. Her throat muscles are working. She lets out a breath as she rolls it closer, her fingers trembling as she searches for something. She stops suddenly and turns towards me, her beautiful brown eyes searching my face.

"Did he suffer, Brooks?"

My jaw tightens and it feels as if my teeth will crack beneath the pressure. We were struck by a nest of insurgents as dawn began its approach. There were too many of them and only a handful of us. Jake was caught on the other side of the rock ledge, and we needed to retreat.

He broke cover, running for a better position to take out the PKM machine gun that was spewing heavy fire, but new shots rained down from somewhere above. The shot hit him right in the neck. His head jerked back and he spun around, eyes already glassy with shock as his hand went to the wound. He pulled it away, staring at his bloody palm.

For a moment I thought it just winged him, then blood spurted from his mouth in a cough.

"No!" I yelled, watching helplessly as the light leached slowly from his eyes and he fell to the ground. "Jesus, no!"

"Man down!" Kendall shouted hoarsely and ran over, hunched, skidding to the ground while I emptied my gun with a roar, bullets firing towards the new target as my teammate dragged him to cover.

"No," I say in a rough voice to Jamie, swallowing the bile in my throat. "He didn't suffer. He was gone in an instant."

"Just like that." Her jaw trembles with the beginnings of anger. It churns in her eyes, making them darker. "Here one moment," she chokes out, "and gone the next."

Like a light winking out in the dark. "Just like that."

Jamie nods, visibly trying to compose herself. "You need to take off your shirt."

"It's fine." It's already unbuttoned, revealing the army green cotton tee shirt beneath. I lift it up at the hem. My belt is already undone, pants pushed down a little to reveal the wound where the bullet ripped through my side. It left a long laceration, like a comet skimming through my skin in a blaze of fire. "Just give me a couple of stitches so I can get out of here," I say through gritted teeth, holding the pain at bay.

"It needs more than a couple of stitches. Lie down."

"I'll sit, thanks."

"Take off your shirt and lie down," she orders, anger rising in her tone, replacing the grief.

I shake my head and it only serves to piss her off even more. "Just fix it and let me out of here."

Jamie curses and spins around, grabbing for the surgical scissors. With the implement in hand, she snags my shirt and cuts it in violent jerks until it hangs loose from my chest.

She slams them back on the tray and pushes my sleeves down both arms, ripping the fabric away and dumping it on the floor.

"Murphy."

She's snapping on surgical gloves and searching for fresh gauze packets when my hand drops on her shoulder. "Stop. Call for the nurse. She can deal with the stitches."

Jamie shrugs me off. "I can do it." She searches her tray. "Goddammit, where's the freaking gauze?" Her voice rises. "Doesn't anyone know how to pack a trauma tray in this freaking shithole?"

She finds it underneath, apparently where it doesn't belong. After tearing it free from the packet, she presses it against my wound, and my intake of breath is sharp.

"Hold that there," she orders and turns.

"Murphy, stop."

"I'm trying to do my job here, okay?" She jabs a syringe into a bottle and liquid fills the little plastic tube. She turns back to me, her eyes level with my chest.

They widen as she seems to notice my tattoos for the first time. Both my arms are sleeved with dark images—and bright ones too. Ones with colour. Teal. Pink. Green. Orange. An entire life inked into the limbs. Then her eyes find the lettering across my chest, and I brace.

I know the typewriter font is more familiar to her than her own face because she's not breathing right now.

The tattoo matches her necklace. An exact replica.

LITTLE WARRIOR.

The syringe in her hand clatters to the floor.

Her eyes shoot up, looking at me as if she's seeing me for the first time. I stare back, wordless, swallowing around the lump in my throat.

Jamie's hand trembles as she reaches for her ever-present necklace, grasping it tight in her fist. "Bear?" she croaks, saying it as if she's willing it not to be true.

My nostrils flare. Hearing the name on her lips fills me with an ache that stabs at my heart. "I'm sorry."

Her brows snap together, and she takes a step back. "I don't understand." She looks me over as if she's fifteen again and peering through the fence, searching for the boy inside the man. "Is it really you? All this time?"

Fuck. I have no idea what to say or how to make this right.

"You knew," she says, realisation in her expression. "You *knew* it was me. But when Jake introduced us, you acted as if you had no clue who I was. Why? Why didn't you say anything?"

"Jamie." I swallow, unable to bear the hurt in her eyes and the ache in her voice. I blink, my gaze shifting over her shoulder at the wall like a damn coward. "Maybe we can talk about this later."

"Later? *Later?*" Her hands fist, her fury palpable. "You left me!" The words hit like a slap. "You were my best friend. You made me need you, and then you left as if I didn't matter at all, leaving me with nothing but a note!"

I reach for her, and she physically recoils. "Don't touch me."

"Jamie." I reach for her again, feeling like the biggest piece of shit alive. "Please. Let me explain later, okay?"

"I said don't touch me!" she yells and shoves at the cart beside her. It slams into the cupboard behind it and tips over, its contents smashing across the floor, rolling in every direction.

"God." I rise from the bed with a wince, holding the gauze to my side. "Don't cry."

"I'm not crying!" Jamie swipes at her face with the sleeve of her shirt, and it comes away wet. "All this time." She backs away from me. "You knew who I was and didn't say a word. God, you are such a bastard, Kyle Brooks," she spits. "I fucking hate you."

"Jamie." I grab for her hands, but she knocks me away.

"I waited for you. Every day I sat by that stupid fence and I waited like a sad, pathetic idiot, but you never showed."

My eyes burn at the image. At what I did to her. "Let me explain."

Jamie takes a deep breath and lifts her chin. I can physically see her tucking away the anger and the hurt, and I'm so fucking proud of her strength, but the expression she leaves behind is one of indifference, as if the bond of friendship we once had meant nothing, when it was the one thing that got me through the death of my mother. The *only* thing.

"I don't want your lousy explanation," she says in a hollow tone. "Save it for someone who gives a shit." I flinch as if the words are pointed darts that jab at my skin. "Just stay away from me."

Wood comes in, the best friend that I once used to be before I threw it away. She brushes past him. "Stitch Brooks up, would you? I can't bring myself to touch him."

She walks out of the room, her stride determined, and yet she glances behind her, just once as she meets my eyes before turning away. It's enough for me to know I can't ship home without trying to fix this.

~

"Jamie?" I knock on the door of her room the next afternoon. I know I should be giving her time, but we fly out tomorrow. Time is something I don't have right now.

I knock again, banging my fist a little harder. I know she's in there. I saw her go in. "Jamie? Can we talk? Please?"

Nothing.

It feels like I'm seventeen all over again and the fence a barrier between us. The only thing that got her talking all those years ago was a taunt. "Are you going to hide from me in your room all night? I never figured you for a timid mouse."

Nothing.

"The Jamie I knew would never back down from a fight."

The door opens so hard it almost rips from its hinges. She stands before me, expression blazing, but it doesn't detract from the dark, puffy circles beneath her eyes from a sleepless night and hair dirty from an obvious lack of washing. She needs a damn shower. She's still wearing yesterday's uniform, for fuck's sake. I know because it's stained with my blood.

I remember the morning I first saw her at the mess hall. Jake was talking with her as if he'd known her a lifetime, his eyes on hers like she was the only person in the room. Then he introduced us from across the table.

"Kyle Brooks, this is Jamie. Jamie Murphy."

The name sent my heart knocking around in my chest. I jerked so hard my knees banged into the table and spilled coffee all over my tray. I mopped at it with a napkin while I tried hard not to stare. Was it really her? Or just someone with the same name and colouring?

Every day I wondered what had become of my best friend, hoping she was happy. That she was doing something important with her life. Something *safe*. I imagined what she looked like all the time. Glimpses through the fence showed brown eyes and hair that was long and wild. Would it be short now, cut in a business-like style that suited her profession, or did she keep it long? Were her hands still as painfully delicate as they were when she held mine beneath the fence?

The female soldier that sat across the table from me was achingly beautiful. The kind of beauty that didn't belong in a place where every-thing was stark and ugly and brutal. Her hair was thick and braided in a long rope that she somehow twisted into a knot at the nape of her neck. Her eyes were large in her face, the chocolate brown richer than I remembered, coloured with flecks of amber.

Then her hand grasped the necklace, and I knew. It was really her, and anger bubbled up inside. I was furious. *Livid.* Jamie inside a warzone? No. *Hell no.* This was no place for her, and not because she was a woman on the front line. I wasn't a sexist asshole. I was just someone who knew she'd already been through too much and didn't want to see her go through anymore.

Then she stood with her barely touched breakfast tray, her shoulders back and chin high, and I realised just how petite she was, despite the lean muscle and feisty attitude. Her face and body had been battered just like the first time we met, yet she somehow appeared five times taller than she was, just from the strength she carried around inside herself.

"I'm not the same Jamie you used to know," she hisses at me, pulling me from the memory. "And I don't want to fight with you. I don't want to even look at you."

She goes to slam the door closed. I wedge my boot in the way, stopping her. "Too bad."

Her brows fly up to her hairline as the door bounces off my foot. "You can't come in here."

"So let's go for a walk."

"I'd rather chew off my own feet," she bites out.

There's the little warrior I know. I would laugh if we both weren't hurting so much. "This is just like old times."

"There are no *old times*." She tries closing the door again, pushing against the boot that remains lodged in her way. "You were never a real friend anyway."

The barb hurts, even though I know she's just lashing out. "Yeah? Well you were mine. The best."

Jamie laughs, but it's not a happy sound. "Let me clue you in, Brooks. Real friends don't walk out on each other. So what we had..." she shakes her head "...not real."

"It was real for me." I remove the boot and take a step back, risking the door being slammed in my face. "I wouldn't have survived if it weren't for you," I tell her, the admission painful but true.

Jamie goes to close it and looks at me, hesitating. The internal struggle is written all over her face. I can tell she wants to ask and yet doesn't want to—all at the same time. "How could it be real if you never told me about your mother?"

The familiar pang of loss echoes through my body. I rub at the tension in the back of my neck. "Cancer doesn't just affect the person with the disease. It affects everyone around them too. It's this big, black cloud that's waiting for you when you wake up, and it's there with you when you go to sleep. There's no escaping it. But with you I could forget she was dying. I could pretend there was nothing wrong. I couldn't do that with anyone else. You gave me that. I know that makes me a coward, and I'm sorry." I swallow, my chest expanding as I take a deep breath. "Just … some days I needed that, you know? It got me through when nothing else did."

"Bear." Her voice is a cracked whisper. Then she presses her lips together, remembering she's supposed to be mad at me. "I get that. I do. But she died and you still left."

Hurt flickers visibly in her eyes. I put it there, and years later it's still there. A wound that never healed. "I'm sorry. I've apologised to you a thousand times in my head. It was selfish to leave with just a note, but I don't know if I could've left otherwise, and I needed to go. The memories of who she was hit me everywhere I went. At school before she got sick, where she'd pick me up after finishing work. At rugby, where she'd cheer me on from the sidelines so loud I could hear her clear across the field. But then the cancer came, and I saw her every time I passed by the local medical centre. I saw her catching her breath whenever we went shopping, leaning against the trolley as she waited for the dizziness to pass. I saw her at the beach, sitting with me on a towel as she watched the waves crash against the shore one last time before she died." My voice grows hoarse. "She was everywhere I turned. So I ran."

"But it didn't work, did it?" Jamie says, a sad knowledge in her eyes because she gets it. Of course she gets it.

"No." My throat aches and my breathing becomes heavy, as if

someone is sitting on my chest. The admission is painful as fuck. "It didn't work. You can't outrun memories. Not when they're inside you."

She reaches for me and stops herself. "You should go."

I nod slowly. "You're right. I should. We ship out tomorrow. I thought you'd want to know so you could say goodbye. To Jake."

"I don't—" she starts and stops. "I'm not sure I can."

"You can, Jamie. You'll regret it otherwise."

Her voice turns bitter. "I'm sure you know all about that."

"I do know. You need to say goodbye. For you."

"Don't tell me what I need, Brooks."

I shake my head. "Always fighting, huh?"

At least with me. It was hard not to envy the easy way she and Jake got along, as if they were caught inside each other's orbit. I didn't make it easy for Jamie here, and I'm sorry for that, but it was easier to keep her at arm's length rather than confess who I really was and risk losing her a second time. Instead, I kept sniping at her, enjoying the way she returned each volley like a champion. Jamie's sharp mind and wicked sense of humour came alive when provoked.

She shrugs, one hand still on the door knob. "What can I say? You bring out the fight in me."

"I like the fight in you. It means you haven't given up."

"Don't, Brooks."

"Don't what?"

"Talk to me as if we're friends. We used to be a long time ago, but we're not anymore."

"Dammit, Jamie." I swipe a hand down my face, scratching at my newly formed beard while I ignore the thundering ache in my side. The painkiller is wearing off. "Let me fix this."

"There's nothing to fix."

"I can't leave knowing you're pissed at me."

"You don't have a choice."

The door slams in my face.

18

JAMIE

I'm conscious of every breath as I fumble with the shirt buttons on my freshly laundered uniform. When I'm done, I tuck it inside my pants and adjust my belt. My boots are by the door of my room. I collect them, along with a thick pair of socks from my drawer.

Seating myself on the edge of the bed, I slide the socks on my feet, followed by the boots. I pretend not to notice the way my fingers tremble as I tie the laces. It takes me a second to get them right.

Standing, I walk to the mirror. My reflection stares back, and it's like looking at a whole other person. Sometimes it's easier to cope that way. If you pretend you're standing on the outside of your life, looking in; it's like watching everything happen to someone else. And if you do it often enough, it becomes second nature.

I weave thick sections of my hair into a braid. After tying an elastic around the ends, I wind it into a knot at the nape of my neck. I'm just finishing when a knock comes at my door.

My lungs expand as I take a deep breath. Each step feels painfully slow as I walk to answer it. The door swings open and Wood stands on the other side, his uniform fresh and face grim. "Ready?"

"No."

He aims for a sympathetic smile, but it falls short of the mark. He just looks constipated. "Then let's go."

I step outside. The morning sun hits my face and flutters my hair, pulling loose strands from my braid and flicking them across my brow. I brush them away as we walk towards the truck, covering my eyes from the pale glare with a dark pair of sunglasses.

The trip is quick. Too quick. What feels like mere seconds later, we're arriving at the airfield. The C-130 Hercules is on the tarmac, the big charcoal beast open from the back end and being loaded with bags. Other soldiers arrive alongside us, the rest of them already out by the plane. Me and Wood step out of the truck and make our way towards them.

He swings a bony arm over my shoulders and gives me a jostle. "You okay?"

"I've had better days."

"We'll be home soon," he reassures me, squeezing the tense muscle around my neck before letting go. "Then we can hit the beach every day and the bars every night."

That was my plan with Jake. How can I laze around and drink beers while he's lying somewhere in the ground, cold and alone in the dark? I can't do it without him. My eyes sting and my voice turns thick. "Can't wait."

My lack of enthusiasm is clear. "It'll be good for you, Murphy. A bit of relaxation and recuperation will be good for both of us."

His comment pokes at my selfish little bubble, reminding me I'm not alone in my grief. "What about you, Wood? You okay?"

He looks at me before his gaze bounces off towards the distance, where the sun meets the mountains as it climbs into the sky. "Yeah," he says, but there's something off in his tone, something that niggles at me. I push it aside for later because my focus has narrowed on a truck that's making its way along the tarmac in our direction. It pulls around, performing a measured U-turn before easing to a stop about twenty yards away.

My stomach knots in a sick lump as the soldiers milling around me form a guard of honour at the ass-end of the plane. Pulling the sunglasses from my face, I tuck them in my pocket and take my place in the line, Wood to my right.

My peripheral vision shows a soldier stepping out from the back of the truck. Then another, and another, and I try not to look. Instead, I stare over the shoulder of the soldier standing opposite me, my focus on the distance as I inhale deeply. I hold it in my lungs for a moment before letting go. The air pushes past my lips in a shaky puff.

God, why is it so hard to breathe?

The soldiers from the truck start for the plane, and I can't stop myself. I look, and my knees almost give out beneath me. Kyle and Ryan lead the small procession, the rest of Jake's team behind them as they carry the casket towards us. It's draped with the Australian flag— the red, white, and blue a bright beacon of colour in a sea of desert camouflaged uniforms and a terrain of thick, drab dust.

Their steps are slow and heavy. As they get closer, I raise my arm in a salute, as does Wood and the surrounding Australian soldiers in the guard. My eyes sting and I mash my lips together as I fight back a sob, but I keep my spine straight, my shoulders true, and my hand pressed hard to my forehead, honouring the fallen soldier as they take him home for the last time.

"Did someone just say the magic word?" Jake asked as he took a seat beside me.

"Home?"

Jake grinned. "No place like it."

Kyle's eyes find mine as they pass me by, and the battle inside them breaks me. Tears blur my vision, rolling their way down my cheeks, yet I see him. I see the boy I used to know. The best friend that stopped me from giving up. The one who ran when life got too hard because he didn't know how to lean on me the way I leaned on him. The one I thought about every night for years, wondering what had become of him. Always wondering.

The small procession keeps moving, and we remain saluting, silent and still, as they walk up the ramp and onto the plane.

I never got to say goodbye. I wasn't ready. But I've learnt that death doesn't wait for you to catch up. People like Jake sacrifice their lives for something they believe in with their whole hearts, and yet the world keeps turning, the sun continues to rise in the east and set in the west, and life goes on, regardless of those who get left behind.

I lower my arm as the soldiers disperse, and Wood slings an arm around my shoulder, pulling me close until I'm engulfed in his warmth. He presses a hard kiss to my forehead. I hold on, just for a moment, my fingers curling into the front of his shirt.

"I've forgotten why we're here, Wood." The war was something I believed in. I trained like a caped crusader on a quest to save the world because I thought I could make a difference, yet I feel like everything I'm trying to accomplish here is for nothing. All I've found in this savage land is pain and loss and a brutal disregard for human life. "What are we even fighting for anymore?"

He shakes his head and relaxes his hold, freeing me from his embrace. "I honestly don't know."

Kyle steps back out of the plane, sunglasses now covering his eyes and shirtsleeves rolled up, revealing his large forearms and inked skin. He grabs one of the bags that rest by the ramp, and I know I need to go to him. He reached out yesterday to make amends, not wanting to leave me the way he did before. Yet here I am, making him do it all over again, forcing his hand. I need to let it go. Kyle has just lost one of the best friends he has. My anger has no place here.

"Give me a minute," I tell Wood and make my way over.

Kyle

I wasn't sure Jamie planned on ever talking to me again. Leaving the way I did was an asshole move. I wouldn't be surprised to see her cross the street if she saw me coming the other way. Maybe not even piss on me if I were on fire. Hell, she'd probably add accelerant and watch me burn. So I do a double-take when she starts towards the tarmac in my direction. I'm not sure what to expect. Jamie can be unpredictable. I'd wave a white flag if I could. Instead, I settle for setting down the bag in my hand and flicking my sunglasses to the top of my head, giving her my attention.

Jamie reaches me and steps close, leaving barely any space between us. Her hands tremble as she reaches up and palms my bearded cheeks. I stare down at her, surprised and waiting for her to speak first. She's struggling. I can feel it. "I'm sorry," she says when she finds her voice.

My tone is gruff, the apology knocking the air from my lungs. "For what?"

Regret darkens her eyes. "For yesterday."

"You don't need to apologise for that."

"I do." She lets me go and moves back a step. "I've been thinking only about myself. When you left I was so damn angry. All I thought about was how could you do this to me? Hadn't I been through enough? How was I supposed to tackle this life without you there by my side? I lost you just when I was starting to find my feet again, but I didn't even think about the fact that you lost me too, and you lost your mother, and I'm sorry for that, Kyle. I'm so sorry. I have no right to be angry."

Grief climbs my throat. I swallow it down. "Don't. It wasn't your fault. I'm the one who fucked everything up. Leaving was a mistake."

A colossal one. I knew it the moment I left. But I couldn't turn back. I had nothing. No belongings. No money in my pocket. No one I cared about except for Jamie, the girl from the other side of the fence. I would have stayed if she asked me to, which was all the more reason for me to leave. Writing her the note was a coward's move, but I didn't know how else to tell her. She probably tore it into tiny bits of confetti and left it for the birds.

I returned home after my first army placement, the very first chance I got. I confronted the memories and went to her house. I even knocked on the door.

"Jamie's not here," her foster mother said when I asked if she was around. Sue, I thought her name was, but I couldn't remember.

"Is she out?" I questioned, glancing over my shoulder as if expecting her to return at that very moment, walking up the path behind me.

"She's not out. She's gone."

"Gone?" The thought sent my stomach into freefall. "Gone where?"

"She left for the army." Sue rolled her eyes heavenward. "Crazy girl, that one. Looking for a fight wherever she could find it. Maybe that place will give her some of the discipline she lacks."

"The army?" I kept repeating her words back at her like an idiot.

Why would Jamie join the army? Did she do it looking for me? I rejected the idea immediately. The girl was stubborn, her pride a rigid iron bar. The last thing she would do was chase down someone who left her, unless she wanted to punch me in face so bad it was worth enlisting for.

"Yeah, the army," Sue repeated. "You just missed her actually."

"When did she leave?"

"Three days ago."

Three goddamn days? I walked away feeling sick and ended up wasting my leave getting sunburned at the beach during the days, and drinking with random army mates during the nights, before crashing on the couch of an old friend from high school.

I returned to base with a pounding headache and food poisoning from some questionable bar food we ate the night before.

What the hell was I doing with my life? I joined the army to find my purpose, and yet I felt more adrift than a sailor lost at sea. I needed something more. Something that pushed me beyond my limits. Something to give my life meaning. So I made the decision to join the SAS, the toughest regiment in the entire army. Maybe it would be the answer for me.

It wasn't as simple as filling out a document and completing a transfer. The SAS wanted only the best. Soldiers with mental, moral, and physical stamina. I wasn't sure of my mental or moral fibre at that point, but I could handle the physical.

Selection was three full weeks of torture. They treated us like convicts, depriving us of food, sleep, and dignity. We trekked for days through mountainous terrain while delirious. Half dropped out from injuries alone.

I reached my breaking point towards the end. Jamie was the sole reason I made it through. She was the kind of girl who never gave up, and damned if I wouldn't either.

I began my eighteen-month employment training back home in Western Australia, at Campbell Barracks in Swanbourne. It was there I met Jake Tanner and Ryan Kendall. Jake lived off base, but Ryan had the room next door to mine. They were close, having grown up together. They would finish each other's sentences and laugh at inside jokes that left you clueless.

"So are you guys together or what?" I ribbed, leaning up against the door frame of Ryan's room as they sat at a small table, playing cards. "You don't need to hide it. The walls here are thin." I rapped at the drywall with my knuckles to emphasise my point and gave them a wink. "I hear everything."

"Dude." Jake just laughed and showed me the back of his hand, pointing to a faint scar along the meaty part of his palm. "Blood brothers."

"Wow." My brows rose slowly. "Cool. You're like a really small … gang. I didn't realise people actually still did that."

Ryan snorted. "Christ, Brooks. We were kids."

Jake shot Ryan a look of mock sadness. "What are you saying? It means nothing to you now because you're all grown up and stuff?"

Ryan looked between the both of us. "You're both as bad as the other." He set his lousy hand—I know because I peeked—facedown on the table. "You know what I think?"

"What?" I asked.

"I think you're jealous." Ryan reached across and snagged something from the bench beside him. A small dagger. He stood and waved it in my direction. "You want to join us?"

"You get any closer with that thing, and I'll use it to cut your balls off. You girls can keep your little gang."

"Sleep with one eye open, Brooks," Ryan called out when I walked off to report for duty.

I responded with the middle finger, and their laughter trailed out behind me.

We became friends after that, but it took weeks and a massive bar brawl before they truly accepted me.

It was Friday night and the day had kicked my ass, literally, because I took to the boxing ring that afternoon against Jake and came out a stupefied loser. I thought I had the edge. I was bigger. Stronger too, because I lifted heavier in the gym. I figured I'd go easy on him, but his affable personality lulled me into a false sense of security. When it came to training, Jake morphed into a goddamn ninja, blindsiding me with his jack-be-nimble athleticism. He came at me with his pretty blond hair and dazzling white teeth, and sucker punched me right into the ropes. I saw stars.

I also lost against him in the rifle range for a third time that month. Jake had the eyes of a bat and the type of preternatural calm you felt in the eye of a hurricane. The dude was Captain freaking America.

Loser paid drinks, so there I was at the heaving high-end bar, emptying my wallet on expensive craft beers because Jake claimed it was all he drank. All lies I discovered later when I found cheap shit lager stocked in the fridge at the cottage where he lived.

The problem with the fancy brews was the alcohol content. It was off the charts. I was shit-faced. We all were. But we weren't *falling off our chairs and barfing on our shoes* shit-faced. We were just loud and jolly. Letting off steam. Two women sat at the table beside ours, reviving themselves with an after-work wine. They were pretty, garbed in office attire, and didn't seem bothered by our noise. I'd been throwing flirty eye-contact at the brunette for the past half hour and getting good reception, though the blonde was just as hot. I literally had no preference. Tall or short, slim or lush and curvy. Come one, come all, basically. It wasn't about notches on the bedpost. I just loved women. Their soft skin. The sweet, feminine scent. The silky hair and smooth legs.

Fuck, I could feel myself getting hard thinking about everything they had to offer. I would have happily settled down with one, but I must have had 'player' tattooed across my forehead because they never lingered the next morning. No one wanted an army trooper. We weren't considered a 'stable choice.'

Whatever. I was a catch. The brunette seemed to agree. She was flicking her long hair so much it almost whipped her friend in the face. Some egotistical ponce seemed to like it and approached their table. He had the bearing of a thug, but he was dolled up like a total dude. The cologne wafted from his person in thick clouds, making my eyes water. Ryan literally gagged.

"Can I buy you both another wine?"

The blonde was polite. "We're good, thanks."

He ignored her reply and clicked his fingers for a server. "I'll get a bottle for the table."

The girls shared an eye roll, but they didn't verbally decline the offer. He took a seat. "What's your plan for the evening, ladies?"

The three of us openly watched the exchange, tossing back our beers as we waited for the crash and burn.

"Just a quiet one," the brunette replied. "We were actually planning on leaving soon."

"You can't leave now." He planted a hand on her thigh—and, dude, there was a line between flirting and being a creep, and he crossed it the moment he got dressed in his navy button-down with … what the fuck were those? I squinted. Flamingos on his shirt. What a winner. Nothing said 'I'm manly enough to throw you down and fuck you senseless' like a bunch of pink birds with stick legs, sinister red eyes, and giant black beaks. "I just got here," he added, as if the party was just getting started.

He ordered a bottle, and two more friends joined him, one of them having to drag a chair to the table. Introductions were made while the hand on the brunette's thigh slid higher and then inward.

I saw the moment Jake clocked the move because his eyes narrowed. The woman flinched, clearly uncomfortable. Flamingo didn't seem to care. He shifted his chair closer and dived his hand right inside her skirt.

The brunette gasped and hissed something in his face. I didn't catch the words. I was already setting my beer on the table, ready to stand and flex some muscle, but Jake was already on the move.

"I believe these ladies are ready to leave," he said to the table in a tone that dared anyone to disagree.

Flamingo lifted his meaty chin, taking the challenge. "Who are you? Their bodyguard?"

I stepped up beside him and folded my arms, trying not to sway as I swallowed a hiccup. "He's your worst nightmare."

Flamingo's laugh tore through the room, and Ryan snorted so hard behind me he began to choke. "That was lame," he coughed.

The brunette pulled herself free, her blond friend already grabbing both their bags. They shot grateful looks our way before skirting around their table and disappearing into the night.

"That was some bullshit," Flamingo spat in our direction, taking our measure. "Dumbass army cunts. So busy taking it up the ass you wouldn't know how to fuck a woman if you tried."

"Oh hell no." Ryan grabbed his drink and stood abruptly. I don't think he realised how shit-faced he was because he staggered, clipping his foot on Jake's chair. The amber liquid in his glass flew forward in an arc, drenching part of Flamingo's shirt. It also flooded the lap of his thug friend beside him, who charged from his chair, flicking out a knife before anyone could blink.

I kicked out my leg, making impact with his fist before he got a full swipe at Ryan's gut. The knife flew from his hand, nicking him in the process. He howled and came at me.

I was still smarting from my loss to Jake, so my fist slammed into his gut extra hard. I watched him go down with a wheezy exhale. Flamingo took offence and clipped me in the jaw. Jake lunged, grabbing him by the collar and slamming him into our own table. I felt the entire bar rattle and shake when he crashed to the floor in a pile of snapped timber and wasted beer.

Broken glass crunched beneath boots when his friends came back for more. I seized one by the throat and took a powerful swing. The bone-cracking blow sent his head snapping sideways, and he crumpled when I let go. Flamingo grabbed me from behind in a chokehold, growling with rage.

"Stop creeping on women in bars, you sleazy sonofabitch," I wheezed, seizing his arm and tossing him over my shoulder. He crashed into another table. "Newsflash. It's called sexual assault."

He rose on his hands and knees, gasping. "I barely touched her."

Security pushed through the crowd, but they had no clue how to calm the escalating situation. Punches were being thrown. Innocent bystanders got caught in the melee and joined in. The knife made a return, slicing through the cotton of my favourite shirt. "You're gonna pay for that," I growled at Flamingo's buddy.

I lunged and someone swiped my feet out from beneath me. I hit the ground, my head clipping the leg of a broken chair and tearing skin. Blood leached down my forehead and into my eye as the knife-wielder made to plunge his weapon in Ryan's back.

I kicked out at his knee. He crashed sideways, losing his weapon in the fall as Ryan turned, realising his near miss. I made a grab for it, kicking it away. It skittered across the booze-soaked floor, landing in a dark corner beneath a booth by the wall.

The wail of distant sirens pealed through the air. People scattered, leaving behind a warzone of splintered glass and smashed furniture.

Ryan reached out a hand. I took it and he launched me from the sticky floor. We both staggered a little as a big booming laugh busted from his chest. He slapped me on the back, quoting the movie *Babe*. "That'll do, Pig. That'll do."

I was inducted into their little girl gang after that, the brawl seeming to cement my place. But six months later I was still trying to best Jake at the rifle range. I was sure I had him that particular day. It was late in the afternoon, the sun behind us and no breeze to speak of. I shot up from my prone position on the ground, kicking up dust as I did the running man on the spot. Victory was finally mine.

"Maybe you should check the targets before you go celebrating, hotshot," Jake suggested.

"No need. Today's my lucky day. Drinks on you tonight."

Except the joke was on me. When our targets were returned, Jake had pipped me by one shot. One single lousy little shot. "Fucking golden boy," I muttered, crumpling the sheet in my fist.

"The only time you'd ever beat me is if I were dead," he said with a laugh, his face covered in dirt and the late sun creating a halo around his blond head.

Jesus fucking Christ. I rip myself free of the memories to find my eyes pricking with heat and Jamie standing on the tarmac in front of me saying something I missed completely. "What?"

She cocks her head. "You were staring off into the distance. Are you okay?"

I want to say I'm fine, but that would be an injustice to Jake—as if he weren't important in my life. "No."

Jamie puts a hand on my forearm and squeezes. She's making the effort to forgive—or at least trying to—and I'm grateful. I want our friendship back. I'm not gonna lie. I need it right now.

"It hurts to see you hurting."

"Then I'll stop," I quip, trying for a light-hearted tone.

"I'm sorry." She gives me another squeeze before letting go. "I know Jake was like a brother to you."

"It hasn't sunk in yet. I keep turning around to tell him something funny and he's not there." I tug inside my pocket, pulling out a bit of paper. I hand it to Jamie and she looks at it. It has my email and phone number. "I know it's selfish to ask, but would you—"

"I'll try." She pockets the scrap of information. "I'm not really great at communication, Brooks."

"It feels better not to talk. To anyone. About anything."

"Okay."

"What are you doing?"

"Sitting here, not talking to you. Trying to see if it feels better."

"You're better at it than you think." The plane starts up. I pick my bag up in my left hand and cup her face with my right, tracing my fingers across the soft skin of her cheek before I let go, raising my voice to be heard over the engines. "Will you still come back to WA for your leave?"

She hesitates. "I don't know if I can."

"Come." I start walking backwards, hating to leave her here, especially with Jake gone. I know she doesn't need me. She has Wood. My replacement. I'm not jealous. Not even a little bit. Okay, maybe I am. But he seems like a stand-up guy. Maybe not as great as me. But he'll do, I guess. "We can hang out. No fence this time."

"About the fence." She scrunches her nose. "I kinda burned it to the ground."

I stop. "Ummm what?"

"I'll tell you about it some time."

"Over drinks. My shout."

Jamie nods. "In that case, I only drink from the top shelf."

Typical. Like Jake and his damn craft beer. I resume walking backwards. "Can I just ask you one thing?"

The wind picks up and blows hair across her face. She tugs it free and shrugs her response.

"Why did you join the army?" I shout to be heard.

"I was trying to find myself, just like you."

"And did you?"

"No." She hugs her arms around her middle. "Did you?"

"No."

Someone yells at me from behind to get a move on. I raise my arm in a brief, casual salute. "Bye, Jamie."

Jamie returns it. "See you later, Kyle."

She's my last image before the ramp of the plane rises up and closes us inside. A lone soldier walking across the tarmac, shoulders straight as she holds all the hurt inside and goes to do her job.

19

KYLE

With my ass planted in bed and my back smushed into my pillows, I slide my MacBook onto my lap, anticipation in my gut. Jamie has sent me an email. I don't know what it is about mail, whether it be electronic or paper, it just feels good to get something personal. To know someone out there thinks you matter enough to tell you about their day.

Brooks,

It's really dusty here today. Like extra dusty.

Murphy

What in the actual fuck was that? It's like I blinked and missed it. I jab my finger on the page-down button, but it scrolls to nowhere.

Not *really great* at communication? The girl sucked ass. She had at least opened the lines though, I guess.

Murphy,

I think you really over-sold yourself about being defective in the communication department. I'd classify that email as hitting rock bottom on the first attempt. The plus side is that the only way to go from here is up.

Just pretend you're talking to me from the other side of the fence.

You remember the fence, right? The one you allegedly burned to the ground ... Please tell me you're coming back to WA after decompression. I'm eager for the story. I need a good laugh.

I'm sure you're in need of one too, so here's a story for you, courtesy of my second deployment to Afghanistan.

Once upon a time, there was a handsome, heroic young soldier on a quest— Just kidding. I was actually in the shithole bathroom on base, innocently brushing my teeth, when Ryan barged in. He was wielding an electric toothbrush. Not his, and I knew because his was an Iron Man toothbrush. I'd bought it for him myself. I'd bought one Avenger toothbrush for each member of our team (mine was Thor if you were wondering ... for obvious reasons). Anyway, he switched it on and proceeded to scrub under the rim of the toilet with the bristles as if I wasn't even there.

"What the fuck are you doing?" I asked.

"Hazing the new guy," he said with a grin.

"Dude, you know he could get seriously ill from the bacteria in that toilet."

His reply was quick and to the point. "You didn't."

Can you believe I didn't actually punch him? I gagged and threw my Thor toothbrush in the bin, rinsing my mouth until my jaw ached. It wasn't the same brush I was using when I started my first deployment with the treacherous asshole (clearly) but I felt it paid to be cautious. I had to spend the rest of my deployment using a crappy, generic brush that did my teeth no justice at all.

The motto of my story, Little Warrior, is trust no one (except me obvs). Also, protect your toothbrush as if it's your very own child and everyone around you is a homicidal kidnapper.

Your (wise and wonderful) friend,

Brooks

There's no mention of Jake in the email. It feels wrong to avoid any talk about him, but the pain is too raw. His funeral is tomorrow and my heart is heavy. My dress uniform is dry-cleaned and hanging in my closet. A stark reminder of what's to come.

Jake will be buried with full military honours at Karrakatta ceremony. The service won't be televised, but it's going to be videoed for those that can't attend. There's a helluva lot of people wanting to pay their respects—the Prime Minister, the Minister for Defence, the Defence Force Chief, the Chief of Army, and hundreds of soldiers, family, and friends. Jake was loved, and he's missed from our team like an amputated limb that keeps giving phantom pains.

~

BROOKS,

I see your healthy ego managed to double in size over the years.

On another note, your story made me throw up a little in my mouth. Ryan is evil. I like him. I hope he continues to bust your chops on the regular.

It's still dusty here.

Murphy

PS What toothbrush did you give Jake? I'm betting it was Captain America.

~

I TUG off my army hat and seat myself on the edge of my bed, the funeral over. Ryan steps into my room. I glance up before resuming my solid stare at the floor, elbows on my knees.

He sets himself down beside me and lets out a long breath. We're both now staring at the floor. "Fuck that was hard."

I want to curl myself into a ball and cry like a damn baby. I settle for loosening the knot of my tie. "Yeah."

Ryan swallows. "Jake was …"

"I know."

He slaps a hand down on my knee and pushes himself up. "Get changed. We'll go drink."

He leaves my room.

Ryan is *not* okay. He's shut down. A total brick wall. All he talks about is returning to Afghanistan. The walls are closing in here. He wants to get back over there and do something, and I know the feeling. Hopelessness. Anger. Futility. As if being stuck here not actively fighting in the war is a dishonour to Jake's memory.

~

MURPHY,

The size of my (healthy) ego is in proportion to other important parts of my body. Just an FYI.

Yeah. He got Captain America. I used to joke that the sun shone out of his ass so it seemed appropriate. I know life isn't meant to be a competition, but he won everything. You can imagine the constant blows my (flagging) ego had to suffer through. The bets I always lost. The money. I was trying to save for a house.

I took great satisfaction in discovering his shitty efforts in the kitchen. He even burnt ramen. I know because I was at his cottage when he did it. Granted we'd had a bit to drink, but it's only noodles. Not haute cuisine!

He put them in the bowl, added the flavour and vegetables, and stuck it in the microwave. I was raiding his cupboards for snacks while we waited (the two-minute cooking time was too long) when this nasty burning smell invaded his little kitchen.

I grabbed the bowl out, and DUDE! He forgot to add water. Even 1 knew you had to add water.

We still ate it (after adding water and re-cooking it). We were hungry.

So ... One more week of deployment. Have you made a decision about where you're spending your leave? (hint hint: here)

Your (well-endowed) friend,

Brooks

~

It's eight a.m. and I'm at the butcher's when my phone dings from my back pocket. Having spent five minutes trying to choose between pork, berry, and truffle chilli sausage, or lamb, mint, and halloumi sausage, the distraction is a welcome relief. What the hell is truffle chilli anyway? Or halloumi for that matter? Who the hell even cares? I just want to barbeque some meat for fuck's sake, not entertain the Queen.

"Give me a minute," I tell the guy behind the counter. I step away and the customer behind me takes my spot, shooting me a dark look for taking too long. I've formed quite the queue with my indecision. Not that it matters what I choose. I'm planning to visit Fin for dinner at the cottage. Word on the street is that she isn't eating. Tonight is my attempt to feed her. Myself too because it's been hard to care about food since losing Jake just a few short weeks ago.

Grief seems to rip your taste buds out along with your heart. Nothing tastes good, but I force it down my throat, same as Ryan does. Our bodies need to function so we don't fall down on the job.

I tug my phone free. A notification from Messenger sits on my screen. It's from Jamie, the message a first. My brows wing up in surprise, yet I can't help the smile that steals across from face.

Jamie Murphy: I'm returning to WA for my leave.

I delve inside our conversation settings on the screen, adjusting our names to our old nicknames for each other. Then I stab out a reply, hitting delete more than once because my fingers are too large for the tiny, stupid keypad.

Bear: You made the right choice.

Dots appear. She's replying. I press my back against the wall of the butcher's, letting all the impatient customers in the store go before me. It's hard not to yell at each and every one of them. Who cares about standing in line for an extra fucking minute or two when there are good people out there fighting for their country? *Dying* for their goddamn country? How can they not see how lucky they are? Why are they not grateful for every minute of life they have?

My phone dings, Jamie's message calming the anger burning in my chest.

Little Warrior: I didn't book the flights. Wood did. And they're non-refundable.

So he gave her no choice. I bet that riled her cute, stubborn ass. Way to go, Wood.

Bear: Send me your flight details. I'll pick you up from the airport.

Little Warrior: Erin can do that.

I pout like a toddler being denied his favourite toy.

Bear: But I want to.

Little Warrior: It makes sense for Erin to do it. We're staying at her place after all.

"Mate, you want to order those sausages now?"

I look up from my phone. The store has cleared. All the impatient customers are probably stuck in their cars now, tapping their fingers against their steering wheels, stuck in Saturday morning traffic as they fight their way home.

"Yeah, sure. One sec."

Bear: Fine. I'll give you a day to settle in. Also, what is halloumi?

Little Warrior: It's a salty type of cheese.

It hits me then. Afghanistan is almost four hours behind us. It's four a.m. back on base. My fingers tap the question out quickly.

Bear: What are you doing awake?

She doesn't respond straight away, so I tuck my phone back in my pocket and step up to the counter, ordering the lamb and halloumi. Next up, the bakery. I ask for a freshly baked loaf of white bread.

"Sliced?" the server asks.

"Sure, thanks."

"Thick or thin?"

"Thick please, mate," I reply, because I like carbs. They help me push harder in the gym, and that place has been my second home of late.

After tucking the food away in the saddlebags of my motorcycle, I swing a leg over and kick up the stand. I know I told Jamie that Jake was a shitty cook, but I wasn't much better. Sausages on buttered bread was my signature dish. My only dish, pretty much, and only marginally better than burnt ramen.

I turn the key. The engine responds with a throaty growl, vibrating deep down inside my soul, soothing me the tiniest bit. The Harley is big and black. A beast. She's also brand new. I might appreciate vintage machinery as much as the next guy, but I also appreciate my bike staying underneath me—thank you very much—the parts where they're supposed to be rather than littering the road behind me.

After arriving back at the barracks, I toss the bread on the counter of the small galley kitchen. The sausages go in the little fridge. I tug my shirt over my head and toss it to the floor. I'm switching out my jeans for gym shorts when my phone dings. I tug them on and grab my phone from the counter.

Little Warrior: I can't sleep. I should probably get a workout in, but I can't seem to move. Tell me about that house you were saving for?

A heavy sigh escapes me. I hate the thought of her stuck there. It leaves me feeling helpless, which is the absolute worst. If my emails or messages help bring even the smallest smile to her face, then it's got to be better than nothing … right?

I take a seat out on the tiny balcony of my lodgings at the barracks. There's room for two craptastic little chairs. They're white, plastic, and have seen better days, having been stuck outside in the elements for well over a year. I take a seat in one, the sun hitting my bare chest as I kick my legs up on the railing and cross them at the ankles.

Bear: It's going to cost me a bit, this house.

Little Warrior: Why's that?

Bear: Because I want to live by the beach. My bedroom has to have a balcony that overlooks the ocean. I want to lie in bed at night with the doors wide open while I listen to the waves crash against the shore.

Little Warrior: You like the beach?

Bear: Yeah. I've never told anyone this, but sometimes I'll grab a towel and go crash on the beach at night. It helps me sleep. Don't know why. It gets a bit cold in the early hours, but nothing beats waking to the hazy pink and orange across the horizon. I want to be able to do that every day without getting sand stuck in my crack.

Little Warrior: Poor little Bear, getting a bum rash from sleeping on the beach.

Bear: Careful. You cracked a joke. Isn't that your quota for the year?

Little Warrior: Ha!

She laughed. It makes me feel like I've achieved something important.

Bear: So this house has to have at least five bedrooms. And it doesn't have to be some impressive mansion. Just a home. I don't need to compete with the neighbours on either side of me. My dick is plenty big enough.

Little Warrior: Five?!?! That seems a little excessive.

Bear: I want kids. Lots of 'em. I haven't told anyone this before either, but I want to be a dad. So bad.

I want to find a girl and fall in love. I want to know what it feels like to look at someone knowing I could never live without them. I want to get married. I want to watch her walk down the aisle towards me, my heart busting from my chest at the knowledge she was mine. I want to feel my babies growing inside her belly, and watch them grow with her by my side. I want to fill that house by the beach with all their little personalities. Take them camping. Teach them about the Earth, and life, and what it means to be a good person. I want it all.

Little Warrior: How many kids?

Bear: At least four.

Little Warrior: FOUR??

Bear: Yep. Maybe even five, but that's a big ask. It's not me who has to grow them.

Little Warrior: Three girls and a boy. That's what you should have.

Bear: I only get one boy?

Little Warrior: The world can only handle so many male Brooks at one time.

I laugh, pushing back on my chair.

Bear: I'm going to take that as a compliment rather than a joke. You have exceeded your wisecrack quota after all …

Little Warrior: You would make a good dad.

Her response fills me with pleasure.

Bear: I agree. I'm pretty great.

Little Warrior: I was going to say you had a whole lot of patience. I think "great" is taking it a little bit too far. Don't you?

Jamie's teasing makes me ache a little, but in a good way.

Bear: I'm glad Jake had you. I won't say he was lucky, but he was happy, Jamie.

It takes her a good minute to respond.

Little Warrior: I should go. Time to get up.

Shit. My last comment must have hurt. I rise from my seat and toss my phone on the bed, reaching for my sports shoes. Dressed, I go hit Ryan up for a run. We're gone for a good solid hour and return hot and sweaty, shirts off and tucked into the backs of our shorts.

"I'll be at Fin's place later this afternoon. Going to barbeque some lamb." We climb the stairs to the first floor. "Wanna come?"

"Nah." Ryan doesn't look at me. "I'm tired."

I huff, frustrated. Ryan has been crushing on Jake's sister for years. *Years.* And he's done nothing about it. Not even after she split with her old boyfriend.

"You sure? I swear I saw that shithead's car parked at her house the other day." Total lie. As if I'd be lurking around her street like a creeper. "What's his name again? Igor? Ignatius?" I know damn well his name is Ian. "You know, the guy Jake said you punched out at their family dinner because he threw a glass at her face." I decorate my comment with a clueless shrug. "Maybe they're getting back together. Or maybe he's being a pest and won't leave her alone."

Ryan grunts and opens the front door of the unit beside mine. "I know what you're trying to do, Brooks. You're about as subtle as a turd in a toilet bowl."

"Then grow a ballsack and come eat with us."

"Like I said, I'm tired."

"Whatever, dude."

He pauses, his jaw going tight. "Don't whatever me like a damn girl."

My brows rise. "Oh, *I'm* the girl here? That's rich."

Ryan's nostrils flare. I've pushed him into feeling something. Good. That's one brick I've managed to knock from his stupid-ass wall. Only a thousand more to go.

"One more wisecrack from your ugly face and I'll knock you the fuck out."

I lift my chin. "Do it if it makes you feel better."

Ryan comes at me in the blink of an eye. He grabs me by the throat and shoves me back against the side of the door, his face red with fury. My head cracks hard against the timber frame. "Nothing will make this shit feel better." He shoves me again. "Nothing."

My throat clicks as I swallow, my eyes starting to burn. *Fuck.* A deep shuddering breath rips out of me. As if he senses the crack in my composure, he lets me go and walks away. "Just leave me the hell alone."

"Consider it done," I rasp, not giving him the satisfaction of rubbing at the ache in my throat.

He stops and turns. "You know what your problem is?"

I don't, but I'm pretty sure he's about to clue me in. "You keep trying to fix everyone around you. Maybe you should try fixing yourself first."

"I'm not broken, Kendall."

Ryan snorts. "Mate. You try covering it all up with your loud attitude and shitty wisecracks, but you're barely held together with duct tape. We all are. Isn't that why any of us join the damn army in the first place? We're hoping it's going to perform some kind of miracle and piece us back together. But newsflash, Brooks, it doesn't. It only makes the cracks inside us bigger."

20

KYLE

I wake with a start when my phone dings. I roll over in bed, swiping a palm across my eyes and down the side of my face as I reach for it.

Little Warrior: I'm home.

Damned if my insides don't do an excited little leap. I yawn, scratching at my chest before I tap out a reply.

Bear: Like home home? Or home Australia home?

Little Warrior: I'm at Erin's apartment.

I rise up on one elbow, coming awake fully.

Bear: Why didn't you tell me?

She could have messaged when she flew into Townsville. Or from the airport before she left for Perth. Or when she got on the plane. I've been counting down the days like a kid at Christmastime.

Little Warrior: I'm telling you now.

Bear: Are you rolling your eyes at me? What time did you get in?

Little Warrior: Yes. And yesterday.

Bear: YESTERDAY?!?!

Little Warrior: Don't get your knickers in a knot. We got in late last night.

Bear: Another joke? Who ARE you?

Little Warrior: Har har. We had a couple of drinks at the airport bar before we flew out.

There's a blanket ban on alcohol during deployment, for obvious reasons, so you lose your tolerance for it. Coming back home is an exercise in building it back up again, so one or two drinks probably tipped her right over the edge.

Little Warrior: And maybe a couple more when we arrived.

I glance at the time. It's six a.m.

Bear: I'm coming over.

Little Warrior: I thought we were going to catch up tomorrow. You were going to give me a day to settle in, remember?

Bear: I think you're making up stories. Besides, it's time for breakfast. You can make pancakes, right?

Bear: Hello?

My chest tightens with impatience. I'm eager to see her. To resume the friendship we once had. I know it won't be the same. We've grown up. Changed. But the Little Warrior she used to be is still inside her. I see it in her emails and messages. The cheeky side is starting to show through more as she gets comfortable talking to me again. So is the stubborn. Jamie's the type that if you told her not to do something, she would not only do it twice, she'd take pictures too, all while giving you the middle finger.

I jump in the shower to wake myself up. When I'm out, I rub the towel over my naked body as I pad through my little unit, checking my phone like an eager puppy waiting for his treat.

Little Warrior: I think I just fell asleep standing up.

I shake my head, laughing as I toss my damp towel on the bed.

Little Warrior: You can come over I suppose.

Bear: Gee, when you say it like that …

Little Warrior: Stop pouting and come over. Pretty please with a cherry on top. Is that better?

Bear: Maybe. But I can sense you rolling your eyes again.

Little Warrior: Do you want pancakes or not?

I laugh to myself as I set my phone down. I'm pulling on a plain pair of black boxer-briefs when she responds with the address. Tugging on a pair of navy cargo shorts and shirt, I grab my keys, wallet, and phone before heading out.

Bear: I'll bring coffee.

I knock on Ryan's door and open it without waiting for an invitation. He's lying on his back on top of his sheets—a prone lump—naked and staring at the ceiling.

"You won't find the answer there," I quip.

"The answer to what?" he asks, his voice gravelly with exhaustion, the kind that settles so deep in your bones you struggle to sleep at all.

"To whether she loves you or not."

"Goddammit, Brooks." Ryan reaches for the pillow behind his head and fires it in my direction. I deflect it with ease and it drops harmlessly to the floor. Stepping over it, I swipe the set of keys from his bedside table. "What do you think you're doing?"

"I want to borrow your car."

"No."

"Too bad." I dangle his keys from my finger with a smirk. I don't actually expect Jamie to cook breakfast. It'll be easier to buy a tray of coffee and pastries and bring them to her, but not so easy to juggle it all on my bike. "So thanks."

I turn and leave, whistling as I go.

"Scratch her and I'll put you in the ground," he yells, half of his sentence muffled because I've already shut the door.

Ryan owns a black vintage Mustang. Beautifully restored, her muscled lines sleek and glossy, her powerful engine a siren song. He keeps her in storage during deployment, tucking her away beneath a heavy cover as if she's more precious than the crown jewels of England. If I so much as get a dent on her gleaming paintwork, I may as well keep driving across state lines and disappear into a whole new life.

The traffic this early is sparse, and I'm at Erin's apartment just over half an hour later, juggling hot coffee and breakfast as I knock on the door.

It opens and Jamie stands there in short denim shorts, a little white tank top, her hair down in a messy tangle around her face, and her hand gripping the doorknob as if it's keeping her upright. She also has sunglasses covering half her face. She tilts her head up to look at me. "Brooks."

"Murphy." I mock squint. "Is that you under all the hair and shades?"

"Funny." Her nostrils flare as she breathes deep. "You brought coffee."

"I said I would."

She steps back, waving an arm out wide. "You may enter."

I walk inside. It's not a large apartment, but it's classy. The kitchen cupboards are bright white, the counter a glossy granite and overlooks the living area. The coffee table is decorated with used shot glasses, a half-empty bottle of vodka, and an almost empty bowl of crackers; only the dregs remain.

The couch is a light beige fabric and covered in blankets and a squashed pillow. "You slept on the couch?" I ask, setting my goodies down on the kitchen counter, along with my wallet and keys.

"Wood did. I shared a bed with Erin."

I grin and waggle my eyebrows. "Did you now?"

"Oh stop it and give me one of those coffees."

I grab one from the tray and hold it aloft. "Only if you give me a hug."

"We may be friends, but we're not the hugging kind."

"We *are* the hugging kind because I just said so. Now give me one before I drink all the coffee and leave you with none."

"It's too early to be a bossy asshole," she complains.

"Just like it's too early to be a stubborn poophead."

Jamie huffs and slides one arm around my middle, giving me a weak squeeze before letting go. "There. Now gimme."

I sigh and hand it over. "That was pathetic."

"You're pathetic," she retorts before taking a sip and groaning like it's manna from Heaven.

I take another coffee from the tray, her insult sliding off like Teflon. "Where's Wood and Erin?" I ask as she shuffles towards the couch like an old woman, fingers curled around her takeout cup.

"The beach. They've gone for an early swim. Wood couldn't wait to get in the ocean, and Erin wanted to clear her head after our drinking fest last night. She has to work today."

I follow, walking over to the window and peeling back the blinds. Jamie hisses like a vampire and scrunches herself back into the cushions. I turn around and chuckle at her whimpering form.

"That was mean, Brooks."

"What? It's a beautiful day outside. Not a cloud in the sky. Let's have something to eat and go for a walk."

She shuts me down. "No."

"C'mon. The fresh air will help your hangover."

"I'm not hungover," she croaks. "Just tired."

I take a seat beside her, setting my coffee on the little table in front of me. I flick the ridiculous sunglasses from her face. They're not hers. It's not her style, so they must belong to Erin.

"Wow," I say quietly and brush my hand across her cheek, looking into her eyes. They're red and slitted, and even the bags beneath them have bags. "You look like hell."

Jamie turns her head away and looks out the window. "Well that's not nice."

I rise from the couch and collect the box of pastries from the counter. I bully her into eating one while I take the other three. We finish our coffees and after putting the rubbish in the bin, I take her hands and pull her to her feet.

She sighs deeply. "You're such a bully."

"Yeah, what an asshole. Bringing you breakfast and making you eat it. I should be shot."

We both pause at the horrible slip, and I don't miss the pain that flickers across her face before it disappears. Her voice wavers. "I don't want to be here, Brooks."

"What do you mean?" My brows pull together. "Here? In Erin's apartment?"

"No." She shakes her head. "Here."

"Perth?"

"Australia. I want to go back to Afghanistan."

I suck in a breath. "Why?"

"I feel like I don't belong here. They said it would take time to adjust being back home, but on base is where most of my memories of Jake are. Being here makes it feel like I'm losing him."

"Jamie," I say quietly, tugging her close. I wrap my arms around her while hers remain limp at her side. She feels fragile against me, as if her bones will shatter like glass at any moment. I press my lips to the top of her head, breathing in the vanilla scent of her hair, along with the over-powering odour of booze and crackers. I'm pretty sure there's a few crumbs lodged in the strands around her scalp. "You can't lose the memories inside your heart." The words feel like an empty platitude, but I don't know what else to say. Jake is gone and it's just too fucking hard to take.

"I know that," she retorts, her voice muffled as she speaks into my chest. "It's just … I feel this weird kind of panic whenever I think of him. So it's easier not to. But that means pushing him out, and—"

"And that's why you feel like you're losing him."

"Yes." Her fingers clutch at the sides of my shirt. "Stupid, huh?"

"There's no such thing as stupid when it comes to grief. We all deal with it in our own way."

Jamie releases my shirt and steps free of my hold. "How do you deal with yours?"

"Shitty wisecracks and a loud attitude apparently," I mutter.

"What?"

"Nothing." I turn her around and nudge her towards the solitary little bedroom in the whole shoebox of an apartment. "Go get some shoes on your feet. We're going walking."

We're gone for almost two hours, walking along the Swan River. I have to keep slowing my pace. Jamie's handicapped by her shorter frame and her hangover. We don't talk much, but it's a comfortable silence. When we return, Erin has already been and gone to work, and Wood has messaged Jamie to let her know he's gone out for groceries.

"What do you want to do now?"

Jamie toes off her shoes by the front door. "Shower and sleep."

"We can do that."

"You don't have to stay."

"You kicking me out?"

She looks at me. "No. But I don't need you spending your day off babysitting me."

"True." I shrug. "And you are kind of a bore."

"Speak for yourself," she retorts.

I go to the fridge and grab a couple of waters, handing her one before I crack the lid on mine and tip my head back, throat working as I guzzle half the bottle in one go. When I straighten, Jamie's looking at me. "What?"

"You look just how I expected you would in all my years of imagining it. I can't believe I didn't see it when I met you over on base."

I waggle my brows. "You imagined how I looked? Were they sexy images?" My lids lower to half-mast. "I'm betting they were."

"Stop!" Jamie cries, laughter sputtering from her lips. "We're not like that!"

I chuckle. "I know." I take another sip of my water. "Go shower, stinky."

She walks off with an eye roll.

"Try not to think of me while you're soaping yourself up in the shower!" I call to her back.

Another laugh. "Gross, Brooks."

I take a seat on the couch, playing on my phone while she cleans up. Getting bored of the game, I send a message to Ryan.

Kyle: Dinged your car. Oops.

His reply is instantaneous and makes me laugh.

Ryan: What the fuck?

Kyle: Yeah, sorry 'bout that. It's pretty bad. We hit a roo.

Ryan: You WHAT?

Kyle: You know kangaroos, right? The furry things that hop about the countryside eating grass and leaves and shit.

He seems to cotton on then, realising I'm just stirring up shit.

Ryan: You're such a motherfucker.

Kyle: You should have seen your face!

Ryan: You know you can't actually see my face, asshole.

Kyle: I know. But I'm betting it's good.

Ryan: You're never borrowing my car again. You know that, right?

Kyle: Don't be a baby.

He stops talking to me after that, and I set my phone down, realising the shower has stopped and the bedroom door is closed. I get up and knock gently. Jamie doesn't answer, so I open the door slowly, prepared for a shoe to come flying at my face because she's in the process of getting dressed, but it doesn't happen.

I peek in. She's on the bed, lying on her belly, braless in another white tank top and pale pink underwear that highlights the curve of a round, toned backside. A gentle snore emits from her lips.

I walk over and take a seat on the edge, kicking off my shoes. I peel off my shirt and climb on beside her, bunching the pillow beneath my head. As if sensing the warm, heavy weight at her side, she snuggles close, burrowing in just a little. It feels nice, so I close my eyes.

I'm woken by a hand on my shoulder, giving me a gentle shake.

Fuck.

I come awake with a start, reaching for the gun beneath my pillow. It's not there. I turn, coming face to face with a pretty blonde. I open my mouth to speak, and she puts a finger to her lips, tipping her head at the sleeping form beside me.

Nodding my understanding, I peel myself from the bed, nice and slow, as if Jamie is a bomb about to detonate at the slightest provocation.

After tugging on my shirt, I check the time on my watch. Jesus, it's five p.m. We've been asleep for *hours*.

Shutting the door behind me, I follow the blonde out. She continues to the kitchen, where Wood stands by the stovetop, pushing something around in a frypan with a pair of tongs.

"Good to see you back, Wood," I tell him, reaching out a hand.

He shakes it. "You too, mate," he says and goes back to his sizzling pan.

I give my attention to the female beside him. "You must be Erin."

A chopping board sits on the counter in front her, vegetables chopped in a pile on its surface and a very sharp looking knife beside it. She picks it up. "And you must be the infamous Bear."

I wince. Erin was there when I left, and she was probably just as pissed about it as Jamie was. Still, I offer a hand in an effort to be polite. "I'm Kyle."

She looks at it as if it's an insect that crawled into her neat pile of broccoli. Wood gives her a nudge, and she sets her deadly weapon down and takes my hand with a sniff. "Erin."

"The only reason she's not stabbing you right now is because Jamie's sleeping like the dead," Wood tells me as he turns pieces of browned chicken over with his tongs.

My brows pull together. "What do you mean?"

"It's been a long time since she's slept like this," Wood admits, his eyes flicking towards the bedroom, worried about being overheard. "We think it might be because you were with her."

My brows pull together. I don't like the idea of her not being able to sleep. "You think?"

Erin sighs, a heavy, unhappy sound. "It seems so."

I give her my attention, knowing I need to do the right thing and clear the air between us. "For what it's worth, I'm sorry, Erin. I shouldn't have left Jamie the way I did."

"Your apology isn't worth shit," Erin snaps. "Jamie cancelled her sixteenth birthday party because of you." She picks up the knife and severs a carrot in half. "You know how often every little girl dreams of her sixteenth birthday?"

"Erin," Wood says in a tone of rebuke. "You know Jamie wasn't the kind to dream about parties."

"Well, I dreamt about the party for her. Planned it. Helped her pick out a dress to wear that cost her more money than she ever dared to spend." The knife points in my direction. "You didn't see the way her eyes lit up when she tried it on because it didn't just make her look beautiful, it made her *feel* beautiful too." Erin huffs and goes back to chopping her carrots until they're lying in a little butchered heap. "Then she never showed up at my house, so I had to go looking for her. I found her sitting on the floor of her bedroom, your stupid letter clutched in her hand. We had to cancel the whole thing. Do you know how that made me feel? I was the one who convinced her to invite you because she was scared you would reject her. Reject her!" Erin says with a harsh snort. Shame sours my stomach like curdled milk. "Only you did worse than that. You fucking left her!" Her words lash me like a whip across my back. "I was the one who stuck around to pick up the pieces while you—"

"Enough!" We all turn at the blunt sound. Jamie is standing by the door in her tank top and knickers, hair mussed and face pale.

"Now you've gone and woken her!" Erin snaps.

"Erin!" Jamie walks over, eyes on her friend, her voice sharper than the knife now resting on the chopping board. "Can you imagine what it would be like for you if I died in Afghanistan? How would *you* feel if I never made it home?"

Erin pauses as if imagining just that. Her bottom lip quavers. "I'm not sure I'd handle it, to be honest."

Jamie jabs a finger in my direction. "That's how Kyle is feeling right now. One of his best friends just died right in front of him, and while I appreciate you sticking up for me, it's unnecessary, and your timing is horrible. He doesn't need your shit right now."

Erin pales as if slapped. She looks at me after a long moment, regret burning bright in her eyes. "I'm sorry."

My jaw works. Jamie's arrival back in Perth had kept my grief deep below the murky waters for most of the day. Not taking up all my thoughts for once. It had been like it used to be when we were younger, talking and teasing, with me pretending everything was okay. But now the grief is rising all over again. I swallow, wanting to say something flippant. Joke it off like I always do. But I can't. My heart is aching too much right now.

"Forget it," I rasp and reach for my wallet and keys. "I should get going."

"Kyle, wait!" Erin calls out.

I wave her off without turning around. I open the door and step outside the apartment and into the hall. Jamie follows, shutting the door behind us. She grabs for my hand. I tug it free. I can't handle her gentle touch right now. I'm pretty sure I'll fall apart if she so much as wraps her fingers around mine.

"I'm sorry," she says. "I wasn't expecting Erin to unleash like that. I mean, I knew she was pissed when you left, but she never said anything more about it. I figured she was over it."

I jab at the down button for the lift. "I'm pretty sure she's not."

"I won't ask you to stay, but can I see you tomorrow?"

"It's Monday tomorrow. I have work," I say to the lift doors as they open with a *ding*.

"Maybe later?"

I step inside and turn. "A long day of work," I emphasise, being harsh with her in my need to escape and lick my wounds.

"Kyle, please." Her eyes are dark and pleading, and dammit, I fold like a cheap suit.

"Dinner," I say, jabbing the button for the ground floor as the doors begin to close. "I'll pick you up."

21

KYLE

"This feels weird," Jamie declares as we arrive at a romantic candlelit table, led there by a waiter who's too busy flourishing proper linen napkins and brandishing hardcover menus to notice our bemused expressions. The restaurant lighting is so dim I'm surprised the couples seated at the surrounding tables are able to read them. "Like a date."

Pink rose centrepieces fill delicate crystal vases, and music plays softly in the background. I'm pretty sure it's the theme song to *Titanic*. Celine Dion is giving her all (albeit softly due to the low volume), zealously letting us know that her heart will go on and on and on.

"Incredibly weird," I agree, wincing as the waiter pulls out Jamie's seat.

She sits down, giving him a baleful glare as he tries to lay a napkin in her lap. She snatches it from his outstretched hand, muttering, "I can do that, thank you very much."

The whole situation is more awkward than the time when I was thirteen and tried to tongue kiss Margaret Ainsworth (an older woman at fourteen) for the first time and accidently gave her a sloppy lick on the nose. To give me a bit of credit, we were out the back of the rugby sheds after a night game and it was pitch black. I couldn't actually see where her lips were. Though I probably shouldn't have come at her like a dog, my mouth wide open and tongue hanging out.

I talked up a big game, but I'd never actually kissed a girl before then. My sexual experience at that point was relegated to feverish little nocturnal emissions with my hand beneath the heavy blankets of my bed.

Margaret avoided me forever after that night, and everyone at school wanted to know why. I never thanked her for not blabbing, but I figured it was in her best interests not to. Who would admit to getting licked on the nose? It spoke of her lack of experience when she gagged and rubbed at her face, running off into the night rather than taking pity on me and giving me a few pointers.

"Sorry." I give the waiter an apologetic look and take Jamie's hand, tugging her from the delicate wooden chair. The heavy napkin drops from her lap and lands beneath the table. "Let's get out of here."

We flee the restaurant as if our asses are on fire, laughing like naughty school kids skipping class.

"What made you pick that place?" she asks as we start down the street.

"I didn't. Ryan said it was …" My eyes narrow and my lips pinch tight. "Sonofabitch." I tug my phone free of my pocket and tap out a message, keeping it direct and to the point.

Kyle: You'll pay for this, asshole.

Ryan: You should see your face!

Kyle: Har har

I deserved that. That's the problem with dishing out shit. You have to be prepared for it to come back tenfold.

We keep walking until we find a rowdy outdoor bar with twinkling fairy lights and tables crammed with patrons. The menus are written in chalk on big boards, and you have to order your food at the counter. It's much more my style, and the way Jamie's shoulders loosen as we wait at the bar for a table tells me it's much more hers too.

There's lingering tension after last night, so I aim for small talk while we share an extra-large plate of nachos and a pitcher of margaritas. "So … you want kids? You never said."

"Kids can be cool. I love their innocence and their honesty."

I reach for another corn chip. "How many you want?" I ask, before tossing it in my mouth and crunching down.

Jamie finishes her drink. She tops up my glass before pouring herself another. "None."

I pause my chewing, unable to fathom the desire to be childless. "None? Kids are great, Murphy. You get to do fun stuff with them that you can't do as an adult, like animated movies, water slides, toy stores. If you're sitting down, you've got someone to play fetch for you. And you get to have macaroni and cheese all the time because that's all they eat."

Her expression is aghast. "Brooks, I fear for the health of your future children."

I laugh. "Seriously though. Those chubby little faces. The way their eyes light up when they see you, as if you're their whole world." My voice turns wistful. I can't help it. "Their little arms wrapping around your neck at night while they beg you for another bedtime story. I can't wait."

Jamie hesitates. "I can't be in the army and have kids, Brooks."

"Why the hell not?"

"Deployments. Reassignments. That's no life for a family. For kids. I'm not one of those women who can do it all."

"You don't need to do it all. You'll have a partner by your side doing it with you."

She snorts as if it's something that will never happen. "Relationships aren't for me, Brooks. There won't be any partner."

Not if it can't be Jake. She doesn't speak the words, but I see them written across her face.

It doesn't take a psychologist to understand that the men in her life always leave. She's trying to protect herself, and I get that, but knowing I'm a contributor to her current state of mind makes me feel like an ass. "You don't know that."

"Yes, I do," she says and picks up her drink, gulping half of it down in one swallow.

I'm hoping time will change her mind, but Jamie has Jake up on a pedestal, which is worrying. I mean, the man wasn't entirely perfect. There's the whole noodle thing. And who knows, maybe he would have run faster than Usain Bolt at the first sign of commitment. Maybe he kicked small puppies when no one was watching. I know he donated to the RSPCA once a year, but it could have been guilt money.

"Okay, so maybe you wind up a sad old cat lady, but there's nothing in the rule book that says you have to re-enlist," I say, trying for diplomacy. I stuff a loaded corn chip in my mouth, chewing and swallowing while she shakes her head at me, her own mouth full. "The army doesn't have to be your whole life. You don't have to be a combat medic forever. Do something else."

Jamie swirls a chip in the bean cause, her chin jutting out a little. "I don't want to do anything else."

Stubborn little ass. I refrain from reaching across the table and shaking some sense into her head because she'd probably karate-chop me into next week. I settle for changing the subject, delving into deeper, darker waters with my next question. "What about your mum? You don't talk about her."

Jamie picks up her drink and takes a large sip. "That's because there's nothing to talk about. She signed away all her parental rights for a wad of cash that she probably blew through in the first year after she left. Last I heard she was somewhere in Europe. She emails occasional-ly." Jamie shrugs. "But I don't read them."

I open my mouth to speak, and she cuts in over the top of me. "And don't go telling me I should. I don't have unresolved issues when it comes to my mother. I made my peace with her leaving. Some people just aren't born to be parents, and that's something I actually understand."

I open my mouth again and her brows snap together. "Why are you attacking me with your probing questions, Brooks? Why don't you tell me about your dad, huh? You never talk about him either."

"Well, if you ever let me get a word in, I was about to tell you that I get the whole thing with your mother."

"Oh." A sheepish expression crosses her face as she goes to refill my glass. I put a hand over the top. "I'm driving. Plus I have work tomorrow. You finish it."

She tops her glass, emptying the pitcher. "So, your dad?"

"He lives in the Northern Territory. He's remarried. Has young kids."

"So you actually do have brothers and sisters?"

"Yeah, two brothers. I've never met them. Dad left the first time Mum got cancer. I guess he didn't envision his future being endless hospital visits, trips to chemo, and a house smelling of antiseptic because we always had to be careful of germs. Mum banning every type of unhealthy food from the kitchen was the last straw. They fought. He yelled something about feeling imprisoned. Then he left."

Jamie reaches across, taking my hand. "I'm sorry you had to go through that."

Dad leaving is old news. Just like her, I've made my peace. "We're better off without people like that in our lives."

"Agreed."

With dinner finished, we pay at the counter and walk back to my bike. Jamie climbs on the back after it settles beneath my heavy weight. Her arms slide around my middle as the engine roars to life, her hands linking at my waist. I place a hand on both of hers and turn my head, giving her a sideways glance. All I catch with my eyes is her profile, but there's a smile on her lips. One of anticipation.

"You good?" I ask loudly.

She grins. "Giddyup, cowboy."

I laugh, feeling carefree and happy for the first time in weeks, and with it comes an overwhelming sense of guilt. Guilt that I'm still alive and Jake isn't. That I'm here with Jamie when it should be him instead. But spending time with her has made the loss easier to bear. She makes me realise how important her friendship is to me now that I have it back. It's something I'll never let go of again.

I take the scenic route back to the apartment, navigating the beach streets, giving Jamie time to appreciate the ride.

"I don't want this to end," she says at the next red light, her voice fighting to be heard and husky from the chilled night air.

"Me either."

But the light turns green, and minutes later I'm pulling up out the front of Erin's building. I tug my helmet free and glance up to the ninth floor. The lights are on, the blinds open. I switch off the engine. "Wood and Erin stayed in tonight, huh?"

"Yeah," she says, climbing off, handing me the spare helmet. "Wood has smarts. He's helping Erin with her business plan for the retreat she wants to buy. The one I was telling you about a couple of weeks ago."

"Business plan." I waggle my brows. "That's what the kids are calling it these days?"

"Brooks!" She jabs me in the shoulder. "You can take the smallest thing and turn it into an innuendo."

I grin. "That's my superpower."

"Not everything's about sex."

"It should be."

She rolls her eyes, but I can see the amusement in the pull of her lips. "They're just friends."

"That's not how it looked last night."

"How would you know how it looked last night? You were with them all of five minutes."

"Five minutes was long enough to see the way they communicated with each other without even talking. Their body language was positive, Murphy. Erin might have been in a pissed-off mood, but the vibes between them were so bright even I could see the sparks, and I can be pretty obtuse to that kind of thing sometimes."

"You're seeing things."

Me thinks she doth protest too much, but it won't be me getting the fright of my life to wake and find Wood playing hide-the-sausage with Erin.

~

MY PHONE PINGS from the bedside table. I lean up on my elbow and peek over the edge of my paperback, checking the screen. It's lit up in the dark, a bright neon light that makes me squint.

Little Warrior: You awake?

It's almost midnight, which means I've been reading for an hour. A Shane "Scarecrow" Schofield book by Matthew Reilly. It's intense. Scarecrow is a legendary Marine whose exploits make our jobs seem like a walk in the park. It's farfetched fiction, but I can't seem to put it down.

Bear: No. I'm sleeping. Go away.

It's been a few days since our dinner, and tomorrow is the weekend. Well, it's now, I guess, considering it's Friday evening. My day was long—work and training. I've been in bed for an hour reading, doing my best to ignore the protest in my muscles every time I shift. My prone position has made them seize like rusty old bolts in an ancient, worn-out engine. It's a shitty reminder that age is slowly creeping up on me.

Bear: Unless you're trained in the delightful art of massage. Then come on over.

Knowing full well she won't be borrowing Erin's car to come over and massage my wonderfully muscled body, I toss my phone on the bed and go back to my book. I'm re-reading the same paragraph twice when my phone pings again.

Little Warrior: What should I bring tomorrow?

Bear: These are the questions that keep you up at night?

Little Warrior: Actually, yes. They are.

Erin waved an olive branch during the week, broaching the idea of a gathering (safety in numbers, I think). I met her halfway and organised a barbeque at the beach for tomorrow afternoon. She's feeling remorse for her attack earlier in the week, and the idea is her attempt to make amends. To be honest, I don't blame her for what she said. The timing might have been a bit shitty, but I appreciate her standing up for Jamie. Everyone can use a friend like that.

Bear: Just bring whatever. Food. Booze.

Little Warrior: I need specifics.

Bear: Then I'm not your guy. Ask Wood. Or Erin.

Little Warrior: What are you bringing?

Bear: Food. Booze.

Little Warrior: I hate you.

Bear: You wound me.

Little Warrior: Nothing wounds you. It's like you're made of Kevlar.

Bear: If you're referring to my abs, then yes, they're hard and mighty. I'll let you touch them tomorrow if you like.

Little Warrior: All I did was ask a simple question …

I take pity on her. I can be exasperating sometimes but it's fun to tease, and Jamie makes it so easy. Ryan can complain about my shitty wisecracks until he's blue in the face, but it keeps me from spiralling into a deep dark pit of despair and anger. Jake should be here. It's so fucking unfair that he's not. If I can just keep pretending to be the man I was before he died, then maybe one day it won't hurt so much, and maybe the anger will fade.

Bear: I'm bringing sausages, bread, and beer, so maybe you could bring some green stuff.

Little Warrior: You mean a salad.

Bear: That's what I said. Maybe bring snacks too.

There'll be a few of us there, including the guys from my team—Monty, Tex, and Galloway. Ryan bailed out, and I know it's because Finlay will be there.

Little Warrior: Should I bring togs?

Little Warrior: Never mind. It's a beach. I'll bring togs.

Jamie hasn't met Fin before, and she's nervous. It won't be easy for her. I know because it's not easy for me. Jake and Fin are incredibly similar in appearance. It's hard to look at her and not see Jake too. It makes the loss even harder. It's a conscious effort to breathe around it.

Our team shoulders the heavy weight of blame for losing Jake, but Ryan is suffering worst of all. The thought of looking Fin in the eye, of apologising for letting her down, is almost intolerable. I know, because it made me physically sick for days.

But Fin is just like her brother—kind, compassionate, and wise. There's no blame. Just an incredible pain and a desperate need to talk. To share stories that bring an ache to my chest. To keep his memory alive.

Bear: You'll be fine. It'll be fun, ok? And if it's not, I'll just toss you in the ocean and that will at least ensure one of us is having a good time.

Little Warrior: You're such an ass.

Bear: You're right. You need to choose better friends.

Little Warrior: I would, but you're like a barnacle. I can't seem to pry you loose.

Bear: You can't see it, but I'm actually crying right now.

Little Warrior: Goodnight.

Bear: You're welcome for the help btw.

Bear: Hello?

22

JAMIE

Kyle walks over when we pull into the parking lot, taking the space next to his bike. He's wearing nothing but a pair of board shorts and flip flops, and I can't help but notice the hair on his chest. It glints blond in the sun.

He rubs his fingers through it when he reaches us, catching the direction of my gaze. "Wanna touch it?" he teases. "It feels better than it looks."

"It looks like you got a piece of carpet and glued it to your chest," I retort as I step out of the car, holding my container of green bean and avocado salad. It doesn't. The hair isn't thick. It looks manly and … nice. Not that I'd ever admit it. Kyle's head is big enough. "So I'll pass."

"You're so mean," he complains as I bump the car door closed with my butt.

"I can't help it," I reply as he takes the salad container from my hands. "You bring out the immaturity in me."

"I make you feel young," he corrects and peers through the clear Tupperware lid. "Wow, Jamie. This looks really good."

His compliment eases some of my nervous tension. I was going to make a Greek salad and changed my mind. Olives and red onion aren't for everyone. But we had no avocadoes, so I sent Wood out to buy some early this morning, trying three different stores before he found ones that were ripe enough. "You think?"

"You'd be surprised at how much I think. I do it almost every day."

I'm laughing at his jest when I open the back-passenger door and reach in for the canvas bag that holds all of Erin's picnic paraphernalia: paper napkins, plates, plastic wine glasses, seasonings, and sauces. It also contains a nice bottle of sauvignon blanc that took me fifteen minutes to choose. I lug the bag over my shoulder while Kyle greets Wood and Erin. He does it with no reservations towards my old school friend. The man can't seem to hold a grudge. It's impressive. Kyle is a good person. A really good one. And I'm feeling lucky to have him back in my life.

I slide a baseball cap down on my head and link my arm with his as we walk down to the picnic area by the beach, Wood and Erin following behind us. Both the sky and water are crystal blue, the sand white, and the grass thick and green. "It's a perfect day." And just like that, Jake's grinning face swims in my mind, reminding me that he doesn't get to do this anymore—swim at the beach, hang out with friends, and grill meat on a barbeque—and my heart aches. "An almost perfect day."

Kyle unlinks his arm and slides it around my shoulders, jostling me as we walk towards the grill he and his friends managed to nab on a busy Saturday afternoon. "Jake lived for days like this." His voice is gruff. "He'd be glad we're here doing this. Enjoying the beauty in the world. But yeah, there won't be any more perfect days, Little Warrior. Just days like this one that remind us to be grateful we're alive."

I slide my arm around his lower back and squeeze tightly, grateful for the comfort he offers and wanting to offer my own. It's all I can do. I don't know what else to say.

"Is she here?" I ask, my eyes skimming over the group as we get closer.

Kyle nods his head towards the back of the grill, where the grass meets the sand.

Finlay is sitting on the ground, arms curled around her knees as she stares out at the water. Her frame is slender, her hair fine and pale. She turns her head in our direction, and I falter. If it wasn't for Kyle's arm, I'd have tripped over my own feet and tumbled face-first into the grass.

"She looks just like him," I breathe, trying not to stare. But I do anyway, and my heart thumps hard in my chest. "Oh, Kyle." I turn my head away, blinking for just a moment, glad my eyes are hidden behind my sunglasses.

He sets my salad down and takes the bag from my shoulder, placing it beside it, while I take a moment to pull myself together. When I'm good, I turn back and force a smile, greeting Jake's old team, introducing them to Erin because they already know Wood. Two of them are married, and we're introduced to their wives. One has a baby. A little girl called Olivia who looks about twelve months old, maybe less. She's dressed in a pair of pink bathers with a cute ruffled skirt. Kyle snatches her up. "There's my precious little princess," he croons and blows a raspberry into her neck.

Olivia giggles and looks at Kyle as if he hung the moon. One of her chubby hands slaps his cheek when he makes kissy faces at her. "You're my favourite girl, Ollie."

"You better not let Monty hear you call her Ollie," warns Monty's wife, Wynn. "He hates it."

Kyle grins. "Now you're just giving me ammunition. Hey, Monty!" he calls out across the group. Monty is chatting with Wood and Erin, my friends already taking their seats in the portable chairs we brought, beers in hand like two peas in a cosy little pod. For a brief second I wonder. Then I push the thought away, giving Kyle a dirty look he doesn't even notice. He's the one who put the thought in my head with all his talk of *vibes* and *sparks*.

Monty stops talking and looks over.

"I'm taking Ollie for a swim," Kyle hollers his way.

His brows snap together. "Mate, call her Ollie one more time …"

I almost laugh. Does Monty not know his friend?

"C'mon, Ollie." Kyle tickles her little belly. "Let's go show off your cute little tush while we paddle in the water."

He starts off with her in his arms and glances over his shoulder. "You coming?"

I look to where Finlay sits, knowing I have to put on my big girl pants. "In a minute, okay?"

Kyle nods while Wynn chases after him, red wine in one hand, hat in the other. She slaps it on Olivia's head and starts back. "Would you like a glass?" she asks me.

"Thanks. I brought some white though, so I might have some of that."

Wynn walks back over to Monty while I pour two wines and take them over to where Finlay is sitting. I take a huge gulp before seating myself cross-legged beside her. The wine does nothing to calm my nerves.

"Hey," I offer, the word sounding lame and croaky on my lips.

"Hi." Finlay smiles slowly, and I can only look at her bright green eyes—Jake's eyes—for so long.

I hold out the glass. "Would you like a wine?"

"Thanks," she says, taking it, cocking her head. "Do I know you?"

"No." I shake my head. "We've never met." I hold out a hand. "I'm Jamie."

She takes it. "Fin," she says in reply before letting go.

There's a moment of awkward silence between us, and we both look out over the beach, watching as Kyle reaches the shoreline and plonks himself down. He sits Olivia on his lap, and tiny little waves splash over them. She screams in delight, slapping her hands in the sand, trying to grab at the water before it recedes.

"I saw you with Kyle when you arrived. You're friends?" she asks, glancing at me before her gaze returns to the ocean.

"We are. Old friends."

"Oh. That's nice. Did you …" She starts and stops, taking a deep breath. "Did you know my brother, then? Jake?"

"I did. We met … through the army." I hesitate on the words. I can't tell her I met Jake with the sole intention of losing my virginity, that our connection began as a one-night stand. It's not that I see anything wrong with what we did, but I don't want to overshare, or flat-out lie either. "Actually, we met the night before I shipped out for basic training and caught up again during deployment."

Finlay looks at me again. Really looks at me. "You're Jamie Murphy."

My nerves startle in surprise. "You know me?"

She nods, swallowing, hands wrapped around her wine glass like it's a hot mug of tea. "My brother and I were close. We talked about everything. He mentioned you. More than once."

My heart begins to race. "What did he say?" I blurt out and immediately wish I could take the words back. It's horrible timing to ask a question like that. "Sorry, I shouldn't have asked that. It's just ... Jake meant a lot to me," I explain, hearing the vulnerability and hesitation in my voice when I speak his name.

"Please don't apologise," she says, her expression both kind and incredibly sad as she looks at me. "I get it. And it's okay. I like talking about Jake, even though it's hard. I'm scared that if I stop, then he'll just fade away like he was never here."

Her eyes fill and my vision blurs. "Fin." I grab blindly for her hand, taking and giving it a squeeze. She squeezes back, blinking as she regains her composure before letting go. "Jake didn't give too much away, but it was more a case of the way he talked about you." She sips her wine, her gaze moving back to the ocean again. "I remember this one Christmas when he was twelve. He'd been begging my parents for a surfboard for the entire year. It was a shortboard. I think he called it a Thruster. It was designed for quick turns and shredding," she says as if I know what all that means. I don't. Surfing is something I've never tried because sharks. "It cost about six hundred dollars, so it wasn't cheap. They wouldn't buy it for him. Jake went through hobbies like we go through underwear, you see, and it cost my parents shitloads of money. I don't know if it was because he got bored or because he just had this huge love of living and wanted to try his hand at everything he could. It's almost as if he knew." Finlay mashes her lips together, throat working.

"You don't have to—"

"I do." She takes another sip of her wine, and I do the same, finishing off the glass and setting it aside. "Anyway, he promised to take out the trash for the whole year. Empty the dishwasher. Mow the lawns. And he did. For the entire year. They bought him the board. You should have seen his face when he woke and found it wrapped and standing against the wall by the tree. He had that exact same face whenever he mentioned you."

I bring my knees up to my chest, wrapping my arms around them. I want to bury my head in them and cry for the ache of what will never be, but I don't. I hold on to my tears, my grip precarious.

"Anyway, he took the board out in the ocean that very afternoon and accidently snapped it in half on the rocks," she says, and both of us laugh a little through watery eyes.

"Oh my god! What did your parents say?"

"Jake shit himself. He didn't tell them for a week. He had to fess up when we all came to the beach for a family picnic and they told him to bring his new board. Dad went all silent and scary, and Mum's eye twitched for the entire afternoon and into the night. He not only had to keep mowing our lawns over that summer, he had to mow our elderly neighbours' lawns too."

It's a great story and hearing it somehow makes Jake more human than superhero. But it also makes the loss feel worse. I've been trying to pack him neatly away in a little box filed under 'memories' and 'what could have been,' and yet my heart still opens the lid, every single day, and the contents churn inside my gut.

"Jake was an amazing person," I tell her, wanting to offer something in return. "He kicked our asses at poker all the time. He was good like that. Good at everything, really. We played for jelly beans most of the time, but he shared them all with me. Sometimes I'd be going about my day and some would fall out of my pocket when I hadn't even realised he slipped them in there."

It's not a funny story, but it's one that stuck with me because it made me feel special. Even a little giddy. I was falling for him *so hard.* How am I supposed to let that go?

Kyle grabs Olivia's arm and waves it at us from afar, beckoning. "Would you like to go for a swim?" I ask Fin.

She wipes at her eyes. "You go. I'm going to go help the guys fire up the grill."

"Are you sure?"

Fin nods. "I'm sure. It'll be nice having something to do. I've been so caught up in my own head lately."

"I get it. I lost my dad when I was sixteen," I share, and I'm not sure why. Maybe it's this sense of connection I'm feeling with her. "It's hard watching life move on around you while you're experiencing this horrible sense of loss, of knowing nothing will ever be the same. I know you worry about Jake fading with time, and maybe he will a little, like my father has, but he'll never leave completely. He'll be there in everything you do. I know, because I carry my dad with me everywhere I go, and now I carry Jake too."

"Thank you, Jamie. I needed to hear that."

"I think I needed to hear it too," I say, loosening my arms from around my legs and stretching them out in front of me, feeling a little wrung dry. "Maybe we can talk a bit more later? After we eat?"

"Sure. That would be great."

We both rise, wiping away the sand from our backsides. Fin squeezes my shoulder briefly before moving off to the grill while I peel off my shorts and tee shirt. I toss both on the grass and start towards the shoreline wearing a plain black string bikini. I'm not into bright colour or fuss, unlike Erin, who decided on a similar style of swimwear except hers are covered in white sequins that gleam with a purple lustre in the sun. I'm used to plain army green or camouflage, so wearing anything with colour feels like I'm drawing attention to myself, and that's the last thing I feel like doing in my present state of mind.

Kyle watches me walk towards him, pumping little Olivia's arms up and down in a cheer. "Yay, yay, yay," he chants, being silly. "It's Aunty Little Warrior."

I plop myself in the wet sand beside the two and find myself bopping the cute little lady on her tiny button nose. "You can call me Jamie."

"Ja!" she says.

"Aunty Jamie," Kyle tells her then points to his chest. "Uncle Kyle."

"No." I shake my head and point to his chest, making sure I have Olivia's attention. "That's Uncle Bear. *Bear,*" I enunciate clearly.

"Bah," she says, and Kyle grins so she says it again, delight on her face. "Bah."

"Holy shit!" I squeal when a wave rushes up and over us, gurgling and splashing cold water over my legs, lap, and butt.

Kyle covers Olivia's ears, his eyes widening on me in censure. "Don't swear in the front of the baby."

"Oops."

"Monty will kick my ass when we get back if she starts spouting swear words at everyone."

"Kyle! You just did it too."

He bites down on his lip, scrunching his nose. "I did. This parenting sh—stuff is hard."

"Well, it's good you're getting your practice in, I suppose, considering the poor woman you decide on marrying is going to end up ruining her vagina for the entire soccer team of kids you plan on having. And kids are expensive too, right? Not to mention all those push presents you'll have to buy."

Kyle cocks a brow in question while Olivia beats at his thighs with her little fists. "Push presents?"

"Yeah. Every time your better half pushes out a giant baby from her vag—and I say giant because I'm pretty sure you were born the size of a toddler—you have to give her diamonds."

"And what do I get?"

"A screaming baby."

"Huh. That doesn't seem fair."

"Fair? Oh boy." I grab a handful of sand and dump it onto his lap, right over his crotch.

"Hey!" he says, doing his best to wash it away while holding a squirming little human.

"Do me a favour and just buy her the damn diamonds, would you? I don't need you crying all over me because she divorced your sorry ass."

He covers Olivia's ears again, hissing, "Language."

We paddle in the shallows for a little while longer, until there's no ignoring the scent of barbequed sausages in the air. My stomach growls louder than a lion, so I stand up and wade in further, dunking myself in deeper water to rinse the wet sand from my backside. When I stride back out, Kyle plonks Olivia in my arms and does the same.

I tuck her into my side, but she starts to whine. I'm used to holding babies from my trips to East Timor and Afghanistan, but they were easy because I had a purpose. They needed health checks, not loving attention.

I give her a little jiggle. "You hungry, little Ollie?"

She looks at me, all big brown eyes and wispy hair, and doesn't like what she sees. She doesn't like being held by a stranger. Her little mouth opens and a cry of fear comes out. Suddenly it's Arash all over again, and the terror on his sweet young face. The way he looked at me as if I could fix everything. His cries when I failed him.

I begin to sweat—a cold sweat in the middle of a hot day—and my eyes dart to the water, desperate for Kyle. He's walking back to us, hair plastered to his face and neck.

Olivia seems to sense my panic and lets out a huge wail, whipping her head around as she looks for someone familiar. "Hey now," I say with a slight tremor, giving her another jiggle. "It's not that bad, is it?"

Oh yes it is, her face says, her bottom lip wobbling and poking out.

Kyle reaches us and I hand her over. "Here," I growl, anger starting to replace the sudden rush of panic. He takes her, brows high as I stomp off, showing Olivia that I'm a baby just like she is—only I'm a bigger one.

"Jamie! Wait." He jogs a little in the thick, dry sand, Olivia bouncing in his arms as he catches up. "What the hell was that?"

"I told you I never wanted kids," I snap, arms swinging and legs burning as I power up the beach towards the grassy knoll. He keeps pace, damn him and his stupid muscled legs. It's from stealing the stair climber in the gym on base all the time. Every morning I came in he was already on it, smirking like a giant poophead. "I'm not even cut out to hold a damn baby."

"Jamie, dammit, would you stop?"

He places a hand on my shoulder, and I see we're starting to draw attention.

I stop. "What, Kyle?"

He's breathing heavy as he stares down at me. Olivia squirms and he shifts her to his other side, patting her little bottom to keep her settled. "Is this whole thing about Arash? I know you were close with him, and I know leaving him behind must weigh on your mind. How could it not? But we're not raising kids in a warzone here. They get a better life."

My lips pinch tight. Fucking perceptive bastard. I start walking again, and Kyle follows alongside me. "Those kids are screwed from the moment they're born. How can I have kids of my own, knowing there are babies over there that have no one?"

"Jamie—"

"It's not right," I sputter.

"It's not," he agrees softly. "But we can't adopt them all. We can't even adopt one. Their laws won't allow it. So is it such a bad thing to have your own? Raise them to be good people. Encourage them to do something meaningful with their lives the same way we're trying to?" He rubs a loving hand down Olivia's back. "You think Monty and Wynn plan on raising a monster here?"

My eyes flick to the baby in his arms as we reach the fringes of our little group. She couldn't look more like an angel if she tried, but she's one of the lucky ones. There are so many out there who aren't. I lift my chin. "The day I can adopt an Afghan child is the day I'll have kids."

Kyle sighs, squinting at me with the sun bright in his eyes. "Stubborn little ass."

"No swearing in front of Ollie."

"Shit," he mutters.

Monty comes over and plucks his daughter free. She squeals and beats her fists against her daddy's chest as he carries her away. "Stop corrupting my little princess with your wicked ways, Brooks. She's too young for all your nonsense."

"All my nonsense?" Kyles call after him. "How old are you again? Eighty? C'mon, Jamie." He takes my hand. "Let's go eat."

23

———————

KYLE

J'm pulling into the carport beneath my unit block when my phone begins to vibrate in my back pocket. I switch off the engine and tug my helmet free, digging for the device.

It's after midnight. I've been out playing pool with Ryan because the walls have been closing in like a bad Indiana Jones movie. It's hitting home that Jake is never coming back. In fact, the longer he's gone, the worse it seems to get. Not even my Matthew Reilly book has been keeping the ache at bay. It keeps rising up like indigestion, burning my throat.

Frustrated earlier tonight, I threw my paperback at the wall, and Ryan opened the door, popping his head in.

"You okay?"

I was tired. I didn't have it in me to brush him off. "No. I'm not fucking okay." I tucked my hands behind my head and looked at him. "How's that for a shitty wisecrack, huh?"

"Christ." Ryan stepped inside my room and took a seat at the edge of the bed, his body facing out towards my little balcony. "I was wrong to say that the way I did." He rested his elbows on his knees and linked his hands together. "The truth is, I like your shitty wisecracks. And I get why you do it. We're men. We're not supposed to cry. We're not supposed to show weakness." He huffed out a breath. "Especially here. God knows, they do their best to train any kind of emotion out of us." Ryan turned his head, looking at me. "So many of us come back from Afghanistan like blocks of ice. All the humour, the grief, the joy—it all shuts down. And it's not that we're incapable of feeling anything. It's the training. But you've managed to avoid all that, and I don't know how."

"It's just practice, Kendall. You keep cracking jokes long enough, it becomes second nature, just like the training."

"I'm not that fucking funny."

"That's true. My kitchen counter has more humour than you."

Ryan chuckles and shakes his head. "C'mon. Too much deep conversation rots your brain." He rises to his feet. "Let's go play some pool."

The ringing of my phone brings me back to the present. I check the screen. It's an unknown mobile number, but I answer it anyway, remaining seated on my bike. "Kyle Brooks."

"Brooks, it's Wood."

"Hey, Wood. Everything okay?"

"Yeah, yeah. Is Jamie with you? She's been gone a little while, and she's not answering her phone."

My brows pull together. "She's not with me. Maybe she's gone out with some friends?"

"She doesn't really have many of those."

That's because she has more prickles than a cactus. "You have reason to be worried?"

"She left in Erin's car and the unopened bottle of vodka on the counter is missing too."

I stay seated on my bike, my helmet resting on the seat in front of me. "Wood, she's not stupid enough to drink and drive."

He huffs out an audible breath. "I'm not so sure."

"Well something must have happened?"

"She might have overhead me talking to Erin about something."

"About what?"

"About not re-enlisting. I'm leaving the army, Brooks."

My nostrils flare. "And you let her overhear you talking about it? Fuck's sake, Wood. She's supposed to be your best friend," I snap. "Shouldn't she be the first one you talk to about this?"

"After losing Jake?" he gripes back. "You really think that would have been a good idea?"

"It would have been better than her hearing it secondhand. You're a goddamn asshole."

"Great, thanks," he barks, clearly agitated. "But I already know that."

"I'll go look for her. If I find her, I'll let you know."

"Thanks. If she comes home, I'll let you know too."

I hang up, tucking my phone back in my pocket. I start the engine of my bike and put my helmet on before pealing back out of the carport.

I'm furious with Wood. So fucking mad I can barely see straight. He should know better than to talk about it with Erin before saying anything to Jamie. It would constitute the worst kind of betrayal in her current state of mind.

I make my way down dark, quiet streets until I find myself in a familiar neighbourhood. My bike comes to a stop outside Jamie's old house. Sue's place. I switch off the engine and tug my helmet free, swinging my leg over and climbing off. It's quiet, no lights on to indicate anyone's awake. I make my way around the back of the house, a flood of nostalgia sweeping me up and carrying me away.

Jamie's right. She did burn the fence down. The one in its place isn't new anymore, but it's different—the timber a little darker, the posts a little lower than they used to be. The big tree she sat near is still there, the branches overhanging the house behind it where I used to live, where I watched my mother die.

Jesus.

I swallow the lump in my throat and force myself to look around. She's not here, so I leave quickly.

After getting back on my bike, I try the beach next, the place where we had our picnic two weeks ago. We've been back since, swimming. There are good memories here, but no Jamie.

Think, Brooks. Where the hell would she be?

Knowing Jamie, she's likely in the one place I wouldn't expect her to be.

Walking to the parking lot from the beach, I climb back on my bike and make my way to Karrakatta Cemetery over in Nedlands. It's only minutes from Campbell Barracks. I would have driven straight past her. When I pull into the parking lot, I see Erin's car and relief loosens the knot of tension in the back of my neck.

The cemetery is incredibly large, the grounds containing hundreds of war graves, some dating back to the First World War, and the Vietnam War. I make my way on foot until I'm not far from where Jake was laid to rest mere weeks ago. I come to a stop. She's there, sitting cross-legged beside the freshly turned earth, though I barely recognise her, even from behind. Her long hair is straight, hanging in a sleek dark sheet down her back. Her torso is wrapped in a strapless black and lace top that could be mistaken for underwear. Slim black pants cover her legs, and heels sit in a haphazard pile of buckles and straps on the grass beside her.

She's saying something. I hear her voice drifting towards me but not the words. Lifting a vodka bottle, she takes a generous swig before tipping a little onto the turned earth.

My eyes burn. *She's saying goodbye.*

I should go but I can't leave her like this. I walk a little closer and a twig snaps beneath my feet. I freeze to the ground.

Jamie turns and my breath lodges in my throat. Her face is made up like I've never seen, her eyes smoky and dark, reminding me that she isn't just one of my best friends, she's also an incredibly beautiful woman. One who's hurting. Her expression is lost as she tries to focus on me, mascara tracking down her cheeks in a messy trail of tears.

"Bear?" she croaks, squinting in the dark. "Is that you?"

My jaw locks hard, grief a tidal wave that seems to rise up out of nowhere, swamping me. "It's me."

"Well don't just stand there like a giant lump." She slurs her words a little. "Come have a drink with me and Jake."

I walk over, dropping down on the damp ground beside her. It rained earlier this morning. Moisture clings to the grass and soaks into the ass of my jeans.

Jamie holds out the vodka and then narrows her eyes, snatching it back, hugging it to her chest as if it's liquid gold. "Unless you plan on being a pooper party and … wait." Her nose scrunches up. "A pooper party. No. Party pooper," she says with a sense of victory, jabbing her finger at me.

"Give me the vodka, Jamie."

She hands it over slowly, her expression wary.

I snatch the bottle. My rational self tells me to take it, and Jamie, and get the hell out of here. But *fuck it.* I bring the bottle to my lips and tip it back, throat working as I guzzle down a massive mouthful.

Jamie whoops and snatches the bottle back while I wipe my mouth with the back of my hand, the high-quality alcohol burning its way down my throat. She tips the bottle towards Jake's grave marker. "To my first love," she slurs before taking a hefty gulp. Jamie hands it back to me. "My first kiss. My first everything."

An odd twinge hits me in the gut. "Jake was your first?"

"Yep." She giggles, a bright drunk sound that cuts through the quiet night. "Don't I look hot? This outfit is just like the one I wore when I met him for the first time in some random bar."

I take another swig from the bottle. And another. "You look …" Broken. So beautiful and broken it makes me ache.

"Hot. Right?" Jamie attempts a wink and just ends up tipping over with a shriek and a giggle. She stays flat on her back, her eyes on the sky. "Erin dressed me that night. I wanted to look like I knew what I was do—" She hiccups. "Doing. I wanted to lose my virginity before joining the army," she sing-songs before giggling again and turning her head to look at me. "And Jake, well he knew exactly what he was doing," she croons. "I couldn't have picked a better man if I'd tried."

"Jamie," I start and stop.

She squints one eye. "What?"

I don't know. Her confession makes me feel weird. I'm glad it was Jake and not some sleazy asshole, but the image of someone else touching her … My mind rejects it like a hot poker is prodding me in the gut. I shake my head, confused. "Nothing."

I take a long swig of the bottle, drinking down more than one mouthful. It works. Warmth spreads through my belly and down to my limbs, making the odd sensation disappear.

Jamie's eyes return to the sky. "Wood is leaving the army, Kyle. Did you know?" She stretches her arms up high, giving the world a double-thumbs-up. "Good for him," she slurs. "Him and Erin. You were right. They were playing hide-the-sausage and now they have each other, and I have no one."

"Wood is an asshole."

"Yes!" Then she slaps a hand to her forehead and rises awkwardly from the grass. "Wait. No." Jamie shakes her head. "No pity parties allowed. Jake would be pissed."

"That's my girl. Look at you." I tip the bottle back again. "Growing up into a smart young lady."

She snorts. "You're such a dick."

"At least I'm a funny dick, unlike you."

"Oh, hey now." Jamie crawls over to me on her hands and knees. "No need to be mean."

She snatches the bottle and loses her balance, falling into my lap, a pile of hair and limbs, one of which elbows me in the gut. "Ooof."

Jamie rolls and looks up at me. "It's okay, though. You know why?" She gestures me close, putting a hand to the side of her mouth as if she's going to tell me a secret. I dip my head down, my face close to hers. "I don't need anyone," she whispers and then giggles. "Wait, that's not it. Nobody needs me," she corrects. "But that's okay. Don't feel sorry for me, Bear," she slurs, reaching up to slap my cheek. "I'm tougher than old leather." She takes a swig from the bottle and splutters, sitting up, bits of grass clinging to the sleek strands of her hair.

I take the vodka and tip it back, almost finishing it off in one go.

"Make sure you leave some for Jake!"

I stop, my chest burning as the alcohol spreads through my veins. Stretching out my arm, I upend the bottle over the freshly turned earth. My head hangs low as the last mouthful sinks into the ground. I swallow and rise to my feet, a little unsteady. I can handle my liquor. Usually. But that was a lot downed in a short amount of time.

Jamie sets a hand down on the dirt, her fingers digging in a little. "Goodbye, Jake." Her voice cracks, and she takes a moment, closing her eyes. "See you on the other side."

Goddammit. Tears blur my vision as I reach out a hand.

Jamie takes it, standing, and she looks at me.

"Bear?" she whispers. "Are you okay?"

My jaw works. "I'm fine."

Jamie

I might have had a bit too much to drink, but I'm not blind. Kyle is not fine. He doesn't brush my question off with a funny joke or a cheeky smile. Instead, he's tense and unsteady, and I've been so wrapped up in my own grief, I haven't been there for him at all. Not one little bit.

"Kyle." A lump of shame lodges in my throat. I've been so stupid. So damn stupid. Kyle is just like me. Strong on the outside yet bruised on the inside, where no one can see. Not unless they look deep below the surface, and I've barely even looked beyond myself.

"You keep talking like nobody needs you, Little Warrior, but I do. I need you."

I slide my arms around his middle, sobering a little. Instead of pulling me close, his own arms hang loose by his side. I press the side of my face to his chest. It's hard and warm, and he smells of motorcycle grease and a little sweat. I don't care. It's more comforting than chicken soup on a rainy day. "I'm here."

He shudders in my hold.

"I'm here, Kyle."

He pulls me to him, his arms slowly winding their way around me until he's holding me so tight I can barely breathe. He tucks his chin on the top of my head, his voice gruff. "You leave in two days." I feel the rumble of his chest against my face as he speaks. It's oddly soothing.

"I know, but I'm not going anywhere, okay? I might be leaving, but I'm not going anywhere."

Kyle lifts me until we're eye level, my legs dangling from the ground. I look at his face as if seeing it for the first time. He looks tired and a little worn at the edges. There are crinkles around his eyes, as if he laughs hard and often. His face is tan, his beard short, and his expression stoic. It's the face of a man who's experienced the worst and the best of what the world has thrown at him and come out the other side stronger, still holding on to the belief that happiness exists. That there's something better out there just waiting for him to reach out and grab it.

"It's you and me, Little Warrior." His voice chokes and tears start rolling down my face. My heart aches. It *aches* for him. It aches for his mother, who will never know the man her boy grew up to be. Someone who's fighting hard to let go of the hurt, and the loss, hiding the battle inside him like the soldier he was trained to be. "You and me against the world."

I nod, my hands cupping his soft, bearded jaw. "You and me, Bear."

He nods in return. "Where do we go from here?"

"Right now?" The thought of going back to Erin's apartment ties my stomach in a knot. I'm not ready to face them yet. "I don't know, but I'm not ready to go to sleep, and we're all out of vodka."

He sets me down. "I've got an idea."

Kyle

We leave our respective rides behind and take a cab along Marine Parade, pulling to a stop in the parking lot by Cottesloe Beach. Patrons spill from the hotel across the road, raucous laughter and loud voices echoing down the street.

"Good thinking," Jamie says, lurching out of the cab while I pay the driver, spiky heels dangling from her fingers. "I love this place."

I shut the door and grab her shoulders, turning so she faces the beach. Waves crash against the shore, the whitewash bright in the darkness. "Not another bar." I point towards the sand. "Let's just hang out for a while."

She turns back towards the hotel. "With a six-pack at least. Don't be a party pooper, Kyle."

"Don't you mean a pooper party?"

"Har har." Jamie totters across the road in her bare feet, dodging a passing car and a rowdy group of people. "Hey, baby," one of the men in the group calls out to her. "Come say hi."

She doesn't even hear him with the way she's motoring across the path towards the entrance. "Say hi to this," I growl, giving him the finger as I stalk past their group. If only Ryan could see me now. He'd probably piss himself laughing.

I find Jamie sitting on the ground by the entryway, her expression heartbroken as she tries to buckle her shoes. She looks up at my approach. "They won't let me in with bare feet, Kyle," she whines, glaring at the bouncer as if he's single-handedly ruining her life.

"Stubborn little donkey," I mutter, knowing I'd have better luck pushing a snowball up a hill than tell her what to do. I sigh a heavy sigh and crouch, helping her buckle the fiddly little straps. "There."

I pull her to her feet, and we buy the damn six-pack. She already has a beer in hand when we cross the street, the lid flicked off and bottle to her lips. A car comes flying towards us, careening unsteadily on the road. "Shit!" I slam an arm hard across Jamie's chest, shoving her back as it shifts direction at the last second, accelerating as it passes us. The occupants whoop and laugh, and a familiar male sticks his head out, waving his middle finger. "Say hi to that, asshole!"

"Immature little fuckers," I growl.

"Hey, dude!" someone yells from behind us. "That was some shit! You two okay?"

I turn and wave the good Samaritan off, adrenaline knocking around in my chest. "All good, mate."

Jamie's face is pale. "What the hell was that?"

I take her hand and lead her across the road. "That was you being drunk and not paying attention to your surroundings."

She blinks. "Are you saying that was *my* fault?"

My nostrils flare. I have the patience of a saint when it comes to this woman. "No, Jamie. I'm simply pointing out that the asshole population is out in force tonight and you're completely oblivious." Christ, she could have been hit and flung metres down the road. I rub at my chest. Is this what a heart attack feels like?

Jamie purses her lips. "Whatever."

We reach the sand, and she sets her beer on the grass, bending at the waist to unbuckle her shoes. The bottle tips, its contents spilling out in a foamy mess as she teeters, almost tipping until I grab her by the shoulders.

"Right on, Bear."

"Sit your ass down."

"Well, geez, since you asked so nicely." She plonks her butt on the grass, and once again I'm crouched at her feet. Only this time I'm smart enough to toss the heels far and wide once I get them off.

"Hey!"

"Fuck those fucking shoes."

Jamie stares off in the direction they disappeared in, her mouth falling open. I can't help but laugh at her shocked expression. She shoves at my knees, and I go down backwards in the sand, a deep belly laugh ripping out of me until I'm gasping for air. Jamie rises up and over me. Her hair spills down and tickles me in the face. "You just threw my shoes."

"I know. And I'd do it again too."

Her mouth opens and closes like a fish. Then she starts to snort and splutter, and it sets me off again, which is how I find myself at three a.m., half-drunk and lying in the sand, laughing my ass off as Jamie sits on top of me, cackling like a crazy loon.

"Kyle?" She leans down, her small calloused palms brushing at my cheeks. "Don't."

"Don't what?"

"Don't cry."

I wipe at my face, finding it wet with tears. "Ahhh fuck. I'm okay."

Her own eyes water, and her words slur a little. "It's okay to not be okay."

"Then let's not be okay, together, okay?"

Jamie squints, her brows pulling into puzzled lines as she tries to make sense of what I just said. Then her expression suddenly clears. "I've got a great idea." She jumps up, a sudden energetic bean. "Let's go swimming."

She reaches behind her back with a grunt, arms straining as I rise to a sitting position. Suddenly her little black top is off and flying at my face.

"Jamie, what the fuck?" I catch a flash of a lacy black strapless bra before she's off and running towards the shoreline. "Oh shit." Reckless little turkey. She'll end up drowning in those monster waves.

I'm up and running in the blink of an eye, peeling off my shirt and tossing it behind me. "Jamie!"

I'm getting close when she stops, hopping about as she tugs off her pants. They drop in the small surge of water. It leaves her in nothing but a tiny black lace thong, baring her round, toned ass to the chilly night air.

I peel off my jeans before diving in after her, catching my breath at the shock of cold. She surfaces, hair plastered to her face and makeup smeared beneath her eyes, somehow making her look even more badass and mysterious than she did before. Her teeth chatter and her arms hug her front, covering her pretty chest. "Fuck, it's cold."

"C'mere," I tell her, rising to keep my head clear as a wave crests over us.

Jamie wades towards me. I fold her up in my arms, and she presses her face into my neck, clutching at my shoulders. "Whose stupid idea was it to go swimming?"

I laugh but it's a little strained. There's a half-naked woman pressed against me and a bright hot jittery feeling in my stomach that I can't make sense of. My voice comes out a little strangled. "We should get out."

"We should," Jamie agrees, except she doesn't move and neither do I. We just stand there wrapped together, waves crashing over us, teeth chattering and goose bumps on our skin.

"Kyle?" Her voice is soft. She pulls back to look at me. "Can I ask you a favour?"

"Anything."

"Don't come see me off at the airport when I leave."

My brows pull together. "Why not?"

"Because I'm not sure I'll be able to get on the plane if you're there. I can't take another goodbye right now."

I nod slowly, freeing a hand from around her waist to swipe water from my face. "If that's what you want."

But two days later when I'm finished playing with explosives all day at work, and just an hour before Jamie's due to board her flight for Townsville, it hits me that she's leaving and I won't see her again for a really long time. Something makes me panic at the thought.

Ditching my uniform, I change into jeans and a tee shirt, grabbing my keys and wallet as I race outside.

"Where's the fire?" Ryan calls after me, going somewhere himself as he opens the door of his Mustang.

There's no time for a retort. I need to see Jamie. I rev the engine and pull out with a squeal, accelerating to a limit just beyond acceptable. I'm pulling away from a red light, opening up a huge lead with the car behind me when a blue light flashes through its windscreen.

"Shit, fuck, goddammit."

I pull over, ripping off my helmet when the officer approaches. "Have you got any idea how fast you were going?"

Absolutely none. "No, sir."

"Where do you work?" he asks.

"Campbell Barracks."

The officer looks me over, lips pinched. "Give me your licence."

I tug my wallet free and hand it over.

"Beeeeeep, beep, beep!" sounds a horn. I look up as Ryan's Mustang growls past, his arm out the window as he waves, teeth flashing in a grin.

"Asshole," I mutter.

"Any reason for the speed?" the officer asks as he does a visual check of my licence.

I crack my knuckles, trying to fight the impatience. "I need to get to the airport."

"You got a flight to catch?"

"No. I have a friend heading back to base in Townsville. I wanted to say goodbye."

He looks up, brows winging high. "This person army too?"

"Yes, sir."

"Poor bastard," he mutters and hands my licence back. "Slow down next time."

The officer starts back to his car. I shove my helmet back on and zoom off, a little slower this time. By the time I find a parking space and jog my way through the airport, her flight is already boarding.

"Jamie?" I holler, looking through the crowd as I reach her boarding gate. "Jamie?"

"Kyle?" My breath whooshes out when she waves from the line. I know she asked me not to come, but I swear her eyes brighten a little when she sees me. She glances behind her at Wood before stepping free of the queue and coming towards me. "What are you doing here?"

"I know you said not to come, but I was out this way anyway," I lie, because I can't think of a good goddamn reason why I'm standing here right now like an idiot. I glance over at Wood before looking back at her. "Are things between you and Wood okay?"

Jamie shrugs. "We're on shaky ground I guess. I'm happy for him,

Kyle. He's found something better than the army, but I don't know. Every time I look at him, I want to punch him in the face."

"Should make for a fun flight," I quip.

She rolls her eyes. "Right?"

I jerk my chin in the direction of her gate. The line is dwindling as everyone boards. "You should go." I don't hug her. I'm not sure I'd let go otherwise. Instead, I palm the sharp line of her jaw, brushing a thumb across her cheek. "Safe travels, Little Warrior."

She starts walking backwards and my hand falls away. "Later, Bear."

Jamie disappears down the boarding ramp and I take a seat by the window, elbows on my knees, hands joined in a fist and pressed to my mouth as I watch the plane taxi down the runway and lift into the sky, taking Jamie away. It's not until her plane fades into the distance that I get up and walk away.

24

JAMIE

ood puts his hand on the handle of the passenger door. "Are you sure you don't want to come in?"

I've pulled to a stop in the drop-off zone at the Townsville airport. It's been months since I was here, arriving from post-deployment leave in Perth. It feels like only yesterday and yet a lifetime ago—all at the same time. Wood is done with the army. His transition to civilian life has been processed. He's now flying to Perth via Brisbane, his relationship with Erin becoming official. They're moving in together.

"I'm sure. I don't handle goodbyes all that well, you know that. The last goodbye I attempted ended up with me drunk and diving half-naked into a bitterly cold ocean."

Wood snorts, knowing of my escapade. It's not something you can easily hide when you return home at five a.m. dripping wet, wearing nothing but a thong and a man's tee shirt that almost reaches your knees, wet pants bunched in your hand, and bare feet. Not to mention Kyle's insistence on walking me to the apartment door, shirtless, his jeans drenched because the waves came up and almost washed them away. Laughter bubbles up inside at the image of Kyle in nothing but his boxer-briefs, scrambling after them with a shout. I dropped to the sand in fits of laughter and had to go dunk myself back in the ocean again to rinse off.

"It's hardly the same thing."

"It feels like it," I say, which is a struggle to admit. Talking about feelings without alcoholic lubricant is hard. I'm not just army. Or a combat medic. I'm a female in a sea of dominating males who think the length of their dick is an acceptable form of measuring respect. I can't appear soft. I don't have that kind of luxury. And it's hard to change that the moment the uniform comes off. I'm not a switch. And I'm not sweet. Nor am I feminine. But it doesn't mean I don't care, even though it comes across that way sometimes.

Okay.

Most times.

"Jamie—"

"You'll miss your flight."

Wood lets out a heavy breath as if I'm testing his patience. "Just walk me to the gate. There's something I want to give you. A present."

"You mean, apart from a black eye and a split brow?"

"That was years ago!"

I smirk, starting to wonder if Kyle is rubbing off on me. "What can I say? I hold a grudge."

"Fuck's sake." Wood knows I'm only teasing, but he's giving the impression that the end of his tether has been reached. He jerks the handle of the door and opens it.

My chest gets unexpectedly tight. "Wait!"

Wood pauses—half-in and half-out of my little Toyota Corolla—and looks at me over his shoulder.

"Move it along!" the parking attendant booms, dipping his head down so I can better see his pissy expression through the car window. "You're holding up the other cars in the line."

I wave him off with a faux apologetic smile while Wood gets out. The attendant walks to the next car, impatient to exert his authority over the blue BMW sedan behind me.

"Wood!" He closes the car door and ducks down, resting his forearms on the open window. "I'll park, okay? Just … get your damn bags out and I'll meet you back here."

His nostrils flare. "Forget about it, Jamie. I wouldn't want to put you out."

Shit. How do I even have any friends at all? It makes me question the judgement of the ones I *do* have. Why do they stick with me? Do they see something I don't? Or do they just enjoy a challenge? I need to do better.

"I'm sorry." My jaw tightens and I tap my fingers on the steering wheel. Doing better is *hard*. "I want to walk with you to the gate. Just don't …"

"Don't what?"

Leave being pissed at me. I love Wood as if he were my own brother. It's been me and him since training began. A team. And now we're not anymore. Everything's changing, and I don't like it. Change is for the birds.

"Don't what, Jamie?" he prods.

Gah! "Just don't give my present to someone else."

Leaving my car in the short-term parking lot, I walk towards the entrance of the airport, phone in the back pocket of my jeans and keys in hand. I don't own a handbag. They always felt like a feminine accessory that never suited me, but they do seem practical. I seem to acquire more necessities as I get older. Things like eye drops for late nights working and lip balm for chafed lips. Tissues and mints. I used to just suck it up, but I'm slowly starting to realise I don't have to. Chafed lips and red eyes don't make me tough. Having a few tissues handy and fresh breath doesn't make me soft.

I make a resolution to go buy a bag after leaving the airport. A nice one. One with leather and pretty buckles. I could even take a photo of it and send it to Erin. She would shit herself. The thought buoys me as the doors *whoosh* open, ejecting cool air as I step inside, flicking my sunglasses to the top of my head.

I make my way over to the departures section, where my best

friend waits beside two extra-large suitcases. "You've got a lot of baggage, Wood."

"That's my whole life in these things."

He collects one and I take the other, and we start wheeling them towards the baggage drop-off. "Well, when you put it that way, it just sounds sad."

Wood bumps me with his shoulder, pushing me off course. "Hey!"

He shrugs. "It kinda is, I guess, but that's army for you, right? When you're single and living on base, the last thing you waste money on is nice furnishings and artwork for the walls."

"You're looking forward to having your own place, aren't you?"

"Hell yes. Erin wants to rent, but I want to buy. We're in a bit of a standoff about it, but we need to decide soon before her lease runs out."

"Trouble in paradise already?" I force myself to tease. It still feels weird, the two of them together. A little awkward even. Probably because I got blindsided by it, which is partly my fault for burying my head in the sand like a stubborn ostrich.

"Buying will eat up a bit of savings, but owning property will go a long way towards getting a business loan for her spa retreat in the mountains. It makes sense."

We reach the gate and I check the time. Boarding isn't for another hour. "What should we do? Buy you a book? Some magazines? Get a coffee?"

"I could eat," he offers.

"Let's eat."

Erin video calls Wood while we're seated together at the gate, juggling coffees and bacon burgers. He answers with barbeque sauce smeared across the side of his mouth. Along with his mussed hair and stupid grin, he looks ridiculous. I don't tell him and Erin laughs. "You got a bit of something …" She points to the side of her mouth.

Wood wipes at the wrong side, holding the phone back far enough for her to see both of us. "Did I get it?"

"Yeah, you got it." She looks at me and we share a smirk. Our first since their relationship blew up in my face. It warms my insides and makes me realise that maybe I'm not losing both of my friends after all. Maybe literally, to distance, but not figuratively.

"I miss you, Jamie."

I let out a breath. "Miss you too."

"When are you going to come visit us?"

Us. God. It's still weird. "As soon as I get leave. Make sure you set up a room for me in your new house."

"I will. I'll give you the room you always wanted and never had." Amusement lights her eyes. "White canopy bed, pink frills, rose wallpaper. A pretty display of barbie dolls."

"Change the barbies to GI Janes and I might consider not burning the entire room to the ground."

She laughs and Wood steps in, mouth full of bacon burger. "Don't worry, Murphy," he tells me. "I won't let her in the house with any of that girly crap."

"Oh my god, Wood." I cover my eyes from the train wreck about to unfold before them.

"What?" he asks, sounding genuinely lost.

"Girly crap?" Erin sounds a bit pissy. "What are you saying, Colin? You want to cover our house in desert camouflage and live in squalor?"

"I didn't say that. Murphy? Did I say that?"

I uncover my eyes and look away, sipping my coffee, happy to leave Wood swinging in the wind on this one. "Don't drag me into your domestic, dude."

"You didn't have to say it. It was *implied*," Erin continues. "I mean, I'm a girl. I'm a freaking girly girl. Does that make me crap too? Will you not let *me* in the house?"

"Erin," Wood says in a soothing tone. "You're being a little dramatic."

Her intake of breath is so sharp she almost chokes on it. "Dramatic?"

"Do you *want* to die today?" I mutter to my idiotic friend. Erin might be dramatic, but it's who she is. Even I, a relationship noob, know you can't call your other half out on their personality flaws. Those are things you learn to live with, not change.

"No, I don't," he mutters back, his lips barely moving. "Help."

I set my coffee down on the vacant seat beside me and get to my feet. Bending, I wave into the phone. "See ya, Erin. Gotta go pee."

"Don't leave me," Wood hisses quietly as I start towards the female restroom. "Traitor," he calls to my back.

The insult slides off like Teflon. I'm actually giggling to myself when I push open the door until I find the line of women waiting six-feet-deep to use the loo. My bladder sends me a threatening message. Freaking airport toilets. My phone starts to ring, causing every impatient civilian in line to turn their head and look at me.

I tug it free of my jeans pocket and look at the screen. It's Kyle. And a video call at that. It's probably bad etiquette to answer, right? I hit the decline button and leave a message by way of explanation.

Little Warrior: I'm in the loo.

Bear: And you're on your phone? You're so gross, Murphy.

Little Warrior: Says the man who plays on his phone while taking a dump.

Bear: I do not!

I actually have no idea if he does or not, but if I've learnt anything from Kyle, it's to fight fire with fire.

The bubbled dots appear as I move forward in the line, indicating another incoming message.

Bear: Stop trying to ruin my sexy image.

I laugh under my breath.

Little Warrior: You can't ruin what you never had.

Bear: Someone's had their morning coffee.

Little Warrior: How can you tell?

Bear: Because you're on fire this morning. Gotta go. I'll call again in a little while. Need to tell you something.

Little Warrior: Tell me what?

Bear: Later, impatient one.

Little Warrior: You're the worst.

Bear: And yet here you are, talking to me anyway.

He got me there. I tuck my phone away and squeeze my pelvic floor muscles while I wait for a free stall. After finishing my business and washing my hands, I return to find Wood has ended his call with Erin. He's also demolished his burger and is busy eating half of mine.

I rip it from his long bony fingers. "What the hell?"

He sneers around his mouthful. "Some friend you are."

I retake my seat, taking a bite of what's left, chewing and swallowing before I speak. "You walked right into it. You have a lot to learn about women, young Padawan."

He has the nerve to snort. "It's not like I can learn anything from you."

"Oh that is it." I grab my now cold coffee and stand. "Good luck. Though you've probably got a better chance of surviving potshots in Afghanistan than Erin."

"Fine. Fine! I'm sorry. I don't know what I was thinking. You're all woman, Murphy. A hundred percent woman," he adds, laying it on far too thick, but I let it go. "Teach me everything you know."

"Get me another coffee and I will."

Wood returns with two more cups, steam rising from the little vents. He hands mine over, and I lift the lid to make it cool faster. "Right, so?"

I shrug, bringing the cup to my lips and blowing on the hot brown liquid. "I don't have time for charts and graphs and diagrams, Wood. Teaching you everything about women requires a two-week master-class, minimum. You board in less than ten minutes."

"Just give me one thing."

"Okay." I think for a moment. "If Erin says she's fine, don't believe her. She's not fine at all."

"I already know that one," he points out, smug. "I learnt it from you. What else?"

I sigh. "Use your actions to show her how you feel, not your words. Erin appreciates the little things, like flowers and you bringing home her favourite takeout when she's tired, so I guess that makes you lucky that she's easily impressed."

"That's a good one. What else?"

I rub my lips together, thinking. Then I tug my phone free and pull up Kyle's contact. *I'll call again in a little while.* My brows pull together. What does he want to tell me? And why can't I stop thinking about it?

"What?" Wood prompts as the flight attendants put the call out for boarding.

I put my phone away and look at my best friend. "Just ..." My hand fumbles for his and I give it a squeeze. "Appreciate every minute you have together, okay?"

The lump in my throat is huge. I gulp down a mouthful of coffee as we both stand. It burns my tongue. In fact, it scorches my throat all the way down, but it doesn't hurt half as much as Wood leaving right now.

I toss my half-empty cup in the trash beside my seat, knowing I won't be able to stomach the rest.

"C'mere," Wood says and pulls me towards him, folding me up in his arms.

I return the hug, sliding my arms around his waist. "I can't believe you're actually leaving."

"I know. This is one of the hardest things I've ever had to do. Leave you here."

"I'll be fine."

"Ha!" His chest vibrates against my face. "Fine. Sure."

"I will," I insist, pulling myself free. "I promise."

Wood collects his carry-on and stands in front of me, his chest heaving with a deep breath. "I guess this is it. Call me every day, okay?"

"Once a week."

"Every second day."

Tears prickle behind my eyes. This is why I don't do goodbyes. "God, whatever, Wood. Just go already."

He starts walking backwards, towards the gate entrance. "Hey, Murphy! About that gift."

I hold up arms. "Yeah about that!"

"It's in the glove compartment of your car." The sneaky SOB. Trying to distract me from feeling sad by hiding presents in my car. "See you soon," he says, grinning.

"Later, Wood."

After his boarding pass is scanned, he turns and gives me a brief casual salute.

I return it and then he disappears down the ramp.

Gone.

My eyes fill, causing my nose to fizz and burn. I blink and turn away, making my way back through the airport, oblivious to those around me. Families rushing for flights, couples walking arm-in-arm, business people powering along in dark suits, wheeling carry-on suitcases behind them.

His present is sitting right there where he said it was. It's wrapped perfectly in bright yellow and white stripes, the paper thick and sharp, the edges precise. I tear it open and toss the wrapping to the passenger seat. It's a flat box with a lid. I open it, pushing tissue paper aside. It's a white tee shirt with block print on the front that reads MY BFF HAS A LIGHT SABRE AND HE'S NOT AFRAID TO USE IT in black.

I'm laughing when my phone dings with a message. It's from Wood. It's a selfie with his stupid, grinning face. He's standing in the crowded aisle of the plane, pointing to his shirt, the hoodie he was wearing this morning unzipped and hanging from his shoulders. His shirt is the same except black with white font that reads MY BFF HAS A BLACK BELT AND SHE WILL TAKE YOU DOWN.

My eyes well up. Again. *God, Wood. You're such a damn loser.* I quickly tug my shirt free, not caring who sees, and replace it with his. It fits perfect, maybe a little snug. I put my sunglasses on to hide my eyes and take a quick selfie, sending it with a message.

Jamie: Your shirts are stupid and ridiculous. I love them.

Wood: Erin said they were stupid too, but I knew you'd love them. You're the sister I never had, Murph. I miss you already.

I sit in the car a long moment, just taking a breath. When I look up through the front windscreen, I see his plane rising into the cloudless sky, the morning sun gleaming across the sleek white metal as it lifts higher.

"Miss you already too, Wood," I say softly.

I'm in the car driving back to base when I remember I'm supposed to be buying myself a handbag. I change direction and start for Castle-Town Shoppingworld. It has a Witchery, and I remember Erin once saying that I could do no wrong in that store. The amber light ahead turns to red when my phone chimes brightly from its dashboard holder. It's Kyle. I slow to a stop at the light and answer the video call.

I briefly catch his face before returning my attention to the road. "I'm driving. Can you call back in ten?"

"No can do. I have to head out."

I glance at him quickly. "Okaaaay then," I draw out slowly as the next set of lights change to red. I'm catching all of them today. "What did you have to tell me?"

I pull to a stop and look at my phone screen. There's tension on Kyle's face. And a smudge of dirt. Sunglasses sit perched on his head, and he's dressed in desert camouflage. My stomach takes a nosedive to my toes. "Wait. You're in Afghanistan?"

"Yeah."

"And you're only just telling me now?"

"About that." He rubs at the back of his neck, wincing.

I'm tempted to hang up on him, but he deserves a piece of my mind first. I rip the sunglasses from my face. "You can eat a dick, Kyle."

"I'm sorry."

The car behind me beeps its horn. I look up. The light is green. "Shit," I mutter and accelerate, glancing at him quickly. "I thought we were friends. Why didn't you tell me?"

"We barely got any notice."

"It takes five seconds to send a message." My chest hammers with hurt. "You know what? Who cares anymore? If you can't be bothered, then neither can I."

My hand reaches for the red button.

"Jamie, wait! Just pull over for a second, okay?"

The intensity on his face is a little unnerving. I make sure he sees my glare before I put my indicator on, pulling to a stop just off the road. After putting the car in park, I give him my attention.

"What, Kyle?"

"I'm sorry. I should have told you sooner." He looks away. "I didn't know how. Coming here without Jake feels so fucking wrong." His head drops for a beat before he looks at me again.

"I'm sorry too," I say softly, and the urge to wrap my arms around him and wipe the desolate expression from his face rises inside me. But I can't, and it hurts that I can't.

Kyle cocks his head, his gaze on mine. "Why are your eyes red?"

"They're not red."

"Yes, they are."

I tip my face to the rearview mirror. They are a little. "It's dusty today."

"I call bullshit. There's no dust in Townsville."

"There is today."

His lips press in a hard line. "Did someone upset you?"

I let out a breath. "Wood left this morning. I just dropped him at the airport."

"Shit," he mutters.

"Brooks," I hear Ryan say from somewhere behind him. Kyle turns his head. "We gotta go."

"Go," I say when he turns back.

"I'll call you in a couple of weeks."

"Sure. Okay."

"Don't be mad at me, please?"

"I'm not mad. I promise." Which is true. I'm not mad. Just sick. Two weeks means he's headed out on a mission. The last one his team went on— My stomach churns and I can't finish the thought. "Take care of yourself. Please."

"You too."

My hands white-knuckle the steering wheel when he hangs up. Erin better be right about her 'shopping is therapy' mantra because I'm about ready to drop a truckload of cash right now at a whole bunch of retail stores.

25

KYLE

Bagram Airbase
Afghanistan

Little Warrior: My deployment schedule's been posted.

Bear: When?

Little Warrior: Can I video call?

My heart does this weird leap, like a horse at the starting gate. I rub a hand over my chest as if I can force it to calm down. It's just Jamie. The girl I've known since forever. I miss her is all, but I miss home too. I miss the colours. Everything is brighter back in Australia. More vivid. The water is clear blue, the sun a brighter shade of yellow, the grass lush and green.

We've been here two months now, and there's been too much time to sit around and think. We have one reconnaissance mission under our belts. I'm eager for another. They make the time here move faster and leaves us feeling like we're actually achieving something.

Bear: Sure, just give me a minute to get undressed.

Little Warrior: Please don't.

Bear: So that's a no for naked video?

Little Warrior: Can you see me rolling my eyes right now? That's a hard no.

Bear: You just said hard.

Little Warrior: …

Bear: Fine but you're missing out. I've just done a thousand push-ups at least. My muscles are fully jacked right now.

I haven't. I've been lying in bed trying to summon the energy for a run. It's hot out. And truth be told, it's difficult without Jake. A gaping hole has been torn in the team. They've filled it, but Jake is a man not easily replaced. Nathan has the unfortunate honour of taking his place, having been hand-picked by our squadron commander. He's young and cocky, as opposed to my mature and cocky, but that's off the field. On patrol he's eagle-eyed and focused. The man is no weak link, but it doesn't make our hearts any less heavy.

I roll over and sit up as Jamie replies, the three bubbled dots appearing and disappearing as she types.

Little Warrior: I can't believe you just said jacked.

Bear: I say a lot of cool words. Are you going to video or what? I'm taking off my shirt.

The video call comes in, and I hit the green button to answer it. There's an odd pull inside me when Jamie appears. There's a natural earthiness about her that's more inviting than a cold beer on a hot day. Her face is tan and familiar. It's late afternoon and she's in her unit, her uniform on with her hair loose. It ripples over her shoulders and down her back like whiskey—rich, silky, and lush. My brows snap together when I find myself tripping down a path that is decidedly non-platonic. *What the hell?* It's just goddamn hair.

"I see you're wearing a shirt." Her voice is husky and a little grumpy. She's tired.

"You sound disappointed."

"Relieved mostly. Don't want my eyes getting rug burn from looking at your hairy chest."

I laugh, loving when she makes the effort to joke. It's cute. She's like an angry kitten revealing her playful side, and she would literally punch me in the nuts if I ever voiced the thought. I slide a hand beneath my cotton tee shirt, rubbing at the modest expanse of hair. "It's hardly a carpet, but I can wax if you prefer it smooth," I joke.

Her eyes goggle. "You would wax your chest?"

"Fuck no." I physically recoil. "Have you seen The Forty-Year-Old Virgin? They damned near ripped his nipples off."

She props her phone up on the kitchen counter and sets about making a coffee. "That's because they were supposed to put Vaseline on them first and didn't." She snorts. "Amateurs. I could do yours if you like. I think I'd enjoy making you cry like a little baby."

"Like you know how to wax a man's chest."

Jamie pauses her action of spooning coffee into her mug and looks me in the eye. "I am a female, Kyle, in case you can't see past the shapeless fatigues. We're pretty much born knowing how to wax our own vaginas."

I lean forward into the phone, my lungs suddenly feeling a little tight. "You wax downstairs?"

"Oh good lord." She rolls her eyes and pours a dash of milk in her coffee. "I'm not having this conversation with you."

"You started it."

She presses her lips together, but I see her fighting the urge to laugh. "And your point is?"

"Don't start a conversation you aren't prepared to finish."

Jamie nods and brings the mug to her lips, blowing carefully on the hot liquid. "I'll remember that in future."

"So is that a yes?"

"Yes to what?"

"The waxing." I hold back a laugh. A little payback is in order, I think, for her hairy chest comment. "Do you go full Brazilian? Or do you leave a little landing strip? Or am I way off base and you're a full-blown furry native?"

She splutters, setting her coffee down before she spills it. "What in the actual fuck, Kyle? It's none of your business!"

"Of course, it is. I'm your friend. Friends talk about this stuff, right? I have no preference if you were wondering. Us guys aren't as choosy as you women—"

"I wasn't wondering."

"—seem to think. In fact, I don't mind a bit of hair. It's like the framing of a Da Vinci painting. It's—"

"Oh my god. Okay! Okay! I'm sorry I implied that your chest was a rug."

"Apology accepted," I reply in a haughty tone as she picks up her phone and starts walking with it. "But don't ever diss on my chest again or I'll start asking what other parts you wax and when I say parts, I mean—"

The screen goes black.

Jamie hung up on me.

I tip my head back and laugh.

Bear: I was going to say eyebrows. I swear.

Little Warrior: You were not!

Bear: Totally was. Why? What did you think I was going to say?

Little Warrior: I'm not even going to say it.

Bear: This conversation is a safe space, Jamie. You can say anything. I'm not here to judge you.

Little Warrior: You know if I was there right now I'd punch you.

Bear: Feisty women are hot.

Little Warrior: I'm going to pretend I don't know you when I get there.

Bear: When are you getting here again?

Little Warrior: Well I was videoing to tell you until you got all dirty.

Bear: How dare you? I shower every day.

Except on missions. There are no showers in the mountains nor across the rocky terrain. There's no shaving. There's no room to pack ten pairs of clean socks. You get dirt and dust inside your uniform, or mud and sludge in your pants and boots from walking through thigh-deep creeks, and it stays there until you return to base. The days are long when you spend them caked in dirt. The nights are even longer and usually spent either guarding the camp or dreaming of cold beer, thick juicy steaks, hot showers, and sinking your cock inside a warm and willing female.

I push the last particular thought away with a curse, tossing my phone and rubbing at the back of my neck as I stand and leave my bunk. Sexual frustration on the front line is an absolute sonofabitch.

Little Warrior: I'll be there in a week.

My head tips back, a harsh breath pushing past my lips. The thought of her coming back here fires every protective instinct I possess. I know she can take care of herself, but it's different here. This place takes from you and doesn't give back. It's not gentle. It's not compassionate. It's war. And the only thing predictable about war is that there will always be war. Jamie's done enough. She deserves a little happiness.

Bear: So soon?

Little Warrior: I put my hand up to replace Wood. I don't have family. Or children. It's easier for me to leave last minute.

Easier for everyone else, I want to say, but I don't. When Jamie wants to do something, she does it, stuff the consequences.

Bear: Then prepare to have your ass handed to you at poker.

Little Warrior: Nice try but you always lose. Funny how you conveniently seem to forget that.

A faint smile forms on my lips. I miss her. Messages aren't the same. I tap the button on my phone, bringing up my photo album. I scroll to the only photo of Jamie that I have. It's from our barbeque at the beach. She's sitting on the sand in her bikini. Her hair is tousled and damp and sticks to her neck, her nose a little sunburnt. I've caught her in a rare laugh, her hand stretched out towards the phone as she tries to hide her face from the camera.

It's my favourite photo in the world. It reminds me that humanity can be unspeakably destructive, but it can also be incredibly resilient. It can be hurt, and damaged, and suffer incredible pain, and despite it all, it can thrive. It can laugh and love and dance and be extraordinarily beautiful.

Little Warrior: I want to ask you a question.

I close the image, Jamie disappearing as I reply.

Bear: Shoot.

Little Warrior: Have you ever thought about leaving?

Bear: The army?

Little Warrior: Yes, the army.

Bear: I think about it every damn day.

Little Warrior: What would you do?

Bear: I honestly don't know. Raise my kids. Be there to pick them up from school. Take them travelling. I want to be a good dad. The dad I always wanted and never got. Why do you ask? Have you been thinking about leaving?

Little Warrior: God no. This is it for me. The army is my life.

I heave a deep sigh and rise to my feet. There's no arguing with her about it. She's too damn stubborn. Maybe I could show her instead. Show her what life can be like outside of regimens and rules and hierarchies. Show her that the army is a job, not a life.

Bear: I'm taking you away after your deployment. Be ready. You're mine for four whole weeks.

Little Warrior: A holiday?

Bear: Road trip.

Little Warrior: Wait, what?

Bear: We're going to travel down the entire coast of Western Australia. We'll do it all. Dive at Ningaloo Reef. Swim with whale sharks. Hike the gorges.

Little Warrior: That actually sounds amazing.

Bear: That, my clueless friend, is what life is really all about.

Little Warrior: Ahhh, I see what you're trying to do here.

Bear: Then let me.

Little Warrior: You can try but it won't work.

Bear: It will work. Trust me, okay? I know you blame yourself for your father's death. I do the same with Jake. But you can't find forgiveness in war. Believe me, I've tried. We need to somehow let go. The only way I can think to do that is in living the best way we know how. Wouldn't they want that for us?

It takes a minute for Jamie to respond.

Little Warrior: They would. You're right. I trust you, Bear. Let's do it.

My chest swells as if a heavy weight has been lifted from it. I set my phone aside, and Monty appears in my open door, rapping on the side to catch my attention. "Briefing at 1700 hours."

I nod, rubbing a hand over my head, knowing I need to set my thoughts aside and focus on getting through this deployment. "Roger that."

"Let Kendall know. Not sure where he is."

"Will do."

He leaves and I find Ryan in the communication room, sitting at the computer. His hand is on the mouse but his eyes are closed. I squint a little at the screen. His emails are open. They're his private business, but I look regardless. There's one from Finlay. He's clearly fighting against the urge to open it.

I prop my shoulder up against the doorway. "Did the big bad soldiers tucker poor little Kendall out?"

His fingers jolt on the mouse, and his head jerks my way, eyes flying open. He shuts his email down and gets to his feet. "I could do with some sleep. No one gets any rest bunking with you, asshole. You snore like a wounded elephant in heat."

My brows fly up. "How would you know what a wounded elephant in heat sounds like?"

"Easy. It sounds like you."

I tip my chin towards the computer. "Heard from Fin?"

"Why do you ask that?"

"You just got that look on your face."

"What look?"

"The look you get whenever you're around her or when someone mentions her name. You know—the puppy eyes."

"Puppy eyes?" he growls. Ryan shoves me as he walks out the door. Being the rock-solid bastard I am, I barely budge an inch, and it only irritates him further. "Fuck off, Brooks. You don't know what you're talking about."

But I do. In the months leading up to deployment, Ryan barely stayed on base. He spent his time with Finlay, and it made me so fucking happy. They were starting to heal, and they were doing it together, until Fin was accepted into a research program with the Climate Change Research Centre in Sydney. For four years.

She planned to turn it down, wanting to stay close to Ryan. He didn't take the idea well. He doesn't want to hold her back from her dreams. I know, because I nursed his drunken ass at pool while he told me all about it. I get it, but he can't see past his warped sense of duty. He thinks he's doing the right thing, but the right thing is to let Fin choose, and when she chose him, he broke off their burgeoning relationship. He's been like an angry grizzly ever since.

"Hey!" I call out.

He turns around.

"I wasn't here to stalk your ass. Monty called a briefing at 1700 hours."

"Good," he mutters, cracking his knuckles as he walks off.

~

Two days later finds us scoping the back of the mountains behind a suspect village for evidence of enemy presence. Our task is not to engage fire but gather intelligence.

Ryan crouches ahead, examining what looks like a weapons pit. The ground has been flattened and an etching in the rocks gives a pretty good indication the Taliban are occupying the area. He signals for me and Nathan to join him.

Just as I'm climbing the rocky outcrop, a bullet zings past our heads, slamming into the tree behind us.

"Sonofabitch," Ryan growls and folds himself behind the thick barrier of rock, assuming a firing position.

I crouch, rushing forward when another shot rings out. My arm explodes in a ball of blistering fire. "Fuck," I curse through clenched teeth, sweat breaking out over my entire body. "I'm fucking hit."

Galloway runs over, ducking low, as Ryan reaches me, his face hard and pale.

"Where?"

"Right arm," I pant, already smelling the thick metallic stench of blood. A quick glance shows exposed bone and muscle tissue. *Sonofabitch.* "It's my goddamn elbow."

Ryan inspects the injury, relief lightening his worried expression. "Suck it up, Brooks," he ribs as he reaches for gauze and bandages. "It's just a scratch."

I try to laugh but it comes out choked, my eyes scrunched against the pain. "Fuck you, Kendall."

"I'd appreciate it if you didn't." He chuckles as if the whole damn incident is amusing, but I can read what's going on behind his dark eyes. For a moment, it was Jake all over again. A few inches to the left and a little higher and I could have been gone too. The fact that I'm not is enough to leave me weak with relief. "Your firing arm is gonna be out of action for a little while."

We lock eyes, a silent acknowledgement of what this means. It causes another sharp burst of pain, this one inside my heart. This type of injury requires delicate surgery to piece muscle and bone back together. I'll have months of physiotherapy ahead of me to get back to the standard of fitness the regiment requires. It means I'm going home.

"Fucking hell, Kendall," I mutter with quiet frustration.

I close my eyes, tilting my head to the sky. After several deep breaths, I open them again, the pain and disappointment shuttered, tucked away for another day. "I'm gonna have to learn how to use my left hand to jack off now."

Ryan tries to smile at the joke and gives up, handing me a green whistle for the pain instead.

Monty inches towards the both of us while Tex sets up a satellite communication, sending a request for a medevac. "We don't know what the fuck we're dealing with out there. Could be one or two rogues, but from the intelligence we've gathered so far, which isn't much, it could be fucking hundreds. Let's retreat to a pick-up position for Brooks, and then we can formulate a plan."

"Fuck this shit," I growl, hating to leave them in the middle of an operation. We train hard for this, living and breathing it every day. Being rendered useless to my team is a slap in the goddamn face.

~

Bear: Change of plans.

Little Warrior: What do you mean?

Bear: I'm in Germany.

And trying to type from my hospital bed with my left hand is its own special kind of hell. My bed is on a vertical incline, my back propped up with pillows, my giant thumb hitting all the wrong keys and deleting every second letter.

Her reply is immediate.

Little Warrior: How bad is it?

Of course she would know why I'm here. She's a combat medic. My injury required a specialist orthopaedic surgeon. I've been patched up good as new. Well, almost. It's going to take a while for the bone and tissue to knit back together, and after that, physiotherapy will be my new best friend.

Bear: Just a scratch.

Little Warrior: They don't send you to Germany for a scratch. Tell me what happened or so help me God, I will go AWOL and hunt you the fuck down.

Bear: I got shot.

My phone starts ringing. Jamie is requesting a video call. I answer and she appears on the screen. It's late at night where she is and her lights are off, save for a dim glow from the lamp beside her bed. It sets a warm halo around her head, making her eyes appear darker. "Kyle?"

"I'm okay. I promise."

She puts a shaky hand to her forehead, expelling a sob.

"Don't cry, Jamie." Not with me stuck here unable to do a damn thing about it. My chest squeezes into a tight knot of misery. "Don't. I'm fine."

"I'm not crying," she chokes out, tears falling thick and fast down her cheeks. "You're an asshole."

"Hey, what did I do?"

"You got shot!" Jamie shouts, swiping at her face.

"Just a little bit."

The pink cotton tee shirt she's wearing stretches tight as she reaches across her bed for a tissue. There's a hole in the neckline and the armpit, and combined with her tousled hair she somehow still manages to look like ice cream on a hot day. I avert my eyes from the exposed tan skin of her belly as she plucks a tissue free. "What happened?"

I scratch at my beard. "It was just a rogue shot. Some asshole got lucky."

Jamie blows her nose and tosses the tissue aside. "Tell me everything."

So I do, not allowed to leave anything out, and promising to show her copies of the X-ray as soon as I can. "Kyle, it's your *right* arm," she says as if I somehow forgot.

I tip my head back on the pillow. "I know that." She sniggers a little and I know exactly what she's thinking because everyone's been thinking it. "Laugh away, chuckles, but this does *not* affect my ability to jack off. I could load and fire a rifle with my left hand while blindfolded and hit a moving target in the time it took my team to find their own dicks."

Jamie laughs outright and it's so much better than the tears. It dies off slowly and she sighs. "I won't get to see you."

"Not until you're back home for our road trip."

Her expression is dubious. "Will you be healed enough by then for that?"

"Wild horses, Jamie."

"I can do most of the driving."

My lips curl into a slow grin. Oh yeah. This is happening. "Because driver picks the music, right?"

"Yup."

Jamie's into the eighties, mostly bands like Cold Chisel and The Eagles because they were her dad's favourites, though she cracks out a few Madonna tunes when she thinks no one is listening. I'm pretty sure "Material Girl" is her favourite, but I can deal with it because it gives me something to tease her about. "So we're actually going to do this? Because now that I'm out of action, I've got a shitload of time to plan it."

She slowly nods her head. "I think we're actually going to do this."

26

JAMIE

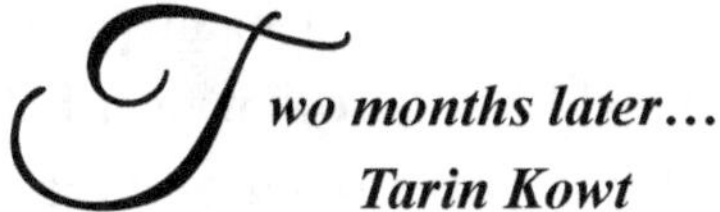

wo months later...
Tarin Kowt

I WAKE SLOWLY, rolling over with a moan. My body is wiped. Every part of me aches, including my heart. I've been up for seventy-two hours straight—dealing with the aftermath of a suicide bombing.

With time I've learnt there's only one way to cope: push it all deep down inside. I know it sounds heartless, but I can't think of them as people with lives and families and feelings. I would choke, otherwise. The only way I can do my job in this kind of scenario is to focus on treating the injury and nothing else.

Sometimes they slip through the way Arash did, and they haunt me at night when I'm trying to sleep. I'm still showing his photo to everyone I can, in every village, on every patrol, in the hopes of finding him. But it's a needle in a haystack. Those hopes sink a little lower with every 'no' I get. My comrades think I'm crazy. It's just one kid in a sea of thousands. But I can't shake the responsibility I feel for

261

him. For the situation I helped put him in. I couldn't save his father the same way I couldn't save mine, and he's all alone.

I should let him go, but I've tried and I can't seem to do it. How could I ever have a family of my own knowing all the while Arash is growing up with no one?

My phone dings. I reach out a hand, grabbing for it with my eyes closed. It slips from my fingers and thumps to the floor.

"Shit," I mutter and roll back over in bed, peeking over the mattress with slitted eyes. It's fallen faceup, a message notification from Kyle on the screen. Too tired to physically pick the device up, I reach an arm down and open it from the floor.

Bear: Guess what?

Little Warrior: You're mad and I'm not?

Kyle has been home for just over seven weeks now. He's on light duties while he recovers, which is getting to him. I can't blame him, but swimming with saltwater crocodiles would be more fun than his bitching lately. He's been keeping himself busy by pissing everyone off. The good news is that they have recruits due in soon. Sprinkling his crabby attitude all over the new soldiers will keep him occupied while he heals.

Bear: You're so childish.

Little Warrior: That's rich coming from you.

Bear: Fine if you don't want my news …

I roll my eyes.

Little Warrior: Please tell me before I expire from anticipation.

Bear: Ryan and Fin are having a baby.

My stomach dips in shock. I collect my phone off the floor and roll onto my back, my eyes stuck on the words for a long moment while they sink in.

Little Warrior: For real?

Bear: Yes for real. Apparently she was already pregnant when we left on deployment, three months along already. I think it was part of the reason why she turned down the research program, but she never got a chance to tell Ryan before he left. She's over six months along now. Time goes so fast!

Jake is going to be an uncle. It makes me ache horribly, my nose fizzing and eyes burning with loss all over again. Not for me this time but for him. For what he's missing out on. What this place took from him.

Little Warrior: I hadn't realised they'd patched things up, but I'm happy for them, Kyle.

Bear: Does it sound stupid if I say I'm jealous?

My brows knit together, confused. Kyle is jealous of Ryan? Does he have feelings for Finlay? I brush my fingers across the screen, suddenly unsure what to do with this information. I don't know what to say.

Bear: Jamie?

There's a buzzing in my ears, the kind that makes me lightheaded for a moment. It passes when I take a breath.

Little Warrior: I'm here. It doesn't sound stupid. I'm just not sure it's a good idea.

Bear: What's not a good idea?

Little Warrior: Fin and Ryan have deep feelings for each other. They're having a baby together.

Bear: Yes, and?

I shake my head, thoroughly confused.

Little Warrior: Nothing. Never mind. I should get up.

Bear: It's Sunday. Aren't you off today?

Little Warrior: It's been a big few days here. I've got to go clean my rifle.

Bear: Can you do me a favour and check in on Ryan for me?

Little Warrior: Sure thing.

I run into Ryan a few days later. He's walking out of the briefing building as I'm walking past on my way to the small gym on base.

"Hey, Murph," he says. He's looking a little rough around the edges, but there's a hint of a smile on his lips. He steps in alongside me, and we walk together.

"Kendall. You're looking … happy?" He immediately frowns. "Or not."

"No, I am. I think." He glances at me, a wry expression on his face. "I don't know how to feel some days. I'm all over the place."

"Well that makes sense."

His brows rise. "It does?"

"Of course it does. You're going to be a dad. Congrats by the way."

His chest expands. "Thanks. Let me guess, Brooks has been flapping his gums harder than an old woman at bingo on a Sunday afternoon."

I laugh. "He might have mentioned it."

Ryan rubs at the back of his head as we walk. "It was unexpected, but I'm starting to get excited. I never thought I'd have this."

"Have what?"

"A family. I just wish …" He swallows and heaves a dejected sigh. "Jake is missing out is all."

I come to a stop outside the building that houses our gym equipment. He stops with me, and I reach up, giving his shoulder a squeeze. "I know. I'm sorry."

"There are days I find myself happy, and then I get pissed at myself because how can I be happy when he's gone? I guess that's why I'm all over the place."

"He would want you to be happy, Kendall," I say softly. "Don't take that from him."

"Yeah." Ryan nods. "I know. He would want the same for you too, Murph."

I wave a hand around at the bland, dusty compound. "This is my happy."

"Geez." He winces and then grins at me, clapping me on the back as he starts to walk off. "You need to get a life!" he calls out as I push open the door.

"The army is my life," I mutter to myself as I make my way towards the treadmill for a five-minute warm-up, and somehow saying the words aloud sounds a little sad. Everyone is moving on around me and it feels a little like I'm getting left behind.

I shake the feeling off and blast the incline button. The machine tilts slowly and my thigh muscles begin to burn. *This is where I'm meant to be.*

❦

TIME PASSES SLOWLY HERE, days turning into weeks and weeks into months at the pace of tortoise. I fill it with hospital shifts, patrols, emails and messages. Wood checks in regularly, as does Erin. And I speak to Kyle almost every day I'm able to. Sometimes I have to use the communications room, depending on where I'm stationed. Sometimes I get to use my phone.

I'm spending my last few weeks with a platoon who rented an Afghan house. It's the highlight of my second deployment, spending time with the locals. It's hard finding privacy as the only female here; I've been heating up water for makeshift showers, taking them early before the men wake. I check my emails every few days. Most are general updates, like the one from Wood I find in my inbox late this afternoon.

Murphy,

I've sent you some links to the houses we're going to look at next week. There are five. Have a look and let me know what you think. I'm still trying to talk Erin into buying so I need you on my side with this!

I have to run so this isn't long, but I miss you. I kinda hate being over here while you're over there. I won't lie, it's hard getting used to life outside the army again. I wake up reaching for my rifle and it's not there. Don't get me wrong. I don't want to go back. But I feel naked. As if I've been stripped of my identity. I'm trying to just take each day as it comes.

How is it going over there? Are you coming to visit when you get back?

Wood

There's no other word to describe the internet service over here except absolute shit. It takes forever for the links to load. I check all the houses, cursing every time the screen freezes. Most are pretty run-down. The kind that need new kitchens and flooring and a good coat of paint.

Wood,

They're all the same as each other except for the third one. It would have a decent view of the water if you added a little front porch. Also, not cool asking me to take sides! You're on your own.

It's same old here. Nothing has changed.

You only want me to visit so I can help work on your new house. I'm coming to WA when I'm done here, but Kyle and I are doing a road trip, so there goes your cheap labour. Sorry not sorry.

Jamie

～

I'm in my last week when good news comes in from Kyle. He's emailed an image of him holding Fin and Ryan's baby with the message, *Isn't he cute?*

It's a boy. He's the image of Ryan with his dark cap of hair and wide brown eyes, but it's the man holding him who's captured my attention. Kyle is looking down at the little blanket-wrapped burrito with an expression of pure adoration on his face, and the puzzle piece falls into place. It's not Finlay he wants. It's the baby. He wants what they have. I should have realised.

My heart gives a little tug. He looks good with a baby in his arms. His big hands hold tight to the precious bundle, cradling him snug to his chest.

I type back a quick response and hit send, unable to help myself. *Not sure who's cuter.*

He must be near his computer because he responds a bare minute later. *Careful. You just said something nice. And you totally think I'm cute. I knew it.*

A smile tugs at my lips. *You caught me in a rare moment. What's his name?*

Jacob, he replies.

A familiar ache rises up inside me. *Jake would love that.*

His response takes a long while to load. *He really would.*

I type another reply. *How are Fin and Ryan doing?*

They're doing really good. How are you doing?

Lonely. I miss Kyle. I miss Wood. And Erin. My little family. I miss them all so much I go to bed feeling hollow at night.

Everything is good. I have three days left here, then I'm back to base and packing up for home. How goes the planning for our road trip?

We're all set.

I'm looking forward to it. When I was home, I wanted to be here so bad. And now that I'm here I want to be home. And not Townsville, but home. It's this constant feeling of being torn, of feeling like I don't quite belong anywhere. I don't know how to fix it, but maybe our road trip will help me work it out. *Then I'll see you soon.*

His response is short, but it sends an odd little flutter through my belly. *I can't wait to see you, Jamie.*

~

I'M up before dawn the next morning, stepping out into the quadrant as Sergeant Marsh comes towards me, suited up and ready to finish today's final task. The sun is yet to hit the horizon, but it's not far off. Pale blue and gold start to colour the sky. "You good to go?"

I heft my pack over my shoulders. The heavy weight of it presses me into the ground. I'm careful to keep the struggle from my expression. I don't want special treatment. There's still a huge percentage of male soldiers who resent us, but my team accepts me. "All good."

Our convoy arrives in Kandahar over an hour later. The city is the second largest in the country, the population a little over five hundred thousand. There's been recent bombings in the city outskirts.

My rifle is at the ready as we get out and walk, my eyes skimming every nook for injured civilians. My arms ache from holding it as an hour turns into another. From my peripheral vision, I see a figure running and turn my head. It's a child. A young boy. There's something familiar about him. My pulse kicks up a notch. His clothing is worn and dirty and splattered with blood.

"Arash?" I call out.

Connor turns and slams a hand in my chest. "Shut the fuck up, Murphy."

Shit. I step around him and start moving forward, keeping low. "Arash?"

"Corporal Murphy! Get your ass back here," Connor growls as I move off in the child's direction.

"Just give me a minute," I call back, moving forward, my eyes on the little boy as he picks up his pace, dust kicking out behind him.

"Goddammit," I hear Connor yell, but I don't stop.

"Arash!" I call again, starting to run, chasing him down.

I'm getting close, passing an open alleyway when I'm grabbed from behind.

"Hey!" It's a group of local Taliban, turbans wrapped around their heads and guns in hand. They're holding American M9 Berettas. I slam the butt of my rifle into the nearest face and another rips it from my grasp.

A hand slaps over my mouth, and I'm dragged backwards by two solid men. They each have an arm, their fingers digging in hard enough to bruise. *Sonofabitch.* The kid was a decoy. *How could I have been so stupid?* My team was right. Searching for Arash took up too much space in my head, leaving me careless.

Using their grip as leverage, I lift up and kick out to my right. The Taliban soldier drops to his knees, his hand loosening. I turn, swinging hard, and my fist cracks into the face of my second attacker. He lets go, cursing in Pashto, the local language in Kandahar.

I start running towards the opening of the alley when my bun is grabbed from behind by a third soldier. Tears spring free at the sudden pain. I'm yanked backwards so hard I land on my ass. I grapple with the man, but he's yanking me so fast my feet can't gain purchase. The pins fall and my hair spills down. He grabs another handful, pulling me with both hands, dragging me along the ground.

"Let me go, you goddamn asshole!" I shout, twisting, reaching out behind me and clawing at his hands.

Shots fire from the alley. It's Connor. The rest of my team would be close behind him, cursing my idiocy. Bullets rain down, and one soldier jerks in a dance as blood sprays outward. He drops to the ground. Dead.

"Murphy!" Connor shouts.

I'm lifted up and tossed into the bed of a dirty, old pickup truck. Two soldiers jump in behind me, firing back as the vehicle accelerates with a wild lurch. I kick out, knocking one of them clean out of the truck. He lands in the dirt, stunned for a minute, before he gets up and jogs after us. The other soldier pins my arms down from behind as he leaps back in, landing right on top of me. His knees punch into my stomach and I grunt. "You'll pay for that, you little bitch," he growls in English as we pick up speed.

His fist slams into my head with a *crack*. Pain erupts, stars exploding as my vision blurs, blood filling my eye. The metallic stench is thick and vile, bringing back memories of crunched metal and shattering glass. I barely take another breath before he comes at me again, punching me in the jaw. I'm hit again and again. A rib fractures, and I wheeze in agony, my head lolling to the side.

I swallow, gasping. I won't go out like this. *I won't.*

My knee jerks up, catching him in the crotch. He hisses, pulling away, and I use the diversion to kick him in the face. His head snaps sideways and he snarls, leaping on me again.

"Bitch!" he shrieks and flicks open a short, sharp blade. He jabs it into my shoulder.

Fire explodes and I cry out. He yanks it free and jabs again. And again. I scream and lift my head, biting his shoulder clean through his shirt. Blood fills my mouth, tangy and vile. My belly heaves, but I don't let go.

My head is ripped back by the soldier behind me, his fist tearing the hair from my scalp. He presses a gun to my temple and I still immediately, the only sound my heavy breathing and the jarring engine of the truck. The metal is cool and hard against my skin. "Move and you die."

The soldier above me slices through the fastenings of my armour and rips it free, tossing it over the side of the moving truck. He starts on my shirt next, yanking through the buttons, tearing the tee shirt underneath. Air hits my exposed chest, blood pooling into my neck and over my white sports bra.

My breath comes in gasps, panic setting in. I squeeze my eyes shut, gagging on blood and bile. He grabs at my breasts with his free hand, sliding beneath the fabric and pinching the soft flesh with a sickening grin.

I can survive this, I tell myself. But I'm not going to sit back and take it.

I open my eyes, taking deep breaths as the soldier above me claws at my belt, clumsy in his haste. He gets it open and unzips my pants, snarling as he looks up at me. His eyes are dark. Angry. He's not doing this for fun. This isn't pleasure. This is degradation. A lesson. He yanks them down, the knife in his hand nicking my belly and thighs as my underwear is exposed.

The truck jerks to a stop behind an old quala as he pulls himself free of his pants. I force myself to remain calm as he leans up over me, the gun still pressed to my forehead as he yanks my underwear to the side.

My nostrils flare as I glare hard into his eyes. "Go to hell, you ugly sonofabitch."

I punch upwards with my legs, using every bit of strength I have. The soldier above me slams forward, crashing into the one behind me. His knee smashes into my nose and blood spurts down my face.

There's a tangle of legs and arms as I scramble to my hands and knees, swiping blood from my face so I can see.

The soldier who held me down still has the gun. I grab for it but he won't let go. I slam his arm into the side of the truck, once, twice. It drops to the floor of the bed, and I snatch it up, slipping in a pool of blood.

A guttural growl wrenches from deep inside as I turn, firing at point blank range. The first soldier goes down. And the second. The driver is already out of the truck, gun out and running low around the front of the hood.

He fires off a shot through the front windscreen. The bullet goes right through the back windscreen. I'm already ducking down as glass sprays outward, splintering my face and chest.

I rise up fast, returning fire. The first bullet catches him in the leg and he stumbles. I adjust my aim. The second catches him in the head, blood and bone shattering as he drops.

"Murphy!" The shout is long and loud. I turn. It's Connor. He's running straight for me, an expression of horror on his face.

I stumble in the bed of the truck, the gun falling from my fingers. I blink through the blood in my eyes, swiping it away with the back of my hand.

I need to pull myself together.

I need to …

He reaches me before the rest of the team, leaping up onto the truck like an Olympic vaulter. "Jesus." His voice is shaky, his eyes darting over me, from the stab wounds in my shoulder and down to the bloodied nicks in my flesh and exposed underwear. "Murphy."

"I'm fine. Just …" I grasp my pants, pulling them up from where they hang half down my hips. My fingers slip on the zipper. "Help me," I whimper. "I don't want them to see. I don't want …"

"I got you." Connor steps in close and slides the zipper up swiftly, fastening my button and belt. "You're okay," he says in a reassuring tone.

"I'm okay," I repeat, clasping my shirt together as he fixes me up, covering the wounds on my shoulder. There's nothing more I can do. The buttons are gone. "Don't tell anyone, Connor."

He pauses, looking at me. "They're going to see."

I swallow. "Not how bad."

"Did they rape you?"

"N-n-no." Dammit. I swallow, pushing everything down inside. "No," I say in a firmer tone.

"Murphy?" I peek around Connor. It's Sergeant Marsh and the rest of the team, breathless, slowing from a jog as they reach us. The team spreads out, scoping the area, checking the downed soldier and the two sprawled behind me, both of them piled on top of each other.

"I'm fine, sir. A minor scuffle." Connor tries to help me down from the back of the truck, and I nudge him away, sweat breaking across my brow as I climb down myself.

Marsh takes me in. "I'm calling in a medevac."

"No! I'm good. Just get me back to camp. I can fix myself up."

"Your shirt is covered in blood, Corporal Murphy."

"It's not all mine." His expression remains unconvinced, but I'm not going back on a Hawk. I'm not leaving my team for something that wouldn't have happened had I been male. The lone female playing soldier tucks tail and runs back to base the minute she gets hurt? It's not happening. "It's not, Sergeant," I reiterate, forcing myself to meet his eyes. "It's just a couple of punches and a torn shirt. It looks worse than it is. I just need some ice for my face."

Sitting in the truck on the convoy back to camp is a welcome relief. Connor sits in the back with me, handing me gauze for my shoulder. I slide it inside my shirt, pressing down hard, my stomach rolling over with a queasy thump.

Marsh orders me to get cleaned up when we return. "Connor, go help her."

Once in my room, I push my shirt over my shoulder, inspecting the wounds in the small cosmetics mirror I keep in my bag. They're small and shallow. The worst concern is infection. "Bring me my first aid kit." Connor pulls it from my pack and hands it over. "Can you get me a wet cloth?"

He ducks out of my room, and I whip off my torn shirt, lightheaded from the pain. The cuts on my belly, hip, and thighs, need nothing more than a bit of antiseptic and some butterfly tape. I quickly wrap a towel around myself and sit on the bed, pulling out everything I need.

Connor returns, shutting the door behind him. He walks over and crouches in front of me, the damp cloth in his hands. "What can I do?"

My lower jaw trembles. "Don't be soft me with me, Connor."

He nods. "Okay."

"I need you to stitch up my shoulder."

Connor's eyes widen a fraction. "Are you insane?"

"Do I look insane?"

"Maybe a little. Murphy, I've never done this before."

"It's easy." I swallow the thick bile in my mouth. "I'll walk you through it."

I instruct him through cleaning the wound, the anaesthetic injection, and each stitch, watching him pull the needle through my skin. It's not neat, but it's not a complete mess either. I probably could have done it myself, but I'm not freaking Rambo—alone and in the damn mountains.

He finishes by covering them up with waterproof gauze so I can shower, his breathing a little shaky as he straightens. "I need a drink."

A laugh bursts out of me, the sound a little hysterical. "What I wouldn't give for a shot of whiskey right now."

"Or a bottle," he mutters as I stand, fighting back a wave of dizziness. He's looking me over like he wants to cry. "You're a fucking mess, Murphy."

He brushes his palm down the side of my face, and I wince. His touch is gentle, and it has me fighting back tears at the pain it evokes. I'm holding on by my fingernails right now. "Bruises fade."

"Only the ones on the outside."

I lift my trembling chin. "You can go now, Connor."

He hesitates.

"I'm fine."

He shakes his head. "You're not fine."

I swallow. "Maybe I'm not, but I will be. Okay?"

Connor exhales deeply, his eyes searching mine before he turns and leaves, shutting the door quietly behind him.

Camp is subdued over the next two days. My body aches everywhere. My face swells up like a balloon, both eyes almost closed from the hit I took to my nose. My fractured ribs are taped, and my body is mottled with deep, dark bruises. It hurts to get dressed, and Connor sneaks into my room each morning to plait and pin my hair for me before I can attempt it myself. "I have two little sisters," he tells me in a light-hearted tone. "I have so much practice I could even put your hair in a French twist if you wanted. But if you tell that to anyone in the team, I'll take you out while you're sleeping."

I find myself staring down every soldier who looks at me a little too long with pity on their face. Most of them show respect, but there are a few with irritated expressions. We were warned about what happened to females over here. The requirement to be extra vigilant. Our brief training in Kuwait before my first deployment included a lecture on female assault. It happens. But it happens everywhere, right? I was trained for it. I dealt with it. I'm not crying on their shoulders. Isn't that enough?

I'm fatigued when our convoy returns to Bagram Airbase. I'm placed on immediate medical leave, and after a briefing my commander advises the incident isn't significant enough to report. He slaps my file on his desk. "You're going home in two days."

"Sir, I've obtained permission to fly direct to Perth."

I won't have to fly back to Townsville first.

He nods. "Godspeed, Corporal Murphy. You're dismissed."

My ribs scream as I lift my arm, snapping off a sharp salute. I return to my bunk and start packing, putting my phone on the charger. It died while I was gone.

Lying down on my bed, I switch it back on to a flood of messages from Erin and Wood. Most are simple updates about what they're doing because they know I've been off base. It's hard to read about normal life when mine's been anything but, though I get through them. There's a few messages from Kyle too, but his are different. They're a little more personal.

I send off replies to all three, letting them know I'm back on base. I add another just for Kyle, sending him the link to my flight information.

Little Warrior: My flight details have changed. Can you pick me up from the airport?

His reply comes in an hour later.

Bear: You're coming two days early?

Little Warrior: I'm coming straight in, not diverting to Townsville. But I won't have my stuff for our road trip.

Bear: We can just buy what you need here before we leave. Is everything okay? How was camp?

Little Warrior: Camp was fine.

Bear: Jamie?

Little Warrior: Yeah?

Bear: I miss you.

My eyes well up and my face scrunches, flooding my entire body with pain. I curl into a ball on my bed, shuddering as I hold the sobs at bay. I need to hold on. Just a little longer.

Little Warrior: I miss you too.

He takes his time replying, the bubbled dots appearing and disappearing for at least two minutes.

Bear: Hurry home, okay?

I close my eyes, hugging the phone to my chest, and I fall asleep.

27

JAMIE

our days later...

MY LEGS ACHE from lack of use as I walk from the plane and up the narrow ramp. I'm tired of travelling, but the flight attendants took one look at my battered face and army uniform when I boarded and they bumped me into business class. I didn't even get to appreciate the finger of whiskey they brought me, or the comfortable quiet surroundings, because I crashed before takeoff, sleeping the whole flight home.

I field constant stares from civilians as I step into the arrival gate, my eyes searching for Kyle. I take my time scanning the mass of people, but he's not here. I swallow disappointment and keep my chin high as I collect my bag and walk the length of the airport, leaving through the arrivals entrance.

The doors whoosh open, and I see him then, my eyes picking him out in the crowd of people coming and going. He's jogging towards the doors, towards me, his expression agitated as he dodges around slow-moving travellers.

276

My heart climbs to my throat as I take him in, every part of him so wonderfully familiar. He's dressed in civilian attire of white cotton tee shirt, dark jeans, and boots. He's always bigger than I remember. So much larger than life. His eyes are searching for me in the leaving passengers, the hazel in them illuminated by the orange glow of the setting sun. The line of his jaw is stubbled from a weekend of free time, and his hair needs a cut. There's a slight curl to the ends, their colour golden from time spent outdoors.

My jaw trembles and I mash my lips together, starting towards him. I know the moment he sees me. His step falters until he comes to a stop. "Jamie?"

I swallow a sob. "Kyle."

People flow around him as he stills, his eyes raking over me. "What ..." He trails off, his expression horrified. I keep moving, blinking wildly as I reach his side.

He touches my face, his fingers gentle as they trail across my mottled brow and down my cheek. The bruises are still a riot of purple and green across my face and down my neck. The swelling took days to go down. "What happened to you?" He sounds breathless, his words stilted as if it's a struggle to speak.

An emotionally charged huff leaves my lips. "It's good to see you too."

Kyle grabs me then, his arms wrapping around my waist, lifting me. My legs dangle from the ground as I clutch at his shirt, relief bubbling up inside me so big and bright it's a wonder I can see. I had no idea how much I needed him until I saw his familiar face in the crowd and felt the comfort of his arms around me.

Kyle buries his head in my neck, breathing me in as if he missed the scent of me. He pulls back and lets me go, slowly setting me on my feet with care, his expression turning hard. "Who did this, Jamie?"

"It was nothing," I reply, wanting to downplay the assault. I can't revisit it right now. I just can't. Not even for Kyle. "Just a minor scuffle."

"Who?"

People stare as they move around us. "Can we do this somewhere else?"

Kyle's nostrils flare. He snatches up my bag, slinging it over his shoulder, and takes my hand. We wind our way through the parking lot until we reach the beautiful black Mustang. Ryan's car. He releases my hand and unlocks it, tossing my bag in the backseat like it's a sack of wheat. Slamming the door closed, he turns.

I go to open the passenger door, and he thumps a hand against it, stopping me. My brows pinch tight. I turn and his palms slap down on the car, boxing me in. "Kyle."

"You wanted to do this somewhere else." He jerks his chin towards the mostly quiet parking area. "This is somewhere else."

I shake my head, holding on to my composure by my damn teeth. "Later."

Kyle leans in close, his nose almost touching mine. "Who did this?"

Frustration bubbles up my throat. I turn my face away. "Kyle, please."

"Tell me!" he roars, his fist slamming down on the hood of Ryan's car behind me. His strength is enormous. I've no doubt he's dented the Mustang. Ryan will lose his shit, but Kyle seems oblivious to his imminent death. His anger is so palpable it vibrates through my body, making me shiver. "Dammit, Jamie. Who?"

"The Taliban." I look up, meeting his eyes. "They grabbed me in Kandahar."

He stills, his only movement the rapid rise and fall of his chest. "They grabbed you?" His face pales as his gaze roams down my neck —to the bruises that trail their way inside my shirt. "Jesus. Did they …" He takes a shuddering breath, his bottom jaw trembling. His voice lowers as if it pains him to voice the words. "Did they touch you?"

"No." I shake my head. "I mean they tried, but no."

Kyle steps back, hands fisting. He looks pissed off and devastated all at the same time. "Why didn't you tell me?"

"I'm telling you now."

"Fuck," he mutters. He roars it a second time. "Fuck!"

I grab his shoulders, rubbing them with my palms as if soothing a wild beast. I've never seen Kyle like this. So riled. His temper unchecked. He looks ready to pick up Ryan's car and throw it clear across the lot. "I'm okay. It looks so much worse than it is." Which is a lie, because I'm in agony right now. I need a pain pill, a bottle of water, and bed.

"How did this even happen?" He turns and stalks two, three, four steps away, shoving fingers through his hair before turning, pinning me with his eyes. "Where was your goddamn team?"

"It wasn't their fault." My mind returns to the child. His dirty tunic, the dark curled hair, the soft cheeks. My eyes fill. I turn my head from his hard gaze. "I thought I saw Arash. I needed a better look. I should have been paying attention."

"Damn straight you should have been paying attention."

My brows snap together at his rebuke. "Fuck you, Kyle. I got away."

He walks back, his hazel eyes dark with anger. "And how did you do that?"

"I killed them," I say in a voice carved from stone, blanking the images from my head. I acted to save myself, and I'm glad they're dead, but the horror of taking so many lives is a lead weight on my soul. "I killed them all."

Kyle comes to stand in front of me, swiping a hand over his face. I tilt my head upward, meeting his eyes. "God, Jamie. *God.*" He takes my face in his palms, his touch so mindful of my bruises that his fingers tremble against my skin. I'm surrounded by his strength, and his heat, and the familiar scent of him. I can't seem to catch a breath. "You did good," he says, his voice hoarse. "But I wish it was me that killed them all. I would have done it without blinking. Just for laying a hand on you. Fucking bastards." He pauses for a moment, his chest brushing mine with every inhale and his eyes searching my face.

"What?"

"You've got to let him go."

"Let who go?"

"Arash. Let him go. Jake. Your father. Let them all go before it ends up destroying you."

My stomach sinks with a horrible, sick feeling. "I can't."

"You can."

My jaw begins to tremble, and the single word comes out shaky. "How?"

"Like I said before…" his forehead presses to mine, his fingers gentle on my face "…we have to live our lives the best way we know how, knowing it's what they would want for us. You said you trusted me. Do you?"

I nod, my forehead rubbing against his. "I do."

"Good. Because I'm not going anywhere." He hugs me to him and I clutch at his sides, taking my first real breath in days. "We can work it out together."

~

I RISE FROM THE TABLE, collecting my dinner plate. I reach for Kyle's and stack it on top of mine.

We're at Erin and Wood's apartment. Half the place is boxed up, ready for moving day. The other half is a shambles because she's collected a lot of crap over the years. In the middle of it all rests a double-bed air mattress because I'm staying here for two nights before mine and Kyle's road trip.

Erin caved and they bought the house—the one I suggested—on the promise that the first thing Wood did was build the front porch like I told her he would.

I'm currently awaiting Wood's retribution, having come to the conclusion that I like them being together. Not just because they're like two happy pigs in mud, but because the entertainment value has increased twice as much. Except for tonight. Tonight is about as fun as a shit sandwich.

Erin rises from the table. "Sit down," she tells me, reaching across for the plates in my hand. "I'll get those."

"I can handle a few plates, Tennyson."

She grabs them and pulls. "I'm sure you can, but you're a guest, *Murphy*."

I pull them back towards me, and we stare at each other across the table. "Since when did you care about that? Last time I stayed here you made me clean out your gross fridge!"

She yanks back and I wince. "I was hungover and there was a horrible smell coming from inside it!"

Kyle half rises, frowning at my friend. "Erin, careful." He turns to me. "Jamie, give me the plates."

"They're just freaking plates!" I yell.

"And I'm taking them to the kitchen!" Erin yells back.

Wood's calm voice carries across the table. "Erin, sit down and let her take the plates."

"You sit down, Colin!" she shouts in a sneering tone, turning her head to glare at him. "*You* sit the fuck down!"

"I am sitting down." Wood looks across to Kyle. "I'm sitting down."

Kyle nods his agreement. "He's sitting down."

I rip the plates free, and I mean to twist them away from Erin's grabbing fingers, I really do, but they fly from my hands. We watch them fly across the room and crash into the kitchen counter before shattering to the floor, a messy pile of white porcelain shards and half-eaten lasagne. "Fuck," I mutter.

I start for the mess, and Erin runs over, getting in front of me. "It's fine. It's fine. I'll clean it up. Colin? Grab the dustpan."

"Are you sure?" he calls out from behind us, quite possibly signing his own death warrant, "because I wouldn't want to *not* be sitting down in my chair."

I'm surprised her glare doesn't incinerate him on the spot. He stands quickly. "It's packed."

"Dammit, Colin!"

"I'll find it. I'll find it," he says in a placating tone, his palms up in surrender.

I crouch, starting to collect the broken shards in my hands. "I've got it. It's fine."

Kyle crouches alongside me, picking up the smaller, pointier pieces.

"Would you all stop!" Erin shrieks.

"For fuck's sake!" I rise, my ribs screaming in protest at the sudden move.

Kyle stands up beside me, his large hand dropping down on my shoulder. "Jamie."

"*You* stop!' I yell at Erin, ignoring Kyle.

"I can't." She bursts into sudden tears. "I can't. I can't do this anymore. Colin?"

He's already walking towards her, wrapping her up in his arms as she chokes on her sobs.

"Do what?" I ask, feeling as if I'm missing a vital piece of this conversation—or altercation, as it were.

"Pretend everything is fine!" she cries. "You keep going off to war, and you don't even care about how it affects the rest of us. You bottle everything up inside, sending your shitty emails about how everything is fine, and how you can't wait to come home, and gee it was really dusty here today," she snaps, waving her arms around like an inflatable tube guy, "and then you come home so bruised and battered it's a wonder you can walk at all," she yells, her voice rising higher and higher until she's shrieking, "and you expect us to act like it's all normal and everything is fine!" She jabs a finger in my direction. "Newsflash, Jamie Murphy. It's *not freaking fine!*"

My hands tighten on the shards, and I feel them cut into palms.

"Erin." Wood turns her to face him. "Go get your purse."

She looks at him as if lost. "My purse?"

"Come on. We'll go get some ice cream."

They leave the apartment, and quiet hits, the only sound the humming of the refrigerator. I turn to Kyle. He reaches for me and I draw backwards, my breath coming in a choppy hiccup. "I didn't think."

He cocks his head. "That what? People actually care about you?"

"Yes." It sounds stupid and selfish, but I didn't think about that at all.

Kyle turns his back on me and drops to the mess. "Go shower, Jamie. I'll clean up here."

I do what he says because I've had enough fighting for one evening. I take my time, washing my hair and shaving my legs despite the pain that comes with it, but I feel better for it when I'm done.

I use Erin and Wood's room to dress, pulling my white lace bra and matching knickers on over damp skin, my hair dripping down my back because I don't have the energy to dry it off. Wrapping a towel around my body, I peer out the door.

Kyle is sitting on the couch in the dark. There's no music. No television. No Erin or Wood. Just him and a bottle of whiskey. "Kyle?"

He turns his head, showing me the handsome line of his profile in silhouette.

"Can you please help me?"

He rises from the couch, his glass hanging from his fingers as he walks over. "What do you need?"

"My stitches need to come out."

"Stitches?"

"My shoulder."

His eyes drop to the gauze, and he doesn't say a word. He doesn't need to. Anger flares so bright in his eyes it almost lights up the darkened bedroom. His jaw is incredibly tight as he hands me his whiskey. I hold my towel together with one hand and take it in the other, tipping it up to my lips. I swallow a huge mouthful, and fire burns all the way down my throat.

Kyle tips his head towards the bed where I've propped the first aid kit from my pack. "Sit down."

I sink down on the edge of the mattress, gulping another mouthful while he switches on the light and takes out the tweezers and suture scissors. The gauze comes off next. Kyle takes a deep breath, nostrils flaring as he stares at the stitched wounds. His eyes flick to mine. "Stab wounds?"

"Just three."

"Oh just three, huh?" His tone is snide. "*Just* three?"

"Kyle."

He crouches in front of me, bringing us to eye level. "Let me see the rest of you."

I grip the towel tighter, not from modesty, but from the need to hide the extent of my injuries. Kyle literally dented the roof of Ryan's car, and he did it without blinking. Ryan is going to lose his shit when he sees it. I don't need Kyle punching a wall in the bedroom and pissing off Wood and Erin too. "That's not necessary."

He glares, the line of his brow hard. "If Erin didn't say it clear enough, Jamie, we care about you. *I* care about you. Can you understand that? Can you understand the need to make sure you're physically okay, whether you tell me you are or not?" He puts his hands on my knees, branding me with heat as he speaks. "If any of us were injured, wouldn't you do the same?"

Of course I would. I'd probably pitch a royal fit until I got my way. Gritting my teeth, I unhook the towel and let it settle on the mattress behind me.

His eyes take in the fading bruises across my chest and down across the swell of my breasts, disappearing inside the cover of my bra. His gaze falls to my mottled ribs and lower, to the butterfly tape across the cuts to my belly, hips, and thighs.

Kyle closes his eyes as if it physically hurts to look at my injuries any longer. "Jamie," he whispers, his voice cracking.

I swallow the lump in my throat. "I'm okay."

He takes a moment, visibly struggling for composure. When he opens his eyes, he searches my face like he's trying to decide if he believes me or not. I'm not sure if he does, but his gaze drops to the multitude of adhesive strips that cover my body. They're damp, their edges curled. They need to come off. He reaches for the closest one. "You want these gone?"

I nod and look towards the wall, my chest shuddering with the need to cry as he gently peels away tape after tape until it's done. "Do you need more on?" he asks.

I shake my head in a negative response, lips mashed together.

"Okay. Let's get these stitches out." He leans in, his warm breath puffing against my shoulder as he lifts each stitch with the tweezers and slices it with the special scissors. He tugs the suture free and sets it aside, starting in on the next.

"You're good at this."

"I'm good at everything."

I huff.

His eyes flick to mine before going back to his task. "Who did the stitches?"

"Connor."

Kyle's only reaction is the pause of his fingers before he slices another stitch free. "You didn't request a medevac?"

"I didn't need one."

"Of course you didn't. You don't need anything or anyone, right?"

My voice softens. "You know that's not true."

"Do I?"

28

―――――――――

KYLE

The sound of a baby screaming echoes through Ryan and Fin's cottage as I walk up the pathway to the front door. The sound gets closer after I knock loudly with the back of my fist.

It's early Monday morning after last night's dinner fail. It's also the first day of my four weeks leave, and I'm about to start it on a really shitty note.

The door swings wide open. Ryan stands there in uniform, a squalling baby propped high on his shoulder. He looks like he hasn't slept all night.

"Swap you," I say, holding out his keys.

Ryan's hand splays wide across Jacob's back as he reaches for them with his free arm. He pockets them before sliding a palm behind Jacob's neck and his tiny bottom, handing him over.

I take him, holding him out facing me. His screams cut off, and his dark eyes blink wide. "Hey, little dude. Is that you making all that noise?"

"All fucking night," Ryan bleats, rubbing bleary eyes.

"You sound just like your father," I coo at Jacob, swaying him the slightest bit.

He gurgles as if I told a great joke.

"How do you do that?" Ryan asks, shifting to the side so I can come in.

"It's easy." I step past him, tucking Jacob into the crook of my arm as I walk down the hall towards the kitchen. He follows behind. "I just make fun of you. He seems to like it."

Ryan goes straight for the coffee pot. "Want one?"

"Sure." Though I'm not sure I should be lingering for coffee, no matter how desperate I am for a caffeine hit. My buddy isn't the only one who got no sleep last night. I was awake in the early hours after dreaming about Jamie being captured by insurgents. They planned a beheading, and I woke in a sweat before they swung the machete, racing to the toilet to puke. I couldn't sleep after that.

Cuddling little Jacob eases some of the lingering tension. Babies are so sweet and so damn innocent, and this one has a wonderful life ahead of him.

"Where's Fin?" I ask, bringing the little one up to my chest and patting his back. He hiccups against the skin of my neck, and my heart melts into a giant pile of goo. This kid. There's nothing I wouldn't do for him already. I'm going to be the best uncle. The kind Jake would want him to have.

"Asleep," Ryan answers, pouring coffee into two mugs. "So try and keep your voice down. I don't want to wake her."

Ryan slides the mug across the table in my direction. Now is a good a time as any. Fin is asleep and I have his son in my arms.

"So," I drawl, stepping back a little. Jacob's arms flail and I rub warm circles over his back. "I accidently dented the Mustang."

Ryan chuckles low and brings the mug to his lips. "Very funny."

"I'm serious."

He takes a sip, swallowing. "Sure you are."

Well shit. Ryan doesn't believe me. I guess I cried wolf one too many times over the years. "Roof of the car. Front passenger side."

The mug lowers in his hand, and he looks at me. I've never been specific before. Ryan sets his coffee aside and stalks from the kitchen. I follow him down the hall and out the front door. He sets eyes on the Mustang and jerks to a stop.

"Sonofabitch!" he curses with force. "You dented my car. You actually dented my fucking car!"

"Language," I scold, tucking a hand over Jacob's exposed ear.

He turns, his eyes wild and furious. "You know you should have just kept going and driven it over a cliff rather than come back here."

"I couldn't do that to Fin. She would miss me."

"You have a serious set of balls, Brooks," he literally growls.

"Well I don't like to brag, but—"

Ryan takes a step towards me. "Give me the baby."

I take a step back. "No."

"Give me the damn baby!" he yells.

"Don't talk about your son that way. He's not a *damn baby*."

Fin appears, blond hair tousled and sleep shirt hanging around the tops of her thighs. Ryan glares at her. "Cover yourself, woman."

"What the hell is going on? You're out here squawking like a damn rooster and probably waking the whole neighbourhood."

"Brooks here…" Ryan looks at me with nostrils flaring "…dented the Mustang. And now he's going to die. So take Jacob would you so I can get to the killing."

"There'll be no killing." Fin turns to me. "Kyle, would you like a coffee?"

"He doesn't have time for coffee, baby, now that he's about to die and all."

Fin rolls her eyes. "Calm down, Ryan. I'm sure he has a perfectly good explanation." She starts down the hall, and I call her back.

"Here." I pass Jacob over. She takes him, cooing gently as she walks off with him.

Ryan looks at me.

I take a deep breath. "I picked up Jamie from the airport yesterday."

"I know that, genius. That's why you borrowed the car. And on that particular subject, you're never borrowing it again."

I swallow the thick lump in my throat. "Jesus, Kendall. You should see her."

Ryan picks up on the strain in my voice. He cocks his head. "Why?"

"She's covered in bruises from head to toe." I shove my hands in my pockets, hiding the tremors. "Cuts to her belly and thighs. Stab wounds in her shoulder."

"What the fuck happened?"

"The Taliban. They grabbed her in Kandahar."

Ryan curses and turns around, giving me his back. He folds his arms, staring at the car, his voice rough. "Did they touch her?"

"I asked the same thing. She says they didn't."

"But you don't believe her?"

I step up beside him, both of us facing the street. "I want to, but she likes to downplay things. She didn't even tell me. I'm wondering if she even would have had I not seen the bruises for myself."

Ryan nods, his eyes still on the car.

"So I lost my temper."

"I see that." His voice is mild, but I'm not fooled. He's pissed. Seriously pissed. And not at me.

"I'll pay for the damage."

"No." Ryan turns and grips my shoulder, squeezing. "I'll cover it."

He lets go and walks back inside. "Come drink your coffee before it gets cold. I'll drop you at the hire place on my way to work."

~

"YOU'RE STILL ALIVE," Jamie says with no small measure of amazement when I step inside the apartment a few hours later.

I swing around to face her, cocking a brow. "Turns out Kendall thinks my little temper tantrum was well justified."

"Whatever." She walks into kitchen as two slices of bread pop up from the toaster.

I look around. The place is empty apart from the boxes, basic furniture, and Jamie. "Where is everyone?"

"Wood is at Bunnings," she replies, referring to the hardware store as she plates her toast and scrapes it with butter. "And Erin has gone shopping. I gave her my credit card and it cheered her up a little. She's going to pick up everything I need for our trip on the condition I stay here and rest."

"And yet here you are, not resting."

Jamie rolls her eyes. "It's midday. I've been sleeping all morning, and now I'm hungry." She starts adding a small mountain of scrambled eggs to her plate before pausing. "Want some?"

"Yeah, but you eat that. I'll make some more."

"Knock yourself out," Jamie says, carrying her breakfast to the table. I start cracking eggs into the bowl she left on the counter. "Did you pick up the car?" she asks around a mouthful of toast.

"Yep."

"What'd we get?"

"A Toyota Hilux. White."

"How much did it cost to hire?"

"Can't remember," I lie, giving her my back as I pour eggs into the pan.

"Don't lie," she says as I set the bowl down beside the stovetop.

"I'm not lying."

"Tell me."

"No."

"Tell me."

"No."

"I'll show you my boobs."

"Okay." I turn around, folding my arms as the eggs cook slowly in the pan behind me. "Get 'em out."

"Kyle!"

"No. You promised me boobs. I'm not telling until you deliver."

Jamie huffs. "Fine. I don't need you to tell me."

I pop bread in the toaster. "That's what I figured."

She gets up from the table and starts for the front door, snatching up the keys I dumped on the side table when I walked inside. "I'll just check the receipt you probably left sitting in the passenger seat of the car."

"Dammit!" I chase after her.

Jamie gets the apartment door open an inch before I get my hand on it, my arm stretched over her head as I slam it shut. She literally growls as she turns, glaring up at me. "You're impossible."

I wink. "I'm a lot of things."

"Why won't you just let me pay half the cost?"

"Because the whole trip was my idea. It's only right I pay for it."

"That's a bullshit notion, Kyle, and you know it."

"It's not."

"It is."

"Just let me do this. For you."

The beep of the toaster cuts through the room.

She sighs and victory is in my grasp. "You're so stubborn."

My hand drops from the door, and I step back, grinning. "I learnt from the best."

I PARALLEL PARK the Hilux in a spot outside Erin and Wood's apartment building and switch off the engine. It's Tuesday morning, five a.m. I want to get an early start and beat the morning work rush. I literally cannot wait to get my ass out of the city and on the road.

Bear: I'm downstairs.

I toss my phone in the centre console and step out of the Hilux, taking a deep, happy breath. The back is loaded down with camping gear, fishing gear, and hiking gear. There's an esky already loaded with ice and beer, and a mesh bag filled with snorkels and flippers.

Walking around the back, I flick the rubber hooks loose and flip back the tonneau cover, shifting bags and tackle boxes while I wait, making room for Jamie's bag.

Erin appears ten minutes later, clad in pyjamas, her eyes puffy with sleep and face creased from the bedsheets. Wood is behind her, wheeling two large hardcover suitcases. My brows almost fly off my face. "What the hell?"

"Don't even say it, mate," Wood cautions as he reaches the back of the Hilux. He slides the handles down and lifts one, tossing it into the back.

"Careful," Erin snaps.

"There's no room for the other one," I say when the first one fills the small bit of space I kept free for Jamie's stuff. "Does she really need all this?"

Erin's eyes shift to the loaded bed. "Do you really need all that?"

"You can't argue with her," Wood cautions me. "It's too early."

"Colin, you're making me sound like a witch."

"If the shoe fits," he mutters under his breath.

"What did you say?"

His voice picks up volume. "I said we'll make it fit."

"Where's Jamie?" I ask, just as the automatic doors whoosh open, and she steps out carrying a thermos in each hand. Bless her beautiful, caffeine-obsessed heart. She's wearing a white cotton sundress that skims the middle of her thighs. Her thick dark hair is bound into a high knot and mirrored aviators rest on top of her head. My pulse kicks up a notch. I rub a hand over my chest, putting it down to excitement. This trip is going to be epic.

"Morning," she says, reaching me and handing over a thermos.

I bring it to my lips, sipping on piping hot liquid, the perfect blend of coffee, sugar, and milk. "You're the best."

"Say it again."

"You're the best."

Jamie laughs and Erin makes a grumpy *harrumph*. "You freaks are so perky in the mornings. It's unnatural."

The three of us share an amused glance. That's the army for you. The routine is ingrained so deep inside I'll probably wake at sunrise every day for the rest of my life.

"What's the hold up?" Jamie asks, looking to Wood as he lifts the second suitcase, struggling as if it contains rocks, all the while pretending he's not struggling at all.

"All your bags," I reply. "What's in them?"

She shrugs. "No idea. Erin came home with a thousand shopping bags and wouldn't let me lift a finger. She packed it all for me."

"You're welcome," Erin says.

"I already said thank you," Jamie replies as we stand there watching Wood's face turn red as he thumps the second suitcase down. "It's not going to fit though," she adds. "Do I really need all that stuff?"

"Yes. You do," Erin tells her.

I hand Jamie my thermos and help Wood. We make it fit, and just as we're getting ready to leave, he pulls me aside, talking to me as if he's Jamie's father. "Take care of her, okay? No stupid risks, no drunk driving, and make sure she doesn't do anything too strenuous while she's healing."

I don't take offence, even though he should know he can trust me. He's only looking out for her. I'm glad Jamie has friends like him in her life. "You got it, mate."

I put the windows down as soon as we leave the city behind us. The dawn air rushes in, fresh and cool as it whips through the dual cab. We're starting off in Broome near the top of Western Australia, a twenty-four-hour drive away. We'll make our way inland through the ranges before winding our way down along the coast until we reach Esperance at the lower end of the country. It's a huge undertaking, but it's something I've wanted to do for years. A once-in-a-lifetime kind of trip.

Jamie tips her seat back a little and sighs as the scenery passes by in a blur. "It feels good to leave everything behind."

"I feel lighter already," I admit.

"Thanks, Kyle." She turns her head, looking at me.

I glance at her. "For what?"

She waves her hand around. "For this. You were right."

"What?"

"You were right."

"Sorry, what? I can't hear you."

Jamie laughs and I cop a light punch to the arm. She fiddles with the music, connecting her phone to the Bluetooth. "Born to Run" by Bruce Springsteen blares from the speakers, and she kicks back in her seat, sipping at her thermos.

My fingers tap to the beat against the steering wheel. "I thought driver chose the music?"

"Are you complaining?"

I laugh. "Not at all."

We reach the small mining town of Mount Magnet at midday, pulling into the rest stop. After stretching our legs and eating lunch, we get back on the road, arriving at Kumarina, a little town off the Great Northern Highway, population seventy-five, four hours later.

"Stop here for the night?"

Jamie nods. "Sure."

We get a small room at the roadhouse, eat dinner, and crash early on the twin beds. I rise at four a.m. and shake Jamie awake. I want to get to Broome by tonight, another fourteen hours away.

She jerks with a start, reaching under her pillow and coming out with a small blade. "It's just me," I say quickly, and her eyes focus on me in the dark. "Sorry."

Her chest rises and falls in rapid breaths. "Christ." She sits up, swiping a hand across her face, her voice croaky. "What time is it?"

"Four."

After loading up with takeout coffee and filling each thermos, we get back on the road, nothing around us but red dirt, open road, and the occasional road train. The sun hits the horizon an hour later.

Jamie presses the button, and her window comes down. She sticks her arms out, taking a photo with her phone, her expression one of awe. "It's incredible."

The vast sky is lit with a rich, deep orange, the scattered clouds turning a warm pink, their shadows tinged with purple. The colours seem endless, stretching across the Earth as far as the eye can see. "I've never seen a sunrise like it."

We stop an hour later for breakfast, and lunch a few hours after that, before arriving in Broome around seven that night. We spend five full days, pitching a large tent in the local caravan park. We visit the markets, traverse the jetty to jetty walk, and make our way to Gantheaume Point—an iconic peninsula of red rocky outcrops and the turquoise water of the Indian Ocean. We swim at Town Beach, nap the afternoons away, drink beer and grill meat in the evenings.

"I don't want to leave," Jamie says, seated in her camp chair on our final night. Her bruises have begun to fade, and her wounds have turned to thin red scars.

I tip the beer to my lips, my eyes on the water. "I could easily live here."

She turns her head, and I feel her looking at me. "Would you? I mean, when you leave the army. Have you thought about where you would live?"

I contemplate her question. "No. It's a nice dream, but I don't want to live so far away from everyone. What about you?"

Jamie shakes her head. "I'm not leaving the army, remember?"

How could I forget? "So you could happily live out the rest of your life in Townsville?"

She doesn't answer.

We pack up early the next morning and make our way down to Port Hedland, spending a couple of nights. From there it's on to Karijini National Park. We set up camp at the park. "You know Karijini EcoRetreat is here?" Jamie says, sweeping sand from our tent with a grumble. Her shoulder is stronger now, the exercise helping blood flow better, healing her wounds that little bit faster. At least the ones on the outside. I have no idea what's going on inside.

"You want to go glamping?"

"I'm certainly packed for it," she mumbles and I laugh.

Erin packed light on the practical wear, allowing only two pairs of decent hiking shirts, shorts, and a pair of hiking boots. Jamie's suitcases are mostly filled with different types of sandals, pretty dresses, at least a thousand bikinis, and tiny pieces of lace underwear that I try hard not to notice. She hasn't touched the large makeup case, or the hairdryer, or the myriad of other implements Erin thought she couldn't live without.

We spend four full days hiking the gorge, diving in swimming holes and paddling beneath waterfalls before moving on to Ningaloo Reef, where we take an excursion out into deep waters to snorkel with whale sharks.

I plunge into the ocean alongside a small group of international tourists, expecting Jamie to dive in beside me, but I turn and she isn't there. I look back to the boat. She's standing on the edge.

I lift my goggles, resting them on forehead and swiping water from my face. "What are you doing? Jump in."

Jamie hisses something at me I can't hear. "What?"

She leans down and I swim closer, noticing her knees are almost knocking together. "This is a shark-infested ocean. There are great whites everywhere. I can't."

Huh. Jamie appears petrified. I never expected that. Her vulnerability is usually hidden deeper than the crusty layers of the earth. "It's not. There are no sharks here."

"There are," she hisses. "I googled."

"There isn't. You can't give any credit to the rubbish you read on the internet."

"Don't lie." Her eyes skim the surface. "In fact, you should probably get out."

"I'm fine. Trust me." I gesture with my hand. "Look at all the tourists out there." Her gaze shifts further down where they bob about in the water, heads dipped down and snorkels pointing to the sky. "In the absolute slightest chance there's a shark, who do you think it'll grab first?"

"You're not helping." Her lips press together.

"I'll let you swim on my back. If a shark grabs me you'll have plenty of time to get back to the boat. Have you seen my size? I'm a big meal."

Jamie appears to contemplate my suggestion, and when I finally get her in the water, she climbs me like a tree, legs winding around my middle, clinging as we bob about. "Okay?"

Her expression is grim, and her eyes are on the water as if she expects a great white to come shooting up from the deep, its jaws open wide. "Let's just get this over with."

We encounter our first whale shark, and she lets me go, her fear suddenly forgotten as we take in the majestic fish, its length easily thirty feet. We dive down a little and take turns snapping photos with the underwater camera. When we reach the surface for air, Jamie is laughing and gasping with pure joy.

She hugs her arms around my neck, squeezing me with exhilaration. The press of her body is warm against mine in the cool water, and I hold her a little tighter.

"Kyle," she breathes against my ear, her lips brushing my skin and making me shiver. "This is incredible. I can't describe it."

My hands curl around Jamie's hips, indulging in the feel of her warm bared skin, squeezing a little. I hear her sharp intake of breath before she pulls back. She looks at me and there goes that hot jittery feeling inside my stomach again. "You don't need to describe it. I'm right here with you."

She laughs and hugs me again, and my heart swells bigger than the damn sun.

29

JAMIE

After leaving Ningaloo, we head to Carnarvon, spending two days on a fishing charter. I've never fished before, yet I manage to catch two large Golden Trevalley. Kyle only catches one and carries on about beginner's luck. We eat well that night.

From there we move onto Shark Bay. I don't swim there for obvious reasons, even though Google tells me it's mostly home to dugongs and dolphins. We hand feed the latter and picnic on the fore-shore at Denham. We hike more gorges at Kalbarri National Park, about halfway down the Western Australian coast.

A week later we bypass Perth and land in Margaret River, which in my opinion is home to the best vineyards in Australia. We visit cellar doors, stocking up on gifts for our friends, walk the local farmers markets, and stop by Hamelin Bay where we see giant rays from the shore.

Another week later, we travel through Walpole-Nornalup National Park. The trees around us reach at least a hundred and thirty feet high. "Let's stop here," I tell Kyle, pointing to the sign for walking trails. We spend the day hiking and taking photos before heading to our next campsite, pitching our tent in a pretty spot by the water.

After an early night, I wake in the morning with my body sagging into the ground. "What the hell?"

I roll and flail, my air mattress squeaking like a little bitch.

Kyle laughs and I turn. He's watching me, thoroughly amused. "I'm not here for your entertainment," I hiss, my back aching from an uncomfortable sleep.

"Someone needs her coffee."

"Did you poke a hole in my mattress?"

"No, but there's something poking a hole in my—"

"For the love of god!" I rise up, the knife from beneath my pillow in hand. "I'm gonna stab yours just for that."

"No!" He laughs, half-rising from his own bed, warding me off with his massive paws. "That damn thing is probably why you woke up on the ground."

I lunge across the tent, my knife jabbing straight into his inflatable mattress. It tears a long, deep gash in the corner. Air hisses out in a wheezy rush. "What in the actual fuck?" he shouts, falling back with a stunned laugh. "You're such a bitch!"

The knife drops from my hand, and I double over, gasping with laughter while the airbed deflates around him, sinking him slowly to the ground.

"Now neither of us have a bed!"

"Oh well." I tuck my knife away. "We can start on those bottles of red tonight until we can't feel a damn thing, and then it won't matter."

I unzip the tent and step out, my jaw cracking from a yawn that stretches my face. "Bring me coffee!" Kyle orders from inside the tent.

I turn my head, sneaking a glance his way. He's standing over his duffel bag, clad in nothing but a tight pair of bright blue cotton boxer-briefs. It's almost a physical punch. I linger a moment before I look away, back to the ocean, trying to dispel the image, but my mind won't let it go. The wide, muscled shoulders, his tattooed arms, the thick washboard abs, his body scarred from combat and a lifetime of hard and heavy training.

I shiver with a sense of longing and have to remind myself that it's just Bear as I start on the coffee. The same Bear who laughed his ass off when I tripped on the edge of the jetty in Broome and fell in the water. The one who snores like a freight train after one too many beers. The one slowly turning into a mountain man because he hasn't shaved since we left. The very same Bear who tips his head back each night in his camp chair and makes me scratch his head with my nails while he sits there and whimpers like a little girl.

I snicker to myself.

"What's so funny?"

Kyle has stepped out of the tent, shirtless and barefoot as he does the button on his hiking shorts. We're climbing Monkey Rock today. I hand him a full mug of steaming coffee. "Nothing you'd ever understand."

"Ha!" He sets down his mug and stretches.

My eyes fall to the tattoo on his chest. *Little Warrior.* "Kyle?"

"Mmm?"

"You never told me why you got that tattoo," I say, and his eyes follow the direction of my gaze.

He rubs it with the flat of his palm. "I wanted a reminder."

"A reminder of what?"

Kyle turns and looks at me, his voice gruff. "Of the one person who got me through the darkest time in my life."

My heart thumps furiously, and I brush across the inked words with tentative fingers. His skin is wonderfully warm. "I did that? For you?"

He takes my fingers, seizing them in his fist. "You did that."

"But you weren't there after your mother died."

"Watching her die was the hardest part."

"I didn't even know she had cancer, Kyle. If I knew I could have …"

"You could have what?"

"I don't know." Something feels different. Something that makes panic bubble up inside my throat. I step back, pulling my hand free. I need space. I need to think. "Make me some breakfast? I want an early swim."

I step around him and walk inside the tent, cursing Erin as I shove through an endless array of string bikinis. There's not a single substantial pair of swimmers in my entire two suitcases.

I spend the day reading on the beach, occasionally watching Kyle as he does stuff around camp—including patching the hole in his mattress. He plugs the electric air pump into the Hilux, and I watch as his bed swells with air.

When he's done he looks over at me, his expression smug. He carries it towards the tent and disappears inside.

We planned our hike for late afternoon, so when four o'clock rolls around, I get my walking gear on and spend ten minutes searching for my boots. I step outside the tent to ask Kyle if he's seen them and find him by the car, ready to go, his back to me and phone pressed to his ear.

"How many did you say?" he says and pauses.

"Six? Jesus H."

After a moment he speaks again. "No, do it. Let me know the cost, and I'll wire the money. Can you get the photos?"

I start back for the tent.

"I don't know, but make them good," he replies, his voice fading out as I step through the unzipped flap. Kyle pokes his head in minutes later. "What's the hold up?"

I stick my feet inside a slip-on pair of tan-coloured sandals. "I can't find my boots."

His eyes drop to my shoes. "You can't wear those."

"Well Google says it's only a thirty-minute climb."

"Yeah, a steep one. With a shit tonne of snakes."

"I'll be fine."

A little under an hour later my calves are on fire, burning as we climb the steep granite, my toes digging into the slippery sole of my shoes in an effort to keep them on my feet.

"You doing okay?" Kyle asks from behind, his voice a little breathless.

The top is in sight. I tilt my head, offering a smirk before I pick up my pace to a jog as if it's nothing, all the while my lungs are burning and my legs are ready to collapse beneath me. "Better than you," I tease, turning around as I dance backwards.

His eyes widen. "Jamie, look out!"

I look behind me and hit the brakes, the edge far closer than it appeared just moments before. I try to stop but my feet catch on rocks and I start to skid, slipping. My legs give out and I hit the ground, sliding. I turn on my belly, scrambling for purchase, rocks tearing at my palms, but there's nothing to grab hold of.

Fear explodes.

"Jamie!"

Kyle yells my name, but I'm going over. Sliding at a furious pace. With my arms outstretched in front me, I grab at loose rocks and dirt, trying to halt my momentum, clutching for anything. Dirt gets in my eyes, impeding my vision as I go off the edge.

There's a momentary sense of weightlessness, and I jerk to a stop. Kyle is on his belly, his hand wrapped around mine so tight the bones in my fingers crush together. I tilt my head, my legs dangling as I look down at the rocky outcrop at least fifty metres below.

"Look at me!"

I turn back at the shout, blinking through the dust. His face is red, sweaty, his teeth gritting as he pushes himself backwards, slowly pulling me up, his arm straining and veins popping. A shout wrenches from him as I'm dragged upward. With one hard yank, I'm up and over. We both land on our backs, breathing heavy, eyes on the sky as what just happened sinks in.

"Holy shit," he rasps, rubbing hands over his face.

"I almost went over." My voice is scratchy, choked with dirt, and my body begins to shake, my lower jaw quivering. "That was so stupid. So fucking stupid."

Kyle moves in an instant, rolling on top of me, his heavy weight pressing me down, grounding me. "Jamie."

"I almost went over," I choke out again, holding both palms against my head, fingers trembling as I gasp for air.

"You're okay." Kyle palms my cheeks, his grip almost painful. "You're okay."

I don't feel okay—my heart is hammering a mile a minute—but I nod anyway. Maybe saying it will make it true. "I'm okay."

Kyle sits up, bringing me with him onto his lap, hugging me to him. His strength surrounds me, yet I can't stop trembling. He loosens his grip. "You're shaking."

I know, but I can't make it stop.

He lets out a ragged breath while he wipes at the dirt on my forehead, brushing it from my face and hair. "Jesus Christ, Jamie." His eyes are fierce. "Don't ever do that again."

"I won't."

"Promise me."

It's not a question but a rough command, and even though I can't predict the future, or what will happen, there's a need deep inside to wipe the fear from his expression. "I promise."

Kyle slides his palm around my neck, his calloused skin scraping across my own. He hesitates for the slightest moment, then he lets out a sound. It hums across my skin, sounding something like a growl before he closes the distance between us, his mouth covering mine. My body tightens and butterflies erupt in my stomach. His lips press hard as if he needs to reassure himself I'm still here and breathing. They soften slowly as the scorching sun beats down on us, and he draws back before I can recover from the shock, his warm palm slipping away until it no longer holds me to him.

"Kyle?"

He expels a breath, his eyes on my mouth before looking away. "I shouldn't have done that. I just reacted. You—"

"Don't."

Kyle shakes his head. "It's just adrenaline. It'll wear off." He looks at me briefly before his eyes shift to the edge of the big rock. "We should go."

He shifts me from his lap. The rejection stings like sunburn even though he was the one who kissed me. "You're right." I get to my feet, ignoring the confusion in my heart and the hand he reaches out to help me up with. "We should go."

My brows knit when he crouches and slides the sandals from my feet. "What are you doing?"

"These stupid things almost got you killed," he mutters before rising. He heaves them over the edge, one after the other.

My mouth falls open as they soar through the sky before dipping into the forest below, so far down the impact is soundless. "Kyle!"

"Fuck those fucking shoes."

Laughter bubbles up, bursting free. "You owe me two pairs of shoes now."

He huffs. "I'll buy you a thousand pairs. But no heels or sandals. Just boots. That's all you're allowed to wear from now on."

Our return to camp is a quiet one, Kyle giving no indication of what he's thinking. Usually I'll cop some teasing after a hike. He'll dig at my stamina, asking me if I'm worn out and need a nap. Or he'll shove a handful of dirt down the back of my shorts if I beat him to the summit. But not today. Kyle is subdued, his expression shuttered.

I use the camp facilities to wash my face, and when I get back to our tent, he's leaving for a shower. I pour two hefty glasses of red wine, a Merlot blend from our visit to the Vasse Felix winery in Margaret River. The cellar door was stunning, fusing a rustic charm with a modern edge. We spent hours tasting wines without spitting. Getting drunk beneath the hot afternoon sun. I remember laughing until I ached.

I can't quite pinpoint when the weight on my chest began to lift. Weight I've been carrying around for what feels like a thousand years. Maybe it was then. Or maybe it was watching the sunrise as we drove through the red rocky ranges. Or when the giant fish caught on my hook, and Kyle abandoned his own line and grabbed me from behind, pulling me into his front to keep me steady, laughing and encouraging me as I reeled it in with a shout.

It could have been anywhere along the way, but as I take a seat in my camp chair, wine in hand, my shoulders feel so much lighter, even though there's tension humming through my veins.

Did we do the wrong thing? I touch a finger to my lips. Something has shifted between us. The air feels different as I stare out across the water, sipping at my wine.

I turn my head at the sound of the tent zipper. Kyle steps out in a clean shirt and shorts, his hair damp and drops of water still clinging to his skin.

He walks over to the glass of wine I poured him and left on our little camp table. He tips it to his lips, gulping down the entire contents in one go. He pours another and downs that too before looking at me. "Refill?" he croaks.

I hold out my half-empty glass, and he comes towards me with the bottle, filling it until it almost spills over. "Shit."

"It's fine." Kyle watches as I bring the wine to my lips, sipping gently until it recedes to a more manageable level. Then he goes back to the camp table, pouring himself another, emptying the bottle. He sets it down, but he doesn't pick up his glass. He just stands there, his chest rising in a deep breath.

"Kyle?"

"Mmm?

"Are you okay?"

"Am I okay?" He laughs but the sound isn't quite right. "Of course I'm okay. I'm just thinking about all the shoes I have to buy you."

Kyle is trying to make me laugh, but it just makes me want to cry because he's hurting and I'm the reason why. It's not just my careless actions on our hike. It's Kandahar too. I hurt him by not leaning on him. By keeping him in the dark. Would I have told him what happened if I knew he would never see the bruises? I don't know, and that answer scares me because if I keep shutting Kyle out, I'll lose him. And I can't imagine a life without him in it.

"I'm sorry," I say, but the words sound trite and useless.

"It's not your fault. I'm the one who threw the shoes."

"Not about that."

He turns his head, waiting for me to expand.

"I was stupid and reckless. Just like I always am. I need to stop thinking I'm invincible because it's exactly that attitude that keeps hurting those I care about. You're my best friend, Kyle. I don't want to lose you. I don't …"

"You don't what?"

My heart pounds heavy in my chest as I set my glass on the ground beside my chair. I rise and walk over, taking his hands in mine. "I don't know what I'd do without you."

Kyle lets out a shaky breath, blinking moisture from his eyes. "You scared the absolute shit out of me, Jamie. You went over that edge, and I thought that was it. I don't know what I'd do without you either."

"I'm sorry."

"Stop apologising."

"I'm sorry."

Kyle grabs me to him, his fingers digging into my arms as he ducks his head, his lips slamming down on mine. My mouth opens beneath his with a gasp. He sweeps his tongue inside, kissing me with wild, pent up aggression. I moan deep in my throat, responding, my blood heating as he grips me tight, anchoring me against him as if he's hungered for me for too long.

Oh god.

I fist his shirt in my hands, kissing him harder, deeper, surrounded by him, consumed and dizzy. His palms slide down my arms until he's gripping my ass. He squeezes, groaning as he kisses me.

I'm overwhelmed, shivers erupting across my skin. I wrap my arms around his neck, shoving one of my hands into his hair. The strands skim through my fingers while his tongue strokes mine, and I love how soft they feel, how silky.

He grips me tighter, liking it, and kisses me deeper than I've ever been kissed before. My body sags against his and he takes my weight, lifting me until I can't feel my feet touching the ground. My legs wrap around his middle, holding on as he turns and sets me down on the table. It creaks, barely holding my weight. Neither of us notice.

Kyle tears himself free, my name a ragged groan on his lips. He takes a breath, and another, his forehead pressing to mine. "What are we doing?"

A tremor runs through me. I swallow, caught up in the most intense feeling I've ever known. "I don't know," I answer honestly, my voice a rasp that I barely recognise.

His lips touch mine. A soft kiss. And another. "Maybe we should stop." But he kisses me again like he doesn't want to stop, his mouth drawing away with pained reluctance. "Until we work it out. I don't want to …"

I nod, my nose bumping his. He doesn't want to wreck anything. Us. Our friendship. "I don't either."

He strokes my bottom lip with the pad of his thumb. It makes me ache for more. His eyes lift to mine, his voice gruff. "You're so beautiful."

"So are you," I whisper.

Kyle's lips curve slowly. "You think I'm beautiful?"

I sigh at his teasing tone. It's his way of getting us back on familiar ground, but I can't work out if it's relief I'm feeling right now, or disappointment. My shoulders lift in a shrug, and I force a playful expression. "Eh, you're okay."

Kyle laughs and lifts me off the table, setting me back on my feet. His hand takes mine, linking our fingers as if he needs some part of himself touching mine. "We should eat something. I'm hungry."

"You mean *you* should eat. You just polished off that entire bottle of expensive wine."

"You helped. Besides, didn't we buy two bottles?"

"We bought a whole case. It's supposed to be a gift for Ryan and Fin. You know, after you dented his car."

He lets me go and steps away, and the sudden distance leaves me cold. "He doesn't really need it, does he?"

We move around camp the same way we've done a thousand times before. Getting plates, tongs, heating up the little grill, chopping onions. But Kyle's eyes follow me tonight. I feel them studying me when he thinks I'm not looking.

It sets my skin buzzing as I slice tomatoes and rinse chopping boards and dry my hands on the tea towel that hangs off the tiny hook of the table. We eat together, and he cleans up after we're done while I take a quick shower, washing off the grime and sweat from the afternoon hike.

Each task is one I've done so many times before, but it feels as if I'm doing it all for the first time. Even the face staring back at me from the mirror looks different. A little more tanned. Eyes a little more seasoned. The bruises faded. The girl inside me gone. She left a long time ago.

The air is charged when I return to the tent, dressed in a cream cotton camisole with lace trim and a little pair of matching sleep shorts. The set was something I thought foolish of Erin to pack. It's flimsy and feminine, and I haven't worn it before now because it felt too delicate for a camping trip. But my eyes kept returning to the set each time I opened my case, making me question myself. What's wrong with wearing something pretty once in a while? I don't have to be practical all the time, do I?

The pale fabric sets off my tan and highlights the long dark length of my hair, and the slide of the soft cotton against my skin feels incredibly good.

Kyle is already in bed, the sheet pulled to his waist. One arm is tucked behind his head, the other resting flat on his stomach. His eyelids lower when I step inside the tent, seeming to watch my every move.

My eyes shift to my own bed, the mattress flatter than a corn tortilla. The fitted sheet is curled in at the corners, bunching in the middle. My eyes shift back to Kyle. "Did you even try patching my mattress when you did yours?"

He shrugs and a smirk lingers on his lips. "No."

"You're so mean."

"Says the crazy woman who stabbed a jagged hole in my bed just for funsies."

I look to his lovely pumped-up airbed, my voice hopeful. "Share?"

"Nope."

My mouth falls open. "I take it back. You're not mean. You're completely heartless."

"Ask me nicely and I'll share."

"You want me to beg?"

His voice turns a little husky. "I'd love to see you beg."

My chest feels a little tight. I turn and hang my towel up on the line we strung through the middle of the tent when we set up camp. "Please," I mutter.

"You can do better than that," he replies, and my lips mash together.

"You know what I *can* do? I can come over there and slap that smirk right off your stupid face."

"Wow, how quickly you turn. One minute I'm beautiful, then I'm just okay, and now my face is stupid?"

I stomp over to my pathetic corn tortilla and lie down with a huff, yanking the sheet right up and over my face. "Can you get the light?" I mutter from beneath the covers, my back digging into the hard ground.

The rustling sound of Kyle moving around reaches me. Moments later the tent falls into complete darkness. Then my sheet whips back and I let out a little shriek.

"Come on, Little Warrior." He slides one arm beneath my shoulders and the other beneath the backs of my knees. He rises, lifting me with ease.

"Kyle!"

He sets me down on his bed, the air mattress bouncing as he slides in behind me. After tugging the sheet up, he snakes an arm around my middle and pulls me backwards, settling my back against his front. His nose rubs against the heated skin of my neck and he sighs. "Go to sleep, Jamie."

30

———

KYLE

I wake surrounded by warmth and the sweet scent of vanilla. My eyes blink open slowly. I'm wrapped around Jamie like a koala, my palm beneath her camisole, splayed across her belly.

My pulse kicks up a notch, stirring a hunger inside me that demands to be fed. I rub my hand over the smooth skin, knowing I shouldn't, but I can't seem to help myself. She's soft and warm and so unbearably enticing.

My palm slides over her hip, skimming just beneath the loose waistband of her sleep shorts. She feels so damn good. I shiver, my cock beginning to harden from the simple pleasure of touching her skin. God help me, I want her. But our friendship is too important. We both agreed last night. So why wasn't that enough to stop my eyes from following her as she moved around camp as we cooked dinner and ate it by the pale light of the moon?

"Kyle?" she murmurs, starting to stir.

I take a deep shuddering breath and roll to my back, my hand sliding free with reluctance.

"Yeah?" I croak, tucking an arm behind my head and sighing deeply.

"Why are we lying on the ground?"

"Because the airbed deflated overnight." I'm suspecting my repair job was a bit shit. But I'm not all to blame. Jamie played her part in making the hole long and jagged. The square patch that came with the repair kit barely covered the edges.

"But you fixed it, remember?"

"Are you complaining? Because you're the one who stabbed it, *remember?*"

"You suck," she mumbles into her pillow.

"I would prefer that *you* did," I retort, my chest rumbling with laughter because she makes it too easy.

Jamie rolls, and in the blink of an eye she's straddling my hips, her forearm pressing down on my throat and her knees on my arms. She leans down, her tangled hair a long curtain that pools around my neck and chest. "You wanna try saying that again?"

Ah hell. My cock is now harder than stone. It takes all my strength to keep my hips from surging upward, but I won't back down from a challenge.

"Suck," I say with a squeaky wheeze, and she presses harder. I curl my leg around her hip and shove, rolling her onto her back. I grab her wrists and pin them to the ground. "My ..." Her teeth grind together, a growl rising up from inside her chest as she shoves against me. I don't budge. Instead, I grin down at her, watching her hiss like a fiery hellcat. "Dick."

"Arrrrghhhh!" Knowing she can't push back against my strength, Jamie slides her left wrist above her head, dragging one of my arms with her and putting me off balance. She hooks my feet with her own and thrusts upward and over. It tips me off, sending me sprawling across the tent ground.

Fuck me. That was brilliant. I tip my head back and laugh, but Jamie is apparently not done. She leaps on me; a terminator programmed to kill or die trying. I laugh as we roll across the tent until we're wedged into the corner. Jamie lands on top and we take a moment, both of us gasping as if we just finished a sprint.

"That was hot," I rasp.

Jamie stares at me, a million thoughts seeming to flicker across her face before she ducks her head and kisses me, hard and swift, pulling back before I can respond. We look at each other for a long moment, my blood pulsing and body parts heating. There's nothing but the sound of our breathing and the ocean waves crashing against the shore, when I fist her camisole and drag her lips back on mine.

My tongue thrusts inside her mouth and my hand snakes around her neck, sliding into her silky hair, holding her with a firm grip. She kisses me back, her hips pushing against mine until she's all I feel.

I groan inside her mouth, my lips mashing harder, needing more, deepening the kiss until everything goes dark inside my mind. There's only this. Her. An endless pleasure that I never want to end.

Jamie breaks the kiss and buries her head in my neck, her breathing ragged. "I can't." Her lips move against my neck when she speaks, making me shiver.

"You can't what?" I prompt when she trails off. It's as if she can't think straight. I take great satisfaction in her muddled tone, knowing I'm not the only one feeling whatever this is.

"I don't know. We shouldn't …"

Jamie pulls back, straightening, her eyes glazed in a way I've never seen before. Her lips are swollen and hair tangled, her nipples hard and pressing against the thin cotton of her camisole. She's so incredibly sexy, the image one I won't ever forget. It makes me realise that there's no putting our friendship back the way it was. Not now. Not for me. It's too late. Like Julius Caesar once said, "The die is cast."

I know her touch. And her taste. And her scent. Every time I look at her, I'll be thinking of it, and wanting more of it, until I slowly lose my mind.

"Hell," I mutter, rubbing a hand across my eyes.

I know she can feel my erection. It's pressing against her, hard and obvious. Desperate for friction. "Maybe we should go for an early morning swim," she suggests. "Try and clear our heads."

I don't want to clear my head, I say on the inside, wanting to stomp my foot like a child denied Christmas. *I want to stay here and kiss your mouth until I can't breathe. And then I want to kiss you everywhere else.*

But this time it's Jamie being the voice of reason, and I have to respect that. "A swim would be good," I force myself to say.

Jamie climbs off, leaving me cold and bereft. She crouches, giving me her back as she starts digging around in her suitcase. "What do we have planned for today?"

More of what we just did sounds like a good plan. Dammit. My sigh is heavy. "I think we were going to hang here for another night, but ..."

She rises and turns, togs in hand. "But what?"

"After that hike..." I rub a hand across my chest as if reliving the heart attack of yesterday "...I wouldn't mind packing up camp and moving on. Maybe we should make our way to Esperance today." It's a five-hour drive and the last stop on our road trip. The thought sets off a pang inside me. This holiday has been the best experience of my entire life. I don't want it to end.

It's not just the travelling. It's Jamie. She's changed. The furrow between her brow has slowly disappeared, and she laughs all the time. Teases me more. I'm hoping this trip has showed her that there's so much more to life than the army.

"Okay," she says, nodding and turning away.

I get to my feet, brushing sand from my hands and clothes, and start for the entrance, giving her privacy to change before I pause. "Jamie."

"Mmm?"

I rub a hand across the back of neck. "About that kiss ..." I want to tell her it wasn't just a kiss for me. That it felt like more. But everything inside me is a jumbled mess, and I don't know how to say it.

Jamie holds up a palm. "I was the one who kissed you, and I'm sorry. I shouldn't have," she says in a tone that's far too breezy for my liking. "It's already forgotten."

My brow furrows. *It is?* "Well, okay then," I say with a nod, tucking those unsure feelings away. "Good."

We pack up camp after our morning swim, eating a quick breakfast before getting back on the road. There are loads of wineries in the area, so we stop at a couple on the way, not taste-testing so much the way we did last time. We stock up on more wine and a range of different cheeses and olives.

"What about this?" Jamie asks, looking across at me as she holds out her phone. She's been Googling as I drive, her legs kicked up on the dash of the Hilux, the wind rushing in and blowing hair across her face.

I give her phone a quick glance. There's an image of a suspended walkway over a huge granite outcrop. "It looks like a walk?"

"Granite Sky Walk," she says.

My eyes return to the road. "How far?"

"About an hour, I think."

It looks safe. The structure looks sound and fenced. Nowhere for Jamie to potentially slide right off. "Reckon you can handle it?" I ask, setting the challenge, because after yesterday my calves are tight and sore. Stretching them out will be good but it's going to hurt.

"Pfffft. I could trek the Kokoda Trail walking backwards with a blindfold on."

"I'd pay to see that."

"How much?"

"A hundred."

"Make it five."

"Deal."

She laughs and points in front of her as we near an intersection. "Turn left up here."

I flick the indicator on. "You're the boss."

"What?"

"You're the boss."

"I didn't quite hear you. What was that?"

I shake my head, laughing. "You've been spending too much time with me."

Jamie turns her head out the window, giving me her profile, yet I still see the slight curl of her lips. She looks cute today, a little rough around the edges, which is incredibly sexy. Her tank top is loose and pink, and she's knotted it at the side. Her denim shorts show off her toned legs. She's paired it all with a thick pair of socks that bunches up above her ankles, and her worn hiking boots, found beneath the deflated airbed when we packed up the tent this morning.

"I like spending time with you," she says quietly.

Her admission sets my heart pounding a little harder. "You do?"

"Mmm hmm." I glance across at her. She looks at me, grinning before turning her head out the window. "I couldn't imagine doing this with anyone else."

Neither could I. Diving with the whales, I let her climb my back until she felt safe in the water. On our deep-sea fishing charter, I abandoned the fish I'd just hooked to help Jamie reel in her own. And when she went over the edge of that mountain, I dived to my belly and would have gone right off the edge with her if I hadn't managed to snag her hand. I would do anything for her.

The thought is like a lock tumbling into place. Jamie isn't just a friend. I'm in love with her. With the tangle of her hair and her unbending opinions, her dark eyes and playful words. I'm in love with her stubborn and ridiculous attitude, and the way she makes me laugh until I can't breathe. I'm in love with the tiny hint of vulnerability that peeks out from beneath her wild, fearless heart.

Jesus Christ, I'm in love with my best friend. The revelation wipes the smile clean off my face, and I veer right off the road, actually feeling a bit stupid for not seeing it sooner.

"Kyle!"

I jerk the steering wheel. "Shit."

"Are you okay? You've gone pale."

I keep my voice low. Casual. I even tap my fingers to the beat of the music. "I'm good. I think I'm just hungry."

Jamie drops her feet from the dash and rustles around in the satchel at her feet. We keep it packed with snacks and water and a first aid kit. A habit really. We're soldiers. Always prepared.

She comes up with a small bag of popcorn, a salty/sweet combo. My favourite. She opens the bag, but instead of giving it to me, she tells me to open wide as if I'm a toddler about to get the aeroplane spoon.

I shrug and do what she says.

"You need to turn your head a bit more."

I turn my head further, still keeping my eyes on the road.

Jamie laughs until she can't breathe.

"Dude! What?"

She gasps a little more. "You look like those clowns at the carnival I went to all the time with Dad."

"Yeah?" I perk up with interest. She rarely talks about him, and I get that. But I like how the good memories she has are floating to the surface. "He used to take you?"

Jamie's smile is bittersweet. "All the time. We ate ourselves sick on dagwood dogs and fairy floss. I would scream myself stupid in the haunted house and ram everyone on the dodgem cars for hours until he dragged me off kicking and screaming. I can't believe I forgot about that."

"Sometimes the bad memories take up too much room. We start seeing more of the good ones when they start to fade."

"How philosophical of you," she says and pegs a bit of popcorn at my face. It hits me in the cheek.

"Hey! You're supposed to get it in my mouth."

"Well yours is big enough. I can't believe I missed it."

"If mine is big, then yours is the Grand Canyon." Another bit of popcorn hits me in the face. "Try again."

I open my mouth, and it flies past my face and straight out the open window. Jamie laughs her ass off.

"You suck at this."

"I really do."

Jamie tries again and gets it in. We both cheer as I crunch down on the salty, sweet treat.

We arrive at the Sky Walk soon after. I let her walk ahead, allowing myself the opportunity to ogle her ass, one I've actively avoided in the past. It turns out to be a bad idea. The round cheeks bob and sway with delicious torture as she moves, making me hard as stone.

I shove past her, mumbling something about her being slow as a fucking tortoise. She almost topples. I get ahead of her, hoping it will clear my head, when she hooks a foot around my ankle, sending me tumbling to my knees. I grab at the railing and she hikes her way around me. She even kicks me a little, though she makes it look like an accident.

"You're so heartless," I call to her back, pulling myself upright.

Jamie gives me the finger without turning around, and I hide the laugh. I even love the way she doesn't take any of my shit.

We make camp later in the evening, planning to settle in for a few days, before we dress with a bit of effort and make our way to the Condingup Tavern. It's a local country pub, the interior made of dark stone and wood. It's also the place Jamie decides to get ridiculously, and unapologetically, drunk as fuck.

It starts with a game of pool. Bets are placed and loser has to buy the beer. I win the first and watch, smug grin in place while I sit on my stool, as she stalks to the bar and buys the cheapest draft on tap.

"You're such a sore loser," I say when she returns with two full schooners.

Jamie downs the whole glass and sets it on the bar table beside us. "Are you trying to summon my inner bitch, Kyle?" Her brow arcs and damned if she isn't looking at me with a glimmer of something deeper and darker in her eyes. Something that sets off a tingle of lust down my spine. "Because she doesn't play nice."

God, why does that sound so hot? I rise to my full height so she has to look up at me, a challenge in my eyes. "I can handle anything you bring to the table."

Her voice turns a little husky. "Then let's get to it. Best out of three."

Jamie wins the next round and whoops loud, drawing attention. A lot of attention. I don't miss the eyes that follow her around the table while I walk to the bar. I don't like it either. Not one single bit.

I return with a high-end brew. She downs hers again while I sip slowly at mine because I'm the one driving us back to camp.

"Best of five," she says, watching as I sink my last remaining ball into the left corner pocket.

"Nope. We agreed it was best out of three."

"There was no agreement. It was simply a suggestion."

I shake my head. "The agreement was implied."

Her eyes narrow. "No it wasn't."

"Yes it was."

"No. It wasn't."

I sigh. Wilful little witch. Maybe I'm not in love with her stubborn parts so much. That particular flaw can go suck a bag of dicks. "Fine." I hold out a hand, giving in because I'm a sucker. "Best of five."

We both shake on it. Settled, she grins and picks up her pool cue. "You're going down, Kyle Brooks."

"Oh contraire, my little babe in the woods. You're the one going down." I grab my own cue, chalking the end of it. "And you're going to love every inch of it."

Jamie smirks a little too soon because I win the next game, making that three out of four, while she gets drunker by the minute. I don't question it. She had a rough day yesterday. There's nothing wrong with letting loose a little. Or a lot, as the case may be. I'd join her if I wasn't driving us back to camp tonight, but at least this way I'm able to watch out for her.

She fights dirty in her attempt to win the next game, even though I've already won the bet. When I take a shot, she leans down in my line of vision. Her low-cut top gapes, affording me a glimpse of black lace. *Fuck me.* My shot goes wild and her head tips back as she laughs. "You're so easy."

I really am.

Jamie takes her turn, sinking the ball, and when I'm up next, she sits herself on the edge of the table, her ass high and firm in those dark blue skinny jeans of hers. I remember the feel of those cheeks in my hands, so round and supple. Hunger hits me in a dizzying wave. My cock jerks and the shot hits the edge and bounces back.

"Why didn't I do this sooner?" she says in a cheeky tone.

I shake my head, trying to clear the fog of lust. "Because you're not a total bitch?"

She laughs and wins the match.

"Time to go," I say, finishing off the last mouthful in my glass. All her teasing has left me hot under the collar. I wouldn't mind returning to a cold dip in the ocean and another beer.

"How 'bout best out of seven?" she asks, squinting as if the sun is in her eyes.

"How about no?"

She sighs. "Who woulda thought?"

"Thought what?"

"That underneath that…" she waves a hand over me "…that…" her eyes heat a little, and she blinks and tries again "…that sizeable exterior lies the heart of an old stick in the mud."

I take her hand in mine and pull her in behind me as I lead her out the door, a protective gesture, one that brings her close, which only makes the hungering ache in my groin pulse harder. "You have no idea what lies beneath this sizeable exterior of mine."

"Maybe you should show me." Jamie winks and it comes off a little too exaggerated because she's completely drunk.

"I would but I'm a total prude."

She *pfffts* me as she climbs inside the Hilux.

We arrive back at camp, my ears ringing because she played "Dirty Deeds" by AC/DC over and over in the car, singing at the top of her lungs while shaking her head around, her long hair whipping me in the face. I would have got it on video had I not been driving so I could share it with everyone I knew.

Jamie turns on the battery-operated string lights that she strung around our camp at every site we visited. And after ducking inside the tent, she comes back out with a bottle of sauvignon blanc and a different change of clothes. Something she hasn't worn before. It's black and silky, with thin straps and a short skirt that floats around her upper thighs. It's even sexier than the little number she wore to bed last night. The one that almost made me choke on my tongue. Though this one is in a whole other league. It almost looks a little like a … I squint. "Are you wearing a negligee?"

"Negligee?" Jamie stops mid-pour and looks down at her little slip, swaying a little. "No. It's a dress."

"No." I shake my head, my eyes roving over her exposed skin, my body heating so rapidly it's a wonder I don't combust into a pile of ash. Her mascara has smudged a little beneath her eyes and she's braless, her nipples poking through the flimsy fabric. She looks downright sinful, like thick chocolate frosting. "That's underwear."

"Huh." She tops up two glasses and brings one to me. "Well, what would I know?"

I accept her offering, wanting to rub the cool glass across my forehead. "Not much, apparently."

Jamie tips her glass to mine with a *clink* before she downs a large mouthful. "Still more than you," she says, her chuckle husky. "Drink up, Brooks."

"Are you trying to get me drunk so you can have your wicked way with me?"

Jamie takes another gulp and sets her wine aside before grabbing the handles of my camp chair. She leans in until her nose almost touches mine. "Yes."

My breath leaves my lungs in a shudder, my fingers gripping so tight to my wine it's a wonder the glass doesn't shatter in my hand. I turn my head and swallow down the entire contents, gasping when I'm finished. I feel the liquid buzz through my blood, but it doesn't help. Not a single bit. I set my glass aside and face her. "You don't mean that."

"Oh, but I do." Jamie leans in further, her lips brushing my ear when she speaks. "I've been thinking dirty thoughts about you all day long."

Sweet baby Jesus. I tip my head back with a groan, my heart thudding an erratic beat. Dirty thoughts are my favourite. It's like she knows it with the way she bites down on my lobe before drawing back, a sinful look in her eyes.

"You shouldn't be saying things like that," I rasp, even though I want to hear every single one of them in explicit detail.

"I shouldn't?" She gives me this smile where her lips tilt up at the corners and her eyes go all hooded, like she knows me. Like she knows what I want. Like she knows exactly how to give it to me. An evil seductress. It's a side of her I've never seen before. And I like it.

"Jamie."

She climbs onto my lap, spreading her legs over mine, surrounding me with heat and exposed skin. "Mmm?"

"You're drunk."

"No I'm not."

"Yes. You are."

"No ..." Jamie ducks down and kisses the juncture where my shoulder meets my neck. My cock begins to fill. She nibbles her way upward before reaching my earlobe again. She flicks it with her tongue, making me groan. "I'm not."

"We shouldn't."

Her lips tickle my neck, and her hands find their way beneath the hem of my shirt. "No?"

God, why are you testing me like this? I extricate her hands before they trail their way up my chest. The effort pains me.

Jamie tugs herself free of my grip and her palms slip beneath my shirt again, hitting bare skin. God, her touch feels so good. Her fingers glide over my chest and I begin to unravel. My hips roll and thrust upward. "Jamie."

She rubs herself against my hardening cock. "You want me."

"I do," I admit, taking a deep shuddering breath. There's no denying it. "So much. But not with you drunk like this. You don't know what you're doing." I might have a dirty mind, and I might have been thinking about what I want to do to her for longer than I care to admit, but I'd prefer her sober, at least. I'd prefer her to know who she's sleeping with.

Jamie looks at me with eyes that seem suddenly clear. "I know what I'm doing."

"Do you really? Because I'm not a saint," I caution in a hard voice, my body pulsing with need and my resolve tumbling like a deck of cards. "If you come at me like this, don't expect me to do the right thing."

"Why do you think I drank so much tonight? Because I want this and I don't have the damn courage to ask any other way. I don't *want* you to do the right thing. I want you to be dirty." She shifts closer, her voice dropping to a husky whisper. "I want you to be rough. I want to feel you until I can't feel anything else, and I—"

Her words break off when I fist her hair and bring her face to mine, my lips seizing hers. She opens her mouth, and my tongue rubs with hers. The kiss is hard and deep and a little furious, the need for more making both of us desperate.

My hands grab her hips, yanking her closer, my palms sliding across the delicate silk fabric of her negligee. Hers slide in my hair, fisting and tearing at it. My heart is slamming against my ribs when I pull back, drawing a rough moan from her lips.

"Get this off," she rasps, grabbing at my shirt.

I lean forward a little, tugging it over my head. It's flying across our campsite when I kiss her again. She smells so damn good. Sweet and fresh, like fruity wine.

Her palms rub the bare skin of my chest while mine slide upward along her bare thighs, our kiss becoming more frantic the higher they climb. They skim beneath the flimsy black fabric and over lace under-wear until I'm gripping her bare hips. Squeezing. Hungry.

"Your turn," I breathe against her mouth, tugging at her slip, knowing our camping spot is private enough for no one else to see but me.

Jamie draws back, lifting her arms as I slide the material up. It glides over her smooth, taut skin as I peel it off, tossing it behind me. It leaves her in nothing but a tiny black lace thong that hugs her skin like gift wrap waiting to be torn off.

She says something but the words don't register. My eyes are on her tits. They're a perfect handful, her nipples a dark, dusky pink. I lick my lips, wanting to run the flat of my tongue over each one in turn, sucking them inside my mouth like the sweetest candy.

Jamie runs her palms over them, touching them the way I need to. A whimper escapes me, and my voice becomes rough. "You better be sure about this because we're about to hit the point of no return."

"Oh, I'm sure."

I slide a hand around her bare back, shivering at the feel of her naked skin. The other splays across her chest, sliding downward, until soft warm flesh fills my palm. "Oh Jesus, you feel so good," I groan, forgetting how to breathe. I dip my head and a take a nipple between my lips, sucking it deep inside my mouth.

Jamie lets out a moan, her hips tilting forward. I look up. Her head has fallen back, her eyes glazing over and hair spilling down until it drifts across my knees. She's so incredibly sensitive. So unrestrained in her pleasure.

I kiss my way across her chest until her mouth shifts to her other nipple. She gasps, a sweet needy sound that almost breaks me. I draw back with a final lick, leaving reddened beard marks across her beautiful, scarred skin.

A powerful, primitive surge overtakes me. It's overwhelming. Intense. I've never wanted anyone the way I want her, here, right now. "We need to take this somewhere else."

Her hands tighten on my shoulders. "Here is good."

We have a quiet spot by the beach, nestled between a few shady trees, private from nearby campers. But anyone could walk past. I can hear the voices of other travellers, the clinking of their glasses, their laughter faint.

I take her ass in my hands and rise from the chair, bringing her with me. She wraps her legs around my waist, her mouth latching on to my neck as I start moving. Her tongue flicks at me with hot, sweeping lashes and I almost stumble.

"Where are we going?"

"Tent," I grunt.

"The wine!" Jamie stretches an arm out towards the bottle on the little camp table. I walk her over to it. She grabs it by the neck, putting it to her lips and tilting upward, taking a hefty swig. "Mmm, so good." She kisses me, her tongue sliding in my mouth.

"You taste delicious." I jerk my chin at the bottle. "Give me some of that."

Jamie tilts it against my lips and wine floods my mouth, heating me from the inside out. She draws the bottle away and I swallow.

The alcohol slides down my throat as I step inside the tent, my eyes falling to the newly repaired airbed. *Fuck.* That won't do. "Grab that towel," I tell her, jerking my head to the large beach towel hanging from the line. She yanks it free and I take her back outside, setting her down on the grassy patch between the beach and the tent.

I take the towel, spreading it out before taking the bottle, swigging a mouthful and setting it aside. Then I look at her.

31

JAMIE

"Come here," Kyle says, his voice a rough command. My heart stops. There's hunger in his eyes, a craving that makes everything that came before this moment just … fall away.

I walk towards him, my legs unsteady like a newborn foal. He takes my hands, pulling me flush against him. The heat of his body is intense, the press of chest against mine heady. He releases my hands and trails the rough pads of his fingers down my ribcage, his thumbs brushing the undersides of my breasts.

"You like that?" he murmurs.

I can only nod and moan as he slowly sinks down to his knees before me, his palms sliding down my sides. "Oh god," I rasp when he presses a kiss to my belly, his tongue flicking at me. His kisses move lower, and his fingers tease along the edges of my thong.

"Kyle." My voice is desperate. "Touch me."

He tugs the tiny scrap of underwear to the side, baring me to his gaze. He lets out a shuddering breath as his hand fumbles between my legs. Then his thick middle finger rubs against the slick skin. I sway, lightheaded, the pleasure sharp and sweet. I know he feels how wet I am, because his lids lower and his nostrils flare. "God, I need to taste you. So bad."

"Please."

Kyle ducks his head, fisting my underwear as his tongue flicks out, licking along my seam. My entire body jolts as if zapped by electricity. I gulp in air, panting as my head tips back, my hands clenching in his hair, pulling lightly on the soft strands.

"So good," he mumbles against me, licking again.

His tongue pushes in further, flattening against the hard nub of my clit, rubbing me in slow, steady strokes. I look down and my insides clench. My best friend has his head between my legs. He's fucking me with his mouth and tongue. We shouldn't be doing this but it feels wicked and good and I don't want him to stop.

But he does. I whimper as Kyle draws back, licking his lips, his hands going to the elastic of my thong. He hooks his fingers in the sides and looks up at me, his eyes glazed and voice a rasp. "Let me take these off."

"God, yes, please."

Kyle slowly inches my underwear down. He rises to his feet as I step out of them. His muscles bunch as he lifts me and lowers himself down, setting me on my back on the towel. He nudges my inner thighs, spreading my legs and kneeling down in front of me, taking a moment to just look at me.

"Kyle," I moan on a long, shaky breath.

He doesn't bring his mouth to me. He lifts my hips, bringing me to his mouth as if I weigh less than a feather.

"Oh god."

Kyle sucks me inside the heat of his mouth and there's nothing delicate about it. His beard scratches the sensitive skin, and his fingers dig into the backs of my thighs. The night is quiet except for the crashing of the waves against the shore, my panting breath, and the sound of him devouring me, his mouth wonderfully relentless.

"You like that, Jamie? My mouth on your pussy?"

His words are crude, but they flood me with fire.

"God yes," I pant, rubbing against him, feverish and needy as I ride his tongue. "I need you inside me."

He rises up over me, looking down at my face as he slides a thick finger inside. I suck in a sharp breath, an orgasm building slow and steady. My eyes close and he groans. "You want me to fuck you?"

"Yes," I gasp, my head tipping back.

His mouth returns, sucking hard as he slides another finger inside me, stretching, curling, thrusting. "How bad do you need it?"

"So bad." My hips rock against his face. "Please."

He stands. I watch as he unbuttons his jeans, lowering the zipper, his eyes burning into mine. He tugs them down, along with his underwear, kicking them away. His cock is thick and juts out. I climb to my knees, taking it in hand, feeling the silky hardness. It jerks at my touch, and his hands fist at his sides.

I lean in, touching my lips to the head. "Jamie," he mutters, gruff. "I'll explode if you do that." My tongue slides around him slowly, and I take him inside my mouth. "Stop." I don't. I take him deeper instead, sucking slow and hard. I need this. I need *him*. "Stop," he growls, pulling himself free. "On your back. Now."

I sink down on the towel, and he drops down over me, his hips between my open legs. He takes his cock in hand and guides himself inside, pushing his way in. Both of us groan as he fills me slowly. Kyle is thick. Big. It's uncomfortably good. I lift my knees and it seats him deep, so deep I feel the pulse of him inside me. I close my eyes, and he thrusts.

"Look at me, Jamie."

He moves again. A harder thrust. And my eyes open.

Kyle is moving inside me, the warm glow of the fairy lights casting shadows across his face. I touch a hand to his chest as if making sure this is real and not a dream. His heart pounds an erratic beat beneath my fingers, his breath uneven.

"You're so beautiful," he tells me, looking down at me as if I hung the moon.

My eyes well with tears, and I don't know why. I'm suddenly over-whelmed—a wild jumble of emotion swamping me something fierce.

Kyle falters. "Jamie?"

The tears spill over, falling down the sides of my face. "Don't stop."

He pauses inside me, his eyes troubled. "What's wrong?"

"Nothing." I rock my hips upward, urging him to move, the jerky thrust causing pleasure to spike beneath my skin. "God, Kyle. Please. Don't stop." I wipe at my cheeks and snake a hand around his neck, pulling his face down to mine. I kiss him, driving my hips into his, mashing my mouth against his until I feel nothing else. No one else. Just Kyle. "Please," I beg against his lips, my hands clutching at his back, fingers digging in, desperate for friction.

"Fuck," he mutters, his voice gravel. He pulls out and punches back in. Again and again. I moan, delirious and shaky, my legs locking around his hips as pleasure builds. My heart is jackhammering in my chest. Strands of my hair cling to my sweaty neck. Every sensation is heightened, every breath harder to take.

Then I'm coming, my eyes squeezing closed, wild vivid colours bursting behind my lids. Kyle sweeps me up in his arms. For a moment I'm weightless, and then he's seated on his knees with me straddling him. Thick biceps wrap around me, clutching me to him, one arm wrapping around my shoulders, the other around my lower back as he anchors me in place.

He thrusts upward, holding me tight, rutting into me with powerful force. It's rough and intense and drives every thought from my head as I ride out the storm, pleasure crashing over me like waves against the shore.

Kyle's lips find mine, kissing me as his body goes hard. He groans into my mouth, rocking and straining, every muscle rigid as he comes.

His forehead presses to mine, and I can feel the pulse of him inside me, the jerks of his cock, the hammering of his heart from inside his chest. His eyes are closed while I look at him, swallowing, knowing this is only temporary. There's no future for us. Just like Jake, Kyle is someone never meant to be mine, and the thought breaks something inside me.

We live two separate lives. We want different things. And there's no bridging the gap between the two. He wants a family, and a house on the beach, and someone who'll love him the way he should be loved. Kyle deserves the world and I can't give it to him. I clutch his shoulders and blink against the burning in my eyes.

"That was …" He trails off as if he can't find the words. His arms slowly wind their way around my back, and he hugs me to him, holding on so tight I can barely breathe.

"Hot?" I suggest, forcing a teasing tone into the word.

His lips tilt in a boyish grin that hits every nerve inside my body. "Really fucking hot."

Kyle pulls out with a slow groan and gets to his feet, holding his palm out towards me. I shouldn't take it, but I do anyway. Tonight I'm going to pretend he's mine and that nothing else matters.

His fingers tighten around my hand, and he pulls me to my feet. He tugs me down to the beach. It's dark out but we hear a few faint whoops in the distance. "Kyle, people can see us."

"We're too far away to see much," he tells me, leading me into the water. The surf is bitingly cold, setting off goose bumps across my skin. He lets me go, and I tie my hair into a knot on my head, not wanting to sleep with it wet. "They're probably drunk anyway."

"Drunk maybe, but not blind."

Kyle hooks a foot around my ankle, and I go down before I can blink, crashing into the water. "There," he says, laughing when my head bobs up, hands wiping at my spluttering face. "Now they can't see you."

"You!" I sputter, checking my hair. I didn't go all the way under so it's mostly dry.

I kick out and he goes under mid-laugh. He comes up choking and coughing.

"Ha!"

Considering myself rinsed, I stalk from the ocean, shivering, my feet splashing through the shallow waves. Kyle lets out a wolf whistle, the sound piercing and loud. I turn, not caring about being naked in front of him. His eyes are on me like I'm steak and he hasn't eaten for days, and it feels good to be wanted. It makes me quiver and tingle and sets off a steady throb of heat between my legs.

Not that I'm telling him that. Instead, I tease him by raising my arms and flipping him the middle finger with both hands.

"Oh you're gonna get it so bad," he growls, lunging from the ocean.

My pulse skyrockets. I turn, actually squealing like a little girl as I run for the tent.

Kyle grabs me from behind before I make it. My limbs flail, kicking out as he swings me up and inside the tent. Damn him and his Usain Bolt legs. He tosses me onto the airbed. I land in the middle, bouncing once, twice.

I rise up on my elbows, and he drops down over the top of me, shaking his head like a dog. Water flies everywhere. "Kyle!"

"What?" He smirks. "I thought you liked being wet."

I gasp. "You're so dirty."

"You love it." Kyle dips his head and kisses me. I moan into his mouth, and my arms slide over his back and down, grabbing his ass cheeks as his tongue moves with mine.

"Again?" I gasp against his lips when the heat of his cock, now hard and erect, presses into my belly.

"You think once was enough?"

I wake in the morning, the sun high in the sky, warming one side of the tent. I shift my thighs, sore, an ache inside that wants more. My cheeks heat as last night tumbles through my mind.

"Ride me, Jamie," Kyle had begged after I used my mouth and tongue, teasing him until he reached his limit.

Those words. Lust flared like a lit match, so bright it blocked out every other thought in my head. I gave him a final lick before straddling his hips, positioning his cock and lowering myself down until I was full. There was a brief sense of relief until need hit me harder and hotter than before.

Kyle's hips surged upward, meeting me on the down stroke. So hot. It was so hot. My hair tumbled from its knot, and he fisted it, dragging me down and kissing me with wild abandon.

I turn my head, pushing last night from my head. Kyle is sleeping, one arm thrown across my middle, a casual proprietary gesture. His eyes open slowly as he wakes.

He looks at me for an endless minute, his eyes searching my face, waiting. I give him nothing because I'm lost. I took something I wanted last night, damning the consequences, and now I don't know how to put everything back the way it was.

His palm moves across my belly, a loving caress. I flinch, and he draws his hand away, resting it on the bed between us. I hate myself for it, but I need perspective. I can't get that here, with him.

I rise from the bed before I do something stupid, like beg him to touch me again the way he did last night. I feel his eyes on me as I dress, snapping my bra in place, tugging a clean pair of knickers up my legs. I reach for a cotton dress, sliding it over my head and tugging it down. Only then do I turn.

There's hurt in his eyes, but he tucks it carefully away.

"I'm going out," I croak.

Kyle rubs a hand over his face. "Where?"

I grab the keys. "Shopping. There's a few things I need."

"What do you need, Jamie?" His voice is low, disappointed, which only makes me hate myself more.

"Girl stuff."

He works his jaw for a moment. "I thought you were on the pill?"

"I am during deployment so I don't get a period, but I go off it when I come home because it gives me headaches."

"Why didn't you tell me?" Kyle asks, rising from the bed and reaching for a pair of shorts. I take in every gorgeous, muscular inch of him before averting my eyes. He's fucking glorious. All encompassing. Like the damn sun. I take a shuddery breath. "I would have … Fuck." He rubs a hand over his head, looking at me, shorts in hand. "I don't even have any condoms. I never expected ... I'll come with you."

"No."

He slides into his shorts as if he didn't even hear me, not even bothering with underwear. He slides the zipper closed and reaches for a shirt.

"Kyle, no."

He pauses. "What do you mean *no*?"

"I can do this myself."

His nostrils flare, his shirt bunching in his hands. "I'm sure you're really fucking capable of doing this yourself, but I'm coming with you."

"No you're not." Damn him and his noble heart, always trying to do the right thing. Not this time.

"Yes I am."

I shake my head. "Please don't argue."

"You're the one arguing." His voice rises. "You're so damn stubborn, and I'm sick of it. Do you think you can just go through life never needing anyone? Is it such a damn sin to ask for help? Will the fiery pits of Hell open up and swallow you whole if you lean on someone other than yourself?" Kyle is angry. So angry his whole body vibrates with it. And it's my fault. I keep hurting him by pushing him away, but I don't know what else to do. "Is that what you want?" he yells. "To be alone for the rest of your life?" I flinch, his barb hitting its mark. Kyle reaches for the keys gripped in my fist. "Give me the damn keys, Jamie. I'm taking you."

I tuck my hand behind my back. "Do *not!*" I caution in a shout, chest heaving and achy, holding on to my composure by the fingernails.

Kyle lowers his voice. "Jamie, please." He holds out his hand, waiting. And I could easily drop the keys in his palm, and he could drive me to the pharmacy, and it could make him feel good about doing the right thing, but I need space. Kyle is too … everything. I can't think with him near me.

He steps towards me, putting a gentle hand on my shoulder. I shrug it off, my voice a scratchy whisper. "Don't touch me."

His arm drops and the light in his eyes dims a little.

I turn my head, vision blurring as I slide my feet into a pair of flip flops. "I'll be back later," I say, stepping out of the tent.

He doesn't come after me. I walk to the Hilux alone and climb inside. Shutting the door, I put the key in the ignition and turn it. The engine rumbles to life and my head drops to the steering wheel. *What have I done?*

The drive to Esperance is a quick one. I make my way past shop fronts until I find a pharmacy. I park and step inside, walking down the back to the prescription counter. A sales assistant stands behind it, jotting down a note on the pad in front of her. She looks up at my arrival, giving me a friendly greeting.

"I need the morning after pill."

"Okay." She gives me a warm, reassuring smile. "Let me get someone for you."

She walks away before I can tell her I don't need someone. Just the pill. But then Kyle is in my head, his voice a sneer. *Do you think you can just go through life never needing anyone?*

Get out of my head, I growl as the pharmacist walks towards me, her hair a sleek dark bob, a sheet of paper in her hand. "I hope you don't mind if I get a few details from you before we put your prescription together?"

Yes I do mind, I want to say, feeling bitchy, but I bite the words back. "Sure."

The pharmacist takes down my name and address. "You're a long way from home."

"Holiday," I offer.

Her knowing nod is enough to make me feel sordid.

"What's your usual means of contraception?"

"I don't. I mean, I don't usually do this."

"Okay," she replies, nice and calm. "Why do you need emergency contraception?"

"Are you kidding me, lady?" I snap, my temper rising.

"We have to ask. Assault happens and we need to be sure you don't need additional care."

"Right." I wince. "I'm sorry."

"That's okay." I'm offered another reassuring smile. "How many hours has it been?"

I check my watch, letting my breath out in a *whoosh*. "About six hours."

She asks a few more questions and leaves me to wait at the counter. She comes back soon after, handing me the prescription. I take it but she doesn't let go. "Your period might be delayed after taking these."

"I know." I'm a medic, not that she knows that.

"Also, it's only about eighty-five percent effective."

"Okay, thanks," I reply tightly, snatching the little packet. Before I pay, I quickly choose a packet of condoms too, just in case, my cheeks heating a little as I add the box to my purchase.

After making my purchase, I leave the pharmacy and climb back in the Hilux, shutting the door behind me. I read the directions on the packet quickly before I take one of the two pills, swallowing it down with a bottle of water. After turning the key, I pull out and find myself driving along the Esplanade, not ready to return to camp.

I park and walk along the water's edge. There are people climbing into kayaks. I pause to watch. It's a beautiful day for it. Clear skies and calm water in the bay. "Would you like to hire one?"

I turn my head. A man is approaching, his gaze running over me. A flirty smile appears on his face. He's wearing shorts and a polo shirt with *Esperance Kayaks* embroidered on the pocket, a clipboard in hand and his feet bare. He's handsome, his eyes green and hair blond. Like Jake. *Jake.* How could I have forgotten about him in the past two days? A horrible sense of betrayal climbs my throat.

"I'm good." I fold my arms. "Thanks."

"Are you sure? I can take you out," he says like it's no big deal.

I look out over the horizon, the calm water at odds with the chaos in my heart. Maybe it's just what I need. "Actually, yes, I would like to hire one."

"Great!"

He takes my name and payment information before walking towards one of the kayaks resting near the shore. "You from around here?"

I shake my head. "No," I say, offering nothing more.

"I'm Graham," he says, holding out his hand.

I give it a brief shake. "Jamie."

"Yeah. I kinda know," he says with a grin, releasing my hand and waving his clipboard.

"Oh." I laugh a little at my stupidity. "Right."

Graham takes the front of the bright yellow kayak and tugs it out into shallow water while I slip my shoes free. I wade into the bay. He holds it steady while I climb in. "Have you done this before?"

"No," I reply, tugging on the little fluorescent life vest he hands me, "but how hard can it be, right?"

He laughs and wades back for the other kayak. I'd rather be alone. Graham is distracting, but maybe that's exactly what I need—mindless chatter with someone who doesn't know anything about me. "It's pretty easy," he says, coming back with his own kayak. He jumps in as if he's done it a thousand times before, which he probably has.

I start to paddle and the tip of the little boat wobbles from left to right. Graham follows beside me. "You're digging the oar too deep. Try going in a long, shallow stroke."

He keeps giving me tips until I manage a straight line. "See?" He laughs. "Easy. You'll be sore tomorrow though."

Not as sore as this throbbing ache between my legs, I say to myself.

"So, whereabouts are you from?" Graham asks, seemingly unable to shut up.

"I'm from Perth, but I'm based in Townsville right now."

"Based? What do you do there?"

"Army."

"Oh right." Graham looks me over with appraising eyes as though assessing whether I'm capable of being a soldier and female, all at the same time, like it's hard. I resist the urge to roll my eyes. "Have you been to Afghanistan?"

"Twice."

"Wow," he says as if it's a miraculous achievement. But we don't choose our deployment. We choose to serve our country in whatever means possible. And sometimes that means during war. Graham lowers his voice, his eyes dropping to the angry pink scars on my shoulder, exposed by the flimsy cotton sundress and thin spaghetti straps. "Have you ever been shot?"

"No," I reply, my voice curt and my stomach tightening in a knot at the turn of the conversation. I wanted mindless chatter, not deep and meaningfuls.

"Have you ever shot anyone?"

My kayak continues to glide over the pretty turquoise water while I rest the paddle across my thighs, gripping it tight to hide the sudden tremor in my hands. "That's a really inappropriate question."

"Why is it? I mean it's probably not the best thing to ask, but no one ever says why."

There's a moment of silence while I think about how best to respond. "Because the depth of the answer doesn't equal the casualness of the question." Movies depict so much graphic violence these days, making it seem like it's easy to kill someone. And the way Graham asked the question makes me think he believes the same. But it's not easy. It takes something from you that you can never get back.

Suddenly I don't want to be on the bay anymore, talking with a stranger. I just want to be with Kyle. With the one person who under-stands me more than anyone else in the whole entire world.

I start towards the shore.

"I'm sorry I asked," Graham says, turning his kayak around, following me, catching up to my side.

"Are you?" He paddles with ease while I jerk my oar in the ocean, hating the clawing feeling inside my throat. "Why did you ask me, then? Are you trying to satisfy your own ghoulish curiosity? Or are you quietly judging me for what I do? Because I'm a combat medic. I save lives, dammit, and I don't need to justify myself to you or anyone else."

32

KYLE

The Hilux disappears with a rev of the engine, and I make my way to the camp table for coffee. I heat the water and add a measured teaspoon of roasted blend to my mug. After pouring the steaming liquid, I give it a haphazard stir before tossing the spoon aside.

Moving to my chair, I turn it outwards, facing the ocean, and take a seat.

I know what I'm doing.

Fuck. I rub a hand across my eyes, squeezing between the bridge of my nose.

Do you really? Because I'm not a saint. Don't expect me to do the right thing.

I'm a fucking bastard.

Jamie was drunk. She didn't know what she was doing. Deep down I knew that, and yet I put my grubby hands all over her anyway.

Dirty fucking bastard.

I want you to be rough.

Of course she did. Being gentle would mean something. Rough sex is simply scratching an itch, isn't it? Jamie was scratching an itch, and

I was handy. How can I blame her for that when I took advantage, ruining everything like a bull in a china shop?

I lower the mug in my hands, my eyes on the ocean, on the two kangaroos that bound across the pristine sand. It's a sight that would have Jamie reaching for the camera. But she's not here to take the photo because I couldn't keep my hands to myself.

What I thought might have been a new beginning for us has quite possibly turned out to be the end. I knew it the moment she flinched beneath my touch this morning, properly sober and in her right mind.

My heart hammers hard with regret.

"Fuck," I mutter, but the curse isn't enough. "Fuck!" I roar, throwing my mug against the tree to my right. It shatters on impact, sending coffee and porcelain shards flying.

"Mate, everything okay?"

I turn, chest heaving with rage. It's our neighbouring camper. A man about fifty or so. We drove past their camp to get to ours, and I nodded an acknowledgement at the time. He waved and smiled, a small group of people behind him seated around a fold-out table as they played a board game.

"Yeah," I rasp, swiping a hand down my face like it's just that easy to wipe the insidious emotion away. It's not, but I manage to push it aside and offer an apology. "Sorry."

"Must have been a real shit brew," he says, nodding towards the broken remnants of my cup.

A huff of laughter escapes me. "Nothing worse than bad coffee."

"True that." He holds out his hand. "The name's Reg."

I shake it before letting go. "Kyle."

"Beautiful spot we got here, ay?" he asks, though it's more a statement of fact than a question. We both look out across the beach, Reg with his hands on his hips. It's a quiet, beautiful haven.

"What can I do for you?" I ask when the silence drags on.

"Thought we might invite you and the missus for a board game at ours tonight." He winks conspiratorially. "Winner gets a bottle of our homemade whiskey."

"Oh, right." I shake my head. "She's not … We …" Fuck.

He claps me on the shoulder. "See you about five?"

I nod. "Sure. Five." Maybe it might be good for us to bring other people inside our orbit. We've lived in such a bubble these past weeks.

"Bring beer," Reg calls out over his shoulder as he walks off. "We'll cook."

Jamie doesn't return until late. I pick up my phone to call her at least a thousand times, but instead I find myself flicking through our photos instead. Starting from the beginning of our road trip.

The first one is Jamie. She's in the passenger seat. It's pushed back and her legs are crossed at the ankle, resting out on the open window. Mirrored aviators cover her eyes and her hair is a messy bun on top of her head. She's grinning while she holds a cigar between her lips, smoke puffing out in a cloud.

"What are these?" she squealed, finding them inside the glove compartment.

I shrugged as she opened the packet. Two were missing. "I bought them for Ryan when Fin had the baby."

She pulled one out, running it underneath her nose, breathing deep.

"You ever smoke one?" I asked.

"Oh sure," she said in a breezy tone.

I jerked my chin towards the centre console, where a bright green lighter sat. "Go ahead," I said. A challenge. "These are the good ones. Cost me my left nut."

"Oh, it's okay. I don't want to waste them."

I grabbed the lighter and flicked it. A flame appeared. Then I said the one thing guaranteed to get her back up. "Are you sure you've had one? Because I wouldn't judge you if you can't handle them. They're pretty strong."

Jamie stuck the cigar between her lips, holding it towards the flame. The end burned red. It was all I could do not to bust out laughing when she inhaled. A deep, hacking cough burst from her lungs.

"You're such a fucker," she said, waving a hand through the smoke as she choked, tears streaming from her eyes.

I laughed. "I need a photo to document this moment."

"I'll do it. You're driving." Jamie took my phone and held it out, chomping down on the cigar between her two fingers, a smirking grin on her face as she clicked the picture.

I swipe through a few scenic ones until I get to the one of Jamie as she went over the edge of the jetty in Broome. It's blurred because I was taking a photo of the water and turned when I heard her shout. I managed to capture the image mid-fall. The one after that is Jamie fully-clothed as she treads water, glaring up at me.

"Are you going to help me out or are you going to just stand there like a big stupid lump and take photos?" she growled.

"Take photos," I said, trying not to piss myself from laughing so hard.

"Kyle!" She spun around in the water, frantic. "What was that? Something just brushed against me. Oh my god. Sharks! Kyle, you bastard." She freestyled towards me and it only made me laugh harder. The water was crystal clear. There was nothing but a few little fish flittering about.

"You watched *Jaws* as a child, didn't you?"

"Stop trying to psychoanalyse me and help me out of the damn water."

I slid into my bed that night and got spiked and scratched. Jamie had filled my bed with a thousand gum tree seeds.

It makes me chuckle even now as I swipe through more of my camera roll, memories hitting me like bricks, one after the other.

I stop on another one. We're at one of the wineries, and Jamie was eyeing off a giant wheel of cheese. I never knew she was a fanatic until this trip. I've even caught her eating it for breakfast.

"I'm buying it," she said.

"How much would you like, love?" the lady behind the windowed display asked her.

"All of it. The whole wheel, please."

My brows almost flew off my face. It weighed at least ten pounds, which meant it would cost her around a hundred and sixty bucks. "You can't buy the whole thing."

An odd expression crossed her face. "There's no such thing as can't."

"You'll never eat it all," I warned her when we returned to camp.

"Watch me." She poured a wine, cut that damn wheel in half, held it up to her face as if it were a hunk of watermelon, and took a huge bite.

"You're an animal."

She stuck out of her tongue, her cheeks bulging with cheese. "Takes one to know one."

I got my phone out and took a photo, showing her the image while she chewed. "Oh my god. I *am* an animal." She swallowed her mouthful. "But guess what?"

"What?"

She tore off another hunk with her teeth and grinned. "I don't care."

I set my phone aside and grab the snorkel gear, knowing I need to do something. Anything is better than sitting here torturing myself with all the ways I fucked up.

Shrugging the mesh bag over my shoulder, I go for a long walk until I find a great spot, spending hours in the water. It's not until I get out that I remember the sunscreen. My back and shoulders feel tender and hot. I shrug my shirt on for the long walk back to camp.

Jamie's there when I return.

"Hey," I say and wince because it sounds lame.

"Hey," she says back.

I set the snorkel gear down. "Did you get the—"

"Yeah."

"Did you take—"

"Yes. All done."

Then why don't I feel relieved? Jamie doesn't want me. Not the same way I want her. And it's not the right environment to bring a child into. Call me old-fashioned, but I want the girl I love beside me where I can take care of her, not pregnant and on the other side of the country, so I should be grateful. Jamie's a practical girl. And she's done the practical thing, which is more than I can say for myself. "Thanks."

"You're welcome."

How fucking polite of us.

"Reg invited us to board game night," I tell her, waving a hand towards the cluster of tents a little way down from us.

"Reg, huh?"

"I said we'd go. Is that okay?"

Jamie nods, the gesture a little stilted. "That sounds good. What time?"

"Five."

"Okay. I'll go shower."

She walks away, grabbing her things before heading towards the shower block. I heave a deep sigh. Yep. That was uncomfortable. She returns a half hour later, towel over her shoulder, toiletry bag in one hand, the other running a comb through her long hair. It snags on a knot and she yelps.

"Let me," I say quietly.

"I've got it."

Frustration rises and she must sense it because she drops her arms, turning her head so I can reach the knotted mass. "Okay. Thank you."

I work at untangling the wet strands. "Jamie?"

"Mmm?"

"I'm sorry about last night," I tell her, trying to put things right. "I shouldn't have put my hands on you the way I did. It was … a mistake." Though it didn't feel like one. It felt like the best goddamn thing ever. "We should try and move past it. You're the most important person in my life." I take a deep breath, working the comb free. "And I can't lose you."

Jamie turns and I put it in her hand. "Please don't apologise. I'm the one who's sorry. This is on me."

"It's on both of us."

Her eyes drop to my mouth for a long moment before she looks away. "Do you think we can go back to how we were before?"

No. But it's Jamie. For her I'd do anything. "We can try."

~

REG INTRODUCES us to his wife, Beverley. "Just call me Bev," she says, sucking on a cigarette as she pours drinks, waving us into their camp. We walk over, Jamie carrying a bowl of salad and me resting a case of beer on my shoulder.

"These are our two boys, Graham and Wil."

Jamie jerks next to me. I shake their hands while Graham sends Jamie a familiar smile. "We know each other."

"You do?" I ask as she shakes Wil's hand.

"We met today."

"Today?" I echo.

"She rented a kayak," Graham explains.

"Oh!" Bev trills, walking over with a glass of wine for Jamie while I set the beer down by the table they have set up. "Both our boys live here, which is why we're visiting. We try and get here at least once a year to see them."

I turn to Jamie. "You rented a kayak?"

She shrugs. "You went snorkelling."

Another two couples join us. Camping neighbours on the other side of Reg and Bev. One is a couple in their early thirties, the other a little older, maybe mid-forties.

Alcohol flows and old seventies tunes play in the background as we team up on a game of Monopoly, me and Jamie buying up Boardwalk and Park Place in quick succession. She sips slowly on her wine as we take each turn, limiting herself to one glass. I take her aside when there's a lull. "Is it okay to drink with the pill?"

She nods. "It's fine."

But she doesn't look so good. "You don't look so good."

She rubs her belly. "I don't feel so good."

I set my beer down. "Let me take you back to camp."

"No, you stay here. I can walk back on my own."

My nostrils flare. "For fuck's sake."

"Fine," she hisses and looks around, seeing Bev watching us. She forces a smile. "But you can come back after, if you want."

"I'm not leaving you alone when you're not feeling well."

"Fine," she says again, and we say our goodbyes to the group, thanking them for the invite and promising to stop by another night before we leave.

Jamie disappears inside the tent while I get her a water. She steps out a few minutes later in her sleep shorts and tank top. I try really hard to forget what she looks like out of them, but it doesn't work. I focus somewhere over her shoulder when I crack the lid on the bottle and hand it over.

She thanks me and pops a pill in her mouth, taking a swallow.

"How many of those do you have to take?"

"Just two."

"Can I get you anything else?"

"No, I'm good. I'm gonna go to sleep," she says, jerking her thumb towards the tent behind her.

"Okay. I'll be in in a minute," I reply and wince—because that makes it sound like I'm expecting something more.

I clean up around camp, wiping down cups, putting stuff back inside containers, switching off Jamie's string lights. It's dark when I step inside the tent. I make out her form in the airbed. She's on the left side, on her belly, facing the canvas wall. Her old bed is rolled up in the corner. I never got around to fixing it. Maybe I should do that tomorrow.

Shrugging off my shirt, I slide in beside her, careful not to jar the mattress too much. I roll to my back with an audible hiss.

"What?" Jamie half-turns. My eyes adjust to the dark, and I make out the little furrow in her brow. "What is it?"

"Sunburn," I reply, my skin throbbing like a little bitch.

"You should have used sunscreen."

"No shit? Why didn't I think to do that? Oh yeah, because I forgot."

"God, you're such a baby when you're injured."

"I am not."

"You are." Jamie rises from the bed and rustles around inside her bag. "Remember your elbow?" She comes back with a tube of something. "You bitched so much back home they banned you from card night."

"That's because they're a whiney bunch of losers that can't handle losing," I point out.

"Roll over."

I eye the blue bottle with wary eyes. "What's that?"

"It's an aloe vera lotion that contains lidocaine."

"Seriously?"

"Yes, seriously," she says as I roll over, giving her my back.

Jamie squeezes the tube, and icy splodges drip their way across my heated skin. I hold back the urge to squeal like a little girl. She's right. I can be a real baby, not that I'd ever cop to it.

"You're the best," I say as she rubs it on. It's instant relief. Jamie always has the best stuff. A veritable wizard of the healing world, her first aid kit full of wondrous, magical things.

I hear the lid of the tube snick closed, and she folds herself back in bed. "There. All done." Jamie gives my back a light pat before her palm moves down my spine in what feels like a long, sensual caress. She snatches her hand free. "Now be quiet. I'm trying to sleep."

We settle back to our respective sides and when her breathing starts to even out, I allow myself to drift off. A heavy *thump* jolts me awake in the early hours. I grab my torch, half-rising as I flick it on. It outlines a kangaroo sniffing out our campsite.

"What is it?" Jamie mutters, lifting her head, her arm sliding from beneath her pillow, knife in hand.

"Put that damn thing away." I shake my head. "It's just a roo."

It slides back beneath the pillow, and she turns to her side, facing me.

I flick the torch off and settle back in.

"Kyle?"

"Yeah?"

"How's your back?"

"Sore."

"Want me to rub some more aloe in?"

"Yes please." As if I'd say no.

I roll to my belly, and she climbs over me this time, straddling my backside. My skin is an inferno, and I hiss when the cool gel hits. She massages it in with slow, gentle strokes this time. My cock hardens beneath me with each swipe of her hands. A groan of pleasure escapes.

"Does that feel good?" she whispers in the dark.

"Yes. So good."

"Roll over."

I hesitate. "Jamie?"

"I can't get your shoulders properly from here."

She shifts up on her knees, and I roll over. She sits back down, straddling me, rubbing herself against my erection as if she can't help it. My groin tightens. "Can you reach them now?" I croak.

Jamie grabs the bottle and squeezes a blob into her palm. She rubs them together and looms over me, her hands working the lotion into the skin of my shoulders. They slide down slowly, her nails scraping the wall of my chest. Delicious shivers erupt. "That feels so damn good."

Her fingers drift lower and lower, and my cock jerks inside my underwear. I know she feels it because she lets out a shaky breath. "What are we doing?"

My voice is hoarse. "I don't know, but I want to keep doing it."

"Me too," she says quietly, and her fingers find the edge of my shorts.

Jamie flicks open the button and slides my zipper down. She shifts down my legs, tugging my shorts and underwear with her. My hard dick surges upward, throbbing and heavy.

"You want this?" I ask, needing her to be sure.

"Yes," she breathes. "I want one more night. Then we can go back to the way everything was before," she says in a desperate tone, as if she's trying to convince herself of the impossible all over again. It didn't work today. It won't work tomorrow. But I can't say no. I'm not strong enough, and I want her too fucking much.

Her head dips down and her tongue snakes out, licking the entire length of my cock. I feel her hot, wet mouth wrap around it, sucking me inside, and my head tips back with a groan. My fingers go to her hair, gripping the strands as she slides down and sucks upward. Just like that, I'm ready to come.

I surrender to her mouth and tongue for an entire minute. Then I sit forward and grasp beneath her armpits, pulling her off and dragging her upward. Any more and I'll shoot through the roof of the tent.

My lips crash down on hers and her mouth opens, an instant invitation. My hot, hungry tongue sweeps in and rubs against hers, my hand sliding up and grabbing her hair in my fist. She moans into my mouth.

I move her onto her back and rise up, peeling her underwear and sleep shorts down, lobbing them into the corner behind me.

"Jamie, roll over, baby. I want you on all fours."

She complies and I get behind her, appreciating the pretty sight of her pussy bared to my eyes, right there for the taking. My palms skate down the naked cheeks of her ass, nudging her thighs. Jamie shifts her knees, opening her legs a little wider, exposing more of herself to my eyes.

I slide a finger over the slick skin between her legs. Finding her opening, I slip it inside and pump slowly in and out. She lets out a moan and her head lowers. My dick throbs, impatient to get in there, but not yet. I need a taste first.

Removing my finger, I spread her cheeks and dip my head, stroking the flat of my tongue over her clit. "Fuck," she pants, dropping to her elbows.

"You like that?"

"More," she gasps.

I spread her open with my fingers and kiss her pussy before licking her repeatedly, my tongue delving in and out with loving strokes. The taste sends me fucking crazy with need. My mouth closes over her clit and I suck hard. Her back bows from the bed and she cries out.

It's not enough. I want more. I want Jamie crying out my name. I want to hear it just once.

I slide a thick digit inside, and another, fucking her with my tongue and fingers.

"Oh god, yes," she hisses, biting her bottom lip, her hips grinding against my mouth.

My fingers drive inside her as I stroke and suck, and the rougher I get, the harder she breathes.

A shudder racks my body. I need to be inside her. Now.

I give her a final lick before drawing back. Grasping her hips, I tilt her ass up slightly and align my cock, pushing in slowly until I'm seated deep inside. Wet heat surrounds me in a tight, snug vice, setting every nerve on fire.

Jamie gasps a shaky moan and shudders.

"Did I hurt you?"

"No. It's good. It's better than good," she says, and my fingers dig into the soft flesh of her hips at the admission.

I draw out and drive back inside, grinding myself against her ass.

"Kyle," she cries out, and that right there is exactly what I wanted.

I thrust again, deeper and harder this time.

"Faster," she pleads.

But I want to savour this and slow my pace instead, rocking against her, teasing, drawing the pleasure out as long as possible. It feels fucking incredible.

"You ass." Her curse is muttered and slightly breathless and it makes me laugh.

"Stop complaining," I say, pulling almost all the way out before I punch back in with a hard thrust. She gasps with pleasure. "You like it any way I give it to you."

"What makes you think that?"

"Because you're always dripping wet when I touch you."

"I am not," she gasps, as if it's a bad thing to be wet. It's not. It's hot as fuck.

"Protest all you like, Little Warrior, but your body betrays you."

"The same way yours betrays you?"

She has me there. I surge forward, unable to tease any longer. My hips slam against her ass, my thrusts measured and forceful, building in intensity until I can't catch my breath.

"Harder," she begs, and I know she's close.

"Say my name."

She pushes against me with every thrust. "Kyle."

I take a shuddering breath and slide a hand around her hip and down, until my middle finger finds her clit. I rub it hard, my pace frantic.

Jamie cries my name again. *My* name. *Mine.* And a surge of pure, male satisfaction rushes through me. Her pussy contracts and shudders around my dick, her body collapsing beneath me.

I slide my finger free and grab her hips, pounding hard, gasping for every breath as her whimpers fill the air around us.

My cock pulses, and I grind against her before pulling out quickly, pleasure hitting like a freight train as I come hard, spurting across her back.

Jamie sinks down, boneless. I follow, spent and sweaty, tucking myself in her side. My head buries in her neck, my sweaty skin sticking to hers as emotion rises like a tidal wave. I try to swallow but it won't stay down. My throat aches with it.

God, I love this girl. *So much.*

She twists slightly and the tips of her fingers flutter gently down my chest, her eyes on mine. "Are you okay?"

No. I'm not okay.

I roll to my back, breathing heavy.

"Kyle?" My name is a wobble on her lips.

I want to reassure her, but I can't because she doesn't love me back, not in the same way. It leaves my insides bruised as if I've taken a punch to the gut. I want to leave the tent, but I can't seem to tear myself from her side.

"I'm okay," I eventually manage to say because above all else, I care about her. And I care about the limited time we have together. I don't want to ruin it by saying things that shouldn't be said.

I rise from the bed, swiping at my face. "I'll get a cloth."

33

KYLE

The drive home from Esperance to Perth feels like a funeral procession, as if someone died. We wave out our windows as we pass by Reg and Bev's camp, slowing down a little. They wave back, Bev pulling a cigarette from her lips to call out, "Drive safe!"

Reg gives a casual salute. "Come back again next year, you two. Same time. We'll be here."

"We'll do our best," I tell him, an empty platitude.

Graham is there having an early breakfast with his parents, dressed in what looks like his work uniform. It's sporty, his muscles seemingly created by a bunch of girly weights in the gym rather than real, hard work. "You should," he says, his eyes on Jamie through the open window. Irritation rises swiftly. Can he not see me right here? I mean, we're not a couple, but he doesn't know that. "I can take you to some of the less populated spots in the kayak."

"We'd love that," I interject with a biting smile.

"Thanks, you guys," Jamie calls, and I tap the accelerator, leaving them behind with a brief honk of the horn.

"Graham is a dick," I mutter.

"You sound jealous."

I snort. "I'm not jealous."

"Mmm hmm," Jamie hums in a patronising tone.

My brows pinch. Am I? "Whether I'm jealous or not is irrelevant. It doesn't make him any less of a dick."

"He looks a little like Jake, don't you think?"

I glance across at her. Because he has blond hair and green eyes? Apart from that, they're nothing alike. It's like comparing a weed in the sidewalk to a giant oak in the forest. "Not at all."

"Just the colouring, maybe," she says.

Is that what she wants? Another Jake? Was it him she imagined touching her these past few nights instead of me? The thought shuts me down, and we don't speak for at least an hour.

Jamie kicks up her legs, crossing them at the ankle and resting them out the open window. Her favourite passenger position. My eyes flick down their long, tanned length, remembering a different position, one with them wrapped around my ass last night as I pounded inside her.

There seemed to be no restraint after the sun went down on our last three nights in Esperance, as if the cover of darkness was a free pass, but only on the unspoken agreement we didn't bring it into the day.

I did my best, but there were times where she made me laugh, and I wanted to swing her up in my arms and plant a smacking wet kiss on her lips. Or slide an arm around her shoulder, hugging her to me while we wandered the local markets, just to enjoy the feel of her body next to mine. Or hold her hand, dragging it onto my lap as we watched a movie at the little theatre, avoiding the thunderstorm sweeping through town.

I've never had that before. Simple affection. Loving gestures. And I know she doesn't want a relationship with me. I'm not expecting her to change her mind, but I can't help this hollow sense of rejection.

"Ugh," I mutter to myself. I need to switch off. "Put some music on?" Usually Jamie is blasting something by now, but she's quiet instead, as if lost in thoughts of her own.

She drops her legs from the window and picks up her phone. Her finger taps the shuffle button on her favourite eighties playlist and "She's Like the Wind" by Patrick Swayze comes on. He starts crooning and the lyrics make me feel worse. "Not that one."

She hits shuffle again. "With or Without You" by U2 starts to play. I give it thirty seconds. "Not that one either."

Jamie huffs and stabs her finger again. "Livin' On A Prayer" by Bon Jovi blares through the speakers. This one I can handle.

I open my mouth to start singing along when she cuts me off. "I swear to god I am *not* changing it again. You can suck a bag of dicks."

"Testy much?"

"I'm hungry," she mutters.

"We only ate an hour ago," I point out.

"Oh gee, thanks," she snaps. "I forgot. Suddenly I'm not hungry anymore."

"What about your giant cheese wheel? You never finished it." She wrapped it with loving care and stored in the esky two days ago. I don't know what she plans on doing with it when we get back. Either take it home in her suitcase or give it to Erin.

Jamie moans. "If I ever see another piece of cheese again I'll barf."

I shout with laughter.

"Shut up," she mutters.

"What happened to your 'cheese makes life worth living' sentiment?"

"I take it back." Her head tips back against the seat, and she literally gags. "Cheese died for me the day I finished two pounds of that wheel."

"Does that mean I can have it?"

She looks at me. "What the hell do you want with it?"

I grin. "I can use it as a bribe to get me back on card night."

She gags again. "It's all yours."

Another quiet hour passes. I think Jamie is sleeping. Her seat is tipped back and my cap sits over her face, blocking out the light. Bored, I reach across, lifting the edge with my fingers.

She slaps my hand away. "Fuck off. I'm sleeping."

"You're such a grouch today."

I hear a mumble from beneath the cap.

"What was that?" I ask, turning the volume down.

"I don't want to go home."

My heart jerks an erratic beat. "What do you mean by home? Townsville?"

Jamie pulls the cap away and tosses it to the floor, leaving her hair in a haphazard mess around her face. "It's not that I hate it there. It's just so … I don't know." She scrunches her nose as if she sucked on a bitter lemon. "Far."

She's due for re-enlistment soon, but the ice between us is thin on that particular subject. No good can come of me skating across it now, so I leave it alone.

Another two hours brings us to the halfway point of our return trip. "You wanna stop for lunch?"

"Maybe we could grab a sandwich to go?"

I stop at the next town. Lake King. Population three hundred and thirty-two. After parking the Hilux by the bowser, I get out and refill the tank while Jamie heads inside to order food. She returns while I'm checking the tyre pressure, carrying two large white packets. "I got us beef burgers," she says, waving them. "And I paid for the fuel."

"Thanks."

We hit the road again after we both use the bathroom. I'm anxious to get home and I'm not—all at the same time. The conflicting emotions make my stomach churn, and I only manage a few bites before I put my lunch to the side. Jamie is my best friend, and I'm in love with her. How am I supposed to let her go?

Jamie

We arrive in Perth around dusk. The sun is setting over the ocean, creating a vivid burst of colour across the sky. I make a show of taking a couple of photos, but inside I feel sick. I've said goodbye so many times before. I can't bear another.

"What's Wood and Erin's new address?" Kyle asks.

They moved out of their apartment while we were gone.

"Bad timing for you. Great timing for us," I teased as we left on our road trip, waving my arm wildly out the window as we headed off into the great unknown. Though, we didn't leave them entirely without help. We recruited Ryan and Nathan on our behalf to do the heavy lifting for us, which means we owe them big.

I recite the address to Kyle, and we pull up out the front forty-five minutes later. Wood is in the front yard wrestling with the electrical cord of a power saw. There's a stack of timber by the frame of a new porch and sawdust covers the front lawn like snow. He pauses, turning at the sound of the car. Then he whoops loudly, dropping the cord. I leap from the car and into his arms, squealing as if it's been a lifetime rather than a few short weeks.

Wood spins me around. "You're back!"

"We're back!"

He plants a hard kiss on my cheek before putting me down, setting me away from him and giving me a thorough inspection. "You look different."

I feel different, though I shrug his comment off. "It's probably the tan."

"No." He shakes Kyle's hand when he reaches us, slapping him on the back. "It's this," he says, turning back to me and jamming a thumb against my forehead. "Your little furrow is gone."

"Hey!" I swat him away. "That hurt." I look towards the front door. "Where's Erin?"

"Inside. In the study I think."

I leave Wood and Kyle to talk while I bound over the half-built porch and step inside. "Erin?"

No answer.

I wander from room to room. It's mostly furniture and boxes half unpacked. I find her in a little nook down the back. She's sitting at a desk, headphones on and pen in hand, mumbling over a piece of paper in front of her.

I sneak up behind and pull the covers from her ears. "Boo!"

"Arrrrghhhhhh!" she screams in a tone so shrill you could hear it from space. "You bitch." She rises from her chair, putting a hand over her heart as if to calm it down. "I fucking hate you. Come here."

Erin wraps me up in a hug and tears spring free. I hug her back. Hard. "I hate you too."

We stand there, swaying a little, hugging. "I can't believe I only get you for one night!"

I step back and she performs an inspection—a different kind from the one Wood did just before. I'm a bug beneath her microscope. "Look at you. You're all stinky and dirty. Did you turn hippy on me?" Erin lifts my arm, taking a peek at my armpits before I swat her away. She looks relieved at the hairless skin before she flicks the tangled strands of my hair. "You need a trim." She peers closer … at my eyebrows. "And you need a wax. I was hoping we could go out drinking and dancing tonight, but look at you. I don't have time for miracles."

Kyle steps inside, wheeling my suitcases behind him.

"I could have got those." An automatic protest.

He gives me a look as he sets them off to the side, flicking the handles down.

"Thank you, Kyle."

Erin gives him a welcoming hug. "How was your trip?" she asks him, drawing back.

"Amazing. We've got so many photos to show you."

She claps her hands. "Gimme."

Kyle nods his head at me. "Jamie can show you. I've got to get going."

Something inside me sinks like an anchor to the ocean floor.

"Will you come out with us later?" she asks. "We're going out for Jamie's last night. Drinks on us for organising the crew to help us move."

"I can't." Kyle and I share a look as he answers, his expression heavy, his tone thick with regret. "Sorry." He starts walking backwards as if he can't wait to leave. "Maybe some other time though."

"I'll walk you out," I say.

"Bye, Erin," he calls out.

"See you, Kyle!"

We pass Wood as he steps inside, wiping dirty boots on the doormat. "Leaving already?"

"Yeah. Got shit to do before I get back to work."

They shake hands again, Kyle giving Wood a slap on the back. "See you next time, mate."

He steps off the half-made porch and stalks towards the Hilux as if his ass were on fire.

"Would you slow down a minute?"

He heads around the side to the back of the Hilux. "I thought you didn't like goodbyes," he says and starts hooking the tonneau cover in place with practiced efficiency. I stand watching him, not knowing what to say because he's right. I don't. But it's not like I'll be gone forever, right?

Kyle makes his way to the passenger door. He opens it, retrieving my satchel. Shutting the door, he gives it to me. Actually, he basically shoves it against my chest, and I catch it before it drops to the ground.

"Well, I'll see you next time, Jamie," he mutters, keys dangling from his fingers.

That's it? I know I'm horrible at goodbyes, but that one was weaker than the shitty beer I bought him at the Condingup Tavern.

He starts for the driver's side. "Kyle?"

He keeps walking.

"Kyle, please."

"Fuck," he mutters, stopping, resting his hand on the hood, his back to me. His shoulders rise and fall for several beats before he turns. The pained expression on his face roots me to the ground.

"I'm sorry." I take a step towards him, but my legs feel ready to give out beneath me so I stop, not knowing what to do or what else to say.

He looks away, blinking. "Yeah," he says, gruff. "Me too."

Kyle raps his fist gently on the hood of the car before he moves off. He opens the door and looks at me. "Message when you get to Townsville, will you?"

I nod. Then he's sliding in the car, the door closing behind him. The engine starts and he drives off. I watch him go and my chest aches. It aches so fucking much. He disappears down the street, brake lights red as he slows before turning the corner, the Hilux roaring as he accelerates away. Then he's gone.

The street becomes quiet. I hear the faint rustle of leaves in the trees, the breeze kicking up a little. It's starting to get cool with the change of season. I rub my bare arms, knowing nothing will ever be the same between us again.

Then, and only then, do the tears start to fall. Faster than I can wipe them away. I have never, *never,* felt more lost and confused than I do right now.

34

JAMIE

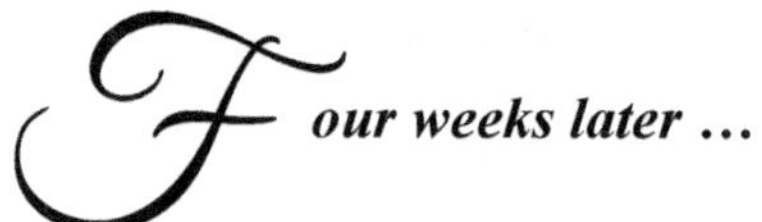 *our weeks later ...*

I ROLL over in my bed, punching my pillow. When did it become so annoyingly lumpy? I settle on my side and close my eyes with a huff, trying to clear my mind, but minutes later I feel it again. The phantom touch of Kyle's arm sliding around my middle. His palm is heavy and hot on my belly, and it slides down, skimming beneath my underwear, sliding between my legs. The pads of his fingers feel rough but his touch is gentle. His warm breath tickles the back of my neck, so real I shiver, alone in my bed, squirming at the raging ache he leaves behind.

A loud crack renders the air, thunder causing the earth to shake beneath my bed as if Mother Nature understands my frustration.

It's still early—around seven o'clock on a Friday evening—but I'm tired. I need sleep so bad my bones ache, but it won't come. I rip the quilt away and scoot off the mattress. I need a pill, that's what I need. The road trip put me off my routine. Once I settle back into my normal sleeping pattern, everything will be fine.

I pad towards the tiny kitchen of my little open-plan unit, bypassing the breakfast table where my re-enlistment papers sit, complete but not yet signed. My eyes fall to the box beside them, and my stomach dips like I'm on the downhill slide of a rollercoaster.

It's taunted me for an entire week, sitting inside its brown package with expectation. The thing is, I'm late. I knew taking the morning after pill would delay my period, but not for this long. It's been easier to bury my head in the sand rather than face reality, but I'm not sure I can put it off any longer. The not knowing is turning me into a basket case.

My phone beeps as rain pelts hard against my windows. I peek through the blinds. It's a heavy downpour, the rain coming in sideways. I flick the blind back in place and check my phone. It's from Connor. He has a unit on base too.

Connor: Party. My place. Beers and board games.

Jamie: Pass.

Connor: Don't make me come drag you.

Jamie: I have a gun and a black belt.

Connor: Good point.

I also have an appointment with a pregnancy test. But instead of taking it, I sit down at the table, staring at my papers. *Just sign them, Jamie. The test will be negative and you can move on with your life.*

But what if it's not?

Then it's not a big deal, I tell myself. These things happen all the time and they get taken care of, right? Easy. A small procedure. I'm strong enough to know I can handle it, so why has a hollow ache taken up residence inside my stomach?

Taking care of it would be the right thing to do, but the right thing isn't all rainbows and unicorns, is it? It can feel real shitty too.

I pick up the pen and I hesitate. I'm not that person. Maternal. Warm. Loving. I'm just not. I wouldn't know the first thing about caring for someone other than myself.

Taking a deep breath, I flip to the last page of my paperwork and I sign with a bigger than usual flourish. I future date the documents for tomorrow, when I'll hand them in for lodgement, and I'm done. I set the pen down. The army owns me for at least another three years. I should be happy. That means three more years of treating the sick and injured. Three more years of saving lives. So why is that hollow feeling stretching ahead of me like a dark, empty void?

Fuck's sake. Take the damn test already, Jamie.

I push the paperwork aside and snatch up the box. I take it, along with my phone, to the bathroom.

I set the box down on the bathroom vanity and send a message.

Jamie: Taking the test.

Erin: YES! I'm on standby.

I broke down in a weak moment last week and called Erin, telling her what really happened on our road trip. She was drunk in the bathroom when she answered, slurping wine while she sat on the toilet. I told her because I wanted her reassurance that it wasn't a big deal. It's what I've been trying to tell myself every time I start to hyperventilate, but maybe it would help hearing it from someone else.

"I'm not actually doing my business right now," she said, slurring slightly. "I came in here to pee and stayed for the peace. Colin started on the renovations for the kitchen today and between the banging and crashing and the pile of rubble on the floor, I thought my best option was to just stay in here and drink."

"Well it's a good thing you're sitting down," I replied, coming straight out with it. "Because I think I might be pregnant." Stunned silence followed, the kind that made me rush to fill it. "But likely not. I'm probably not. I've got a test here. I haven't taken it. I should hang up and go do that. I don't even know why I called you. I feel a bit stupid, actually."

More silence.

"Erin? Are you there?"

"Fark," she slurred in dramatic fashion. "Give me a minute." She had a thousand questions, I knew it. She was just wading through all of them, picking the best ones first. She began to fire them at me, one after the other, as if we were in the final round of a television game show. "Kyle?"

"Who else?"

"When?"

"The last week of our road trip."

"How?"

"What do you mean how? Insert tab A into slot B, you twat."

She kept going without pause at my insult. "Who touched who first?"

"Really?" I rubbed a hand across my face, cringing as I paced along the short length of my kitchen. "That's not what's important here."

Her tone turned bossy. "Answer the question."

"He kissed me." I walked to my bed and turned, flopping down. "I told him I didn't know what I'd do without him and he kissed me."

"Oh my god." Erin moaned vocally and then slurped another mouthful of wine. "That's so hot. And so romantic I could actually die."

I huffed out a breath, somehow finding myself agreeing with her. "It was the best kiss of my life. I couldn't stop thinking about it. Does that make me horrible for saying that? Jake was amazing. We had a … thing. A wonderful thing. But there were no expectations. We barely knew each other. Our history was a one-night stand. Not like—" I broke off, not prepared to follow that train of thought. "Kyle is my best friend."

"Right. And would you kiss me the way you kissed Kyle?"

I snorted. "Umm no, but you're a girl, right?"

"Okay. Would you kiss Colin the way you kissed Kyle?"

I outright laughed. "Erin! It's Wood." I'm pretty sure I'd feel more attraction for a cabbage.

"How long since you've spoken to him?"

I hugged an arm around myself, the phone pressed hard to my ear, my stomach a queasy lump. "Not much of late, but we've both been busy."

"I see."

"You don't see, though. He might have kissed me, but I'm the one who got drunk and slept with him. I did that. Deliberately. Because I wanted to know what it was like to be with him. Just once. Except once turned into more because I'm a greedy bitch who doesn't know when to stop. It's like when you buy yourself a giant wheel of cheese and think you'll just have one piece. Only you realise that piece tastes amazing and makes you feel good inside, so you have another, and another, and then you realise you've almost finished off the whole wheel and you start to feel sick to the stomach and not just because you're a goddamn guts. Erin, I think—" I broke off, needing to catch my breath. "I crossed a line I shouldn't have and nothing is the same between us anymore."

"You know what I think?"

"What?" I asked, holding tight to my phone as I eagerly awaited her advice. I needed her to tell me what to do. I needed moral guidance to set me on the right path. Some gleaming pearls of wisdom to fix everything I broke.

She slurped at her wine before she imparted it. "I think you should keep on eating that cheese."

"Erin! Not helping."

"Okay, I keep forgetting my opinion is only valid as long as it aligns with yours."

"Don't get bitchy."

"Then stop being stupid."

"I'm not stupid. I just don't have my head in the clouds the way you do all the time. I'm a realist. Sue me."

"Fine. Okay. Just forget what happened. Think platonic thoughts."

"Platonic thoughts. Right." I nodded. "I can do that. Like the time Kyle tripped me up on the skywalk because I was moving too slow. Or how he threw pine cones at my head because I wouldn't put my book down and go swimming with him. Or the time he dared me to eat a green chilli because I was dumb enough to tell him the salsa he made wasn't spicy enough."

"Did you eat it?"

"Do you even know me? Of course I ate it. Kyle had to hold my hair back while I barfed into the shrubs, bringing it right back up. FYI, it burned just as much coming back up as it did going down. I thought I was going to die."

"Kyle did that? He held your hair back while you barfed all over yourself like the foolish, competitive dick you are?" She literally sighed after insulting me and sipped more of her wine, smacking her lips. "He saw you at your worst, and he still kissed you. Not sure that's platonic. Come to think of it, he probably tripped you on the skywalk by accident because he was staring at your ass. And the whole pine cone thing? He wanted your attention, and he was willing to face your wrath to get it. You need to work a little harder on this."

"Okay. He laughed when I fell off the jetty and into the water."

"Did he jump in after you?"

"No," I replied, indignant. "He just laughed harder and took a photo."

"Doesn't count. I'd do that if it were Colin. What else?"

"I don't know."

"Because you can't think of a single platonic moment." The triumph in her tone sounded a little too giddy, like she wanted this. "Tell me something about Kyle you like."

"How will that help? Won't it just make everything worse?"

"We need to get to the bottom of what you're feeling. It might help shed some light on the situation."

"There is no situation. And it doesn't matter what I feel, does it? Because there's no way that—"

"Oh my god," she snapped. "A potential pregnancy is not a situation?"

"What is going on in here?" I heard Wood say, his voice faint. "I can hear you all the way from the kitchen. With my drill going."

"Jamie might be pregnant," Erin replied.

"Erin!" I snapped.

"What?" Wood sounded like he was being strangled.

"Do you mind, Colin?" she said to him. "I'm on the toilet." I heard the sound of a door banging shut before Erin yelled, "Bring more wine!"

"Why would you say that?"

"I'm drunk, Jamie. You can't hold me accountable for what I say. Now where were we?" I heard a tapping sound, like fingernails clacking against a bathroom vanity. She was having far too much fun with this. "Oh … We were talking about what you like about Kyle."

"No, we were not."

"Don't make me book a flight. I will come there, and we can have this conversation in person," she warned, and she would do it. Erin didn't deal in empty threats.

"He's …" I trailed off. "This feels stupid."

"Just do it."

"Okay." I closed my eyes, picturing Kyle. He was grinning at me. It was smug, and familiar, and heartbreakingly cute. "I like his smile."

"Lame answer, but okay. What else?"

"He's photogenic."

"Really? I feel like you're not taking this seriously."

"I am. I'm just not good at expressing what I'm feeling."

I took so many photos on our holiday. Kyle is in almost all of them without him even knowing. He's a little rough around the edges, flawed in a million perfect ways, scarred, and yet so incredibly handsome and compelling at the same time. He has this beautiful light in his eyes and a smile that pulls at something inside me, making it hard to look away. And every night I try falling asleep, I find myself looking at all the images, getting stuck on my favourite one from our stop in Broome.

We were walking along the water's edge, barefoot on the sand, and I stopped to take a photo of the sunset over the turquoise water. Kyle stopped with me and I got him in profile, the panorama blurring behind him, bringing him into focus. There was a quiet strength inside him as he looked out past the crashing waves. The kind that said he'd seen the ugly side of life, and experienced the absolute worst of humanity, but he didn't let it break him.

How was I supposed to articulate all that without sounding like a complete fool?

I set the memory of mine and Erin's conversation aside and focus on taking the pregnancy test. I don't bother with the instructions inside the box. I know how pregnancy tests work. I've even read textbooks on all the symptoms, and I have none of them. No tender breasts. No morning sickness. No weird cravings or crazy mood swings. I'm just a little late. And tired. But when is that abnormal?

I finish peeing on the little white stick and set it on the counter. I'm washing my hands at the basin when a loud bang comes at my front door. I jolt, knocking the stick sideways. It flies off the bathroom vanity and smacks into the wall before dropping itself inside the little trash bin I keep beside the toilet.

"Huh." It feels like a sign.

The knock comes again, a fist rapping hard, and someone calls out my name. Who the hell? It's probably Connor, come to make good on his threat. I toss my phone on the bed, braless and dressed in a thin white tank top and pink cotton knickers.

"I'm not home!" I yell and grab my robe, sliding my arms inside the sleeves as I walk to the door, tying it at the waist. I flick on the outside light and unlock the deadbolt, swinging the door wide with an irritated scowl, hoping it will scare Connor off.

Kyle

You big stupid idiot, I curse to myself, standing at Jamie's door, rain pelting me in the back and legs. It runs down my face, plastering the hair to my head as I raise my fist and bang again on the door. Impatient. Edgy. My need for her palpable. I feel it in the breath pushing past my lips. The pulsing in my blood. The burning of my eyes and the racing of my heart.

I told myself I could handle this as I drove off, leaving her at Wood and Erin's. I could forget about being in love. The feeling would fade with time and distance. I busied myself with unpacking all the camping gear, cleaning it all off, and putting it back in storage. I returned the Hilux to the hire company, and I buried myself in work and training until I fell into bed each night, exhausted and yet somehow wide awake, staring at the ceiling.

I tried reading books, listening to podcasts about fishing, and harassing Ryan and Fin into letting me babysit Jacob. I turned up with bags of baby clothes, fur-lined jackets for the winter, and tiny Nikes for when he takes his first steps. I even showed up with a giant box of Lego.

"Choking hazard," Ryan said to me, though he let me inside.

I made my way down the hall to the kitchen where Fin was sprinkling cheese over a pan of lasagne, a glass of red wine in her left hand. "The Lego is for me, asshole," I griped, going straight for the fridge, cold air gushing outward when I opened the door, the Lego box tucked beneath my armpit. "Hey, Fin."

"Kyle."

"And you're how old?" Ryan asked.

"This old," I said, giving him the middle finger before coming out with two chilled bottles.

Fin gave him a look and he gave one back, both of them having a conversation with their eyes that all couples had when they were nauseatingly close. It made me want to kick something. They may as well just dump me inside a cannon and launch me into outer space. At least then I could justify the loneliness.

I growled something and shoved one of the bottles at Ryan before moving to the living area with my beer, setting my Lego box down on the coffee table beside a teething ring, a blue sippy cup, and a little potted plant.

Ryan sighed, a deep, heavy sound before following me into the living area. He sank onto the couch, watching as I ripped open the box, spilling packages of Lego everywhere. "Do you want to talk about it?"

"No, I don't." My tone was snide, but I couldn't seem to help it. I grabbed the thick instruction booklet and opened it to the first page. "I just want to build this goddamn Death Star and drink my beer."

His eyes dropped to the box, which clearly stated over four thousand pieces were bagged inside. "That will take at least twenty-four hours straight."

"Twelve. You're helping me."

"I'm not even into Star Wars."

"Well we can't all be losers like you."

"I've got a better idea." Ryan got to his feet, jerking his head towards the French doors leading outside. "Follow me."

We headed out onto the back deck. I took a seat while Ryan opened the drawer of their little outdoor cooking unit. He grabbed out a lighter and a packet. Pulling two cigars free, he put one to his lips and handed me the other, flicking the lighter and holding the flame out towards me. The end glowed red as I puffed, drawing the smoke inward, letting it curl around my tongue before exhaling in a scented, satisfying cloud.

Ryan lit his own and took the seat beside me, smoke a hazy cloud around him when he spoke. "You're in love with her, aren't you, you great big lump."

I coughed and choked on my next exhale, eyes watering. "First of all," I rasped, scowling, "I'm not a great big lump. Second of all, in love with who?"

"Oh, for fuck's sake. Don't give me that shit, Brooks. I've been where you are. In fact, I recall a certain someone telling me to grow a ballsack once. He also said I wouldn't find the answer on the ceiling when he caught me staring at it. And when I asked him the answer to what, he said to whether she loves me or not." Ryan took another puff of his cigar. "Seems to me you like to go balls out when giving other people advice but you're just a big ol' coward when it comes to taking it yourself."

Smoke huffed from my flared nostrils. "Fuck you, Kendall."

"No. Fuck you."

I rose from my chair, my back to Ryan, the image of Jamie in my head as I leaned my forearms on the timber railing of the deck.

Fucking hell, she was beautiful. A perfectly flawed little asshole, but she was *my* little asshole. I tried so hard not to fall in love with her, but it was like scooping water out of a sinking ship with my bare hands. I was so fucking sunk.

Bringing the cigar to my lips, I drew in a deep mouthful of smoke before exhaling, watching it drift out on the breeze. "You remember that time you said we were all just held together with duct tape? That we were hoping the army would perform some kind of miracle and piece us back together but all it did was make the cracks inside us bigger?"

Ryan stepped up beside me, resting his forearms on the railing same as me, and he looked out into the yard beyond. "Jamie patched up the cracks," he said, his voice gruff because he knew. He'd been there too.

"She's my duct tape."

Ryan snorted and a chuckle rose up from somewhere deep inside me. It built and built until I was laughing my ass off, Ryan laughing alongside me, choking on smoke and shaking his head.

Finlay came out to check on us. "What's going on out here?"

Ryan waved a hand through the cloudy haze. "Brooks found his duct tape," he said, and it set us off all over again.

Finlay looked at us like we'd lost our minds, and I'm pretty sure we had, but it was a good feeling. "Well, good for you, Kyle."

She went back inside, and we went back to our seats and cigars. "You know what I did?" I said, cutting through a comfortable few minutes of quiet.

"What?"

"I got her a present. I was going to send it, but damned if I want to see the look on her face when she gets it."

"What is it?"

I told him, and it took me a good half hour explaining the full story behind it.

"And that set you back how much?"

"The entire deposit I tucked aside for my house on the beach." The very one I talked about all the time. My dream. Every penny earned and squirrelled away, gone because I was a fool who'd do anything to make her happy, to fix what was broken inside of her.

"You're a goddamn idiot," Ryan said.

I suck on my cigar for a moment. "I don't regret it. It was worth every cent and more."

"Jesus, Brooks. Some days I think there may just be a heart inside that egotistical exterior of yours."

"I don't know whether to feel insulted or not."

He reached across and slapped me on the back. "You know what you should do?"

I leant forward, eager for some advice. "What?"

"Hand deliver it."

The thought sent jitters through me. "You think?" I asked, though I knew he was right. I didn't want regrets. I didn't want to wake up one day and realise I should have tried. Jamie was worth the fight. Right to the end.

"There's just one thing you need to do first," he warned, rising from his chair.

"What?" I stubbed my cigar out, getting to my feet.

"Go build your Death Star, you fucking infant."

The front door swings open beneath my hand, and the scowl falls from my face, shock rooting me to the floor.

It's not Connor.

Kyle is standing on the other side of the door, rain pelting him from all directions, hair plastered to his face, a bag slung over his shoulder. He's dressed in a cotton tee shirt and jeans, the drenched fabric highlighting the thick, heavy muscle of his body. Goose bumps run the length of his arms as he stares at me, shivering, water running in his eyes—eyes that hold more heat than a bonfire. They eat me up as if he's starved.

Everything inside me ignites. "Kyle?"

"Jamie," he croaks.

My pulse skyrockets and my heart threatens to pound from my chest. How did I ever think I was strong? Because I'm ready to launch myself at him with just a single heated look. "What are you doing here?"

"I needed to see you," he says, rain spattering his face faster than he can wipe it away. "I know I'm not Jake. I know I'm not the one you wanted."

My brows knit, and I open the door wide so he can step inside, out of the downpour, only he doesn't move. "Kyle—"

"Just hear me out. Please," he begs, swallowing, swiping at his face. "Jake is gone. He's gone. And it still hurts like a motherfucker. I still wake every day wanting to tell him something, or make him laugh just to see that stupid movie-star smile of his because it made me feel like I was part of something special. Then I remember that he's gone and it's like a punch to the goddamn gut." Kyle raises his voice over the din of the rain. "Jake wanted you. I know it. He saw a life with you. Only he never got to have it. And I shouldn't be here, trying to take that life for myself, but I can't help it. I'm a selfish bastard. I'm not good like Jake was. I can be childish and impatient, and I can be really fucking stupid. I have nothing to offer you. But I'm here. Jake might be gone, *but I'm still here*. And I want you more than I've ever wanted anything in my entire life."

Kyle finishes with a heaving breath, and my heart is pounding so hard in my chest it hurts. "Are you done?" I ask, my voice a rasp, hoping he's finished because I need his mouth on mine.

He shoves at the wet hair on his forehead. "I'm in love with you, Jamie Murphy, and I don't even know your middle name."

His declaration steals the air from my lungs. I reach out, quaking on the inside as I fist his shirt and drag him inside. He drops his bag, kicking the door shut behind him, barely catching his breath before I push him against the back of it. My hands grab his face, pulling his mouth down to mine.

"It's Juliet," I say against his lips before I kiss him with impatience, my tongue thrusting inside his mouth, frantic and violent.

"What?" he mumbles, kissing me back. Heat explodes between my legs, along my veins, inside my heart. Our mouths become desperate, tongues rubbing, devouring each other, harder and faster because it's not enough.

I take a breath. "My name. Jamie Juliet Murphy."

He kisses me again, fingers grabbing at the knot of my robe. My hands tug at his shirt. He lets me go, tugging it over his head. It falls to the ground with a wet slap before his lips are on mine again. "What about you?"

"What about me?"

He unknots the tie and my robe falls away. "What's your middle name?"

"Edgar."

My chest shudders with a chuckle that can't get free because Kyle's mouth is back on mine, lips pressing hard, consuming me in the best possible way. He breaks off to peel away my shirt, and my laugh gets loose.

"Shut up," he mumbles, his palms chilled from the outdoors as they land on my boobs, making me flinch.

"I can't help it," I gasp, my head tipping back, a giggle escaping. "It's just so unsexy."

His fingers tweak my nipples, a little too hard, but it shoots pleasure straight down my belly like an arrow finding its mark.

"Kyle Edgar Brooks," I say.

"Do you mind? I'm trying to fuck you here."

My giggles only get worse. "Then you need to do better."

"I think it sounds distinguished," he says, affronted, dropping to his knees before me. "It's the name of my grandfather."

My laughter dies a quick death. "Your mother's father?"

"Yes," he says, hooking his thumbs in the sides of my pink cotton knickers. He slides them down, and I lift my feet one at a time, stepping out of them, my hands holding tight to his rounded shoulders.

"You know what?"

His lips press against my stomach, warm and a little tickly, and I let out a breathy moan. "What?"

"I love it."

Kyle dips his tongue inside my belly button, and my head tips back, my toes curling. "You're just saying that now because you feel like a dick."

"I'm sorry." He rises to his feet, and I tilt my head to meet his eyes.

"I *am* a dick, but I wouldn't lie. I do love it. It's perfect. Your name is perfect."

I stretch up, touching my mouth to his, my hands going to the button on his jeans. His breath is shaky against my lips, and I love it. I love the vulnerability he doesn't hide from me and the need that darkens his eyes.

Lowering the zip, I sink to my knees the same way he did just moments earlier. Kyle watches as I peel the wet denim down his legs, along with his boxer-briefs. He kicks them away and his cock springs free, filling my palms, hard and smooth. I open my mouth, taking him in, surrounding the hard flesh with warm, wet heat.

He groans and his head tips back. "Fuck."

His fingers fist in my hair, tugging, his cock rock solid and his abs shuddering with restraint. I swirl my tongue, whimpering around the hard length of him. The throb between my legs grows bigger, a thrumming steady ache, his pleasure increasing my own.

"You need to stop," he rasps, trying to step free.

I pull away with a lick, taking him in my hand. "I don't want to."

"I'll come."

My fist moves up and down, stroking, and I slide my tongue around the wide, velvety head. "Good."

"Not yet."

Kyle grips me beneath my armpits and hauls me upright. I could fight him, but I'm too far gone. I need him inside me. I'm grabbed and pushed up against the wall behind me, face-first, his breath hot and harsh against my neck. "Jamie," he rasps, his hands everywhere, cupping my breasts, pinching a nipple, the other sliding over my hip and between my legs.

He leaves me for a brief moment. I turn my head, watching as he fumbles through his pocket of his jeans. He pulls a condom packet free and tears it open with his teeth. I take a deep, shuddering breath as he rolls it down quickly. Then he's back on me, thick fingers probing, finding me swollen and wet. I cry out, my legs almost giving out beneath me.

"I want to be gentle," he says, grunting, his breath harsh and hot against my neck. "But I can't. I'm sorry. I can't."

I moan climbs my throat. "I don't want gentle."

Kyle growls and a thick finger pushes up inside me. Air leaves my lungs in a rush as a second one joins the first. His cock pushes up against the crack of my ass as he finger-fucks me until I'm a quivering ball of incoherent need. "Please," I gasp. "Dammit, Kyle." I push my hips back, rubbing, begging.

He removes his fingers, replacing them with the blunt head of his cock. He pushes inside me, driving forward until he's all the way in, grinding against me with a ragged groan.

My hands splay flat against the wall, panting, revelling in the feeling of fullness. He draws back and thrusts in again. It's not soft and it's not gentle. We fuck. Hard. The door rattles and my body shudders and jerks against it. And when it's over my legs give out, leaving me a breathless, boneless mess.

His hands wrap around my hips as he pulls out, and I'm swept up in his arms before I sink to the floor.

Kyle carries me to bed, and we fall in a tangle of loose, sweaty limbs. "That wasn't how I wanted this to go," he says, still catching his breath.

I twist to my side so I can see him. He looks tired, bone tired, like he hasn't slept in weeks. I swipe my thumb across his cheek, unable to stop myself from touching him. "How did you want this to go?"

He tucks an arm around my middle and tugs me closer, pressing our bodies together. "I thought maybe I could take you out on a proper date. Talk to you like a normal person." His mouth kicks up in a half smile. "Instead, I blurt out a bunch of shit and fuck you against the wall like an animal."

My hand falls to his shoulder, fingers trailing down along his tattooed bicep. "I like the way you fuck me."

Kyle lifts up on his elbow, eyes dropping to his groin. "I need to take care of this."

He climbs from the bed and in a blinding moment of clarity I remember the pregnancy test. It sure as shit has been longer than three minutes since I peed on that stick, but I don't know the outcome yet and I don't want him finding it first. I'm not ready to explain. Not yet.

Thinking Kyle is heading for the bathroom, I launch from the bed, chasing after him. Except he goes to the kitchen, tying the condom off and dropping it into the trash bin by the counter. He turns and almost stumbles over the top of me, not realising I was right behind him. "What are you doing?"

I hesitate. "I'm getting a drink. Want one?"

"Got any whiskey?"

I busy myself at the counter, unscrewing the cap of the bottle, pouring in a couple of fingers, putting the lid back on.

Kyle presses up behind me, and I feel the stirring of his cock against the crack of my ass. Need flares between my legs. "Again?"

"I'll be gentle this time," he says from behind me, ducking his head and pressing soft, fluttery kisses along my shoulder. I shiver with pleasure. "I don't want to hurt you."

I bring the glass to my nose, breathing it in as if the scent of alcohol will stop me from melting into a puddle on the floor. "You could never hurt me, Kyle. Not even if you tried."

His palms skim around my waist, warm as they rub across my belly, soothing and gentle. I sink back against him, my mind on the possibility of a baby. Kyle's baby. Part of him growing inside me. Something curls around my heart and squeezes. "Oh god."

He pauses, his lips lifting from my shoulder. "What's wrong?"

I lower the glass and turn, handing him the whiskey.

"Nothing. I just … I think I'll have a water."

We finish up in the kitchen, and Kyle makes good on his promise, being gentle the second time, pouring love into his every caress. We finish and his arm twines around my middle, tucking me close. I tumble headlong into a deep sleep.

"You're going to be an amazing mother, Jamie."

I shake my head. I'm at the beach, walking along the line of the shore, waves rushing up and over my feet, bubbling up against my ankles. Everything is hazy. And somewhere deep down inside my conscious, I know I'm dreaming because I'm not alone. Why else would Jake be talking to me?

I turn my head. He's walking along beside me, hands in his pockets, his face so wonderfully familiar my chest aches and my eyes burn hot with grief.

"I don't want children," I find myself saying to him, swallowing, blinking.

His green eyes crinkle at the corners. "That's what you tell yourself."

"I don't."

"You do, but you think you can only have one or the other. The army or family. As if you can't have both."

"Jake …" I shake my head. "I can't have both. It's not possible."

"But you can't keep going the way you are, can you? Aren't you tired of acting like you're made of armour? Do you really think you can find forgiveness for your past by fighting in some war?" He stops, looking out across the ocean. I stop with him. "Does being caught up in an IED blast balance the scales? Does being assaulted in Kandahar make everything okay now?"

"No." I shake my head, my jaw beginning to tremble. "It doesn't."

He turns his head, watching me with eyes that see right through me. "Do you know why that is?"

"Why?"

"Because it wasn't your fault your father died. How can you not see that? He made choices, same as you did, that led to his downfall, and you're making the same ones. He should have got out before it wrecked him. And here you are, travelling down the same path. If you keep going the way you are, it's going to wreck you too."

"What are you saying?"

Jake starts walking backwards, away from me, his steps slow, his image fading before my eyes. A growing sense of panic climbs my throat. "What are you saying, Jake? That I have to choose? The army or Kyle? How is that fair?" I shout.

He shakes his head at me, almost transparent now. "There's only one thing you *can* choose, Jamie, and when you do, everything will fall into place. You'll see."

I catch the flash of his smile, and then he's gone.

"Jake!" I scream, yelling into the wind, tears streaming down my face. "What am I supposed to choose?"

His voice comes from nowhere, surrounding me. "The one thing you've deserved all along, my precious Jamie." I spin around, searching, but there's no one here. There's nothing, just an endless ocean.

"Jake. Come back," I beg, sobs cracking open my chest. I drop to my knees, fingers clawing into the sand as if I can drag him back to my side. "Please."

"You know I can't do that. There's no changing the past," he says, his voice faint now, fading on the wind. "But you can always change the ending."

I wake with a start, breathing hard, chest aching. I swipe at my face, turning my head. Muted light streams through the partially open blinds. Dawn is here.

Kyle lies beside me, his sleep heavy and deep.

"I'm love with you, Jamie Murphy, and I don't even know your middle name."

He came all this way just to tell me. I fall back on the bed, my eyes burning.

"You keep talking like nobody needs you, Little Warrior, but I do. I need you."

All this time.

"I wouldn't have survived if it weren't for you."

All this time.

My eyes close, my hand going to the silver chain around my neck.

"It's a reminder. So you never forget who you are."

All this time.

Bear.

My Bear.

My hand goes to my mouth, tears spilling out of my eyes, falling unheeded down my cheeks. It's always been him. All this time. I'm in love with him. I'm so in love with him, so deeply, so absolutely, unequivocally in love with him, that I couldn't even see it.

I scramble from the bed, racing for the bathroom. For the trash bin. I grab it, my arm digging inside for the little white stick. My fingers close around it, and I pull it out, giving it a quick glance.

One pink line.

Just one.

I close my eyes, fighting disappointment. I want the baby. I want the family. I want Kyle. But I want the army too. I want it all.

I toss the stick back in the bin and leave the bathroom. Kyle is still fast asleep. I leave him that way. He needs it so desperately. Picking up my robe from the floor, I slip it on and make myself a coffee before taking a seat at the table, pulling the re-enlistment papers towards me, the pen rolling off beside them.

I flick through them, my heart a chaotic mess inside me. What am I supposed to choose?

My head tips back and I swallow, my throat thick as I try to make sense of the whirlwind in my head.

I just want to wake up without this heavy weight on my chest. I want to laugh, and love, and I want to live, just the way Kyle showed me it could be. I want to be … happy.

The internal revelation makes me stutter. Jake was right. It's the only choice I ever had to make. To be happy. And not the happy I tried forcing myself to feel, but the kind that comes without even thinking about it. The kind that comes naturally, from deep down inside.

The heavy weight slides right off my shoulders and tears spring to my eyes, making them hot.

"Jamie?"

I blink them away and turn my head. Kyle is sitting up on his elbow, eyes bleary, rubbing at his face. He looks like everything I never knew I wanted.

"You can always change the ending."

I set the papers back down. They might be signed, but that was yesterday. I'm not going to lodge them. Not today. Not tomorrow. Not ever. Because it's not the army that makes me happy. It's helping people. It's saving lives. It's the hope that I'm making a difference, and that what I did at the end of my life mattered. I don't need to be a soldier to achieve all that, but I need Kyle.

"Did I wake you?" I rise from the table, a smile curving my lips. "Go back to sleep."

His voice is low and drowsy but there's a happy light in his hooded eyes. "Kiss me first."

I walk over, leaning down. Kyle tips his head up, and I kiss him. His hand snakes around my neck, tugging, and I tumble down on top of him, laughing.

"Mmm." His mouth rubs against mine. "You smell like coffee."

"I'll make you one later. Sleep. I'm going to shower."

He waggles his brows. "I'll join you."

"No! Sleep. You need it." I push up off of him, tugging the tie of my robe free from his busy fingers. "I'll give you something really good if you do."

"Now you're talking."

"I know how to speak your language, Kyle."

His laughter trails behind me as I walk inside the bathroom, shedding my robe. Making sure the temperature is perfectly warm, I step inside the shower. I take my time, soaping up my hair twice, leaving the conditioner in, combing it through, shaving my legs, exfoliating all over until I'm buffed and smooth, my skin pink. I step out an entire lifetime later, drying off, telling myself it's a good thing my test was negative. I'm not ready. Neither of us are. We're only just working out how we feel.

Wrapping the towel up in my hair like a turban, I slip on my robe and open the bathroom door, steam trailing out behind me.

My eyes go to the bed but it's empty. I scan my little unit. Kyle isn't here. My brows pull together. His bag isn't by the door. Nor are the clothes he left on the floor. My skin prickles with the heat of panic.

I walk into the kitchen, spinning in a circle, searching. But there's nothing. No evidence that Kyle was here at all. My gaze drops to the table and my stomach dips painfully low. My re-enlistment papers are a crumpled mess. The same papers I dated today, because today was going to be the day I handed them in.

My eyes close and I see Kyle sitting up in bed, watching as I set them down on the table, moving the pen. He doesn't know. He came here declaring his love for me and all he got in return was a signed document telling him I was giving the army another three years of my life, and giving him nothing.

"Fuck!" I shout, running for the door. I rip it open, stepping out, looking left and right, but it's like he was never here.

I run down the full length of the balcony in nothing but a tiny terry cloth robe, past unit doors, past soldiers in uniform, my bare feet slapping against the wet concrete, until I reach the very end, breathless, looking out across the road.

"Jamie?"

I turn.

It's Connor.

"What's going on?"

I race back past him, ignoring his question. Maybe Kyle ducked out for some reason and slipped back in from the other side, using the staircase on the left. I swallow panic as I dash back inside, but it's exactly how I left it. Empty.

I slap a hand across my mouth, holding back a sob.

My phone.

I need my phone.

Where the fuck is it?

I dash about the unit, frantic, searching, until I remember I tossed it on the bed last night right before I answered the door. I find it down the side, on the floor, but it's dead.

I race to the kitchen for the charger, and that's when I see it. I jerk to a halt, my eyes landing on the flat brown package. It almost blends in with the tabletop it rests on. I pick it up, turning it, my name scrawled on the front. I take it with me to the counter, plugging in my phone. After an endless minute, it comes back to life. I go straight to my contacts, dialling Kyle, heart in my throat as I set the audio to speaker. An automated message comes through. His phone is off. *Dammit.*

I hang up and I'm setting it back on the counter when a message *dings*. It's from Kyle. I open it, breathless, sick.

Kyle: Jamie, I'm sorry for leaving the way I did, but I feel like such a fool. I snooped through the papers on your table, and I'm sorry for that too. I got up to make a coffee and they were right there, but that's no excuse.

I came here for no other reason except my need to see you. No ultimatums. But you have this plan of your future in your head, and you're so intent on living it on your own terms. I'm not sure I'm included in that. At least, not in the way I want to be. You're closed up so tight I don't think anyone could break through. Not even me.

I love you, Jamie. I fell in love with you because of the million things you never knew you were doing. But I want to be loved in return. I want the kind of love that's so deep, and so endless, and so consuming, it goes beyond a lifetime. I want forever, and I wanted it with you. But this morning I realised it's not possible and that coming to see you was a mistake.

Please don't call or message. At least not for a while. I need time. And space. And I need to hope we can one day be friends the way we used to be.

You'll always be my Little Warrior.

Bear.

"Damn you, Kyle!" I yell, getting to the end of the message. I rip the charging cord free and throw my phone. It flies across the room, hitting the wall. The screen cracks on impact before dropping to the tiles below.

My back slides down the kitchen cupboards as I sink to the floor, holding both palms against my head as a sob breaks me open, so wide and deep it doesn't make a sound. The next one is loud. And it *hurts*. And the next. Until I'm crying so hard it feels as though I'll never stop.

I can't hold them back anymore.

I can't.

Kyle left me again, but this time it's my fault because I didn't give him a reason to stay. I gave him nothing. I bang the back of my palm against my forehead. "Arrghhh!" *I should have fucking told him.*

I cry until my eyes are swollen and my stomach heaves. I cry until I'm sick. For everything I've ever lost.

For my father.

For Jake.

For Arash.

For Kyle.

When I'm wrung dry, I get to my feet, wobbly like a newborn foal. My stomach rolls over in a slow, queasy thump, and bile climbs my throat. I race for the bathroom, throwing up in the toilet, heaving, gagging, until there's nothing left.

"Jamie!"

Banging comes at my door. It's Connor. This time I know it is. I brush my teeth and wash my face in the basin before walking out of the bathroom, dizzy and tired. "Go away."

"Are you okay? Open up." He bangs again.

I grab the nearest object, a heavy book, and throw it at the door, shouting, "Go away!"

It's followed by blessed peace. I pad over to the beige package, carrying it with me to the bed. It's wrapped with precise corners, neat and perfect. I climb onto the middle of the mattress, cross-legged, eyes swollen and puffy, and peel the tape away from the edges, ripping it open. The brown paper falls away, revealing a black leather-bound folder.

I set it on my lap, flipping the cover. It opens to the first page where a photo sits square in the middle. I bring a hand to my mouth. It's Arash. My eyes swallow up every detail. He looks a little taller, but he still has that cute grin, the very one that says how *cool* he is. He holds a sheet of paper in his hands with writing on it in thick black marker. It's neat and legible, so I know someone has written it for him.

Hi Jamie!

That's all it says. I swallow, fingers trembling as I turn the page. It's another photo of Arash. This time he's standing in front of an old building. There's a fresh white sign on the front, words painted blue that read *Helping Hearts Orphanage.* A red heart sits underneath, surrounded by two hands.

This is where I live.

I didn't think I had more tears left inside me, but it seems I do. They fall down my cheeks, slow and silent. I run my fingers over the image as if I can touch him from here. I swipe at my face and turn the page. Arash is standing by a bed, holding another sheet of paper. The mattress is thick, the bedding clean and fluffy, with two pillows and a stuffed dinosaur in the middle.

This is where I sleep.

I turn the next page. Arash stands beside an open box of toys.

These are all my toys.

I peer close, bringing the page to my eyes. He has the entire collection of Avengers. All of them look brand new. Thor. Iron Man. The Hulk. Black Widow. I even see Rocket peeking out alongside Captain America.

Did Kyle do all this? *Pay* for all this? Suddenly I can't breathe, but still I turn another page because I can't stop. Arash is standing by a pile of books and pencils in the next photo.

This is my school work.

I turn another page. Arash standing next to an Australian soldier. One I don't recognise. He's crouched, bringing him to the same height as Arash, sunglasses on, both of them holding up thumbs.

This is Anderson. His team brought me here.

I start to shake. Another page. Arash with a boy. Both of them appear similar in age, arms around each other's shoulders. It's an awkward pose, but they don't seem to care because their grins are wider than the Sahara Desert.

This is Farjaad. Anderson brought him here with me.

Another page. Arash with a small girl.

This is Hajira. Anderson brought her here with me too.

I turn another. And another. Until I count six kids in total, including Arash. Six. I close my eyes, remembering back to my road trip with Kyle. His phone conversation.

"How many did you say?" Kyle had said before pausing, listening to the person on the other end of the line speak.

"Six? Jesus H."

He paused, listening before speaking again. "No, do it. Let me know the cost and I'll wire the money. Can you get the photos?"

I turn another page. All six kids are in the next photo, their arms around each other in a huddle of bright happy faces. Another sheet of paper is held by Arash.

We are safe because of you.

The lump in my throat is so large I can't swallow around it. I smooth a hand across the page, my finger tracing along their little smiles. But the folder hasn't reached its end, and I can't stop myself from flipping another page, greedy for more. The next photo is Arash standing in front of a mature couple. They both have a hand resting on each of his shoulders.

I am leaving the orphanage in two weeks. I got adopted. This is my new family.

My lips mash together, eyes blurring through my tears. Kyle is killing me. I have never seen such a selfless act of kindness in all my life. Never.

I turn another page. It's Arash by himself. He's holding up another sheet of paper, but in his other hand is the photo that Connor took of us on that bright happy day.

I will never forget you, Jamie. You saved me. Thank you.

I turn the page but there are no more photos, just a simple card with his full name and new address, clearly placed there so I can keep in touch.

I don't leave my unit all day, ignoring the messages that build up from Erin and Wood. The folder doesn't leave my side. I go through it again, and again, and again, until I can't see straight. I sleep with it that night, exhausted, hugging it to my chest, and when I wake in the morning my mind is clear. I know what I need to do.

Thanking my lucky stars I didn't break my phone in my little fit yesterday, I go through my contacts and find Ryan, dialling his number.

"Hey, Jamie," he answers. "How are you?"

I don't have time for pleasantries. I explain everything that happened, and I do it quickly because I'm impatient. He doesn't sound surprised at Kyle's visit, but his voice turns hard when I get to the outcome.

"It was a misunderstanding."

"There wouldn't have been one if you just spoke to him," he says.

I want to protest but Ryan is right. "I know that now. The thing is, he left behind this gift for me. A folder. It's—"

"I know what it is," he replies, interrupting me.

"You do? Because I can't even begin to imagine what it took to make all that happen."

Ryan does not fuck around. "It cost him everything to make it happen. Everything. Do you get what I'm saying?"

I nod, even though he can't see it. "I don't deserve him, do I?"

"He seems to think you do."

"Ryan?" My hand grips tight to the phone. "You'll probably say no, but I need a favour."

His voice softens, gruff. "I'm not a total asshole, Murphy. I care about the both of you. Tell me what you need."

I lay it all out and when I'm done, there's a deep measure of respect in his voice. "I'll get right on it."

"Thank you," I breathe. "Thank you so much."

"You got it, Murphy."

I hang up the phone and set it on the counter, my bladder ready to burst. I make my way to the bathroom. Tugging down my underwear, I take a seat on the toilet, my eyes falling to the trash bin beside me. The white stick is still sitting there, reminding me what could have been. Finishing up, I flush and wash my hands. I dry them off and start to walk out, but something pulls me back, and I don't know why.

I go back to the bin, plucking the stick free. I look at it, giving it a closer inspection. My heart begins to pound when I see a second line this time around. It's so faint it's barely visible at all, but it's there.

I press a hand to my belly, my insides leaping with a mixture of excitement and terror. *Oh my god. Is it real, or just a phantom second line?*

The box is still on the counter. I pick it up, slightly breathless, and take out another test. I drink as much water as I can and wait ten minutes. I can't wait longer than that.

My hand shakes as I pee on the second stick. I stay seated on the toilet, waiting, knickers around my ankles and eyes on the test. The second line appears slowly, and it's still faint, but it's there. *It's fucking there.*

Holy shit.

I'm actually going to have a baby.

Kyle is going to be a father.

36

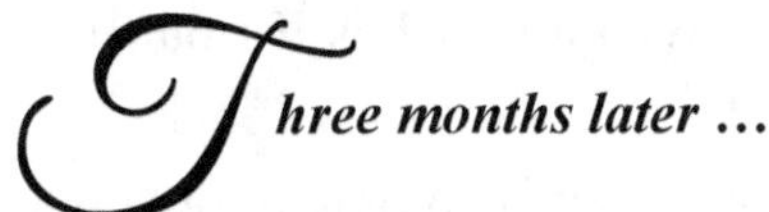 *hree months later …*

THE PLANE CIRCLES in the sky above Perth. We're in a holding pattern over the airport. I heard the grinding of the wheels below my seat a while ago, and my gut is telling me something is wrong. I don't think they're coming down.

I have about (I check my watch) zero time for a crisis. My plan is in motion, and if I'm not there it's going to blow up in my face.

My head tips back and I take a hand from my belly to grip the armrest, expelling a deep, impatient breath. Every day, every hour, every minute, has led up to this moment, and it's been *endless*. I need Kyle. I need him so much.

"We're going to be okay, dear," June, my fellow passenger says from beside me. She pats my hand in a soothing gesture, mistaking my tension for a paralysing fear of flying. June is returning from Brisbane, having attended her eightieth birthday party with family. They live on the east coast and she lives here on her own because it's home. My head tips towards the window, looking down. *Home.*

"Thanks," I say, tilting my lips, hoping it somehow forms a smile. I don't tell her I've been through worse. Planes dipping and lurching to avoid gunfire, coming down in a war-torn country in the dead of night to the deep shuddering *boom* of missiles hitting the earth. That's all behind me now.

I'm officially honourably discharged from the army. They warned me the transition would be difficult, but I never imagined feeling so adrift. Untethered from the harbour. I'm a civilian now, no longer a part of something special. I don't belong anymore.

Bitch, you've got bigger problems, my bladder screams.

Ugh. Aeroplane bathrooms are *the worst.* I unbuckle my seatbelt, rising. I scoot past June, my burgeoning belly bumping the seat in front of me. The male passenger spins around with a scowl as if I punched him.

I restrain my middle finger with effort. There's no time for a brawl. My stomach literally popped in the last two weeks as if I swallowed a balloon. Needing the toilet becomes DEFCON level one when there's no room left for such things like internal organs.

The flight attendant comes rushing down the aisle, a tolerant smile pasted on her face. "Ma'am, please remain seated. The fasten seat belt lights are on," she tells me, actually pointing to them as if I had no idea what they were.

I put a hand to my belly and let out a pained groan. "I need to use the bathroom. I'll be quick."

"I'm sorry but we'll be landing soon. Please take your seat."

My eyes narrow at her false tone of sympathy. I'm just a pesky fly in the ointment of her day. I could make it worse by letting go and pissing all over her navy shoes, but I won't have time to change my clothes once we land. "Is everything okay with the plane?" I ask, my voice rising with alarm so everyone around me can hear. "I'm no expert or anything, but it sounds like the wheels aren't coming down. Do we have enough fuel to be circling the airport like this?"

Suddenly everyone is talking, passengers calling her from all directions. I hold back the smirk and dash down the aisle while she's distracted.

I slam the door closed and turn inside the tiny cubicle. Shoving down my skinny maternity jeans, my backside hits the seat and I let go with a moan of relief, peeing like a racehorse. Whoever said pregnancy was undignified got it one hundred percent right. There is nothing sexy about me right now.

When I'm finished, I fix my clothes and wash my hands, checking my appearance in the mirror. I'm wearing makeup. Not much. Just enough to darken my lashes, tint my lips, and pinken my cheeks. I'm not sure it's an improvement. I want Kyle to want me. I want him to take one look at me and lose his mind with lust, but I feel I'm fighting a losing battle. I'm busting from the bra beneath my fitted tee shirt, my belly is swollen, my skin puffy, and dark smudges circle my eyes. I'm just so damn tired. I fall into bed at night as if I ran a marathon each day.

I dry my hands and leave the tiny cubicle. The flight attendant gives me the death stare as I return to my seat. I give her a little smile and a wave. I can't help it. Baby hormones make me bitchy.

I sit back with a sigh, knowing I'll be needing to pee again soon. It's a never-ending cycle of trips to the bathroom. My hands rub over my belly. I'm not big enough to feel any kicks from the outside, but I feel them on the inside. Tiny little swishes inside me like the wings of a butterfly.

Kyle doesn't know yet. No one does. Erin thinks my test was negative because I lied. To say she's going to be a bit pissed about that is a massive understatement, but what choice did I have? Kyle is the father. Doesn't he deserve to know before everyone else?

The problem was that I couldn't just tell him via a message, not with the way things are between us right now. I've given him the time and space he asked for, but have I given him too much? Is he moving on already? Was his love like a meteor entering the atmosphere—burning hot and bright before breaking apart into nothing?

My hands grip tight to the armrests. If Kyle decides he doesn't want me, well too damn bad. I'll make him want me. Anything else is not an option.

Ryan Kendall

My Mustang accelerates from the lights with satisfying speed. The windows are down and air rushes in, swirling through the car and ruffling my hair. I cherish days like this where there's nothing but the sun in the sky and the road ahead of me. I tilt my head up, passing near the airport. There's a plane coming around, circling low. I glance at my watch before my eyes return to the road. Jamie should be landing any moment, which means I need to hurry.

I punch down on the accelerator, heading towards the barracks. My gaze shifts to the rearview mirror, the cars behind me fading into the distance. I smirk behind my mirrored aviators, flicking my indicator on as I change lanes.

Twenty minutes later, I'm easing into a park and making my way towards Kyle's unit. I bang on the door before checking the handle. It's unlocked. I swing it open, my eyes sweeping the space quickly and coming up empty. Tugging my phone free, I fire off a message.

Ryan: Where are you?

It doesn't take him long to answer.

Kyle: Why?

Ryan: Because I need to talk to you.

Kyle: So call me, dipshit.

Kyle has been a wounded bear for months. Everyone is staying clear, keeping a ten-foot radius around his person as if he'll attack at any given moment.

I grit my teeth and type another message.

Ryan: Just tell me where you are, asshole. I need help with something.

Kyle: Ask someone else.

I start back down the hall, heading for the gym, typing as I walk.

Ryan: I built that goddamn Death Star with you.

It took us all night. Kyle left in the dawn, taking it with him. It's probably in pieces now, trashed in a fit of rage. I can't blame him. I'm pretty sure I was almost as bad when it came to patching up the mess I made with Finlay, but Kyle has been marinating in his misery for months. Jamie's plan better work or I'm going to tie a cement block to his feet and drop him in the Swan River.

Kyle: Whoop-de-doo. Someone get this man a medal.

He includes the hand-clapping emoji. Three of them. He follows it up with a gif of someone stepping up onto the podium at the Olympics, accepting a gold medal. *Smartass.*

I take a deep breath, reminding myself that he's hurting. We always lash out against those closest. I'm just the lucky one stuck in his direct firing line.

I arrive at the gym, stepping inside and looking around. He's not here either. I leave, typing again while I walk. I shoot off a message to Jamie.

Ryan: Have you landed yet?

I get no response. She should have touched down by now. In fact, she should be in a cab already. Why did I ever agree to this? Oh right, I wanted to help. Jamie owes me a case of whiskey. The expensive kind. A whole carton of cigars too. In fact, I'm going to make a list. They both owe me.

Thinking that he's possibly having a late breakfast, I send another message on my way to the mess hall.

Ryan: Are you listening to yourself right now? You're acting like a giant man-child.

Kyle: Resorting to insults? Who's the man-child now?

Fuck him. When I get my hands on him I'm going to strangle him until he's blue in the face.

"Hey, Kendall!"

I look up from my screen, twisting my head. Paul Montgomery, our troop commander, is jogging up behind me. He's in his early forties now, but he's fit and experienced, inspiring confidence not just in our team but across the entire regiment. He's just that likeable. He uses his position of power for good rather than evil, earning my respect and lifelong loyalty years ago. Unlike Kyle, who can go take a long walk off a short cliff.

He falls into step beside me. "What are you doing here on your day off?"

"I wish to God I knew," I mutter and his brows rise in question. "Long story. Have you seen Brooks?"

He shakes his head. "Not today. Why? What's he done this time?"

"This time?"

"He got into it with Nathan at card night last night. I wasn't there, but I heard Nathan accused him of cheating and Kyle flipped the whole goddamn table, grabbing him by the throat and slamming him up against the wall. Took three men to pry him loose."

"Jesus fucking Christ." I swipe a hand down my face, worry a knot inside my stomach. I knew it was bad but this? This isn't him.

"Maybe try the field? Some of the guys were talking about a rugby friendly."

"Thanks, mate," I say, already jogging backwards. "Gotta go."

He gives me a casual salute, and I turn, high-tailing it to where the field is situated between the beach and the barracks. I jog over to the small handful of soldiers on the sidelines, my eyes on the game playing out in front of me. They're caught up in a scrum on the far side, too far for me to make out any one person. All I can tell is that one team is wearing black shirts, the other wearing none.

"Brooks out there?" I ask the group in general, though I know each of them personally.

"He's on the shirtless team." Riggs, the soldier standing closest to me, points in the direction of the fast-moving, hard-hitting bodies. "You can't miss him."

Someone else speaks up. "He's the one who thinks it's a boxing match instead of a friendly."

My eyes pick him out as they get closer. He's a mess. Sweaty. Covered in mud from head to toe because it rained for three days straight this week, the clouds only clearing just last night. He has the ball tucked under his armpit, and he's running for a try.

"How long have they been playing?" I ask.

"Only a few minutes."

He gets closer, the pounding of heavy legs thundering across the earth. The black shirts are chasing him down, pushing him towards the sideline, the shirtless storming up from behind as if they're battling for Winterfell and not just a damn ball.

Kyle is fast, but someone comes at him from the side, taking him in a savage tackle right near our feet. They go down and the ground shudders beneath me.

I reach down and grab his tattooed arm from the pile, using all my strength to pull him free of the scrum. His left eye is already swelling and blood leaks from his nose and his bottom lip as he gets to his feet. *Christ.*

"What the fuck, Kendall," he gasps, bending, hands on his knees as he sucks air into his lungs.

"You need to come with me." I'm already turning, fuming, stalking from the field, done with his reckless behaviour. First it was mildly amusing to see him go down the same path I travelled not long before. Then it was simply irritating. Now it's downright alarming. Kyle is more than a friend to me, he's my goddamn brother, and it physically aches to see him struggle like this. "Grab your shirt."

"I'm in the middle of game!" he yells to my back.

"Now, Brooks," I bark, not even turning, my voice a command as I pull rank, something I hardly ever do. "That's a goddamn order."

Kyle falls into step beside me. I glance across at him. He's shrugging on his shirt, muddying the white cotton. He grabs the hem and uses it to wipe his face, staining it with blood and sweat and dirt, his lips pressed into a thin line. There's no time to get him showered and cleaned up, so I stalk straight to the parking lot. He keeps up with me but he doesn't speak. He's pissed. I reach the Mustang, unlocking the car.

"Get in."

Kyle opens the passenger door, sliding his stinking, hulking body inside. He slams it closed like a sulky child, and my car shudders beneath the force. My hands curl into fists, but I allow the tantrum. Just this once. And only because I pulled rank on him.

He winds down his window, and we drive off in tense silence. He doesn't ask me where we're going or what we're doing. I don't even get a single wisecrack.

I can't deliver him to Jamie like this, but I don't know what to say to snap him out of it.

We arrive at our destination, and I switch the ignition off. The engine ticks over in the sudden silence and my phone *dings*. I check the screen with discretion.

Jamie: Landed. On my way. Five minutes out.

Ryan: We're already here.

Jamie: Shit. Ok. Can you wait just a bit longer?

Ryan: Let me know when you're one minute out.

"Can I just say one thing?"

Kyle sets his jaw. "No, but I'm sure that won't stop you."

"You had a week between booking your flight and going to see Jamie."

"So?"

"That's a whole week you had to think about how you felt. To plan what you would say. An entire week to put your thoughts into actions. You left with your little grand gesture and your speech because you had it all figured out. Was Jamie supposed to have it all miraculously figured out too, just because you did? I know you never expected her to fall at your feet, but you didn't even give her a day. Instead you left because you thought she put the army above you."

"She did," he croaks like a wounded caged animal. "It's all she's ever wanted."

"You're wrong."

"Yeah? Well what would you know?"

"I know you've lost people close to you. We all have. We've all learnt the hard way that loving someone is a risk."

Kyle shakes his head. "Jamie doesn't love me the same way I love her."

"How do you know? You got a chance to take the risk, but you never gave her the chance to take it with you!"

Kyle rubs a hand over his face, his throat working as he swallows, seeming to take in everything I just said. I could probably add more, but it's time to pass the baton. He's Jamie's problem now.

My phone beeps again. I check the screen before tucking the device away.

Jamie: One minute.

"Get out," I tell him.

His brows fly up. "What?"

"You heard me." I jerk my chin at the handle of his door. "Get out."

Kyle climbs out but I remain buckled in my seat, hands on the wheel. He shuts the door and turns, ducking down. He rests his muddy forearms on the open window. "What are we doing here?"

"I'm not doing anything here." I turn the key and the engine roars to life with a throaty growl. I'll never tire of the sound. I start backing out, and Kyle follows after me, brows snapping together, arms splaying wide. "Kendall, what the fuck?"

"You're welcome," I say out the window before roaring off down the street, my duty done.

KYLE

My eyes follow the Mustang as it thunders down the street we just came from. What the hell is going on? Is this some kind of Disney moment, where I get dumped miles from home and have to find my way back, somehow finding myself along the way?

Because Ryan is way off the mark. I *know* the plague is more appealing than I am right now. I *know* I'm being a complete dick. I *know* I didn't give Jamie a chance. Ryan's little 'come to Jesus' sermon was *not* a revelation. I expected too much of her too soon, and when I didn't get it, I acted like a little bitch. He would've done better actually telling me what I could do to fix it rather than pointing out what a colossal shit sandwich I made of everything.

And my text to Jamie? Time and space, my ass. The past three months have been hell. I've been spiralling, sucked down inside a black hole I can't seem to claw my way out of. *I'm so fucking lost without her.*

I shove my hands in the pockets of my rugby shorts and turn, facing the ocean. It's the only place that seems to calm me, but even it holds memories of Jamie for me too. Like the time she dived drunk into the waves in just her underwear—so reckless and beautiful. Or the argument we had on the beach while holding Monty's little girl, Ollie.

"How can I have kids of my own, knowing there are babies over there that have no one?"

Would the folder change her mind? We got six of them to safety, including Arash. Giving each one a chance at a better future. But we can't save them all. And the thought of Jamie turning her back on a family of her own because of that makes me ache.

A car pulls in behind me. I hear the crunch of gravel as the wheels roll over it. I half turn, hands still in my pockets, the breeze from the ocean ruffling my hair. A cab pulls to a stop nearby and the back-passenger door opens. My lungs close up when Jamie steps out, shock rooting me to the ground as she flicks the sunglasses on her face to the top of her head. Her eyes are on me as she closes the door behind her. It's coming into summer yet she's wearing tight jeans, heeled boots, and a thick, bulky coat as if she's expecting snow.

"Kyle," she says. I'm too far away to hear it, but I see my name on her lips.

The cab driver steps out behind her, opening the boot of his car, pulling out suitcase after suitcase, yet she stands there unmoving, watching me.

"Where do you want these, love?" the cabbie asks.

"Can you put it all on the porch?" she asks without taking her eyes from mine.

He bustles about while I stand there trying to recover my breath. How is it she's more beautiful than I ever remembered? Her hair is thick and glossy. Longer than I've ever seen it. Her skin looks warm and tanned, her lips lush and pink. She's literally glowing from the inside out as if she swallowed the sun.

Damn Ryan. Damn him to hell for dumping me here all bloodied and filthy. I look like a train wreck, and I feel worse. I take a step forward and stop, suddenly unsure.

What is she doing here?

Jamie takes a step forward herself before being distracted by the driver. He's unloading boxes from the back seat now, walking between us, oblivious as he goes about his task.

She takes another step, a rueful expression on her beautiful face. "This isn't how I planned everything to be."

I'm confused by her statement. By the suitcases. The boxes. "What do you mean?"

Her next step is hesitant, and I catch a glimpse of fear on her face. I've never seen Jamie so scared in my life. *Never.* That's she scared now, here with me, almost breaks me apart. "I had a whole speech prepared," she tells me, letting out a shaky huff, "and I can't remember any of it."

"A speech?" I echo, sounding dumb as dog shit. I can't help it. Jamie is here as if I manifested her from the dreams she haunts me in every night.

"Yeah." She tucks her hands inside her pockets, mimicking me, and now we're both standing here staring at each other like motionless statues.

The cab driver saunters over. "All done, love."

"Okay, thanks," she tells him, her eyes still on mine like she can't drag them away. I can't make sense of it, why she's here right now, looking at me that way, but it fills something inside me, something that felt so achingly hollow just minutes before.

Her driver mutters something about payment and it seems to jolt her, as if the two of us were caught inside our own bubble and he just popped it. Jamie frees a hand from her pocket, coming out with a crumpled wad of cash. She doesn't even count it. She just hands it over. The man counts it for her, brightening, telling her to have a good day before he walks off to his car. He gets inside, shutting the door and zooming off down the street.

"Kyle." Her eyes roam over my face. "What happened to you?"

I brush her question off with a shake of my head, not wanting to explain. How can I tell her I lost my mind at our weekly card game last night? I acted like an animal. But Nathan was poking at my wounds. Taunting me over Jamie. His piss poor attempt at getting me talk about it as if "card night" was code for "therapy session." I even told them all he accused me of cheating, knowing it would get him kicked from the game.

My plan had been to pound out the frustration in rugby this morning. Instead I'm here, and suddenly Ryan's parting words make sense.

Jamie gestures towards the beach with her chin. "Can we walk?"

"Of course." Whatever she wants, I'll do it with bells on.

She reaches my side and bends, trying to take off her shoes, but she struggles, the bulk of her jacket seeming to get in the way. "Let me," I say, and crouch down.

Her hands land on my shoulders like two hot brands, keeping her steady as she lifts a foot. I slide a boot free and set it aside. The second boot comes off and I set them both aside on the grass. I straighten, close enough now I could lean in and kiss her lips. *Goddamn, she smells good.* I inhale and almost weep like a baby.

Her eyes drop to my mouth like she hears my thoughts. Then her gaze shifts outward, over the horizon, her cheeks pink as if she's flustered. Jamie? Flustered? It doesn't compute.

She starts walking across the soft grass. I fall into step beside her, tucking my hands back inside my pockets. I don't know what else to do with them besides reach for her and never let go.

"I've missed the beach," she says, breathing deep as if the salty air is a magic elixir.

We reach the edge of the grass where it butts up against the sand and keep on walking. I don't have shoes to take off. Our rugby game was played the way God intended, barefoot and primeval. I left them by the side of the field in my haste to catch up with Ryan. "You have beaches in Townsville."

"I never went. They weren't the same," she says as we trudge through thick, white sand. "Not like home."

We reach the shore and start walking north along the water's edge. "And home is here?"

Jamie hesitates, glancing across at me before she answers. "Home is wherever you are, Kyle."

I stop dead, absorbing her words deep inside my skin. She stops with me, looking at me, then down, then out across the ocean. Does she really mean that? Because I've never had anyone say something like that to me in my entire life.

My eyes burn and my jaw works hard to hold back the wild surge of emotion. "Jamie," I croak. "You—"

"Please don't say anything. Let me speak, okay?"

I nod, grateful, because I'm not sure I can articulate anything right now that would make sense, and we start walking again.

"My father told me I was born a fighter. I've spent my entire life trying to prove it. Only I never knew what I was supposed to be fighting for. I joined the army because I thought it might hold all the answers. And I don't regret it. Not for a single second. I wouldn't be who I am today without it. Without you, and Wood, and Jake, and everyone else I've met along the way. I've lived an extraordinary life in such a short amount of time, and I'm grateful. Grateful for all of it. And I could never see that until now. Stupid, huh?" She laughs at herself, hugging her arms around her middle.

My eyes prickle with heat. I reach for her. "Jamie—"

"Hear me out, please," she begs, sounding desperate, stepping back like she needs space to get the words out. "I know you're not Jake. And I know you think you're not the one I wanted. But you are." Her throat works as she swallows, her eyes blinking hard. "Since the first time you sat on the other side of the fence and told me not to cry. I was breaking apart inside, and you were a lifeline. I barely knew you and yet you were all I had in the world. Even after you left, I'd talk to you as if you were still there. I thought about you every day. And I wondered where you were, and what you were doing, and if I'd ever see you again. When you came to visit me in Townsville, you spoke to me as if Jake was the one I couldn't let go, but all along it was you, Kyle. You're the one I couldn't let go. I know you believe he saw a life with me, but it was one that was never meant to be. That life was meant for *you*."

Jamie slips her hand inside mine, twining our fingers together. She takes a step closer, moving inside my space. I dip my head, pressing my forehead to hers, still struggling to believe she's standing here with me. Her nose nudges mine and our eyes meet.

"I love you, Kyle Edgar Brooks." She kisses me, brief, soft, loving. So unlike our frantic kisses of the past. "I'm in love with your impatience and your childish antics." Another kiss. "I'm in love with the way you tease me, and laugh with me, and care for me as if I'm the most precious thing in your life. I think you're amazing."

Warmth floods my chest. Jamie loves me. She loves *me*. Her strong, beautiful heart is mine, and damned if it doesn't make my chest puff out like a goddamn peacock right now. I feel ten feet tall. "Totally amazing," I agree, my lips curving at the corners. Her admission makes me greedy for more. "What else?"

Jamie laughs. "You're really hot!"

Her palms slide over my shoulders and down, resting on my pecs. "I love your big strong body." Her lips brush mine. "And your hairy chest, even though it gives me rug burn every time I kiss it."

I grip her hips, my palms skating around until I get a good handful of her ass, despite the odd bulkiness of her jacket getting in the way. I give the round flesh a good pinch. "Take that back."

Jamie squeaks. "Ouch! You want me to lie?"

"It's not that hairy!"

"Well, you're not Chewbacca, but …" she trails off, suggesting I'm not far off the mark.

I pinch again and she leaps away with a laughing shriek. "Take it back, Jamie Juliet Murphy, or else."

"Or else what?"

I take her hand and pull her back against me. What the fuck is with this massive, ungainly coat? It's in my way. "Or else I won't fuck you good and hard, just like I know you want it."

Jamie's eyes flare with heat. "Kyle."

My thumb skims along the side of her jaw, across her bottom lip. My voice lowers, husky. "Take it back."

"Never," she whispers and I love it. Her stubbornness. Her teasing, rebellious heart. *I want her so bad.*

My mouth comes down on hers, covering her lips, pushing them apart with my tongue. She lets me in with a soft moan, her fingers digging into the skin of my shoulders. We stand there by the water, making out for endless minutes, my cock getting hard and pushing against the front of my rugby shorts, reminding me we're in public and I'm making her grubby.

My tongue rubs against hers, lazy and slow, and when I pull away, I pepper little kisses along her jaw with my lips. "I'm sorry for the way I left you in Townsville. For leaving at all. I'm such a fucking moron."

"It's okay. I get it."

"It's not okay. It was three months of torture."

"I've left the army, Kyle."

My breath catches in my throat. "What?"

"I never re-enlisted. I had that paperwork filled out before you showed up, but I had to talk myself into it. For so long I told myself it was where I wanted to be. Then you showed up out of nowhere telling me you loved me, and it made me realise I'd changed, that my world had grown beyond what I wanted at the age of eighteen." Jamie takes my hand. "Come with me." She leads me up over the sand dunes, back in the direction we came. "I want to show you something," she says, acting as if she just told me she went to the store to buy a loaf of bread and milk, rather than left the career she always insisted was her whole entire *life*.

"Jamie." I squeeze her hand, tugging, slowing her momentum. "Stop."

"I can't. I have something I want to give you."

"It was never my intention to make you choose."

She stops then. "You never made me choose between you or the army. I chose something else entirely."

"What?" I ask, my chest tight from all her revelations. I'm reeling, but in the best possible way.

A bittersweet smile crosses her face, there and gone in an instant. "To be happy."

To be happy.

How simple she makes it sound, as if it were just that easy, but I know that it's not. Leaving the army will change her life, for the better, or worse, I don't know. But it's going to take weeks, maybe months, for the change to sink in. And what if she resents me for it?

Jamie tugs at my hand and we reach the porch of the house where the cab driver delivered her luggage. The house is set beside a small side street, a cul-de-sac that fringes the entrance of the beach. The porch is large, more like a veranda the way it wraps around the back, the large expanse facing out across the ocean.

We stop in front of it, and I scan the exterior. "Are you renting this place?"

It's a one-level house and a little rundown for what you'd expect from a weekend rental. The timber slats on the veranda need replacing, as does the railing around it, but the front door appears oddly brand new—ready for a clean, stained finish. The yard and gardens look like they were beautiful once, but they're overgrown now—a tangle of sweet-smelling jasmine, long grass, and weeds set around two large magnolia trees along the fence line, one of them big enough to climb, its branches wide and lowset.

"No," she tells me, biting down on her bottom lip. "I'm not renting it."

"You know the owner?"

She laughs at that as if I told a great joke. "Intimately."

My brows snap together, a possessive growl climbing my throat. I need to get a hold of myself. We both have a past. I'm just not sure I appreciate Jamie rubbing hers in my face.

"Here," she says, smirking like she knows exactly where my mind went as she takes my hand. She turns it palm up and puts something on it.

I look down at the small slip of silver metal in my hand. "What's this?"

"What does it look like?"

"A key," I say, staring at it, not understanding.

"To your new house."

"My house?" I look up, standing there like a dumb lump as I take in the exterior all over again. "I don't understand."

"What? You think you're the only one capable of grand romantic gestures?"

My heart begins to gallop inside my chest, my fingers curling around the key in my hand until it forms a fist. "Grand romantic gestures are where you fly across the country to surprise someone you love. Or a bunch of flowers and jewellery. They're not houses," I say, struggling to catch my breath. Jamie has winded me with her gift, but I can't accept it. *It's a house.*

"I got your folder, Kyle," she says softly. "I know how much it cost you. I know it's something I can never repay."

"How do you know the cost?"

"How could I not?" she replies, evading my question. Yet I'm not so stupid I can't put two and two together. Ryan has conspired behind my back to get me here, so he's likely the one who told her. I can't be mad—well, I can, but not right now because … a house?

"I have selfish motives. I want to live here with you."

Jamie makes her way up the three steps and turns, looking out. She beckons me. I hesitate, dumbfounded by her bombshell. She wants to live here? With me? My heart pounds as I climb the stairs, and when I turn to take in the view, my vision blurs. This is all I ever wanted—not some colossal mansion with all the latest gadgets, but a charming house by the beach I could turn into a home with someone I love.

I swallow around the thick lump in my throat. "I don't know what to say."

"Don't say anything yet. I have one more grand gesture."

I rub a hand across my heart. "I'm not sure I can take anymore."

"Deep breaths, babe," she tells me. "This is a big one."

Babe. The endearment goes straight to my dick. I love it. "Bigger than buying me a house?"

"Not physically," she mutters beneath her breath, though I hear it anyway. "At least I hope not."

A flash of nerves crosses her features before she dips her head, her dark hair falling forward in a thick sheet and her eyes on her hands as she fumbles with the zipper of her jacket. Her fingers shake and it isn't like her. Jamie has always been assertive and sure.

"Hey." I take hold of her elbow, making her pause. Whatever this grand gesture is, I don't like how apprehensive it's making her. "What is it? What's going on?"

Jamie takes a deep, determined breath and slides the zipper down. It snags at the end and she lets out a curse, jerking at the clasp. "This is *not* how I planned this in my head."

"That's the second time you've said that."

She huffs, jerking some more. "Are you sure you want me? Because I suck. I suck so bad right now. I wanted to make this perfect and instead it's about as romantic as a dog taking a shit."

"Make what perfect?"

Jamie throws up her arms. "This!" she yells at her jacket.

"Here, let me."

Jamie

Kyle pockets the key and takes over, his chuckle low and deep. "It's not funny," I hiss, my bitchy hormones coming out to play.

It shouldn't be this hard. The plan was to present him with a house and a baby in that freaking order—a tender moment we could cherish together for as long as we lived. But I've never been in a proper relationship before and romantic gestures feel foreign and stupid.

"I'm not laughing," he says, fiddling with the clasp of my zipper, his chest shuddering as he holds it in.

"You are too."

He ducks his head for a closer examination. "Don't be childish."

"But I learnt it from the best."

Kyle tilts his head, looking up at me. I poke out my tongue. He laughs out loud. "I love you, Jamie Juliet Murphy. Please don't ever change."

"I love you too, Kyle Edgar Brooks."

Please don't ever leave me.

The clasp breaks apart beneath his large fingers, and I don't even care. The jacket is hot and clunky, making a sweat break out across my brow. I'm about ready to toss it in the bin. I only needed it to cover the bump until I could say what I needed to say.

I slide the jacket free and set it on the railing to my right. Then I turn back. Kyle's gaze slowly runs the length of me and back up again, halting at my belly, stuck.

He exhales an audible breath, his eyes wide. "That's a …" He shakes his head, swiping a hand over his face. "You're …" His eyes find mine. "Jesus fuck."

The relief of finally sharing the news is overwhelming. My chest wells up and a big fat tear forms, spilling over, rolling down my cheek.

"Oh, baby. Don't cry." He steps forward, smoothing his thumb across my cheek, wiping the tear. "You're pregnant?" he asks, his eyes searching mine as if the evidence isn't proof enough.

"No. I just ate a really big burrito," I reply. I'm aiming for sarcasm, but the words come out all weepy.

Kyle's laugh huffs out, a little hysterical. He's stunned, but I know it's in a good way when he takes my cheeks in his hands, his fingers trembling against my skin. "We're having a baby?" He kisses me, his mouth smacking against mine before he draws back. "We're … I'm going to be a daddy. Fuck me. *Fuck me.*" His lips hit mine again, once, twice, before he sinks down before me, eye level with my belly. My pregnancy tee shirt is fitted and pale pink cotton. It stretches wide across my abdomen, and he's reading the words printed across the front, silently to himself. *I'm creating a tiny human. What's your superpower?*

He takes hold of the hem and looks up at me in question, his eyes full of wonder. "Can I?"

Of course he freaking can. So much yes. I try to convey all that in a single nod because I can't speak.

Kyle pushes my shirt up, underneath my boobs. It bares my stomach to the cool breeze off the ocean. He takes a deep, shuddery breath and places his two big palms on my burgeoning little belly. They brand me with their heat, making me shiver.

His voice is gruff when he speaks. "How far along?"

"Eighteen weeks."

"Was that … Christ, I can't do math right now." His hands smooth across my stomach before winding around my hips. He takes a handful of my ass and presses his lips to the taut skin near my belly button.

"The road trip, yes."

"The pill …"

"Didn't work."

Kyle rises to his feet until I'm tilting my head to look at him. His lips curve into a grin of pure male satisfaction, his eyes dancing. "My swimmers are too strong for the likes of you." He flattens his palms across my belly again as if he can't stop touching it, his eyes flaring with hunger. "It shouldn't make me hard that I knocked you up, should it? I want you so fucking bad right now."

He winds his arms around my middle and lifts me like I weigh nothing, his big strong body pressed against mine. A wild surge of lust floods my veins and my voice comes out raspy. "I want you too."

Our mouths meet in a tangle of lips and tongues and heat. My arms slide around his neck, hugging him close. He groans deep in his throat, liking it, kissing me like it's the last kiss he'll ever have.

"One down, four to go," he manages to say before his mouth hits mine again.

"What?" I mumble, squirming against him.

"Kids," he replies, setting me down. I stumble, my legs weak and mind in a fog, having no idea what he just said. He grabs for me with one hand, keeping me steady while he uses the other to slide the key inside the lock of the door. He turns it and shoves it open, coming back for me.

I'm swept up in one smooth motion and carried inside. He looks around. The space is open and empty. "Well fuck," he mutters, his eyes searching for furniture, a couch or a bed, but I haven't got that far yet. "This won't do. You're planning on staying here?"

"Yes. I just need to buy some basic items, and I'll sleep on an airbed until I can get some furniture. I thought you'd want something you could renovate. Something you could make ours."

Kyle turns in a circle, still holding me as he takes it all in. "I can do that. We can both live here and work on the house together. I can extend. Add a second level."

"You can do anything you want."

He sets me down, seeming suddenly panicked. "We need to get started. We only have five months."

"Plenty of time."

Kyle looks at me as if I'm crazy. "Jamie, baby." He shakes his head. "Renovations aren't a sprint. They're a marathon. We'll never get it done in time."

"In time for what?" I say simply, thanking Jake from deep inside my heart for helping me see how easy it was to choose happiness above everything else. "We have the rest of our lives."

EPILOGUE

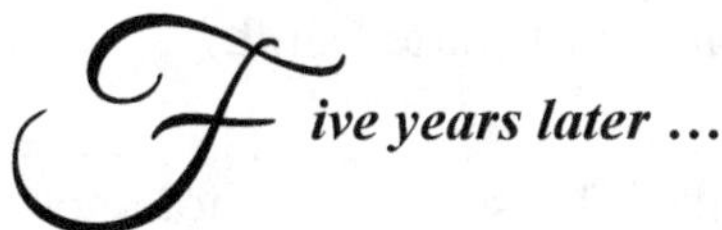 *ive years later …*

THE VIDEO CALL comes in while I'm standing at the back of the ambulance doors, taking inventory. It shouldn't be a surprise because Kyle
video calls every day, some days more than once, yet I still feel a wild
burst of pleasure with every single one.

Wood walks around the side, bandage packets piled high in his
arms. His eyes drop to my phone, and they don't just roll, they roll
hard. "Is that Brooks *again*?"

"Yep," I say it with a long-suffering sigh, acting as if his hovering
is a huge inconvenience, but secretly I love it. Not a day goes by that I
don't feel wanted or loved.

Kyle's face appears when I swipe my finger across the screen. It's a
tiny bit more weathered now than it used to be. The crinkles at the
corners of his eyes are a little deeper, his hair lighter from all the time
we spend in the sun. The road trips. The camping. The surfing. I

haven't lived so much, or so hard, and I know Jake would be happy knowing that.

"Hey, babe," I greet him while Wood climbs into the back of the ambulance with his hoard.

Kyle grins from the middle of our bed, wrapped in nothing but a white sheet, his chest bare and thick muscles bulging. My hormones wobble precariously. I do my best to shut them down. I'm on the clock.

When he speaks his voice is husky from sleep, and I know it's because he just woke up and found me gone, the sheets on my side of the bed cool and rumpled. "Hey, my sexy baby mama."

Wood rolls his eyes again while he re-stocks our supplies. I don't see it, but I feel it. "What's up?"

"Just wanna say good morning and make sure you're ready for our scan at the hospital this afternoon."

I check my watch. It's six a.m. "I've only just started shift."

"So?"

"I don't finish until four," I point out. "The scan is a whole hour after that."

"So?"

I'm four months pregnant with our third baby. I haven't told him, but I'm secretly hoping for a girl. We have two boys already, and they're both the spitting image of their daddy. Little heartbreakers with sun-kissed waves that hit their shoulders, golden skin, and hazel eyes too big for their cherubic faces. I can't deny them anything. "So it's *ages* away yet."

His bottom lip pokes out. "Don't be such a killjoy."

"I'm not!" I turn my head to look at Wood as he ducks down, jumping out the back of the ambulance. "We need more sterile wipes too," I tell him, and he nods, disappearing around the back doors.

"Mmm hmm," Kyle pipes up from my speaker in a suggestive tone. "Say that again."

"Kyle!"

"Wait, pan out a little while you do it."

I stretch my arm out straight, holding the phone high and angling it down because I can't deny Kyle anything either. "We need more sterile wipes," I say again and try to pout my twitching lips.

"Fuck me," he says, exhaling with grin though his eyes are dark with hunger. "I love you in that uniform. Sexiest goddamn thing ever."

I laugh.

"You should swing by home. I feel a heart attack coming on. Might need the paddles."

I laugh a little harder, my heart a melted puddle at my feet because he still takes the time to flirt with me, even when he wakes and has a million things to do before he gets the kids off to day care and himself off to work.

Wood comes back with the sterile wipes in one hand, sticking his finger down his throat with the other, pretending to gag as if he's never been in love and made kissy faces to Erin on the phone while I'm driving us to an emergency situation. "You guys make me sick."

Kyle ignores him. "Lift your shirt. Wanna see my baby."

"Kyle!"

He tips his chin. "Do it."

I untuck the front shirt of my uniform and lift it a little.

"More."

I lift it a little higher, exposing my rounded belly. A groan rumbles from his chest. He flops back against his pillows, one of his hands disappearing.

"Are you hard again?"

He cocks a brow. "If you want me to lie, then no. I'm totally not."

"Kyle!"

"I can't help it. I want to fuck you stupid, get you pregnant all over again. You make me crazy."

My brows fly up, my tone sardonic as I bring the phone a little closer to my face. "Oh, I make *you* crazy?"

"Daddy, daddy, daddy!"

I hear the thundering of little feet against the white oak timber flooring in our house. It's morning time. Malin—his name meaning strong little warrior—is our eldest at almost five and usually the first to wake.

Kyle lets out an *oof* when he jumps on the bed, Malin landing on his chest in a tangle of pint-sized arms and legs. Excited little fingers grab his face. "Can we surf?"

"You have day care today."

His brows snap together in a mulish frown. "Surf."

"No. Day care. And say good morning to your mum. Tell her to have a good day at work."

His face turns towards the screen, and I can't believe I created him, this miniature version of the man I adore. Just when I thought I knew love, Malin came along and showed me just how much of it you can squeeze inside your heart. Kids are incredible. "Have a poopy day, Mum."

They're also little assholes. Though *poop* is his word of the month and not meant with malice. He thinks it's hilarious. "Nothing could be more poopy than your face."

His little laugh peals through the phone and pierces my heart like an arrow. "Dad is taking me for a surf."

"Is that so?"

"Uh huh."

Kyle props his phone against the empty mug on his bedside table so I can still see them both before he wrestles Malin into the bed. "Day care for you."

He lets our boy roll him to his back and pin his arms. A move I taught him, which makes my chest puff proudly. He dips his face to Kyle's. "Surf."

"Day care."

"Day care stinks." Malin sits back on his dad's stomach, releasing Kyle's arms so he can fold his own in a little fit of temper. "Royce stole my Iron Man and broke his leg off before giving him back."

Kyle sits up, nostrils flaring, going from sleepy, sexy male to angry papa bear in the space of a single sentence. "He *what?*"

"Babe," I pipe up and he turns his face to the phone. "You might wanna ask Malin what *he* did first."

Kyle arches a brow at our little baby, our firstborn, who came out of the vaginal canal with a stubborn frown on his face, the only inherent trait that seems to come from me. The cheeky sly behaviour? That's all Kyle. One hundred percent Brooks. "What did you do?"

Malin is chewing at his bottom lip. "Nothin', I swear."

"What *did you do?*"

"Nothin'!"

It's going to be that kind of day, I'm thinking. I interrupt the squabble. "I have to get going. Have a good day, babe. Give Angus a kiss for me," I tell him. My three-year-old is a serious little fellow. I see the same quiet strength in his eyes as his father, as if he's walked this Earth before. "See you later this afternoon."

Wood and I get through our shift. It drags a little because tomorrow we leave on holidays. We're taking the boys on a road trip along the north-east coast, starting at Cairns, the gateway to the Great Barrier Reef. It's made up of red dirt, croc-infested river crossings, ancient rock art, and the lush Daintree rainforest, a world heritage site. We're going to snorkel the biggest reef in the world and walk the famous Mossman Gorge trail, and we're going to finish with five nights at Lizard Island because road trips with kids aren't for the faint of heart. I'm going to need some serious luxury before we return home.

I meet Kyle after shift, and we get through our twenty-week scan with flying colours while Erin watches the kids back at home for us. The good news? We're having another boy. Another Kyle. He holds my hand as we leave, twining our fingers together as the hospital entrance doors *whoosh* open, ejecting us into a warm dusky afternoon.

"You're not disappointed, are you?" he asks me.

"Of course not. If anyone can handle another male Brooks, it's me."

We reach his car in the parking lot, a late model 4WD. It might be newish but it's definitely lived in. Boys have a tendency to wreck their toys, and Kyle is no exception.

I climb in and he reaches across the seat, rubbing a hand across my belly. "I ever tell you I love you?"

I put my hand over his and he takes it, squeezing. "Only every day."

Kyle slides his hand free and grips the steering wheel. He uses the other to turn the key, and the Hilux thunders to life.

Kyle

Erin sends me a message as we make our way home.

Erin: We're all set. So excited!

I take a breath, anticipation thick in my blood, my pulse racing with nerves. I send her a furtive message when we stop at a red light.

Kyle: Five minutes out.

"Did you finish packing?" Jamie asks me.

I haven't started yet. "Of course I have."

"You haven't, have you."

I glance her way, widening my eyes. "Would I lie to you?"

"Yes."

"Ugh." My hand goes to my heart. "You wound me."

Jamie snorts as we pull into the driveway. She's looking around with brows pulled together, our usually quiet street filled with cars. I hit the button on the garage door remote, and it lifts with a slow steady pace. I drive inside and it lowers behind us, offering a warm muted light as I switch off the engine.

"So ..." I clear my throat. "I did a thing."

"You did a ..." Jamie's brows rise high with exasperation. "What now?"

Maybe I deserve that. I hosted card night this week, and we might have got a bit drunk and broke the oven. Though it was Nathan's idea to cook nachos, so it's partly his fault that the door came clean off when I pulled it open. It's the price Jamie pays for having a muscled husband who doesn't know his own strength, though she didn't look impressed when I pointed that out.

I might have also eaten all her donuts the night before last, the very ones she was saving for after her shift. There was no possible way she could prove it, so I blamed the boys. She cried over the empty box, *actually cried*, and I felt like such a piece of shit. What kind of monster eats his woman's donuts when she's pregnant? I ducked out to the local 7-Eleven and bought her another box, though two somehow slipped free and flew out the open window on the drive home. Such a freak accident.

"It's not a bad thing this time," I reassure her. At least, I hope it's not.

The internal door between the garage and the laundry opens. Erin appears, her blond hair set in loose waves, a pearl pin holding them back from her face. She's stunning in her ankle-length lace dress and made-up face. Wood is punching above his weight so bad. A fact I remind him of every time he blames me for Jamie turning up tired on shift, but it's hardly my fault she can't keep her hands off me in the middle of the night, is it? Her sexual appetite for me is almost embarrassing.

Jamie opens her door and goes to step out. I reach for her, grabbing her hand. "Wait."

She stops, turning her head to look at me.

My heart thunders in my chest. "It's just … we've been so busy. And I didn't want to wait any longer."

Jamie shakes her head. "What are you talking about?"

"You'll see."

I let Erin whisk her away and make my way up the internal stairs to Malin's bedroom. I swing the door open, confronted by Ryan, Nathan, Monty, and my two beautiful boys, all of them dressed in suits. Even my sons have a small cream rose pinned to the lapels of their smart black jackets, their hair tied back at the nape of their necks.

Goddamn. I almost tear up.

Malin and Angus hit my legs, hugging me, and Ryan sets a hand on my shoulder, giving it a squeeze. "Time to suit up, my man."

I nod and drop to a crouch in front of my boys, running a hand over each of their heads. "Ready to marry your mama?"

"Uncle Ryan says you give each other a ring," Malin says. "Do I get one too?"

Angus pipes in. "What are rings?"

"I don't know, but whatever they are, you're not getting one," Malin tells him.

Angus flares his little nostrils. "I want one."

Malin sticks out his tongue. "You can't have one because you're stupid."

"Hey, hey, hey!" I cut through the escalating situation, knowing I need my boys on their best behaviour tonight of all nights. "How about instead of rings that you'll both end up losing, we get you a dog?"

They both gasp and look at me, eyes round. "Yes!" they yell in unison, strands of their hair coming loose as they jump about the room, screaming, "Dog, dog, dog!" like they're on a trampoline.

I straighten, knowing Jamie is going to kill me. We discussed, *and agreed,* on getting a dog later down the track, when the boys are older and can take responsibility for its care. "You have to behave tonight though or it's not going to happen," I say in a loud voice, confident my bribery will work. "And that means being quiet and sitting still."

They shut up and race to take a seat on the bed as if we're playing musical chairs and I just paused the song.

Mission accomplished.

"And don't tell your mum," I add.

Monty hands me a chilled bottle of beer, and I put it to my lips, tipping my head back as I take a deep pull, hoping it will cool the bundle of nerves in my stomach. He laughs. "Bit late for cold feet, isn't it?"

"Mate, we have two-point-five kids and a mortgage, and I still wake up waiting for her to realise she made a mistake."

Ryan leans up against the windowsill, his own beer in hand. "Let's face it. She can do way better than you." The room erupts into laughter. Except for me. It's not fucking funny because it's true. Even my boys laugh, though it rings a little false because they don't get the joke. "Seriously, though, Jamie is a lucky woman and the way I see her look at you tells me she knows it."

I nod, feeling emotional, and clink my beer to his, and then Monty and Nathan in turn, before we all take a drink.

Later, after I'm suited up and our bottles are empty, we make our way downstairs through the busy kitchen and living area and out onto the back veranda. I look out over the yard.

Erin and Julie, Jake's mother, have outdone themselves. Fairy lights are strung between the trees and the house, creating a warm, happy glow. White tables and chairs have been set out around the lawn, an array of flowers at their centre. Lacy garlands and paper lanterns hang from branches, and all our friends are mingling about, chatting above the sound of music, glasses of champagne in their hands.

The gates at the far end of our lowset fence are wide open, leading out onto the beach beyond, and a rectangle wooden arbour decorated with lace ribbon, twinkling lights, and cream-coloured roses.

The noise in the yard dies off when everyone sees me standing at the top of the steps, my boys' hands in mine and my best friends beside me. They let out a cheer and a few claps and I speak up. "Thank you all for coming on such short notice. You might have figured it out already, but if you haven't, you're here for a surprise wedding. Jamie and I have been engaged for over four years now, but every time we even think about planning anything, something comes up."

"Or you pop another baby out," someone pipes up from the back and everyone laughs.

"Jamie wants a big family. Who am I to deny her?" More laughter. "Anyway, it's almost time, so if everyone can make their way out onto the sand, bring your glasses, and we'll make this happen."

I take my place by the arbour, taking a minute to introduce myself to the celebrant. Malin and Angus stand in front of me, Ryan to my left, followed by Monty and Nathan.

Music begins to play. I chose the song. "Nothing's Gonna Stop Us

Now" by Starship. Corny as fuck but I don't even care. It's perfect. An ode to Jamie's love of the eighties.

Our crowd of friends turn their heads as Finlay walks out first. She's wearing the same dress I saw Erin in earlier, and she's holding a bouquet of roses. Fin is followed by Erin, and when Erin reaches the bottom of the porch stairs, Jamie appears, her arm tucked inside Wood's. My breath lodges in my throat. She's wearing a cream lace dress, fitted snug around her chest before dropping to the floor in a sweet, cascade of lace. Her hair is out, long soft waves floating down around her, with a single rose tucked in her ear.

Her eyes find mine and my vision blurs, my hands squeezing too hard on my boy's shoulders.

"Ouch, Dad!"

"Sorry," I mutter, loosening my hold as they start towards us.

I am the luckiest goddamn bastard in the world, is my first thought. *I hope she's not mad,* is my second. Women like planning their own wedding, don't they? Maybe she's feeling a little robbed right now.

They reach us slowly, and the music winds down, leaving only the sound of the waves crashing against the shore as Wood steps off beside Erin.

Jamie turns, facing me. "I'm going to kill you," she mutters, smiling through eyes that are welling rapidly.

"Did I make the wrong call?" I mutter back, smiling at everyone around us to hide the sudden worry.

She hands her bouquet off to Erin as instructed by the celebrant, and takes both my hands in hers. "No. It's perfect. Absolutely perfect." She frees a hand to wipe beneath her eye. "I can't believe you did all this. How do you always manage to surprise me?"

"Not easily. We had a few close calls."

"Like when?" she whispers as the celebrant starts his prattle about love bringing two people together.

"Like your dress. It was meant to be delivered to Erin. Instead they sent it to the billing address. You signed for it, remember? And I told you it was meant for our neighbour."

Her lips twitch. "I thought it odd Mrs. Newbury was getting a dress from Eileen Wu Bridal Couture. I mean, she's ninety-two."

We reach our vows and the celebrant asks for Jamie to go first.

She tips her head to all our friends. "Please bear with me," she tells them. "I didn't know I was getting married today, so I'm not prepared." Laughter follows and she turns back to look at me, squeezing my hands. "I met you on one of the worst days of my life. It was like God knew my life was falling apart and he was giving me something to put it back together again. It wasn't easy to be my friend, but it was like you made it your life's mission to be mine. You were pushy and annoying, and yet somehow, you were all I had in the world. Who knew that boy I met on the other side of the fence would one day be mine? That he would gift me with friends, and children, and a future I could only dream of. I choose you to be my husband, Kyle, and not just because I'm the only one who could ever put up with you…" our friends titter, but I grip her hands tighter, fighting back a well of emotion "…but because I can't imagine a life without you in it."

She lets go and slides the ring Wood gives her on my finger.

"So fucking romantic," I hear Erin mutter on a sigh.

The celebrant turns to me, indicating it's my turn.

I take a deep breath, my eyes holding hers. "Jamie. In you I met the one person I want to annoy for the rest of my life. You're stubborn and reckless, and incredibly lucky to have me. I promise to always be your big spoon and let you press your cold toes against my legs in the morning. I will let you win at wrestling and will always laugh and take photos when you fall off the jetty. I promise to buy you giant wheels of cheese to satisfy your pregnancy cravings and never let the boys eat all your donuts again."

She laughs but it comes out choked with emotion.

"I love you, Jamie Juliet Murphy soon to be Brooks. You're hot in uniform and insatiable in bed."

Everyone laughs.

"Kyle!"

"Sorry. I'll be serious." I let go of her hands to take the ring Ryan offers me. I slide the simple band on her finger. "I give you my heart, Jamie. And from this day forward, I promise you'll never walk alone."

"Ladies and gentlemen," the celebrant speaks out, "Kyle and Jamie have declared before me and before all of you, their family and friends, that they will live together in marriage."

"Mum," Malin interjects, tugging at the elegant skirt of her dress.

The celebrant speaks louder. "They symbolise it by joining hands, taking vows, and exchanging rings."

"Mum!"

"Shhhh, baby," she whispers, her eyes on mine, loving and emotional.

"I therefore declare Kyle and Jamie to be husband and wife." He turns his head, looking at me. "You may now kiss your bride."

I lean in, my lips a breath away from hers.

"Mum! Dad said we can have dog. Can we go get it now?"

Uh oh.

"I want a labrador," Angus pipes in.

"You may kiss the bride," the celebrant repeats, louder this time.

Jamie's lips, painted a pretty pink and so goddamn kissable, press in a flat line. "You promised them a dog?"

"He did," Malin says, the little dibber dobber. "Just before. He did, Mum, I swear."

I cast a panicked glare at my boys before looking at Jamie. "I can explain."

THE END

BOOKS BY KATE MCCARTHY

The Biker and the Thief

The End Game

Fighting Redemption

Fighting Absolution

The Give Me Series

Give Me Love

Give Me Strength

Give Me Grace

Give Me Hell

find out more via

https://www.katemccarthyauthor.com/

ACKNOWLEDGMENTS

To my readers, I thank you for your constant encouragement, and for reading *Fighting Absolution*. Your support inspires me daily, motivates me, and makes me strive do better with each book. I'm eternally grateful for all of you.

To my darling kids, how loved you are. You (and my writing) are what gives my life meaning. Every day I am grateful for you, the two brightest stars that shine in my sky. To all the bloggers, reviewers, and bookstagrammers who have helped spread the word about this book. There are no words to express the level of my gratitude and appreciation of your constant hard work and support. Thank you so very much.

A special thank you to Maree Hunter. You have been there for me through every step of this book (and all the others) but we both know it's been an especially tough year, with lots of learning life's lessons, and I just know this book would not be what it is without you.

My editor, Max. I am so thankful and lucky to have you. You are the reason I continue to grow.

Sali. What are blessing you are. Thank you for your friendship and your exceptional work on this book. You've opened my eyes a little more and I've learned much from you.

Kimberly Brower, my agent. For all the work you have done for me already. I'm excited for the future and for what we can achieve together!

To Nina and the team at Social Butterfly PR. Thank you for everything you have done for me. You have shared so much of your knowledge, and offered so much support and advice, and for that I am eternally grateful.

ABOUT THE AUTHOR

Kate McCarthy lives in Queensland, Australia.

Website
https://www.katemccarthyauthor.com/
Facebook
https://www.facebook.com/KateMcCarthyAuthor
Instagram
https://www.instagram.com/authorkatemccarthy/
Twitter
https://twitter.com/KMacinOz
Goodreads
http://www.goodreads.com/author/show/6876994.Kate_McCarthy

www.ingramcontent.com/pod-product-compliance
Lightning Source LLC
Chambersburg PA
CBHW071734110726
47908CB00006B/1585